BY ELLA CLARK

Indian Legends of the Pacific Northwest (Berkeley, 1953)
Indian Legends of Canada (Toronto, 1960)
Indian Legends from the Northern Rockies, (Norman, 1966)
Guardian Spirit Quest (Billings, 1974)

INDIAN LEGENDS of the PACIFIC NORTHWEST

INDIAN
LEGENDS
OF THE
PACIFIC
NORTHWEST

BY ELLA E. CLARK

ILLUSTRATED BY ROBERT BRUCE INVERARITY

UNIVERSITY OF CALIFORNIA PRESS
Berkeley, Los Angeles, London

University of California Press

BERKELEY AND LOS ANGELES, CALIFORNIA

University of California Press, Ltd.

LONDON, ENGLAND

COPYRIGHT, 1953, BY

THE REGENTS OF THE UNIVERSITY OF CALIFORNIA

ISBN: 0-520-00243-1

MANUFACTURED IN THE UNITED STATES OF AMERICA

Designed by John B. Goetz

15 16 17 18 19 20

CONTENTS

II. LEGENDS OF THE LAKES

III. TALES OF THE RIVERS, ROCKS, AND WATERFALLS

IV. MYTHS OF CREATION, THE SKY, AND STORMS

V. MISCELLANEOUS MYTHS AND LEGENDS

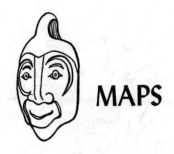

MAPS

PLACES IN THE STORIES

THE INDIAN TRIBES

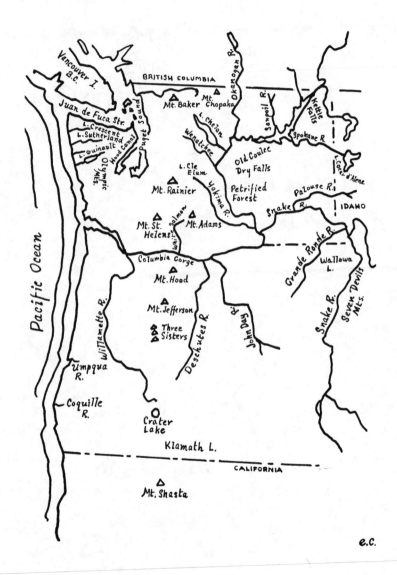

e.c.

Squamish
BRITISH COLUMBIA
Lummi
Samish
Okanogan
Lake
Colville
Makah
Klallam
Skagit
Chelan
Sanpoil
Snohomish
Snoqualmie
Quillayute
Spokane
Queets
Skokomish
Duwamish
Quinault
Puyallup
Nisqually
Palouse
Chehalis
Chinook
Yakima
Klickitat
WASHINGTON
Nez Perce
Clatsop
Wishram
OREGON
Wasco
Pacific Ocean
Warm Springs
Santiam
IDAHO
Kalapuya
Coos
Umpqua
Coquille
Klamath
Shasta
Modoc
CALIFORNIA
e.c.

INTRODUCTION

FROM MOUNTAIN

PEAKS TO

INDIAN LEGENDS

As a lookout for the United States Forest Service, I had a broad view and a grand view. Four snow-crowned peaks rose above the forested mountains: Mount Rainier and Mount Adams, Mount St. Helens and Mount Hood. Up among the peaks, I felt almost in touching distance of the glaciers on Mount Adams.

Before I went up to my perch the first time, my companions at Fire Guard School told me fragments of an old Klickitat Indian myth about a volcanic struggle between Mount Adams and Mount Hood, sons of the Great Spirit, who fought each other because of their love for Sleeping Beauty Mountain. Sleeping Beauty Mountain was across a valley from my cabin; through field glasses I could see a lookout station on the rock which forms her nose. Mount St. Helens was in the story, and the Columbia River also, the bluffs of which could be seen from my lookout tower.

Returning to a library in September, I easily found the old story—several versions of it, in fact. Surely, I thought, there must be a similarly primitive myth about Mount Rainier. But it was many months and several libraries later that I stumbled upon a story about Mount Rainier as it was when the world was very young.

By that time I had uncovered many interesting legends once told by the Indians of the Pacific Northwest, and I have continued to find them tucked away in obscure books. As the bibliography will reveal, most of the tales in this collection have come from government documents, old periodicals, old histories, and the reports of anthropologists and folklorists who have made a special study of the American Indians. Several are from manuscripts of Oregon and Washington pioneers.

From the Indians themselves I heard many of the stories, in my brief visits to fourteen reservations. A few of the legends collected I believe have not before been published; others that I had previously read seemed to have new meaning when I listened to experienced storytellers. Today, these old tales, which have been transmitted orally for countless generations, are known by only a few Indians, most of them more than seventy years of age. In almost every village I visited, someone said, "If you had only come last year! The person who could have helped you most died last winter"—usually at the age of ninety or older.

Many of the younger Indians are either scornful of the tales or apologetic about them. They seem embarrassed by the superstitiousness of their ancestors, unaware that the earliest literature in any European language—English, Irish, Scandinavian, German, classical Greek and Latin—is filled with the deeds of giants, monsters, and superhuman heroes. Readers acquainted with the folk literature of the Old World will find striking parallels between it and the oral literature of the Indians of the Pacific Northwest.

But some of the older people still enjoy their old tribal tales and are accustomed to relating them. Several fortunate and memorable experiences not only filled my notebooks but gave me unique entertainment—stories told in very good English, chants and songs in an Indian language or in nonsense syllables, appreciative chuckles, fascinating mimicry with voices and hands. A skillful Indian storyteller is actor as well as narrator. His facial expressions are lively, his eyes twinkle, he gestures not only with his hands but with his feet, he changes his voice to fit his characters. When one of his characters sings, the storyteller sings. Sometimes a tale that was delightful when I heard it lacked life when put on paper, for the dramatic quality of the person who related it had been lost.

From the hundreds of Pacific Northwest Indian tales that I have heard or read, I have selected for this book chiefly those about features of the landscape of Washington and Oregon—the mountains, lakes, rivers, rocks, and waterfalls. Many are myths explaining the origin of those features. A few are legends with definite settings. Stories about places are only a small part of the total body of tales told by the Indians of the two states; but my experiences in teaching literature for many years make me believe that they are the ones of most interest to the general reader.

My two criteria in the consideration of each tale have been inseparable: Is it authentic? And is it interesting? My approach, in other words, has never been sociological or anthropological; my chief purpose has been to prepare a collection of Pacific Northwest myths and legends that the general reader will enjoy, either as entertainment or as information about an American way of living strange to him.

My opinion that Indian folk tales about landscape features appeal to the general reader is based in part on the fact that many were recorded, obviously with enjoyment, by the "general listener." Such stories form the greater part of those preserved by the early neighbors and friends of the Indians of the Pacific Northwest. Army officers and army engineers, early missionaries and teachers, a Canadian artist wandering through the Northwest to sketch Indians, a poet of the early West, a nineteen-year-old soldier at Fort Klamath in 1865, government physicians on reservations in the 1870's and 1890's, a pioneer rancher and pioneer housewives, an early resort owner on Lake Chelan, hunters in the Cascade and Wallowa Mountains, early historians at Pacific University and at the University of Washington—these men and women showed their interest by recording old tribal tales about the rivers, lakes, and mountains near their homes or seen in their travels.

The stories in the first three sections of the book, therefore, were selected or collected mainly because they center around natural phenomena and geographical features of the Pacific Northwest. In each of these three sections, the tales have been arranged, as far as possible, in geographical order. But these legends of the landscape reveal many of the beliefs of the people who originated and related them. To round out that part of the picture, myths of creation, of the origin of Indian customs, of heavenly bodies, storms, and fire have been included. In the fourth and fifth sections, the arrangement of tales, therefore, is topical, although some of them likewise have localized settings. At the beginning of each section there is a chapter of factual material. In the first section, the chapter "Indian Names for Mount Rainier" is also factual.

Throughout the entire book, the general reader, not the specialist, has been considered: the general reader who likes an entertaining folk tale and who has some curiosity about what our native Americans in the Pacific Northwest thought on subjects which have puzzled people of every land.

Most of the legends from printed sources I have rewritten, chiefly because (1) literal translations, desirable for scientific purposes, seldom make smooth, pleasant reading and (2) the ornate wordiness of most pioneer recorders is not appropriate to folk literature. (For the simple, direct style of Indians accustomed to storytelling in English, see pages 91, 121, 122, 138, 151, 158, 189.) In four stories, references to physiological functions have been deleted. For the harsher and more repetitious aspects of the Indian folktales of the region, serious students are directed to the specialized publications listed in the bibliography.

A complete list of the people who have contributed to this anthology would be very long. Members of pioneer families on both sides of the Cascade Range, librarians in university and public libraries in Oregon and Washington, my colleagues at the State College of Washington in Pacific Northwest history, anthropology, geology, English, and the library—their many courtesies are appreciated; but only my Indian helpers will be named here, in gratitude for their special kind of coöperation.

Mrs. Clara Moore, early in my field research, permitted me to make wire recordings of three of her stories, so that I might study the style of a good storyteller long accustomed to speaking English. Mary Summerlin spent a day with me, sharing much that she had learned from her Colville grandmother, who was eager for tribal traditions not to be forgotten. Harry Shale, Esau Penn, Leven Coe, and Robert E. Lee—each an experienced entertainer of his people—are recognized in connection with their own stories. In the same region, Jack Ward, with one of his father's stories, and Mrs. Rose Purdy, with her unusual knowledge of the guardian-spirit concept, also were helpful.

To them I add Mrs. William Shelton, aged ninety-three when I called on her, Jerry Meeker, aged ninety, Mrs. Rose Seymore, aged ninety-four, Peter Noyes, Eneas Seymore, John Hudson, Ellen Joe Dick, Sam Ulmer, Chief Jobe Charley, and Otis Half-Moon, from the older generation; Mrs. Joe Hoptowit, Joseph Hilair, Andrew Joe, Lucy and Walter Miller, Hattie Wesley, Caleb Whitman, of the middle generation; and young, college-trained Clarence Pickernell—all appreciative of their culture and interested in preserving the best of it. Each of them "dug deep down in his head," as Otis Half-Moon expressed it, for another story, or additional details for some legend already written, or facts about old beliefs and customs.

It is my hope that my Indian helpers will approve of these selections from their oral literature and of this retelling of some Indian Legends of the Pacific Northwest.

I.
MYTHS
OF THE
MOUNTAINS

THE SPIRITS

IN NATURE

"To the Indian in his native state," said Martin Sampson, an Indian grandfather of the Puget Sound region, "everything had life or spirit; the earth, the rocks, trees, ferns, as well as birds and animals, even the hail which fell from the sky, had a spirit and a language and song of its own and might be an inspiration to a warrior."

Each wind was the breath of some being who lived far away in the direction from which the wind blows. To each the Indians gave a name; and every sigh, whistle, moan, or roar of the wind seemed to them to be the voice of its spirit. Echoes, waterfalls and rapids, the roar of thunder, the growth of plants, the changed position of stars—all were caused by the spirits living in them. The spirits of nature control nature, the Indians believed, just as the spirits that live in human bodies control human actions.

Whether the spirits were regarded as good or evil depended chiefly on how they treated the Indian. He tried to win their favor and protection, therefore, and to avoid their wrath. If angered, the spirits that controlled salmon would cause a failure of the season's run of fish; the spirits of the mountains would cause a storm or avalanche or perhaps a volcanic eruption. The spirits living in the rapids of the Columbia River and in the dark pools along its banks might seize the canoe of the man who had angered them. Some spirits, always evil, hid in caves and in caverns below the earth, but roamed forth from time to time to do their wickedness.

The spirit of swamps and thickets could be heard but never seen. It did no harm except that its voice sometimes caused people to become lost, because it kept them from knowing the right direction. The spirit of the dark forest was an evil spirit, a demon. It slept during the day and journeyed forth at night to break canoes, rob traps, and frighten late travelers. Disobedient children were warned that it would steal them.

The spirit of the storm was visualized as a huge bird, known as Thunderbird. The flapping of its wings caused the sound of thunder; the flash of its eyes was the lightning. It lived in a cloud above the highest peak the tribe could see, or in a cave in the mountains. Indians near the coast believed that Thunderbird flew to the Pacific Ocean to get the whales which were its food. Rain clouds and thunderstorms often followed it home from the ocean. The Indians feared Thunderbird and tried not to anger it.

Powerful spirits lived on the tops of the highest peaks. They too must not be angered. That is why the Indians never climbed above the snow line on Mount Rainier. "There is a lake of fire on top of the mountain," warned Sluiskin, the guide of the first men to climb Mount Rainier. He took them only as far as the snow line. "In the lake lives a mighty demon. If you should reach the top, the demon will seize you and kill you and throw you into the fiery lake."

When he saw the climbers returning two days later, he stood open-mouthed, sure that they were ghosts.

Mount Baker (Komo Kulshan) got very angry one time, Indians along the Stillaguamish River have told Nels Bruseth. "Kulshan once got so mad that a big piece fell off and slid way down the mountain. This made a big fire and lots of noise. Kulshan and Shuksan became black all over. The waters in the rivers became black and warm. Fish came floating down the rivers cooked. Lots of Indians and animals fled. Next year most of them went back again. Since then Kulshan has never been mad."

In some traditions, the mountains seem more like human beings than spirits; in fact, three storytellers today begin certain tales with the words, "Long ago when the mountains were people." The peaks of the Cascade Range moved about at will; they had wives or husbands; they had children —the smaller peaks and buttes near them.

Some spirits, of course, had more power than others. Did the Indians before the white man came conceive of an all-powerful spirit, a Supreme Being, a "Great Spirit"? There is disagreement on this matter, not only among the missionaries and teachers who knew and wrote about the Indians in early days but also among anthropologists and mythologists who have studied their myths and rituals in more recent years.

Tyhee Sahale and *Sahale Tyee* (*Tyee* meaning "chief," and *Sahale* meaning "up above") are terms often found in stories recorded by pioneers. They were the words in the Chinook jargon, the trade language of Indians and white men, that missionaries used for the Christian concept of God. In some traditions recorded before specialists were in the field—"In the Beginning of the Nisqually World," for instance—the term "the Great Spirit" obviously refers to a supernatural being, told about in many tribes, who bore a name which means "the Changer." He was called *Dokibatl, Doquebuth, Xelas, Mikamatt,* and other names difficult for white people to pronounce and to spell. This being changed the world of the ancients into the world of the Indian; he was the creator and transformer, but apparently he was not worshipped.

In some other stories, it is not clear whether the "Great Spirit" (or *Tyhee Sahale*) was the chief of the sky spirits, some other powerful spirit, or a native concept of a Supreme Being. The Great Spirit, or the Great White Spirit, occasionally referred to by today's storytellers seems to be a blending of aboriginal concepts with the Christian idea of God.

MOUNT SHASTA

AND THE

GRIZZLY BEARS

"At night, when no wars or excitement of any kind stirred the village they [the Indians] would gather in the chief's or other great bark lodges around the fires, and tell and listen to stories; a red wall of men in a great circle, the women a little back, and the children still behind, asleep in the skins and blankets. How silent! You can hear but one voice at a time in an Indian village."

Thus the poet and adventurer Joaquin Miller described the storytelling custom among the Modoc of southern Oregon and northern California, as he knew it when he lived among them in the 1850's. At such firelight gatherings he learned this story about Mount Shasta, which can be seen from the Modoc area.

Mount Shasta is a snow-covered peak in northern California, 14,161 feet in altitude.

Before people were on the earth, the Chief of the Sky Spirits grew tired of his home in the Above World, because it was always cold up there. So he made a hole in the sky by turning a stone round and round. Through this hole he pushed snow and ice until he made a great mound that reached from the earth almost to the sky. Later, people named it Mount Shasta.

Then the Sky Spirit stepped from a cloud to the peak and walked down the mountain. When he was about halfway down to the valley below, he thought, "On this mountain there should be trees." He put his finger to the ground here and there, here and there. Wherever his finger touched the ground, a tree began to grow. In his footsteps the snow melted, and the water ran down in rivers.

The Sky Spirit broke off the small end of the giant stick he had carried from the sky and threw the pieces into the rivers. The longer pieces became beaver and otter; the smaller pieces became fish. From the big end of the stick he made the animals.

Biggest of them all were the grizzly bears. They were covered with hair and they had sharp claws, just as they have today, but they walked on two feet and could talk. They looked so fierce that the Sky Spirit sent them away from him, to live in the forest at the base of the mountain.

When the leaves dropped from the trees, he picked them up, blew upon them, and so made the birds.

Then the Chief of the Sky Spirits decided to stay on the earth, and to bring his family down from the sky. The mountain became their lodge. He made a big fire in the center of the mountain and a hole in the top so that the smoke and sparks could fly out. When he put a big log on the fire, sparks would fly up and the earth would tremble.

Late one spring, while the Sky Spirit and his family were sitting round the fire, the Wind Spirit sent a big storm that shook the top of the mountain. It blew and blew, and roared and roared. Smoke blown back into the lodge hurt their eyes. At last the Sky Spirit said to his youngest daughter, "Go up to the smoke hole and ask the Wind Spirit to blow more gently. Tell him I am afraid he will blow the mountain over."

His little daughter was glad to go. As she started, her father spoke again. "Be very careful when you get to the top. Don't put your head out. If you do put it out, the wind may catch you by your hair and blow you away. Just thrust out your arm, make a sign, and then speak to the Wind Spirit."

The little girl hurried to the top of the mountain and spoke to the Wind Spirit. As she was about to start back, she remembered that her father had said the ocean could be seen from the top of their lodge. He had made the ocean since the family moved from the sky, and his daughter had never seen it.

She put her head out of the hole and looked toward the west. The Wind Spirit caught her long hair, pulled her out of the mountain, and blew her down over the snow and ice. She landed among the scrubby fir trees at the edge of the timber and snow line, her long red hair trailing over the snow.

There Grizzly Bear found her when he was out hunting food for his family. He carried the little girl home with him, wondering who and what she was. Mother Bear took good care of her and brought her up with their family of cubs. The little red-haired girl and the cubs ate together, played together, and grew up together.

When she became a young woman, she and the eldest son of the grizzly bears were married. In the years that followed they had many children. The children did not look like their father or like their mother. They were not so hairy as the grizzlies, and yet they did not look like spirits either.

All the grizzly bears throughout the forests were proud of these new creatures. They were so pleased and were so kindhearted that they made a lodge for the red-haired mother and her strange-looking children. They built the lodge near Mount Shasta—Little Mount Shasta it is called today.

After many years had passed, Mother Grizzly Bear knew that she would soon die. Fearing that she had done wrong in keeping the daughter of the Chief of the Sky Spirits away from her father, she felt that she should send him word and ask his forgiveness. So she asked all the grizzlies to join her at the new lodge they had built. Then she sent her oldest grandson to the top of Mount Shasta, in a cloud, to tell the Spirit Chief where he could find his long-lost daughter.

The father was so glad that he came down the mountainside in giant strides. He hurried so fast that the snow melted off in places under his feet. Even today his tracks can be seen in the rocky path on the south side of Mount Shasta.

As he neared the lodge, he called out, "Is this where my little daughter lives?"

He expected to see a little girl exactly as she had looked when he saw her last. When he saw the strange creatures his daughter was taking care of and learned that they were his grandchildren, he was very angry. A new race had been created, and he had not known about it. He frowned on the old grandmother so sternly that she died at once. Then he cursed all the grizzlies.

"Get down on your hands and knees. From this moment all of you grizzlies shall walk on four feet. And you shall never talk again. You have wronged me."

He drove his grandchildren out of the lodge, put his daughter over his shoulder, and climbed back up the mountain. Never again did he come to the forest. Some say that he put out the fire in the center of his lodge and took his daughter back up to the sky to live.

Those strange creatures, his grandchildren, scattered and wandered over the earth. They were the first Indians, the ancestors of all the Indian tribes.

That is why the Indians living around Mount Shasta would never kill a grizzly bear. Whenever one of them was killed by a grizzly, his body was burned on the spot. And for many years all who passed that way cast a stone there until a great pile of stones marked the place of his death.

MOUNT SHASTA

AND THE

GREAT FLOOD

The Indians of the Pacific Northwest, and those of some other areas also, believed that before the first Indians were created, the world was inhabited by a race of animal people. In some tribes, chiefly those between the Rocky Mountains and the Cascade Range, the shrewdest and most powerful of these people was Coyote. For further explanation of this belief, see "The Animal People of Long Ago."

Once Coyote was traveling around, carrying his bow and arrows with him. He came to a body of water where an evil spirit lived. Seeing Coyote, the evil spirit rose out of the water and said, "There is no wood." Then the evil being caused the water to rise and overflow the land until Coyote was covered.

After a time, the water went down and the land dried off. Coyote sprang up, took his bow and an arrow, and shot the evil spirit. Then Coyote ran away.

But the water followed him. Coyote ran to higher ground. The water followed him to higher ground. He started up Mount Shasta. The water followed him up Mount Shasta. He ran to the top of the mountain. The water followed him and became very deep, but it did not quite reach the top.

On top of Mount Shasta, Coyote made a fire, on the only ground left above the water. Grizzly Bear saw the fire and swam to the top of the mountain. Deer saw the fire and swam to it. So did Elk, Black Bear, Gray Squirrel, Jack Rabbit, and Ground Squirrel.

Badger, Porcupine, and Raccoon saw the fire and swam to it. Fisher, Wolf, and Cougar swam there. All the animal people stayed on top of Mount Shasta until the great flood was over. At last the water went down, leaving dry land in the midst of lakes and marshes.

Then the animal people came down from the top of Mount Shasta and made new homes for themselves. They scattered everywhere and became the ancestors of all the animal people on the earth.

THE PEAKS OF

CENTRAL OREGON

The Oregon sky line for many miles both east and west of the Cascade Range is dominated by a series of peaks. The following stories and traditions about some of them were recalled by Lucy and Walter Miller, Warm Springs Indians, who had heard them in childhood from their grandfathers, signers of the Treaty of 1855.

The group of peaks called the Three Sisters is a prominent landscape feature in central Oregon. Each peak is more than 10,000 feet in altitude.

The mountains were once people, our grandfathers used to tell us. Mount Adams, north of the Columbia, and Mount Hood, south of it, became jealous of each other because of some girl. So they started quarreling and fighting. At that time there was a bridge across the river, and the two rivals would cross it to fight. Sometimes they fought on one side of the Columbia, sometimes on the other. Coyote tried to stop their quarreling, but they would not stop.

So all the other mountain peaks agreed to help him. From away down in the Klamath Marsh country they marched north for a big council meeting. They planned to cross the Columbia on the bridge and have the meeting north of the river. The Three Sisters marched with the mountain people, and so did Black Butte and her husband.

Black Butte carried on her back a big bag of roots and berries, for food along the way. Her husband carried a deer over his shoulder, so that they would have meat on their journey. One day the sun was so hot and the bag was so heavy that Black Butte sat down to rest. Her husband was annoyed and lay down, pouting. Black Butte was very tired. She was so warm that sweat ran down her face and sides in streams. Those creeks came together below her and formed the Metolius River.

But Coyote did not wait for the help of the mountain people. Mount Adams and Mount Hood were going to have a wrestling match, and Coyote knew that it would turn into a fight. So he made up his mind to keep the two men apart. He wished the bridge to fall, and the bridge fell. Mount Adams could not cross over.

When the mountain people heard that Coyote had broken down the bridge, they stopped marching. They stayed just where they were, and later were given new mountain names. They stopped where they are today—Mount Jefferson, the Three Sisters, Mount Washington, and all the others.

Black Butte and her husband were still resting when the bridge fell, and they stayed there at the head of the Metolius River. Green Ridge, the husband, still lies there pouting. There are plenty of deer on Green Ridge. The plants and seeds Black Butte carried took root. We still go there to dig bitterroot, kouse, Indian potato, and *looksch,* and to gather huckleberries, service berries, little blueberries, and pine nuts. Almost all the plant foods Indians like grow on Black Butte.

2

South of Black Butte and Green Ridge is the mountain group called the Three Sisters. Klah Klahnee, the Three Sisters, was once the biggest and highest mountain of all; it could be seen for many miles. One time the earth shook for days, and the mountain boiled inside. It boiled over, and hot rocks came out of the top of it. Flames and smoke rose high in the air. Red-hot stones were thrown out in every direction. Many villages and many Indians were buried by the rocks. When the mountain became quiet again, most of it was gone. Only three points were left. That is why it was called *Klah Klahnee,* for that means "three points." You can still see the black rocks all around the base of the three mountains.

3

South of the Three Sisters is Broken Top; our grandfathers called it *Tluskh-na-me Pahto.* That means "dirt mountain." South of Broken Top is Bachelor Butte. Our old people called it *Tkh-tkh-ee,* which means "grasshopper mountain."

Three-fingered Jack, north of Black Butte, they called Little *Khla-tee-wap-thee.* Mount Jefferson they called Big *Khla-tee-wap-thee.* That means "slide down and get stuck in the mud." That is what happened when people rode up the mountainside in the spring—the horses slid down and got stuck in the mud.

MOUNT JEFFERSON
AND THE
GREAT FLOOD

Like the Hebrews, Babylonians, Greeks, Norsemen, and other peoples of the Old World, many Indian tribes of North and South America had traditions of the Deluge. The Indians of the Pacific Northwest told several flood stories, the highest peak in the area being the Ararat. The Shasta tradition has already been given; other flood myths appear farther on in this volume.

This flood tradition about Mount Jefferson, the second highest peak in Oregon, was told by John S. Coie, Assistant Professor Emeritus, the State College of Washington. He had heard it years ago from a Portland resident who had spent much time among some Indians of Oregon.

A great flood covered the land. Then the waters flowed away, and the land became dry again. A second time a flood covered the land, and a second time the waters went away. Afraid that another and greater flood might come, the people cut the biggest cedar they could find and made the biggest canoe any of them had ever seen.

When they saw the flood coming the third time, they chose the bravest and finest of their young men and the fairest and choicest of their maidens. They put the young people in the canoe, with enough food for them for many days. Then a flood bigger and deeper than any before swallowed all the land and the people.

For many days and many nights rain fell, and the canoe floated over the water. Once the dark clouds opened up and the young man and young woman saw blue sky, but the clouds closed again. A second time the dark clouds opened, and they saw blue sky. But again the dark clouds closed. When the clouds opened a third time, the people saw dry land. The man paddled the canoe toward it.

This time the clouds stayed open. The rain stopped. The flood waters went down, and the canoe rested on the top of the peak now called Mount Jefferson. When the valleys were dry again, the two people left the canoe and made their new home at the foot of the mountain. All the Indians are their grandchildren and their grandchildren's children.

You can still see the big canoe near the top of Mount Jefferson, for it was turned to rock.

THE CHIEF'S FACE

ON MOUNT HOOD

Mount Hood (11,253 feet in altitude), the highest peak in Oregon, rises from the Cascade Range southeast of Portland.

Years and years ago, the mountain peak south of Big River was so high that when the sun shone on its south side a shadow stretched north for a day's journey. Inside the mountain, evil spirits had their lodges. Sometimes the evil spirits became so angry that they threw out fire and smoke and streams of hot rocks. Rivers of liquid rock ran toward the sea, killing all growing things and forcing the Indians to move far away.

In those days the Indians also were taller than they are now. They were as tall as the pine and fir trees that cover the hills, and their chief was such a giant that his warriors could walk under his outstretched arms. He was the bravest and the strongest of his tribe.

One night a voice spoke to the chief in a dream. "If you do not conquer the evil spirits that live in the mountain, they will some day throw out a river of fire. The river will flood the land, all the people will be drowned, and your country will be ruined."

The chief knew that he must protect his people. He would fight the demons alone. So he took the long journey to the top of the mountain.

There he found a crater, a big hole, which was the home of evil spirits. Scattered around it were some large stones. The chief picked them up and threw them into the crater.

Muttering with anger, the mountain spirits heated the rocks red hot and hurled them back again. The rocks rose toward the sky and then fell a long distance away. The chief hurled more stones into the crater. The demons spewed up hot rocks and smoke and fire.

For many days the battle continued. Then the chief, resting for a moment, looked down upon the land he had left—the land that had once been green and beautiful. The rivers were choked, the forest and the grass had disappeared, the animals and the people had fled.

The heart of the chief broke with sorrow. He had failed to protect his people, and his land was a blackened ruin. He sank upon the ground and was soon buried by the streams of hot rocks.

But some of his people had fled to the tops of the near-by mountains and so were not covered by the rocks. When the earth cooled and the grass grew again, they returned to their country. In time there was plenty of food once more. But the children, starved and weak for so long, never became as tall and strong as their parents and grandparents had been. The people will remain stunted and weak until a great chief comes who can conquer the demons of fire in the mountain. When he comes, the people will be restored to their former size and all the earth will be happy.

Sometimes the old chief's face can be seen on the north side of Mount Hood, about halfway down the mountain. It is a huge shadow, the profile of an Indian head with its scalp lock.

A MOUNT ADAMS STORY

Mount Adams (12,307 feet in altitude), the second highest peak in Washington, stands in the southwestern part of the state. The Klickitat and Yakima Indians called it Pahto. They claimed it as their mountain.

This legend was told by Chief Jobe Charley, with his granddaughter, Hattie Wesley, acting as interpreter. Now eighty-six years old, Jobe Charley heard the story when he was a little boy. When he got his first horse, he rode to Mount Adams and climbed it. Until he saw the eagles up there, he had not believed the story. Many eagles are hatched in the caves on the east side of the top of Mount Adams.

Back when the mountains were people, Sun was a man. He had five mountains for his wives. One was Plash-Plash, where the Goat Rocks are now. *Plash-Plash* means "white spots." Another was Wahkshum, west of Satus Pass. The others were Mount Adams, Mount Rainier, and Mount St. Helens. The Indians called all of them *Pahto,* which means "standing high." Wahkshum and Plash-Plash were once known as Pahtoes also. I will call only Mount Adams Pahto in this story, for Rainier and St. Helens are not important in it.

Sun traveled from east to west, of course. So Wahkshum was the first wife he talked to every morning. Plash-Plash was the second, and Pahto was the third. Pahto became jealous of the other two and made up her mind to get rid of them. Jealous and angry, she fought them and broke down their high heads. All that is left of Plash-Plash is Goat Rocks. All that is left of Wahkshum is the mountain called Simcoe Mountain and the little huckleberry bushes on it. Rainier and St. Helens were so far away that Pahto left them alone.

For a while after she had broken the heads of Wahkshum and Plash-Plash, Pahto was happy. Every morning she was the first wife Sun spoke to. She was the tallest mountain around, and she was proud and strong. But she did not remain satisfied. She made up her mind to go across the river and take what she wanted from the mountains south of her.

So she went down there and brought back all their grizzly bears, black bears, elk, deer, pine nuts, huckleberries, roots, and herbs. From the rivers and creeks she took the salmon and trout and put them in the streams which flowed down her sides. She planted the berries and the pine nuts and the roots all around her. She turned loose the elk, deer, and bears. That is why there are plenty on Mount Adams today.

All this time the Great Spirit was watching. He saw the wrong things Pahto was doing. He thought to himself, "There must be a law that any wrongdoing shall be punished."

But punishment did not come yet. Pahto was so strong and tall that the other mountains said, "We'll not do anything about what she has done. We'll just let it go."

But Klah Klahnee—you call them the Three Sisters—said among themselves, "Pahto is too proud and greedy. We must do something."

They came up north and said to Wyeast, Mount Hood, "Why don't you destroy Pahto? Why do you let her get the best of you? You are tall and strong. Some day there will be people on the earth. When they find that we have let Pahto destroy us and steal from us, they will make fun of us."

That is how Klah Klahnee caused Wyeast to fight Pahto. "If I get the best of her," Wyeast promised them, "I'll take back all she has stolen from us."

But first Wyeast said to Pahto, in a nice way, "I want you to give back half of what you took from us. When the new·people come, those who live in our part of the country should have the same food that people near you will have. I am asking you now, in a nice way, for only half of what you took from us. If you give it to me, the new people will have food."

But Pahto was greedy. "No, I shall never give you anything," she said.

So they fought.

Up to that time, Pahto had had a high head. Wyeast hit her from the east side and knocked her head off. Today on the north side of Pahto there is a pile of fine rocks about half a mile long. These rocks were once Pahto's head.

Then Wyeast thought, "I'll leave here and there a little bit of everything she took away—elk, deer, berries. I'll put some here, some there. Pahto can't have everything." So Wyeast shared with the other mountains.

The Great Spirit saw all that happened. He did not try to help Pahto. "She deserved that punishment," he thought. "She deserved to lose her head because she destroyed the heads of Wahkshum and Plash-Plash. That will be the law. If people do wrong, they will be punished in the same way."

But after Pahto lost her head, she became mean. Whenever she became angry, she would send a big thunderstorm and much rain. In the winter she would send big snows, and in the spring there would be floods. All through the Yakima Valley there were lakes from the big floods. When the first people came to the earth, they lived only on the mountains.

The Great Spirit was watching. He saw all that happened. At last he said, "I shall make a new head for Pahto. Then she will not be so mean."

So he sent down a big white eagle with his son, a red eagle, riding on his right shoulder. He put the two eagles on top of Pahto, to be her head. Then he said to her, "I am sending White Eagle and his son to you, to be your head. Don't have hard feelings toward the other mountains. And don't flood the earth again. Remember that you are the daughter of the Great Spirit."

Pahto answered, "I am glad you have given me the eagles. I will forgive the other mountains, and I will not flood the country any more."

Then she raised her right hand and said, "I did not know that the Great Spirit is my father. I am sorry for all the wrong things I have done."

Then the Great Spirit replied, "I gave the world to you mountains. I put you here and there, where I wanted you to be. Some of you I made high. Some I made low. You should never have destroyed Plash-Plash and Wahkshum."

From that time on, to this day, it is really true, in your belief, in my belief, that the Great Spirit is the father.

WHITE EAGLE: THE
LAW ON MOUNT ADAMS

This legend, which an old Yakima told Lucullus McWhorter in 1924, explains why the Indians objected when white people climbed Mount Adams. Once when a surveying party was climbing the peak, a wind came up and thunder rolled through the mountains. The Indian guide of a hunting party was delighted. "The sacred eagles that guard the mountain are angry," he explained. "They do not want the silence of the hills broken. Perhaps these men will be killed for going where they should not go."

One time Wasco (Mount Hood) and Pahto (Mount Adams) had a big battle. Pahto's head was broken off and pieces were scattered from here to Fish Lake. Even today that is hard country to travel.

Wasco took home with her everything that had belonged to Pahto—all her game and fish, berries and roots. Pahto was left standing headless and useless. She was no longer growing foods. She was no longer a producer of life.

The Great Maker saw all that had been done. And he could see the future. He knew that people were waiting to be born, waiting for the country to be made ready for them. So he brought life back to Pahto. He returned to her all her game and salmon, all her berries and roots.

He gave her a new head to take the place of the one she had lost. This head was Quoh Why-am-mah, the Great White Eagle sent down from the Land Above.

Pahto was now a powerful Law, standing up toward the sky for the whole world to see. Wisdom was in the White Eagle, to watch and guard the whole world. Life was in the White Eagle, to grow foods and give life to the people who were to come.

White Eagle said, "I want two children to sit beside me, to watch toward the sunrise. I will send them to all parts of the earth, to see everything everywhere. They will tell me what they see, tell me what is being done."

In this way the Great Maker sent White Eagle to be the head of Pahto, to be the Law standing high for all the world to see. The two children, two young eagles, were sent to him, and then White Eagle declared:

"Whatever the Great Maker has done, I know. And I know what is to come. There will be birth, and there will be death. There will be sorrow everywhere. When the children grow up, there will be chiefs and rulers in the land.

"But White Eagle will care for all of them. The center of power, the head of the Law, is in me. I will send my children all over the land, to report to me what is going on. My power, my Law, is stronger than all the people who will ever live."

The White Eagle, having come down from the Land Above, holds great spirit power. Life dwells in the mountain. Life is in the water flowing down from many caves and from fields of snow and ice.

Facing the sunrise, the two young eagles sit at either side of White Eagle's topmost crown. San-we Tlah, the Speaker, is on the right, toward the northland. Kay-no Klah, the Overseer, is at the left, toward the southland. They watch everywhere, go everywhere. Flying all over the world, they report to White Eagle all that is being done. Nothing escapes their sharp eyes.

That is why Pahto belongs to my people. Pahto is a witness to our treaty with Governor Stevens. White Eagle always points upward to the Great Maker, who heard the promises of the treaty. That is why I do not like to see the white people climb Pahto. Young Indians used to go to the top, but they made no wrong there.

Standing high among the clouds, White Eagle is always first to be greeted by the Sun. The berries and roots, the game and fish of the mountains and streams were created for us, for we are the first real people of this country. All that Pahto has—all her foods—are free.

That is why I always give freely, why I feed the hungry without pay. It is the Law, the white Law, lifted high where it is painted by the Sun and blanketed by the clouds. Since they are the gifts of the Great Maker, the foods which were planted for his children must all be free.

THE BRIDGE

OF THE GODS

Tribes from central Oregon to northeastern Washington related traditions about a legendary rock "bridge" that spanned the Columbia River "one sleep" below the site of The Dalles. When it fell, old Indians said to early travelers, its rocks formed the Cascades in the river; its fall, two Indians explained to travelers in 1854, was accompanied by quarrels between Mount Hood and Mount St. Helens, who threw fire at one another.

The most familiar version of the myth about the stone arch has been altered so freely that no one now can determine the original tradition, even in the variant written by a Puyallup-Nisqually Indian. The source of the story given here, Lulu Crandall, seems to have been the one closest to the Klickitats, who had this tradition. Mrs. Crandall, who had known those Indians from her pioneer childhood, was a historian of The Dalles area.

Long ago, when the world was young, all people were happy. The Great Spirit, whose home is in the sun, gave them all they needed. No one was hungry, no one was cold.

But after a while, two brothers quarreled over the land. The older one wanted most of it, and the younger one wanted most of it. The Great Spirit decided to stop the quarrel. One night while the brothers were asleep he took them to a new land, to a country with high mountains. Between the mountains flowed a big river.

The Great Spirit took the two brothers to the top of the high mountains and wakened them. They saw that the new country was rich and beautiful.

"Each of you will shoot an arrow in opposite directions," he said to them. "Then you will follow your arrow. Where your arrow falls, that will be your country. There you will become a great chief. The river will separate your lands."

One brother shot his arrow south into the valley of the Willamette River. He became the father and the high chief of the Multnomah people. The other brother shot his arrow north into the Klickitat country. He became the father and high chief of the Klickitat people.

Then the Great Spirit built a bridge over the big river. To each brother he said, "I have built a bridge over the river, so that you and your people may visit those on the other side. It will be a sign of peace between you. As long as you and your people are good and are friendly with each other, this bridge of the Tahmahnawis will remain."

It was a broad bridge, wide enough for many people and many ponies to walk across at one time. For many snows the people were at peace and crossed the river for friendly visits. But after a time they did wicked things. They were selfish and greedy, and they quarreled. The Great Spirit, displeased again, punished them by keeping the sun from shining. The people had no fire, and when the winter rains came, they were cold.

Then they began to be sorry for what they had done, and they begged the Great Spirit for fire. "Give us fire, or we will die from the cold," they prayed. The heart of the Great Spirit was softened by their prayer. He went to an old woman who had kept herself from the wrongdoing of her people and so still had some fire in her lodge.

"If you will share your fire, I will grant you anything you wish," the Great Spirit promised her. "What do you want most?"

"Youth and beauty," answered the old woman promptly. "I wish to be young again, and to be beautiful."

"You shall be young and beautiful tomorrow morning," promised the

Great Spirit. "Take your fire to the bridge, so that the people on both sides of the river can get it easily. Keep it burning there always as a reminder of the goodness and kindness of the Great Spirit."

The old woman, whose name was Loo-wit, did as he said. Then the Great Spirit commanded the sun to shine again. When it rose the next morning, it was surprised to see a young and beautiful maiden sitting beside a fire on the Bridge of the Gods. The people, too, saw the fire, and soon their lodges were warm again. For many moons all was peaceful on both sides of the great river and the bridge.

The young men also saw the fire—and the beautiful young woman who attended it. They visited her often. Loo-wit's heart was stirred by two of them—a handsome young chief from south of the river, whose name was Wyeast, and a handsome young chief from north of the river, whose name was Klickitat. She could not decide which of the two she liked better.

Wyeast and Klickitat grew jealous of each other and soon began to quarrel. They became so angry that they fought. Their people also took up the quarrel, so that there was much fighting on both sides of the river. Many warriors were killed.

This time the Great Spirit was made angry by the wickedness of the people. He broke down the Bridge of the Gods, the sign of peace between the two tribes, and its rocks fell into the river. He changed the two chiefs into mountains. Some say that they continued to quarrel over Loo-wit even after they were mountain peaks. They caused sheets of flame to burst forth, and they hurled hot rocks at each other. Not thrown far enough, many fell into the river and blocked it. That is why the Columbia is very narrow and the water very swift at The Dalles.

Loo-wit was changed into a snow-capped peak which still has the youth and beauty promised by the Great Spirit. She is now called Mount St. Helens. Wyeast is known as Mount Hood, and Klickitat as Mount Adams. The rocks and the white water where the Bridge of the Gods fell are known as the Cascades of the Columbia.

*   *   *

On the Washington side of the Columbia Gorge, in communities where Sleeping Beauty Mountain is a familiar landmark, a somewhat different version of the legend is still told. It was used as the prologue of a centennial pageant, "The Mount Adams Story," given at White Salmon in 1952. Sleeping Beauty Mountain, back in the days when the mountains were people, was loved by Wyeast (Mount Hood) and Pahto (Mount Adams), sons of the Great Spirit. In a volcanic struggle between the jealous brothers, the terrified waters of a vast lake east of the mountains tore a hole through the range and thus formed both a tunnel and the Columbia River. In a second battle between the peaks, the bridge over the tunnel crashed. The ugly old guardian of the bridge, Loo-wit, was granted her wish to become young and beautiful again. She is now known as Mount St. Helens.

For several other versions of the legend, and a modern scientist's explanation of the probable cataclysm in which it originated, see the author's "The Bridge of the Gods in Fact and Fancy," in the *Oregon Historical Quarterly* of March, 1952.

THE RIVER SPIRIT

AND THE

MOUNTAIN DEMONS

The Wishram great-great-grandmother who told this legend in her native language remembered the coming of Dr. John McLoughlin and the establishment of Fort Vancouver in 1825. She was a little girl when the men of the Hudson's Bay Company came to the area; her father was chief of a village a few miles upstream from Fort Vancouver. When she related the following story to Glenn Ranck in 1921, her grandson, her interpreter, was chief of the village.

Long, long ago, quarrels and fierce fighting broke out between the spirit that lived in the river and the evil spirits that lived in the mountains above it. In one of their battles, the mountain demons built a rock wall across the stream and tied to it the chief of the river spirits.

But the river spirit, strong in his anger, broke the ropes. Then he called upon all his powers and gathered together all the river spirits. With their help he cut a hole and then a long tunnel through the rocks. This made a broad stone arch over the river, a wide natural bridge which people and their ponies and their dogs could cross.

The Great Spirit, whose home is in the sky, called together the tribes living on both sides of the river.

"We shall name this the Bridge of the Tahmahnawis," he told them. "It will be the bridge of the spirits, but you people also may use it. As long as you are good and friendly and peaceful, the bridge will span the river. But if you become selfish and greedy, if you quarrel and fight, it will be destroyed. Then the rocks will fall into the water below."

The people crossed over the Bridge of the Gods, and they passed under it in their canoes. Whenever a party of Indians reached this long tunnel, they would fasten their canoes together, one behind the other, so that they would not crash against each other in the darkness. Then they would pray to the Great Spirit for courage and guidance as they paddled through the long, dark tunnel.

For many years the Indians on both sides of the river lived in peace and friendliness. They met together for fishing and hunting, huckleberry picking and camas digging, races and games, potlatches and winter dances. But in later generations bitter feelings grew up between the tribes, and warfare followed. At last, quarrels over who owned the bridge turned into a bloody battle that lasted for days.

Suddenly, in the middle of the night, the earth began to shake and tremble. The mountain demons belched forth flaming thunderbolts. They hurled hot stones and liquid rocks upon the water below.

Angrily the river spirit dashed his waves against the supports of the bridge. The huge rocks began to shake and tremble. Then, with a noise like Thunderbird on the mountain, the Bridge of the Gods fell. Rocks, earth, trees came tumbling into the angry, whirling waters of the river.

On the morning after the fall of the bridge, a grandfather of my people was fishing on the riverbank between The Dalles and the Cascades. He had felt the earth shake and had heard the crash. He had seen the flames and hot rocks thrown by the mountain demons. But he had not realized that what the Great Spirit had warned would happen had come to pass.

While he was fishing, the water began to rise around him. He stepped back on higher ground. The river continued to rise. The fisherman stepped to a higher level again and again as the water rose around him. The river became deeper and broader as if a dam had been built below where the man was fishing.

Then an Indian runner appeared. "The bridge has fallen!" he called out. "The Great Spirit has spoken."

The bridge fell because people had forgotten the commands and teachings of the Tahmahnawis and the wise men. The rocks fell apart because peace between the tribes had been broken. The Indians were punished, and their power was broken. The valley of the Wauna, the great river, was opened for the coming of the white man from afar.

But in the happy days to come, when all tribes are again at peace, when our chiefs and the white men smoke the pipe of friendship, another bridge will span the river where the Bridge of the Gods was in the days of our grandfathers.

THE ORIGIN OF
PUGET SOUND AND
THE CASCADE RANGE

Clarence Pickernell, a Quinault-Chehalis-Cowlitz Indian from Tahola, Washington, told this legend in February, 1951. He had heard it from his great-grandmother. Pickernell pronounced the closing words rapidly, in a rhythm and with a hand movement to suggest the lapping of water against the shore.

One time when the world was young, the land east of where the Cascade Mountains now stand became very dry. This was in the early days before rains came to the earth. In the beginning of the world, moisture came up through the ground, but for some reason it stopped coming. Plants and trees withered and died. There were no roots and no berries for food. The water in the streams became so low that salmon could no longer live there. The ancient people were hungry.

At last they sent a group of their people westward to ask Ocean for water.

"Our land is drying up," they told him. "Send us water lest we starve and die."

"I will send you my sons and daughters," Ocean promised the ancient people. "They will help you."

Ocean's sons and daughters were Clouds and Rain. They went home with the messengers from the dry country. Soon there was plenty of moisture. Plants and trees became green and grew again. Streams flowed with water, and many fish lived in them again. Roots and berries grew everywhere. There was plenty to eat.

But the people were not satisfied with plenty. They wanted more. They wanted to be sure they would always have water. So they dug great pits and asked Clouds and Rain to fill them.

Clouds and Rain stayed away from their father, Ocean, so long that he became lonely for them. After many moons, he sent messengers to ask that his sons and daughters be allowed to come home.

"Let my children return home," he sent word to the ancient people. "You have enough water for the present, and I will see that you have enough in the future."

But the people were selfish and refused to let Clouds and Rain go. The messengers had to return to Ocean without his sons and daughters.

Then Ocean told his troubles to the Great Spirit. "Punish the people for their evil ways," prayed Ocean. "Punish them for always wanting more and more."

The Great Spirit heard his prayer. He leaned down from the sky, scooped up a great amount of earth, and made the Cascade Mountains as a wall between Ocean and the dry country. The long and deep hole left where the earth had been, Ocean soon filled with water. Today people call it Puget Sound.

The people east of the mountains are still punished for their selfishness and greed. Ocean sends so little moisture over the range that they do not have all the plants that grow along the coast. But they still have the pits their grandfathers dug. They are Lake Chelan and the lakes south and east of it.

Ocean still grieves for his sons and daughters who did not come home. All day and all night along the beach he calls to them and sings his mournful song: *"Ah' tah lah' tah lah'! Ah' tah lah' tah lah'! Ah' tah lah' tah lah'!* Come home! Come home! Come home!"

INDIAN NAMES

FOR MOUNT RAINIER

Mount Rainier, 14,408 feet in altitude, is the highest peak in the Cascade Range. It is the heart of Mount Rainier National Park.

In these Indian names for Mount Rainier, the accent is on the second syllable; the k's *are strongly guttural, the* h's *aspirate.*

"Before the world changed, five sisters lived where Orting is now," recalled Jerry Meeker, a Puyallup, ninety years old in 1952. "When Doquebuth, the Changer, came, he changed them into five mountains. One of them was called Takkobad by my people. That is Mount Rainier. I forget the Indian names for the other sisters—Mount Baker, Mount Adams, Mount St. Helens, and Mount Hood.

"Doquebuth said to Takkobad, 'You will take care of the Sound country. You will supply water. You will be useful in that way.' *Ko* means 'water,' " added Mr. Meeker.

In the summer of 1900, a nephew of Chief Seattle told another story about the original name of Mount Rainier, as he sat looking at it from Longmire Springs. It also is said to be a Puyallup myth.

"When Dokibahl [the changer of all things] saw that his work was done, he went and sat on a high mountain. From this he gazed upon his work and then said to the mountain, 'You shall be Ta-ko-bid, because upon you I have rested and you are so near the Divine.' "

Attempts to indicate the tribal names for Mount Rainier by means of our alphabet have resulted in several other spellings, and Indians have given various interpretations of the name. Edward Curtis wrote in 1911 that *Tkomma* in some form was the specific name for Mount Rainier in several Salishan languages; in others, *Tkomma* was the name for any snow-covered peak.

In 1882, twenty elderly Indians from several tribes were invited to the Tacoma office of Elwood Evans, historian and writer, so that they might give him information about place names in the vicinity. When asked through an interpreter, John Flett, about the highest peak in the area, no two of the Indians used the same combination of syllables. *Tehoma, Takober, Takoman* were some of the names spoken. Most of the interpretations of the word referred in some way to the mountain as a source of nourishment, referred directly or indirectly to the streams of white water coming down its slopes.

"The earth is our mother," John Flett explained at another time, "and Tahoma gives us drink, gives white water to the land." A Puyallup woman told an early historian, W. D. Lyman, that the name was *Takhoma,* meaning "breast of the milk-white waters." Another Puyallup informed him that *Takhoma* means any "great white mountain," and that the second syllable was prolonged when Mount Rainier was referred to.

The Reverend Peter Stanup, an educated Puyallup, wrote to Edwin Eells, Indian agent at Tacoma in the 1880's: "The meaning of *Ta-ko-man* is a high, treeless, white or light-colored peak or mound. The name is applicable to any peak or mound as described, but is generally used for one that is distinguished, or highly honored." *Takoman* was mostly used for the peak near Tacoma, he continued, not only because it was held with much respect by most of the Northwest Indians, but also because the syllable *ko* means "water" and refers to the "little lake on top of the mountain. In that lake is a great abundance of valuable shells, from which the Indians made their nose and ear-rings and other valuable jewelry."

Lucullus McWhorter, a pioneer friend of the Yakima and the Klickitat east and south of the mountain, used the spelling *Tahoma* for their name for it, and gave their interpretation as "rumbling like thunder near the skies." Henry Sicade, an educated Nisqually, also wrote that to the Klickitat *Tahoma* means "the great mountain, which gives thunder and lightning, having great unseen powers." The Nisqually name, he wrote, was *Tacobud,* meaning "the place the water comes from."

A ninety-three-year-old Samish woman, Mrs. William Shelton, who lives north of Mount Rainier, told me that her people called it *Takhobah* (the syllables almost equally stressed, the *b* explosive); she said that the word means "hard mountain." A Lummi Indian, Joseph Hilaire, who lives a little farther north, said that the name was *Duh-hwahk* and that it means "clear sky." When the sky is clear, he explained, Mount Rainier can be seen from the ancestral home of the Lummi near Mount Baker. *Kobah,* meaning "high mountain always covered with snow," was the Skagit name for Mount Baker, Andrew Joe told me; *Takobah,* "higher than Kobah," was their name for Mount Rainier.

Dahkobeed, Tahkobed, Takobed, T'koma, Tacopa, Takobet, Takeman, Tacoman, and *Tacob* are other spellings found in scattered sources.

Different tribes not only had different names for the Great White Mountain they lived in sight of, they had different stories about its origin.

MOUNT RAINIER

AND THE

OLYMPIC MOUNTAINS

These first four myths of the origin of Mount Rainier—a fifth is part of the story "Kulshan and His Two Wives"—are also myths about the Olympic Mountains. These mountains rise in the center of the Olympic National Park, which is near the center of the Olympic Peninsula in northwestern Washington. The rugged, knifelike peaks of this section of the Coast Range vary in altitude from 3,000 to 8,000 feet.

The first of the myths given here was related by Peter Rodgers of the Duwamish tribe and was recorded by T. T. Waterman. The second, a Skokomish myth, has been adapted from Edmond S. Meany. The third and fourth, Puyallup and Nisqually, respectively, have been adapted from Henry Sicade. A few details in the third story, including the spelling of the name for Mount Rainier, were contributed by Jerry Meeker.

There are two big mountains in the Olympics. One of them is a sharp peak. He stands southward. His name is Ahstch-a-kud. Another great mountain stands to the north of him. It is like a toothed ridge. That is the man's wife. Her name is Ee-loolth. He had two other wives. One was a small woman, named Bah-bah-deed. His third wife was a tremendous[ly] large woman. Her name is Dah-ko-beed. This was at the time when the Transformer was just preparing to come around the world, to make everything different.

That man Ahstch-a-kud did not know what to do with his three wives. They quarreled all the time. Dah-ko-beed especially was a problem. There was no place big enough for her. She was too big, that woman. Finally he placed her over on the opposite side of the Sound—that is, on the east side. There was room enough for her there. Some people still call her by her Indian name, Dah-ko-beed. Some call her Mount Rainier.

Another wife he put down over by Charleston. She is a little mountain behind Charleston. Bostons [white people] call her Blue Mountain today. To her he gave lots of deer for her food. That small mountain was never covered by the flood. It floated up and stayed dry all the time.

The other wife he set alongside himself in the Olympics. He gave her for her food all those elk that are found over there.

Then everything was fixed. At that time the Transformer turned them into mountains.

Some say that Rainier and one of the other wives still continue their quarreling, off and on, and shoot fire at each other. That is the lightning.

2

Long, long ago, when mountains and stars and rocks were living beings, Dosewallips, a mountain on the west side of Hood Canal, had two wives. These wives were jealous of each other and quarreled frequently.

At last one of them filled her basket with food and plants and crossed over to the other side of Puget Sound. As she passed over the Skokomish River, she dropped a piece of salmon, and it fell into the water. Ever since then, salmon have run up the Skokomish River. Near where Olympia now is, she dropped some bulbs of blue camas. They spread and made a great camas prairie. When the Indians came to the earth, they went there every year to dig the bulbs for food.

At last the woman became weary of traveling. East of where Olympia now is, she sat down. She kept on sulking and nursing her troubles. Sometimes she grew so angry that she thundered, and the other wife thundered back. Once she gathered some fire and threw it across the Sound at the head of the other wife. It burned all the trees off her head, as you can see today.

The mountain that moved away is now known as Mount Rainier. A great hole can be seen on the Olympic Peninsula where she used to stand. The other wife is now known as Mount Constance. The smaller peaks in the Olympic Mountains are the children of Dosewallips and his two wives.

3

Before Mount Rainier was made, a beautiful maiden lived in a valley east of Puget Sound. She married a young man who lived west of the Sound. He already had one wife. And when the new wife joined them, the two women were jealous of each other. They quarreled. After a while they hated each other.

One time when their quarrel was fierce, the younger wife scratched the other woman's face. The husband, too, got scratched when he tried to separate his wives. Then the second wife decided to take her small son and go back to her own tribe across the water.

She put her son in her canoe and also put in plenty of dried fish. As she was about to pull away from shore, she said to the boy, "Takkobad!" She meant by the word, "Don't forget the snow water!" From that exclamation to him she was named Takkobad.

After returning to her childhood home, she was punished for leaving her husband. The Great Changer transformed her into a snow-capped mountain. He made her into a high peak so that all might see it and be warned by it. The little son was changed into what is now called Little Tahoma. It is the highest point on the eastern flank of the great white mountain.

Takkobad's husband also was punished because he did not control his wives and keep peace in his lodge. He was changed into a peak in the Olympic Mountains. Old Indians point to cracks in the mountains behind Jackson's Cove on Hood Canal and say, "There are the scratches Takkobad made on his face."

4

Long ago, the peaks of Ho-had-hun were people. White people call Ho-had-hun the Olympic Mountains. One of the warrior peaks there was named Swy-loobs. He married a maiden peak, Tacobud.

Even after they were married, they and the other peaks kept on growing. They became so large that after a while they were crowded in their small space. Tacobud especially was growing both taller and broader. At last she said to the others, "I will move to a place not so crowded. Then there will be more room for the rest of you."

She spoke to the rising sun. "The people over there have no mountains. I will move across the water and give myself plenty of room. I will take salmon and berries with me, so that the people over there will have plenty to eat."

The peaks of Ho-had-hun had grown so close together that Tacobud found it hard to get loose from them. But she freed herself and moved across the Sound. There she had plenty of room. She grew taller and taller, broader and broader, until she became a giant mountain.

After she had been on the east side of the water for a while, she turned into a monster. She devoured the people who came up on her slopes for berries. She devoured those who came to her forests for deer and elk. She sucked into her cavelike stomach all the people who came near her. Then she devoured them. Their friends and their tribesmen lived in great fear.

At last they asked the Changer to come and rescue them from the mountain monster. When the Changer came, in the form of Fox, he decided to challenge Tacobud to a duel. But first he made a strong rope by twisting twigs of hazel bushes and tying them together. He tied himself to a mountain near Tacobud and then called out to her, "O mountain monster, I challenge you to a sucking contest. I defy you to swallow me as you have swallowed your neighbors."

Tacobud drew in one deep breath after another. She sucked in rocks and boulders and trees, but she could not make Fox move. Again and again she tried, but Fox did not even stir. The rocks which rolled by scratched and bruised him, but he could not be moved. At last Tacobud drew in such a deep breath that she burst her blood vessels. All over her body, rivers of blood gushed forth and flowed down her sides.

Then the mountain monster died, and the Changer made a law. "Hereafter, Tacobud shall be harmless. The streams of blood shall turn to rivers of water. The waters shall have plenty of fish, for the good of all the people who come to the lakes and rivers on the mountain."

MOUNT RAINIER

AND THE

GREAT FLOOD

Long, long ago, when the earth was young, the Great Spirit became very angry with the people and the animals of his world. The Great Spirit lived on the snowy summit of Takhoma.

He was angry because the people and animals were wicked and did many mean things to each other. He decided that he would rid the earth of all of them except the good animals and one good man and his family.

So he said to the good man, "Shoot an arrow into that cloud hanging low over the mountain."

The good man shot an arrow, and it stuck in the cloud.

"Now shoot another arrow into the shaft of that arrow," continued the Great Spirit.

The second arrow hit the lower part of the first arrow and stuck there. The man kept on shooting arrows, as the Great Spirit commanded, and each arrow stuck in the lower part of the preceding arrow. After a while there was a long rope of arrows reaching from the cloud on top of the mountain clear down to the ground.

"Now tell your wife and children," commanded the Great Spirit, "to climb up that rope of arrows. Tell the good animals to climb up after them. But don't let the bad people and the bad animals go up."

So the good man sent his wife up the arrow rope, then his children, and then the good animals. He watched them climb into the cloud above the mountain. Then the good man himself climbed up.

Just as he was stepping into the cloud, he looked back. Coming up the arrow rope was a long line of bad animals and snakes. They were climbing toward the cloud. So the good man took hold of the arrow nearest him and broke the rope. He watched all the bad animals and the snakes tumble down the sides of the mountain.

When the Great Spirit saw that the good animals and the good people were safe around him, he caused a heavy rain to fall. It rained and rained and rained for many days and many nights. All the earth was under water. The water rose higher and higher on the sides of Takhoma. At last it came up to the snow line, up to the high place where the snow leaves off in the summertime.

By that time all the bad people and all the bad animals were drowned. So the Great Spirit commanded the rain to stop. He and the good man and his family watched the waters slowly go down. The land became dry again.

Then the Great Spirit said to the good man, "Now you may take your family and the animals back to the earth."

So they all climbed out of the cloud, and the good man led them down a mountain trail to the place where they were to build a new lodge. As they walked down, they found no bad animals or snakes, and there have been none on Takhoma to this day.

THE LAKE

ON MOUNT RAINIER

When the grandfather of my grandmother was a young man, he climbed Takobed. He climbed to the top in search of spirit power.

Before he started, he made five wedges of elk horn. After he reached the snow line, he used the elk-horn wedges to cut steps in the snow and ice. When one wedge wore out, he threw it away and used another one. At the end of a day of climbing, when he reached the top of the mountain, the fifth wedge was worn out.

On the mountaintop he saw a small lake. He made camp beside it and stayed there all night. Next morning he swam and washed himself in the lake. There he gained spirit power. He felt strong and brave and wise.

Then the mountain spoke to him. "Because you have stayed one night with me, I can talk to you. You will become an old, old man, because of your spirit power. When you are very old, moss will grow on your knees and on your elbows. Moss will grow on your head after your hair has fallen out. At last you will die of old age.

"At the time of your death, my head will burst open. The water from the lake here will flow down my sides into the valleys below. I, Takobed, have spoken. All things will come to pass even as I have prophesied."

When the mountain stopped talking, the young man picked up five shells and started home. Before he had gone far, snow began to fall.

"Oh, I have displeased Takobed. He does not wish me to carry shells away," the young man said.

He threw one shell down, then the other four, one at a time. The snowing stopped. With empty hands but with strong spirit power within him, he returned home.

Years passed. The man became old. When he was very old, everything happened just as Takobed had prophesied. His hair fell out. Moss grew on his knees, his elbows, his head. To his people he said, "When I die, look up at the mountain. Takobed's head will burst open. The water from the lake on top will spill down the mountainsides."

The old man died, and it was as he had said. Takobed's head burst open, the lake on top spilled out, and the water rushed down. It swept the trees from where Orting now is, and left the prairie covered with stones.

White people have never seen the lake on Takobed. My grandmother, who told me the story, remembered when the lake burst and spilled out.

THE MISER

ON MOUNT RAINIER

In 1853, Theodore Winthrop journeyed through the Northwest by canoe and on horseback. In his record of his trip he included this legend of Mount Rainier, which an old Nisqually Indian told him at Fort Nisqually. This fort, a post of the Hudson's Bay Company, was situated not far from the present city of Tacoma.

The old storyteller, Hamitchou, said that he had heard the tale from his father; his father had heard it from his father, long before white men were seen on Puget Sound. Hamitchou's grandfather was the great medicine man who had this strange experience on the mountain.

"But now, alas!" added Hamitchou, "I have no son to hear the tale. I

grow old, and lest this wisdom die with me, I tell the tale to you. May
you and your people not scorn the lesson of an earlier age, but profit from
it and be wise."

A wise old Nisqually once lived along these waters, near where this fort
now stands. He liked to hunt and fish, as all the Coast Indians did. But
more than hunting and fishing, he liked *hiaqua*. Hiaqua are shells from
the northland. My people use them for ornaments and use them where
you use money. The man who has the most hiaqua is the best of all the
people who live beside these waters.

This old man of my tribe could never get enough. He traded deer
meat and salmon for hiaqua, but he wanted still more. He let his wife
have no shells for earrings, none for necklaces. He used none himself for
ornaments. Instead, he hid all the hiaqua he could get.

He would never attend the salmon feasts which my people held every
spring, to celebrate the coming of the salmon up the rivers.

"Feasting is wasteful," he said. "Feasters will come to want. Feasters
will grow hungry."

Whenever his neighbors did run short of food, he sold them elk meat
or salmon for shell money. And he always charged a high price. He would
take shell ornaments from starving women in return for scraps of dry,
tough elk meat. He always had fish and meat to sell, for he knew the
pools where the salmon gathered and the mountain meadows where the
elk fed.

But he gathered hiaqua too slowly. Always he dreamed of finding a
great treasure of it. Again and again he asked the spirits to tell him where
he could find more shell money. Again and again they refused to tell
him. Finally, Moosmoos, the elk spirit, told him there was a great treasure
of shell money on top of Tacobud. Moosmoos told the man exactly where
he could find it.

No one had ever climbed Tacobud, for somewhere above the tree line
was the home of the Tahmahnawis, the spirits. But his desire for hiaqua
made the man brave. Toward sunset he started out to climb the mountain,
alone. With him he took some dried salmon and dried camas to eat, a
stone pipe and some kinnikinnick to smoke in it, his bows and arrows, and
two picks, or spades, which he had made from a pair of big elk horns.

All that night and all the next day he climbed. The second night he
camped just below the snow line. He was cold, but he would not use his
fire sticks and build a fire, for he feared people would follow him and
find the treasure. As soon as the moonlight was bright, he started up over
the snow fields where no man had ever been before. At times he could see
the peak above him. At times he could see, far below him, the waters of
Whulge, the great inland sea. He climbed slowly, floundering through
the deep snow.

At sunrise he reached the top. There he found a huge hole, or crater. In the center of the crater, surrounded by white snow, was a black lake in a purple rock. At the far end of the lake were three high stones. The man hurried toward them, for Moosmoos, the elk spirit, had told him about them.

One stone was as high as a giant man; at the top it was shaped like a salmon's head. The top of the second stone was shaped like a camas bulb. The third stone stood apart from the others; at the top it was shaped like an elk's head with antlers in the velvet.

"Everything so far is exactly as Moosmoos said," the man said to himself.

He was very much excited. The elk spirit had told him that he would find shell money buried in the snow at the foot of the elk-head stone.

He threw down his pack, seized one of his elk-horn picks, and began to dig. At the first stroke he heard some animal behind him give a great puff. Looking around, he saw a huge otter climbing up over the edge of the lake. It was four times as large as any otter he had seen.

The otter stopped a moment and struck the snow with his tail. A second otter appeared at the edge of the lake, then another and another, until twelve otters had climbed up out of the water after their leader. In single file they marched toward the man and formed a circle around him. Each of the twelve was twice as large as any of the otters the man had seen in Whulge.

When the twelve otters had formed their circle, the big leader jumped to the top of the elk-head stone and sat there between the antlers. At a signal from his tail, which he tapped against the stone, his followers puffed big puffs, all at the same time.

The man was startled, but soon turned back to his digging. At every thirteenth stroke of his pick, the chief otter tapped the stone with his tail and the twelve otters in the circle tapped the snow with their tails. From underneath the snow came a strange, hollow sound.

The man dug and dug and dug in the frozen snow and then in the rock under the snow. He became so hot and tired that he stopped to rest awhile and to wipe the sweat from his face. But as soon as he stopped digging, the chief otter turned around and whacked him with his tail. The otters in the circle turned around and, one by one, whacked the man with their tails.

Bruised and still tired, the man began to dig again. He dug and dug until he broke his pick. The chief otter jumped down, handed him his second pick, and jumped back to his perch on the stone elk's head. The circle of otters drew closer round him. They were so close now that he could feel their breath upon him. Still at every thirteenth stroke they tapped the snow with their tails. The sound coming up from below grew more hollow and more hollow.

At last the digger uncovered a big square hole. He stared and stared at what he saw in it. He was almost breathless with excitement and joy. The big square hole was filled with shell money!

When he thrust his hand into the hole, he found he could not reach the bottom of the shells. He laughed aloud. At last he had what he had always wanted. The shells were pure white, small and beautiful, strung on strings of elkskin.

He loaded himself with the hiaqua, putting some strings of it round his waist, some strings over each shoulder, and five strings in each hand. Still the great hole seemed to be filled to the top. He thought he would take home all the hiaqua he could carry and climb the mountain again for more. He covered the hole with stones and covered the stones with snow.

But one thing he did not do. He did not leave a gift for the spirits. He should have put a string of shells round the stone with the salmon head at the top, another round the stone with the camas bulb at the top, and two round the stone with the elk's head at the top. But he was too selfish and too greedy to be thankful.

Staggering under his load of shells, the man started to climb up the side of the crater. At once the chief otter jumped down from his perch. At once the twelve other otters fell into line with great puffs. They marched to the lake, plunged in, and began to beat the water with their tails.

The man was so loaded with shells and the snow was so soft that it took him an hour to reach the rim of the crater. There he stopped and looked back. A thick mist was rising from the lake where the otters were splashing. Under the mist was a black cloud, which grew bigger and blacker as he watched.

"Are the spirits in that cloud?" he asked himself in terror.

He hurriedly started down the mountain, but the black cloud followed him. The cloud became a storm, which threw him down on the jagged rocks and ice. He clung to the hiaqua, struggled to his feet, and started again. The storm grew worse. In the wind and the thunder the man heard the voices of the Tahmahnawis, the spirits, shrieking, "Ha, ha, hiaqua! Ha, ha, ha!"

Again and again the spirits screamed, "Ha, ha, hiaqua! Ha, ha, hiaqua!"

The storm grew darker, louder, more terrifying. At last the man knew he would have to give something to the spirits, in order to quiet their anger. So he threw into the storm the five strings of shells he carried in his left hand.

At once there was a lull in the storm. In the quiet, the man heard the puffs of the thirteen otters, but he could not see them. Then the storm grew worse again, and he heard the voices in the wind and in the thunder screaming, "Ha, ha, hiaqua! Ha, ha, hiaqua!"

Hands of the spirits seemed to clutch at the strings of hiaqua at his waist and at his neck. Terrified, the man threw into the storm the shell money which he wore around his waist. There was a lull for a few seconds, and he heard again the puffs from the otters he could not see. Then the storm grew more frightening. The roar of the wind was louder than the roar of many bears.

The man threw away the shell money which he wore round his neck. Again there came a lull in the storm, and again he heard the puffs of the otters. Then the wind blew him from his path. The thunder roared with a terrifying sound. The voices of the spirits screamed, "Hiaqua! Hiaqua!" The man threw away one of the strings of hiaqua which he carried in his right hand. He threw away the second and the third and the fourth. But the storm continued. For a long time he clung to his fifth string, the last of the hiaqua he carried.

Finally he threw it away. By this time he was worn out by the storm and by the struggle in his mind. He sank into the snow and fell into a deep sleep.

After a long, long time he awoke. He heard Blue Jay welcoming the sunrise. Looking around, he found himself in the place where he had camped and where he had started climbing by moonlight. Around him was a thick carpet of camas. What could that mean? Camas belongs in wet meadows, not on mountainsides, he thought to himself.

Hungry, he looked for his pack of dried salmon and dry camas, but it was gone. Only his black stone pipe remained. When he started down the mountain he found that he was very stiff. His joints creaked and groaned. Scratching his head, he found that his hair was matted and very long.

But he felt strangely at peace with himself and with the world. He had never heard the birds sing so sweetly and the forest hum so cheerfully. He no longer had any desire for hiaqua. Instead, he wanted to see his neighbors.

Walking down the mountainside as fast as his creaking joints would let him, he soon came to the place where his lodge had once stood. But everything was changed. A new and better lodge stood there, and trees he remembered as small were now tall, with many branches.

In front of the new lodge a very old woman was seated on the ground stirring a kettle of salmon over the open fire. If she was his klootchman, his wife, she had grown old during his absence—and also rich. Around her neck and wrists and waist she wore many strings of hiaqua.

He heard her chanting this song as she stirred:

> My old man has gone, gone, gone,
> My old man to the mountain has gone, gone, gone—
> To hunt the elk, he went long ago.
> When will he come down, down, down,
> Down to the salmon pot and me?

Joyfully the man rushed toward her, shouting,

> He has come from the mountain, down, down, down,
> Down to the salmon pot and you!

He had been gone for thirty snows, his wife told him. She had gathered camas bulbs and special herbs, had sold them, and so had earned enough for the new lodge and her strings of shell money.

Soon she and her neighbors learned that the man who had climbed Tacobud was a changed man. He was changed inside. He no longer wanted hiaqua. He was contented with what he had, and he cheerfully shared with others. He showed people where the best fishing and hunting were. He taught them better ways of hunting elk and of spearing salmon. People living near Tacobud and people living along Whulge came to him for advice. He told them what to do to make peace with the spirits who live on the mountain. He became the great medicine man of the Nisqually.

THE ORIGIN

OF MOUNT SI

AND THE FORESTS

Mount Si is a solitary, sharp peak in the Snoqualmie National Forest, east of Seattle. A Suquamish myth somewhat similar to the one given below explains the origin of Mount Snoqualmie, a mass of rock (6,270 feet high) north of Snoqualmie Pass and the Sunset Highway. According to another myth, the Snoqualmie Indians came from Snoqualm, the Moon.

Long ago, Snoqualm, the Moon, was the chief of the heavens. One day he said to Spider, "Make a rope of cedar bark and stretch it from the earth to the sky."

Soon Fox and Blue Jay found the rope and climbed up it. Late at night they came to the place where it was fastened to the under side of the sky. Blue Jay picked a hole in the sky, and the two of them crawled through.

Blue Jay flew to a tree, and Fox found himself in a lake. There he changed himself into Beaver. Moon had set a trap in the lake, and Beaver got caught in the trap. Next morning, Moon took Beaver out of the trap, skinned him, stretched his skin out to dry, and threw the body into one corner of the smokehouse.

The next night Beaver waited until Moon was asleep and snoring loudly. Then he got up, took the skin from the place where it was stretching, and put it back on. While Moon was still snoring, he examined the house and the Sky World.

Outside, he found a great forest of fir and pine and cedar trees. He pulled some of them up by their roots and then, with his spirit powers, made them small enough to be carried under one arm. Under his other arm he put the tools for making daylight. He took some fire from below the smoke hole, put ashes and leaves and bark round it, and carried it in one hand. He found the sun hidden in Moon's house and carried it away in his other hand.

Then Beaver found the hole Blue Jay had made, changed himself back to Fox again, and went down the rope to the earth. There he gave the fire to the people. He set out the trees. He made the daylight. He set the sun in its place so that it would give light and heat to all. The people were happy because of the things Fox brought from the sky.

By this time, Moon had awakened. When he found that the beaver skin had gone and that the sun had disappeared from its hiding place, he was very angry. He knew that one of the earth people had tricked him. Noticing footprints around the house, he followed them to the top of the rope which Spider had made.

"I will follow him to the Earth World," said Moon.

But as he started down, the rope broke. Both Moon and rope fell down in a heap. They were transformed into a mountain.

Today the peak is called Mount Si. The face of Snoqualm, the Moon, can still be seen on one of its rocky walls. The trees which Fox brought down from the sky and planted have become the great forests of the Cascade Mountains.

KULSHAN AND

HIS TWO WIVES

Komo Kulshan, meaning "white, shining mountain" or "great white watcher," was the Nooksack and the Lummi name for the most northern of the high peaks of the Cascade Range. It watched over the land and over the waters of Puget Sound and Georgia Strait. Captain George Vancouver, on his exploring expedition of 1792, named the peak in honor of his lieutenant, Joseph Baker.

Mount Baker (10,750 feet in altitude), the third highest peak in Washington, is in the Mount Baker National Forest.

Komo Kulshan, a very tall and handsome young man, married two wives, as was the custom in his tribe. One was named *Duh-hwahk,* meaning "Clear Sky"; the other was named *Whaht-kay,* meaning "Fair Maiden."

For several years Clear Sky was Kulshan's favorite wife. She was the more beautiful of the two, and she had borne him three children. Fair Maiden was less beautiful, but she was always gentle and kind. At last she won Kulshan's love through kindness, but at the same time she gained Clear Sky's dislike. Clear Sky had a jealous and bitter nature. Soon there was quarreling in the lodge.

One day Clear Sky scolded Komo Kulshan sharply. "You should love me more than Fair Maiden," she added. "I am the mother of your children."

Kulshan smiled and said nothing.

Clear Sky became angry and said to him, "I am going away. I will leave you and the children and go away."

She really did not mean to go. She thought that Komo Kulshan would say, "Don't go away. You are the mother of my children. I love you most. Don't go away."

But Kulshan did not beg her to stay. He did not want her to go, and he loved her. But he was too proud to tell her so.

Instead, he said, "If you want to go, you may go. You may go as soon and as far as you wish."

So Clear Sky packed all her things. She packed slowly for a long time. She took all her seeds and bulbs, all her roots and berries, all her flowering plants. Her children cried loudly when they saw their mother leaving. That pleased Clear Sky. She was sure that when she had gone a little distance, Kulshan would call to her to come back.

She traveled down the mountain valleys slowly, alone. When she had gone a short distance, she stopped and looked back. But Kulshan did not say, "Come home to us."

She went a little farther and stood on a hill to look back at Kulshan and the children. When she stood on tiptoe, she could see them. But still Kulshan did not say, "Come back, Clear Sky."

She went on farther south. She was still among the hills and mountains, mountains not so high as Komo Kulshan. He still did not call to her, though she stretched herself on the tips of her toes. Farther south she stopped on top of a high hill, stood on tiptoe, and stretched herself as tall as she could. Then she could see Kulshan and the children, and they could see her.

By this time she had stretched herself so many times that she had become much taller. Sure now that her husband did not want her to return, she decided to make camp there. She knew that from her camp, on a clear day, she would be able to see her family. So she put down her packs and took from them all the seeds and bulbs and roots. She planted them around her, and there she stayed, to care for them.

Fair Maiden lived with Kulshan for a long time. One day she said to him: "Kulshan, I want to see my mother. I am going to have a baby, and I want to see my mother."

Fair Maiden's mother was an island in Whulge.

"How can you go to your mother?" asked Kulshan. "There is no trail. There is nothing but rocks and trees and mountains between us and Whulge."

"I don't know how I can get there, but you will have to make a way for me. I want to see my mother."

So Komo Kulshan called together all the animals that have claws—the beavers, the marmots, the cougars, the bears, even the rats and mice and moles—and told them to dig a big ditch. The animals with claws dug a deep ditch, wide enough for two canoes to pass. Then Kulshan turned all the water from the mountains near him into the big ditch, until there was enough to float a fair-sized canoe. Today the stream is called the Nooksack River.

Before starting, Fair Maiden gathered many kinds of food to take with her. Then she went down the river and out into the salt water of Whulge.

She ate mussels at one of the islands and left some there. That is why mussels are found on that island today. She ate clams at another island and left some there. She ate camas at another; that is why much camas grows on Matia Island today. She ate devilfish and berries at another island and left some there. At every island on her journey she left some kind of fish or root or berry. That is why the Indian names for these islands are the names of food.

When she got to Flat Top Island, she decided to stay somewhere near it. She stood looking over the water for some time, for it was hard for her to choose the best place. The winds blew round her tall figure and made many whirlpools. The whirlpools sucked in people, even some who lived far away, and devoured them.

Fair Maiden kept on standing there, and the winds kept on blowing round her. At last the Changer came to her and said, "Why don't you lie down? If you stand, the winds will blow, and the whirlpools will keep on sucking in the people. Soon there will be none left."

So Fair Maiden lay down, and the Changer transformed her into Spieden Island. When her child was born, it was a small island of the same shape as Spieden and lying beside it. Today it is called Sentinel Island.

Kulshan, left with his children in the northern mountains, kept stretching upward, trying to see his wives. So did his children. The three of them grew taller and taller and became high mountains. One is

Shuksan, a little east of Kulshan and almost as tall. Some people say the others are Twin Sisters, a little west and south of Kulshan.

A long journey south of them stands their mother, Clear Sky. You know her as Mount Rainier. The seeds and roots she planted there grew and spread. That is why the lower slopes bloom with flowers of every color. Often on a clear day or on a clear night, the mountain dresses in sparkling white and looks with longing at Komo Kulshan and the mountain children near him.

MOUNT BAKER

AND THE

GREAT FLOOD

This story of the Deluge was told by the Squamish, who lived in British Columbia, northwest of Mount Baker, along Howe Sound. "The Lummis also speak of a flood," wrote the Reverend Myron Eells in 1878, "and Mount Baker is their Ararat."

When the Squamish people saw the great flood coming, they gathered on a spot above the reach of the water. There they held a big council. To save their tribe from destruction, they decided to build a giant canoe and tie it to a giant rock. Day and night the men worked, building a boat larger than any of them had ever seen.

The women made the rope for fastening it to the rock. They gathered cedar fiber, tore it into shreds, rolled it and chewed it and worked it into a larger rope than any of them had ever seen. Then they oiled it.

The people fastened one end of the giant rope to the giant canoe, and the other end to a huge rock. Then they put into the canoe every baby and every small child. They placed enough food and fresh water in the boat to last for many days.

Then they chose two guardians for the children—the mother of the youngest baby in the camp, and the bravest and best of their young men. They placed him in the stern of the canoe and seated the young mother, a girl of sixteen, with her baby, only two weeks old, in the bow. No one else tried to get into the boat. No one wailed or wept as the water reached the hilltop where they had gathered. No one wept as the canoe floated away. The people left behind sank beneath the flood.

For days the children and their young guardians saw only a world of water and sky. But the rope held. One morning they saw, far to the south, a speck on top of the water. When the sun reached the middle of the sky, the speck was a big spot. By the time the sun reached the water, the spot was still larger.

When the moon came up, the man thought he saw a piece of land. All night he watched it. In the morning, when the sun came out of the water, the young man saw a mountain—Mount Baker it is called now. He cut the rope and paddled toward the south. By the time the canoe reached the mountain, the upper half of the peak was dry.

On the mountain the guardians helped the children out of the boat. When the waters had gone down and the land below was dry, they made a new camp. They built their lodges in the region between the Fraser River and the Georgia Strait, in sight of Mount Baker. The children lived and grew up. Through them the Squamish people were saved.

In a giant crack halfway up the slope of Mount Baker is the outline of the giant canoe. It has been there ever since the great flood.

THE ORIGIN

OF SISTERS PEAK

The following brief myth was told in August, 1952, by Ellen Joe Dick of the Swinomish Reservation, with Mrs. Joseph Joe as interpreter.

Three sisters built a very high house, a long time ago. They made it tall because they wanted to go up to the sky to see the Creator. They kept building it higher and higher and higher. By the time the house was finished, they could not speak the same language. They could not understand each other. That is why there are so many different languages today.

During the great flood, the three women drifted away. After the flood, the Changer came to make the world over. He transformed the sisters into a mountain with three peaks. It is the Sisters Peak up there by Mount Baker.

OTHER TRADITIONS
OF THE
GREAT FLOOD

"*When the earliest missionaries came among the Spokanes, Nez Percés, and Cayuses,*" the Reverend Myron Eells reported in 1878, "*they found that those Indians had their traditions of a flood, and that one man and his wife were saved on a raft. Each of those three tribes also, together with the Flathead tribes, had their separate Ararat in connection with the event.*" In several traditions, he said, the flood came because of the wickedness of the people.

Tribes of the Olympic Peninsula and the Yakima, who lived east of the Cascade Range, told the flood stories given below. The Skokomish along Hood Canal, the Klallam along the Strait of Juan de Fuca, and the Duwamish, who lived near the present site of Seattle, belong to the Salishan linguistic family, as do several tribes often called Flatheads. The Quillayute and the Chemakum were the only tribes belonging to the Chimakoan linguistic family. The Hoh are generally regarded as a band of the Quillayute.

"Once a big flood came to this world," said Mrs. Rose Purdy, a Skokomish. "My people made ropes by twisting cedar limbs. They tied the ropes to their canoes and fastened the canoes to a mountain near the canal. When the world got flooded, the Skokomish people went higher and higher into the Olympic Mountains. The Olympics got flooded. Some of the ropes broke and the canoes drifted away.

"They kept on going and kept on going—down, down, down. They kept their canoes tied together until they reached the country of the Flathead Indians. They became known as the Flatheads.

"A long time afterward, when there was war around where Seattle is now, the Skokomish people were trapped on the bay. They heard strange people talking in the Skokomish language. When my people spoke to them, they said, 'We are the people who drifted away from here.'

"That is why the Skokomish and the Flatheads speak the same language."

2

Sam Ulmer, a Klallam who lives near the Strait of Juan de Fuca, learned in childhood a similar story of canoes tied to a mountain during the great flood. The mountaintop broke off, he said, leaving the two points now visible at the ends of a saddle-like ridge in the Olympics. "The canoes floated away and came down, after the flood, to the place where Seattle is now. The people in the canoes became the ancestors of the Indians who used to live around there."

3

Thunderbird was so angry one time that he sent the ocean over the land. When the water reached the village of the Quillayute, they got into their canoes. For four days the water continued to rise. At last it covered even the tops of the mountains. The boats were carried this way and that way by the wind and the waves. The people could not guide them, for there was no sun and there was no land. Then the water began to go down. For four days it receded. By that time, the people were scattered. Some of the canoes landed along the Hoh River. So those people have lived there ever since. Others landed at Chemakum, on the other side of the mountains. They have lived there ever since. Only a few found their way back to the Quillayute River.

4

There was a flood in the Yakima country, one time in the early suns, back near the beginning. Before the big water came, there had been wars and blood between the tribes. Even the medicine men had killed people. But there were some good people who remembered what they had been told by the old people who were gone.

One of the good men told the others, "I have heard from the Land Above, the land of the spirits, that a big water is coming—a big water that will cover all the land. Make a boat for the good people. Let the bad people be killed by the water."

The good people held a council and decided to make the boat from the cedar tree, the biggest and best cedar they could find. They chipped it with stone and with antlers of elk and burned it hollow with fire.

When the cedar canoe was finished, it went over the water like a good canoe. Soon the flood came. It filled the valleys. It covered the hills and the mountains. The bad people were drowned by the big water. The good ones were saved in the boat.

We do not know how long the flood stayed. At last the canoe came down where it was built. It is still there. You can see it on the Toppenish Ridge, on the side toward the rising sun.

The earth will again be destroyed by a big water if the people do wrong a second time—if they fight in wars, if they steal and murder and do other wrongs.

THE VALLEY OF PEACE

IN THE OLYMPICS

A great-grandmother of Clarence Pickernell (he is Quinault-Chehalis-Cowlitz) told him she was sure that the following story is a genuine Indian legend. She had not heard this version before, but she had heard a similar one. Eugene Semple, who recorded the version given here, was governor of Washington Territory in the 1880's.

In the days long gone by, the Indians had a sacred place in the heart of the Olympic Mountains. It was a valley, wide and level, with peaks high on every side. The base of the mountains was covered with cedar and fir and pine, which stayed green throughout the year. A small stream murmured through the valley, and flowers of many kinds grew on its banks and spread through the meadows.

It was a place of peace, for it was held sacred by all the neighboring tribes. Once every year, all the Indian nations, even those that at other times made war upon each other, gathered in the Valley of Peace. Coming from all directions, they climbed the trails to the summits of the mountains and gazed upon the beautiful valley below them.

Then they put away their weapons of war, went down to the valley, and greeted their former enemies with signs of peace. There they traded with each other and enjoyed games and contests of strength and skill.

These friendly gatherings were held for many years in the Valley of Peace. But Seatco, chief of all the evil spirits, became angry with the people who gathered there. Seatco was a giant who could trample whole tribes under his feet. He was taller than the tallest fir trees. His voice was louder than the roar of the ocean, and his face was more terrible to look upon than the face of the fiercest wild beast. He could travel by land, in the water, and in the air. He was so strong that he could tear up a whole forest by the roots and heap rocks into mountains. By just blowing his breath, he could change the course of rivers.

This demon became angry, without reason, at all the nations that gathered in the Valley of Peace. One year when they were there for trading and for contests of peace, Seatco came among them. He caused a great trembling and rumbling of the mountains. Then he caused the earth and water to swallow the people.

Not many Indians escaped. A few rushed away in time to save themselves from the anger of Seatco. They returned to their villages to warn their people away from the valley. The Indians never went there again.

THE SEVEN DEVILS

MOUNTAINS

The Seven Devils Gorge, or Hell's Canyon of the Snake River, forms part of the boundary between Oregon and Idaho. On the Idaho side of the gorge, which is said to be the deepest canyon on the North American continent, seven high peaks stand in a semicircle. They are called the Seven Devils Mountains. The Blue Mountains are in eastern Oregon and Washington.

The myth given here was corroborated and details were added by Caleb Whitman, a Nez Perce on the Umatilla Reservation, in August, 1950.

Long, long ago, when the world was very young, seven giant brothers lived in the Blue Mountains. These giant monsters were taller than the tallest pines and stronger than the strongest oaks.

The ancient people feared these brothers greatly because they ate children. Each year the brothers traveled eastward and devoured all the little ones they could find. Mothers fled with their children and hid them, but still many were seized by the giants. The headmen in the villages feared that the tribe would soon be wiped out. But no one was big enough and strong enough to fight with seven giants at a time.

At last the headmen of the tribe decided to ask Coyote to help them. "Coyote is our friend," they said. "He has defeated other monsters. He will free us from the seven giants."

So they sent a messenger to Coyote. "Yes, I will help you," he promised. "I will free you from the seven giants."

But Coyote really did not know what to do. He had fought with giants. He had fought with monsters of the lakes and the rivers. But he knew he could not defeat seven giants at one time. So he asked his good friend Fox for advice.

"We will first dig seven holes," said his good friend Fox. "We will dig them very deep, in a place the giants always pass over when they travel to the east. Then we will fill the holes with boiling liquid."

So Coyote called together all the animals with claws—the beavers, the whistling marmots, the cougars, the bears, and even the rats and mice and moles—to dig seven deep holes. Then Coyote filled each hole with a reddish-yellow liquid. His good friend Fox helped him keep the liquid boiling by dropping hot rocks into it.

Soon the time came for the giants' journey eastward. They marched along, all seven of them, their heads held high in the air. They were sure that no one dared to attack them. Coyote and Fox watched from behind some rocks and shrubs.

Down, down, down the seven giants went into the seven deep holes of boiling liquid. They struggled and struggled to get out, but the holes were very deep. They fumed and roared and splashed. As they struggled, they scattered the reddish liquid around them as far as a man can travel in a day.

Then Coyote came out from his hiding place. The seven giants stood still. They knew Coyote.

"You are being punished for your wickedness," Coyote said to the seven giants. "I will punish you even more by changing you into seven mountains. I will make you very high, so that everyone can see you. You will stand here forever, to remind people that punishment comes from wrongdoing.

"And I will make a deep gash in the earth here, so that no more of your family can get across to trouble my people."

Coyote caused the seven giants to grow taller, and then he changed them into seven mountain peaks. He struck the earth a hard blow and so opened up a deep canyon at the feet of the giant peaks.

Today the mountain peaks are called the Seven Devils. The deep gorge at their feet is known as Hell's Canyon of the Snake River. And the copper scattered by the splashings of the seven giants is still being mined.

II.

LEGENDS

OF THE

LAKES

SPIRITS

AND ANIMALS

IN THE LAKES

The Indians had many myths and legends connected with the lakes of the Northwest. In Lake Steilacoom, near the present city of Tacoma, lived an evil spirit which the Nisqually Indians called Whe-atch-ee. The lake also they called Whe-atch-ee. Because of the demon, they never swam or fished in the lake, but sometimes they would see her from the shore. She would lift her head and right arm from the water, raise her thumb and little finger, close her middle fingers, and say, "Here is my Whe-atch-ee." The Indians would then flee in terror.

In Fish Lake, near Mount Adams, the water is so clear that trout can be seen darting in and out of holes in the bottom. The Klickitat Indians used to believe that these holes were the doors to the hiding place of a great dragon. When angered, the dragon would spit fire from his nostrils and his eyes and then would fly about to spread destruction and famine over the country. In the old days, the Klickitat people were forbidden to fish in the lake, under penalty of death. Even in recent years, Indians would not touch a fish from this lake, and they shunned the trails that pass near it.

Between Mount Adams and Mount Rainier are many small lakes, in a region where the Indians used to go late in the summer for huckleberries and game. In these dark, deep lakes surrounded by tall trees, the Indians believed, lived spirits that had control of rain. These spirits, they said, wanted their waters to be always quiet. If the water should be disturbed in any way, the spirits would be offended and would send down rain upon those who caused the disturbance. The Indians were therefore careful not to throw stones into the lakes. They did not water their ponies in them, and from certain of them did not even take water for cooking.

Some of the lakes in that region were said to have strange animals living in them. These animals were the spirits of beings who had lived ages ago. At night, when all was dark and quiet, the spirits would come out and gather food on the shores. In some of the lakes were the spirits of little children who had lived in the days of the ancient people. Their cries sometimes broke the silence of the nighttime. The next morning the prints of their little naked feet were found in the wet sand along the margin of the lake.

Elks of a strange kind sometimes came out of these lakes, fed on the shores, and then disappeared as mysteriously as they had come. In Lake

Keechelus, northeast of Mount Rainier, a man on a tall horse once appeared, out in the middle of the lake. One of the horses of a band of Indians who were passing just then swam out to the tall horse, and then both disappeared.

Near the shore of Goose Lake, south of Mount St. Helens and Mount Adams, are the prints of two moccasined feet, the toes turned in, and prints of two hands—small, like those of a girl. Many years ago, the Indians say, a maiden fled from an unwanted suitor. She reached Lemei Rock, the highest point in the immediate area. Still pursued, she jumped from the tall rock and landed on the shore of Goose Lake. The Great Spirit was so impressed by her courage he decreed that the prints of her hands and feet should remain there forever. When the water of the lake is low, these prints can be seen, even to this day. And sometimes on a moonlight night the girl's spirit appears for a moment in the middle of the lake.

In a small lake in the eastern foothills of the Cascade Range lived a giant crawfish. His sharp claws could crush the life out of a man as easily as a man can break a robin's egg. Crawfish claimed that he was owner of the lake, of all the fish in it, and of all the roots and berries on its banks. If a man took too many fish or if a woman took too many roots or berries, Crawfish became very angry. He would make the water seethe and boil. He would make waves so big that greedy fishermen and berrypickers fled in terror. If anyone refused to drop the food he had obtained, the waves would seize him and carry him back to Crawfish. The giant would crush him in his sharp claws and swallow him. Then the anger of Crawfish would leave him, and the lake would become quiet again.

In Cascade Lake on Orcas Island, long ago, no fish lived, because of the wrath of Raven. Angry one time at the spirits in the water, he made his powers on the top of Mount Constitution and killed all the fish in the lake. Many snows passed before fish were permitted there again.

Stories about the spirits and animals that lived in the lakes were entertainment around the campfires, when the Indians gathered in the mountains for hunting and berrypicking. There the best storytellers of the groups had a perfect setting for their tales of the strange events that had taken place in the lakes near them, long, long ago.

THE ORIGIN
OF CRATER LAKE

In the autumn of 1865, a nineteen-year-old soldier stationed at Fort Klamath in the southern part of Oregon Territory climbed up to see Crater Lake, which had been discovered by white men only a short time before. On his return, he had a long talk with old Chief Lalek, Peace Chief of the Klamath Indians. The young soldier, William M. Colvig, had learned the Chinook jargon in childhood while playing with the Indian children who were his neighbors. While at Fort Klamath he spent many hours with the friendly old chief, then about eighty years old, and from him learned much about Klamath Indian lore and legendry.

"Why do your people never go up to the lake?" asked the young soldier. "Why are you afraid to look down upon its waters?"

"Oh, you cannot understand," replied the old chief.

"Yes, I can understand," said young Colvig, filling the old man's pipe.

Then Chief Lalek told the following legend, which he said he had learned from his father, who had learned it from his father. Later, Mr. Colvig heard the same legend from other old men of the Klamath tribe, told with some variations.

A long time ago, so long that you cannot count it, the white man ran wild in the woods and my people lived in rock-built houses. In that time, long ago, before the stars fell, the spirits of the earth and the sky, the spirits of the sea and the mountains often came and talked with my people.

Sometimes the Chief of the Below World came up from his home inside the earth and stood on the top of the mountain—the high mountain that used to be. At that time there was no lake up there. Instead, there was an opening which led to the lower world. Through it the Chief of the Below World passed from his home to the outside world and back again.

When he came up from his lodge below, his tall form towered above the snow-capped peaks. His head touched the stars around the lodge of the Chief of the Above World, the all-powerful chief.

One time when the Chief of the Below World was on the earth, he saw Loha, the daughter of the tribal chief. Loha was a beautiful maiden, tall and straight as the arrowwood. Her eyes were dark and piercing; her hair was long and black and glossy. She was beloved by all her father's people, and warrior chiefs from many nations had tried to win her favor.

The Chief of the Below World saw her and fell in love with her. He told her of his love and asked her to return with him to his lodge inside the mountain. There, he said, she would live forever and forever. But Loha refused to go with him.

Then the Chief of the Below World sent one of his warriors to a feast of the tribe, to plead for him and to arrange for a marriage with Loha.

"The maiden shall have eternal life," promised the warrior. "She shall never know sickness or sorrow or death when she becomes the mate of the Chief of the Below World. The great chief demands that she come with me."

But again the maiden refused. And the wise men of the council would not command her to go. Instead, they advised her to hide herself from the sight of the Chief of the Below World.

When the messenger returned to the middle of the mountain and reported the maiden's answer, the Chief of the Below World was very angry. In a voice like thunder, he swore that he would have revenge on the people of Loha, that he would destroy them with the Curse of Fire. Raging and thundering, he rushed up through the opening and stood upon the top of his mountain.

Then he saw the face of the Chief of the Above World shining among the stars that surround his home. Slowly the mighty form of that chief descended from the sky and stood on the top of Mount Shasta. From their mountaintops the two spirit chiefs began a furious battle. In a short time all the spirits of earth and sky took part in the battle.

Mountains shook and crumbled. Red-hot rocks as large as the hills hurtled through the skies. Burning ashes fell like rain. The Chief of the Below World spewed fire from his mouth. Like an ocean of flame it devoured the forests on the mountains and in the valleys. On and on the Curse of Fire swept until it reached the homes of the people. Fleeing in terror before it, the people found refuge in the waters of Klamath Lake. Mothers stood there holding their babies in their arms and praying that the awful war might end. Men prayed to the Chief of the Above World to save them from destruction by the Curse of Fire.

Two great medicine men lifted up their voices. "Our people have done wrong," said one of them. "Because of our wickedness, the Curse of Fire has been sent upon us. Only a living sacrifice will turn away the wrath of the Chief of the Below World, who has sent the Curse of Fire. Who among us will offer himself as a living sacrifice?"

"No young man will want to make the sacrifice," answered the second of the great medicine men. "We old men have but a few more suns to live. We should be the ones to throw our torches into the fiery pit of the Chief of the Below World. We should be the ones to follow our torches into the fire. Then will the sins of our people be forgiven."

The Chief of the Above World heard the voices of the medicine men and spoke to the people from the top of Mount Shasta. "Your wise men have spoken the truth. You have not listened to my voice, though I have spoken again and again. Now you are being punished. Your land is being laid waste."

As his voice ceased, the two medicine men, the oldest and most revered of the Klamath people, rose from the water, lighted their pine torches, and started toward the mountain of the Chief of the Below World. From the waters of Klamath Lake the people watched the flare of the torches move up the long ridge on the east side of the mountain. Brilliant against the night sky, the torches moved on to the top of the cliff which hung over the entrance to the Below World.

On that cliff stood the angry Chief of the Below World. There the medicine men paused for a moment, watching the flames and smoke coming up through the opening. Then they lifted their burning torches high above their heads and jumped into the fiery pit.

The great Sahale Tyee, the Chief of the Above World, standing on Mount Shasta, saw the brave deed of the medicine men. He saw that it was good. Once more the mountains shook. Once more the earth trembled on its foundations. This time the Chief of the Below World was driven into his home, and the top of the mountain fell upon him. When the morning sun rose, the high mountain was gone. The mountain which the Chief of the Below World had called his own no longer towered near Mount Shasta.

Then rain fell. For many years, rain fell in torrents and filled the great hole that was made when the mountain fell upon the Chief of the Below World. The Curse of Fire was lifted. Peace and quiet covered the earth. Never again did the Chief of the Below World come up from his home. Never again did his voice frighten the people.

Now you understand why my people never visit the lake. Down through the ages we have heard this story. From father to son has come the warning, "Look not upon the place. Look not upon the place, for it means death or everlasting sorrow."

THE WAR BETWEEN
LAO AND SKELL:
A LEGEND OF CRATER LAKE

This legend was told by Captain O. C. Applegate to a group gathered around a campfire on the rim of Crater Lake. Captain Applegate was then (about 1900) agent at the Klamath Indian Reservation and was often referred to as the "Sage of Klamath." He had known the Klamath Indians for a long time; as a young man he had been clerk and interpreter for his father, Lindsay Applegate, Indian agent there from 1865–1869.

The Klamath and Modoc Indians called the mountain in which the lake rests Lao Yaina, "Lao's mountain."

Long, long ago, the powerful spirit Lao lived in the lake that lies deep in the top of a mountain. He was chief of many lesser spirits. Among them was Crawfish, a giant with long and powerful arms. He could, if he chose, lift up his arms to the tops of the cliffs around the lake and drag down anyone who dared come too near this spot sacred to Lao.

These spirits had the power to take any form they wished. When they left the lake and wandered over the land, they took the forms of many animals of today. Often they played games on the smooth field on the north slope of Lao Yaina, near the great cliff that overlooks the lake. There they played with the spirits from other places, spirits also in the form of animals.

Another powerful spirit was Skell, who ruled over the Klamath Marsh country. His home was near the Yamsay River. Like Lao, Skell was chief of some of the lesser spirits. When they left the marsh and roamed over the land, Skell's spirits took the form of Antelope, Deer, Fox, Wolf, Bald Eagle, Golden Eagle, Dove, and other wise or swift animals and birds.

More powerful than any of these spirits, more powerful even than either Lao or Skell, was Komoo Kumps, who lived in the sky. He was the Creator and the greatest of all the spirits.

For many years the followers of Lao and the followers of Skell met together peacefully and played together on the slope of Lao Yaina. But at last quarreling and bitter strife broke out between Lao and his followers and Skell and his followers. For a long, long time, fierce war raged, sometimes one side winning, sometimes the other.

After many battles, Skell was killed in the Klamath Marsh country.

His enemies tore his heart from his body and carried it joyfully up to Lao Yaina. Pleased with their victory, Lao and his followers planned a big feast and games on the mountain. They asked all the spirits in the mountains and waters near by to join them in the games on the playfield, and even invited the followers of Skell. The festival day came. When the games began, Lao announced that all would play ball with the stolen heart of Skell.

Now the followers of Skell knew that if his heart could be put back into his body he would live again. So they secretly made a plan for getting the heart and carrying it away to the land of the dead. Some of Skell's followers stationed themselves at different places on the mountainside. Deer hid near the playfield, because he could jump far. Antelope stood ready at the edge of the trees, because he was the fastest runner. Others of Skell's people placed themselves at the best spots between Lao's land and the land of the dead. All the way down the mountain, some of Skell's followers waited.

Lao and his creatures formed a big circle and tossed the heart of Skell from one to the other. Often they threw it into the air. Each time they threw it, Skell's followers laughed at them and teased them.

"Why don't you toss it higher?" shouted Fox again and again. "Even a child can throw it higher than that!"

Then Lao's creatures threw it farther and higher than before. Skell's creatures laughed and teased again.

"Higher! Higher!" shouted Fox.

At last Lao caught the heart and flung it with all his might. It went higher and farther than ever before. It went outside the circle of his creatures.

That was what Deer, at the edge of the circle, was waiting for. He caught the heart of Skell and leaped down the mountainside. Instantly all the servants of Lao chased Deer, shouting and shrieking as they went. But none of them could run as fast as Deer.

When Deer was out of breath, he tossed the heart to Antelope, who was waiting for him. Antelope sped with it eastward, still followed by Lao and his servants. Antelope gave it to Wolf. When Wolf was almost worn out, Bald Eagle swooped down, caught the heart in his beak, and flew to the eastward. Bald Eagle gave it to Golden Eagle, and Golden Eagle gave it to Dove.

Dove carried the heart to the land of the dead and put it in the body of Skell. So Skell came back to life and was ready to wage war again.

When Lao and his followers heard the far-off voice of Dove, they gave up the chase and went back to Lao Yaina. Skell and his creatures followed them there and began fighting again. In a fierce battle Lao was defeated and killed.

Skell's followers carried the dead body of Lao to the edge of the great cliff overlooking the lake. To keep his enemy from living again, Skell ordered that the body be cut into pieces and the pieces thrown down to Crawfish and his creatures in the lake.

Skell fooled the followers of Lao. He caused them to think that Skell, not Lao, had been killed, and that it was Skell's body that was being thrown to them.

"These are Skell's legs," shouted Skell, as his servants threw the pieces into the lake. Crawfish and his creatures swallowed them eagerly.

"These are Skell's arms," shouted Skell. Crawfish and his creatures ate the arms.

"But this is Lao's head!" shouted Skell.

Then he fled for his life and, with the help of Komoo Kumps, the great sky spirit, he escaped from the anger of Crawfish.

Lao's creatures knew that the head was the head of their master and would not touch it. So it remains in the lake today. It is called Wizard Island.

Lao's spirit still lives in the great cliff, Llao Rock, and watches over the lake far below. Sometimes, when the other spirits of the earth and water are asleep, Lao's spirit leaves the cliff and moves down into the lake. There it shouts angrily through the wind and lashes the water into a sudden storm.

CRATER LAKE AND

THE TWO HUNTERS

Moray L. Applegate, who wrote down the following legend in 1898, was a grandson of Lindsay Applegate, the first Indian agent on the Klamath Reservation, and a nephew of O. C. Applegate.

Crater Lake, the Klamath people believed, was the home of one of the most powerful spirits. His lodge was a mountain peak that rose from near the center of the lake. Within the mountain a fire burned always. Through a hole in its top, red flames and black smoke poured forth.

The medicine men of the Klamath, the only people the Spirit Chief let visit the lake, pictured it as a giant cave which led into the interior of the earth. "The cave is deep and bottomless," they said, "—as deep and bottomless as the sky. The mountains around it sink far into the earth and reach toward the clouds. The cave is filled with blue water—water of deeper blue than the sky which looks at itself in the lake."

Through this cave, in the years long gone by, had come the grandfathers of the tribe. They had come from inside the earth, carried up by the flames and the smoke. And to the little mountain in the lake the spirits of the Klamath always returned after their bodies died.

Sometimes the medicine men climbed up to the lake, to hold council with the Spirit Chief. There they were given healing herbs for people who were sick. There they found charms against evil spirits. There they met the spirits of the dead and bore messages from them to the living.

The spirits of evil men flew about in the smoke and steam that escaped from the mountain standing in the lake. They were trying to get away from their fiery punishment, but always the Spirit Chief pushed them back.

The spirits of men who had led good lives were free to enjoy the lake and all the mountains and meadows around it. Some floated in canoes over the lake or fished in its blue waters. Some flew like birds from one mountain peak to another around the rim of the lake. Some hunted the spirits of deer and bear in the near-by forests.

All these things the medicine men reported to their people. "The great Spirit Chief has made a law," they said, "that no living person, except the wise men of our people, shall ever visit the home of the dead and the home of the Spirit Chief. If any man dares to disobey this law, he will die, and his spirit will be sent to the ever-burning fire inside the mountain which stands in the lake."

The Klamath people believed the medicine men—all believed but two hunters. These hunters had killed the fiercest beasts of the forest. They wore at their belts the scalps of mighty warriors. They had overcome all the enemies they had met, and now they feared nothing. They made up their minds to visit the place sacred to the spirits.

The two hunters left their home beside Klamath Lake and traveled through the forest toward the peaks that they knew surrounded the high lake like the rim of a big bowl. They climbed up and up toward the Spirit World, never losing their courage even when they remembered the warnings of the medicine men.

At last they came to an opening in the forest and saw, far below them, the round blue lake. Everything was as it had been pictured to them by their wise men. Over the water and above the mountains which shut in the lake, spirits flew with wings like birds, and as they flew they made happy sounds like birds' songs. In the lake was a little mountain. From the hole in the top of it, flames and smoke burst forth. From the smoke came the screams of the spirits of men being punished for their evil deeds.

The hunters looked and looked in silence, unable to leave the cliff they were standing on. As they watched, the great Spirit Chief, knowing they were there, came up from his lodge in the lake. He called to him a monster lying in the water and pointed to the two men on the cliff.

The huge monster swam toward the men more swiftly than Eagle flies, leaped high, and caught one hunter in his claws. Holding the terrified man before him, he swam back to the peak in the lake.

The other man fled. Swift as a frightened deer, he ran down the mountain, followed by hundreds and hundreds of angry spirits. Running without stopping, he at last reached a village on Upper Klamath Lake.

There he told his people that he had disobeyed the medicine men and the great Spirit Chief. He told them how the monster had seized his hunting companion. Then the man lay down and died, even as the Spirit Chief had foretold. And his spirit was sent to the fire within the little mountain in the lake.

The Klamath people never forgot what happened to the two hunters. Only a few of them ever again dared look upon the deep blue waters now known as Crater Lake.

ANOTHER

CRATER LAKE LEGEND

In 1885, an old chief of the Klamath Indians told this legend to William Gladstone Steel, the man chiefly responsible for having the area around Crater Lake set aside as a national park. Next day the cliff referred to near the end of the story was named Llao Rock. It rises 2,000 feet above the surface of the water, on the west side of the lake.

Before white men came to the West, a band of Klamath Indians were hunting in what is now southern Oregon. One day, as they were climbing a mountain, they suddenly found themselves on the rim of a deep crater. Startled, they gazed in silence.

Far, far below them lay a lake, round like a full moon, bluer than a mountain sky. Within the circle was an island, which had a small crater at its top. High rock walls like the sides of a bowl enclosed the water. No lake they had ever seen was so deep or so blue.

"It is the home of the Great Spirit!" one man whispered.

Trembling with fear, they moved silently away. They knew that punishment always came to men who looked upon the places sacred to the spirits. The hunters walked quietly down the mountainside and camped far away.

Something within one man's heart kept calling him to return. Next day he climbed back to the rim of the crater and there built his campfire. He slept, and nothing wakened him. The next morning he awoke strangely rested and strong, and went down the mountain to join his friends. A second night and a third night he returned to his camp, to sleep alone on the highest cliff. The third night he was awakened by noises he had never heard before. Strange voices rose from the lake.

But the young hunter was not afraid. After returning to his home, he came back to the lake again and again. In time he dared to climb down the steep wall and to bathe in the blue water. Often he spent the night there at the foot of the cliffs. Again and again he returned to look upon the beauty of the lake and to swim in its waters. Sometimes he saw people there. They looked like the Klamath people except that they seemed to live always in the lake.

As time passed, he became stronger than any other warrior in his tribe. "It is because of the spirit power in the lake," he explained to them. Every time he came back from the place, he seemed stronger than before.

So others began to go to the lake in the heart of the mountain. They too would draw strength from a night on its shores. Old warriors began to send their sons to the lake, to prepare for the hunt and for war. First, they slept on the rocky rim of the crater. Then they too went down to the lake shore. At last they bathed in the deep blue waters. They also became healthier and stronger.

But punishment followed. One day the young warrior who had first dared to return to the spot killed one of the creatures that lived in the water. Why he did it, no one knows. Instantly, untold numbers of angry Llaos, the creatures of the lake, set upon him. They carried him to a cliff which hung over the water. There they cut his throat with a stone knife, tore his body into pieces, and tossed the pieces down below. The angry creatures of the water caught them as they fell, and devoured them.

"This will be the fate of anyone who dares to go to the lake," Klamath grandfathers told their children. "Certain death will come to anyone who even looks upon the lake which lies in the heart of Llao's mountain."

THE ELK SPIRIT

OF LOST LAKE

The concept of the guardian spirit, of great importance in the religion of the North American Indians, is explained at the beginning of the fifth section of this volume. "The fact that the young man divulged his guardian spirit," wrote Edward Sapir about the following legend, "is itself indicative of approaching death, for only upon the death bed was it customary to communicate this, the greatest secret of one's life."

In the days of our grandfathers, a young warrior named Plain Feather lived near Mount Hood. His guardian spirit was a great elk. The great elk taught Plain Feather so well that he became the most skillful hunter in his tribe and always knew the best places to look for every kind of game.

Again and again his guardian spirit said to him, "Never kill more than you can use. Kill only for your present need. Then there will be enough for all."

Plain Feather obeyed him. He killed only for food, only what he needed. Other hunters in his tribe teased him and laughed at him for not shooting for fun, for not using all his arrows when he was out on a hunt. But Plain Feather obeyed the great elk.

Smart Crow, one of the old men of the tribe, planned in his bad heart to make the young hunter disobey his guardian spirit. Smart Crow pretended that he was one of the wise men and that he had had a vision. In the vision, he said, the Great Spirit had told him that the coming winter would be long and cold. There would be much snow.

"Kill as many animals as you can," said Smart Crow to the hunters of the tribe. "We must store meat for the winter."

The hunters, believing him, went to the forest and to the meadows and killed all the animals they could. Each man tried to be the best hunter in the tribe. At first, Plain Feather would not go with them, but Smart Crow kept saying, "The Great Spirit told me that we will have a hard winter. The Great Spirit told me that we must get our meat now."

Plain Feather thought that Smart Crow was telling the truth. So at last he gave in and went hunting along the stream now called Hood River. First he killed deer and bears. Soon he came upon five bands of elk. He killed all but one of them, and he wounded that one. Plain Feather did not know that the wounded elk was his guardian elk.

When the elk hurried away into the forest, Plain Feather followed. Deeper and deeper into the forest and into the mountains he followed the tracks of the animal. At last he came to a beautiful little lake. There, lying in the water not far from the shore, was the wounded elk. Plain Feather walked into the lake to draw the animal to the shore, but when he touched it, both hunter and elk sank.

Plain Feather seemed to fall into a deep sleep. When he awoke, he was on the bottom of the lake. All around him were the spirits of many elk, deer, and bears. All of them were in the shape of human beings. All of them were moaning. He heard a voice say clearly, "Draw him in." And something drew Plain Feather closer to the wounded elk.

"Draw him in," the voice said again. And again Plain Feather was drawn closer to the great elk. At last he lay beside it.

"Why did you disobey me?" asked the elk. "All around you are the spirits of the animals you have killed. I will no longer be your guardian spirit. You have disobeyed me and have slain my friends."

Then the voice which had said, "Draw him in," said, "Cast him out." And the spirits cast the hunter out of the water, onto the shore of the lake.

Weary in body and sick at heart, Plain Feather dragged himself to the village where his tribe lived. He slowly entered his tepee and sank upon the ground.

"I am sick," he said. "I have been in the dwelling place of the lost spirits. And I have lost my guardian spirit, the great elk. He is in the lake of the lost spirits."

Then he sank back and died. Ever after, the Indians called the lake the "Lake of the Lost Spirits." Beneath its calm blue waters are the spirits of thousands of the dead. On its clear surface is the face of Mount Hood, which stands as a monument to the lost spirits.

THE DEMONS

IN SPIRIT LAKE

Spirit Lake lies at the base of Mount St. Helens. Because of the Indians' fear of the lake, Paul Kane, a Canadian artist wandering through the Northwest in 1847, could not hire anyone to accompany him to the lake and the mountain. There were several traditions about it. At certain spots, it was said, the sound of waterfalls could be heard from places where there were no waterfalls. Hunters and fishermen and women picking berries stayed away from Spirit Lake, and they warned their children and grandchildren to stay away from the home of demons and the lake of strange noises.

The lake at the foot of the beautiful mountain Loo-wit was the home of many evil spirits. They were the spirits of people from different tribes, who had been cast out because of their wickedness. Banding themselves together, these demons called themselves Seatco, and gave themselves up to wrongdoing.

The Seatco were neither men nor animals. They could imitate the call of any bird, the sound of the wind in the trees, the cries of wild beasts. They could make these sounds seem to be near or seem to be far away. So they were often able to trick the Indians. A few times, Indians fought them. But whenever one of the Seatco was killed, the others took twelve lives from whatever band dared to fight against them.

In Spirit Lake, other Indians said, lived a demon so huge that its hand could stretch across the entire lake. If a fisherman dared to go out from shore, the demon's hand would reach out, seize his canoe, and drag fisherman and canoe to the bottom of the lake.

In the lake also was a strange fish with a head like a bear. One Indian had seen it, in the long-ago time. He had gone to the mountain with a friend. The demons who lived in the lake ate the friend, but he himself escaped, running in terror from the demons and from the fish with the head of a bear. After that, no Indian of his tribe would go near Spirit Lake.

2

An Indian hunter, seeking food for his starving tribe, once followed a giant elk to the edge of the lake. The elk plunged into the water, and the hunter followed him. At once the demons stretched out their long arms and drew him to the bottom of the lake. The elk was only a ghost, which the demons had sent out to lure the man to his death. On a certain night each year, the elk and the Indian hunter appear in the mists over the lake.

3

In the snow on the mountaintop above the lake, other Indians used to say, a race of man-stealing giants lived. At night the giants would come to the lodges when people were asleep, put the people under their skins, and take them to the mountaintop without waking them. When the people awoke in the morning, they would be entirely lost, not knowing in what direction their home was.

Frequently the giants came in the night and stole all the salmon. If people were awake they knew the giants were near when they smelled their strong, unpleasant odor. Sometimes people would hear three whistles, and soon stones would begin to hit their lodges. Then they knew that the giants were coming again.

KWATEE AND

THE MONSTER IN

LAKE QUINAULT

Lake Quinault, Indian property, is a picturesque lake on the west side of the Olympic Peninsula, a few miles from the west boundary of Olympic National Park. Near the mouth of the Quinault River, the outlet of the lake, the Quinault Indians have lived for centuries, in the village of Tahola.

Kwatee, the Changer, appears in two stories in the next section: "How

Kwatee Made the Rivers and Rocks" and "How Kwatee Changed the World." The concept of the Changer is explained in "The Animal People of Long Ago."

When Kwatee, the Changer, was an old man, he traveled down the coast until he came to Lake Quinault. A monster lived in Lake Quinault, a monster so big that it could swallow a cedar canoe. As Kwatee arrived at the lake, he saw his brother out in a canoe and called to him.

But at that very moment the monster stuck his head out of the water, opened his huge mouth, and swallowed the canoe, with Kwatee's brother in it.

Kwatee set to work at once to save his brother. He gathered all the big rocks around the lake and heated them. Then with a pair of tongs he tossed the hot rocks into the lake. When the water was boiling hot, the monster floated on the surface of the lake, dead.

Kwatee then made a sharp knife of mussel shells. He planned to cut the monster open, so that his brother might get out. As he cut, he kept singing, "Don't be afraid, little brother. I will soon set you free."

But when the monster was cut open, the brother did not jump out. Inside the monster's stomach he had been changed into a hermit crab. Kwatee's brother was the father of all hermit crabs in the world today.

Kwatee was so angry that he hurled his tongs out into the ocean and changed them into stone. The tongs were open, and the handle was pointing up. You can see them today—the split rocks near the village of Tahola at the mouth of the Quinault River.

Kwatee continued his journey for a little while longer. Then, feeling old and tired, he knew that he had made all the changes he could make to help the new people who were to come. He climbed upon a rock that overlooks the ocean and sat watching the setting sun. When the copper ball had disappeared into the water, Kwatee pulled his blanket over his face and turned himself into stone.

You can see him today, south of the village of Tahola, sitting on a rock near where Point Grenville juts out into the sea.

THE ORIGIN

OF LAKE CRESCENT

Lake Crescent lies on the north side of the Olympic Peninsula, not far from the Strait of Juan de Fuca. The highest mountain overlooking it is Mount Storm King.

Many, many years ago, the Klallam people and the Quillayute people had a big battle near the shores of the Strait of Juan de Fuca. For two days they fought, from sunrise to sunset. Many warriors on both sides were killed, but neither side would ask for peace.

After watching the bloodshed for two long days, Mount Storm King became angry. On the third day he broke off a great piece of rock from his head and hurled it down into the valley. The rock was so huge that it killed all the men fighting in the valley below him, all the Klallam warriors and all the Quillayute.

Through the valley flowed a small river. The rock hurled by Mount Storm King dammed this stream, and soon at the foot of the mountain where the fighting had been fiercest a peaceful little lake sparkled in the sunshine. For many generations no Indian ever went to the place where the warriors had been punished by death.

The little lake is still there—Lake Crescent it is called today. And Mount Storm King, mirrored in its clear depths, still looks out across the Strait of Juan de Fuca and over the forest-covered mountains on both sides of it. Storm King guards the crescent-shaped shore line and the calm blue waters of the lake he made long ago.

NAHKEETA: A STORY

OF LAKE SUTHERLAND

Many years have passed since Nahkeeta, a beautiful maiden, lived in the northern foothills of what are now known as the Olympic Mountains. Nahkeeta was a gentle girl, greatly loved by her people. She was as pretty and as graceful as the maidenhair ferns which grew in the forest. Her voice was as cheerful and musical as the little stream which flowed from under the waterfall not far from her home.

Her people were canoe Indians. They got most of their food from the salt water, very little from hunting. In the summer, after the salmon had been dried and stored for winter use, the women gathered berries near the edge of the forest. In the autumn, they went to openings in the forest to gather currants and roots and tiger lily bulbs. They almost never went back into the deep woods.

One autumn day, Nahkeeta was gathering roots with her mother and sisters. She wandered back into the woods, enjoying the carpets of ferns, the moss-wrapped logs and moss-draped trees, and the yellow-green light that shimmered through the forest.

After a while she realized that she had wandered far. When she turned round to go back, she found that she was lost. She called to her mother and sisters, but she knew that her voice was lost in the bigness and tallness of the forest. She knew her family would be able to hear only the murmur of the mountain streams. She tried to retrace her steps. Slowly the yellow-green sunlight of the forest faded. Darkness came. Nahkeeta struggled on, often climbing over fallen logs and getting tangled with the vines and ferns and small trees that grew from the old moss-covered trunks. At last, too weary and frightened to go farther, she dropped down on the moss beside a log and fell asleep.

Next morning her people searched for her. "Nahkeeta! Nahkeeta!" they called, again and again and again. There was no answer but the song of the wind in the treetops and the murmur of the mountain streams.

For three days her people looked for her. On the fourth day someone stumbled over a moss-covered log. Beside it, in a pool of blood, lay Nahkeeta's body. Some wild beast had torn it.

Grief filled the hearts of Nahkeeta's people as they buried her body in a valley in the forest. For days, mournful chants and the sad wailing of women filled the air. The people's sorrow was so great that the Spirit Chief's heart was touched. One morning when they arose they were surprised to see a beautiful little lake, its blue-green waters surrounded by white-barked alders. The lake covered the place where Nahkeeta was buried.

The Indians called the little lake Nahkeeta. They said that every autumn the birds hovered over the lake and called, "Nahkeeta, Nahkeeta!" The only answer was a ripple over the water.

Today the lake is known as Lake Sutherland, because the first white man to see it was John Sutherland. Nahkeeta has been forgotten, except by a few old grandmothers of her tribe.

MASON LAKE
AND THE
CRYING LOON

On the east side of the Olympic Peninsula is a small lake, Mason Lake, which the Indians said was the home of evil spirits.

Not far from the lake lived a little boy, a very good swimmer. He spent much of his time in the salt water and on the shore of what is now called Hood Canal. His mother often told him that he must never swim in the haunted lake. If he should swim there, he would anger the evil spirits and they would punish him. But this little boy sometimes did what his mother told him not to do.

One warm day he disobeyed her and went swimming in the lake of the evil spirits. He could see no demons, but he did see many trout swimming about in the clear water. He swam and dived and had much fun all afternoon. He tried to catch the swift-moving trout, although he had no net with him. At last he caught one and swam ashore with it in his hand.

Hungry after his long swim, he thought to himself, "What a fine meal this would make!" So he built a fire on the beach, cooked the trout, and ate it.

The fish tasted good, but one thing the little boy did not know—one of the evil spirits of the lake was hidden in the speckled trout. Just as the boy swallowed the last bite, he was changed into a loon.

Frightened, he flew to his home. Round and round he flew over the lodge, calling to his mother. With the harsh cries of the loon, he tried to tell her what had happened to him. But his mother did not understand. She did not know that the crying loon was her little son. She even tried to beat off the bird with a stick. Fearing she would kill him, the little boy, still crying, flew back over the lake.

To this very day loons give harsh cries of warning to boys and girls who do not obey their mothers.

THE LAKE

ON VASHON ISLAND

Vashon Island, about fourteen miles long, lies near the west shore of Puget Sound, halfway between Tacoma and Seattle.

At the south end of Vashon Island is a large pool at the bottom of a pothole. A hill stands between it and the beach. It used to be a lake, and in the lake lived an evil spirit. On the shore of the lake, many years ago, lived a beautiful girl. The evil spirit wanted her to be his.

But a young man in a neighboring village wanted the girl for his wife. He wanted her to dig camas and fern roots for him in the spring, to pick huckleberries and service berries for him in the summer. He angrily warned the spirit of the lake to leave the girl alone.

One summer day the young man went out on the lake in his canoe. That angered the spirit of the lake. He changed himself into human form, seized the man, and took him down to his home far below the surface of the water.

Far down in the water there was an underground passage that led from the lake to Puget Sound. The evil spirit, still in the form of a human being, got caught in that passage. He struggled and struggled, but he could not free himself. As he struggled, he kicked up mud and made the hills at the south end of the island, and he splashed most of the water of the lake out into the Sound.

Next day, say some people, the young man's canoe was found far out in the Sound, bottom up. Others say that the young man was found unconscious in his canoe and that he lived to tell his grandchildren why there is only a pool where a lake used to be on Vashon Island.

THE LAKE

AND THE

ELK-CHILD

Many years ago, in the foothills of the Cascade Range east of Mount Adams, there was a large lake. In its water the Indians used to catch many salmon and sturgeon. In later years the lake became only a pond in which tules grew. These the Indians gathered and wove into mats for their tule lodges.

In the long ago, the waters of the lake had spirit powers. Whoever drank of it or bathed in it was sure of happiness and wealth and long life. But the ruler of the lake did not like to have anyone come near. The ruler was a huge swan by the name of Hawelakok. She was very selfish. Whenever people came to the lake, she stirred up the water and caused it to overflow. People were drowned if they did not hurry faster than the rising water.

A beautiful maiden of the Wishram people, who lived near the great river, once went alone to the lake to bathe in its waters. She hoped to gain long life and good fortune. She dived in, sure that she could escape from the wrath of the giant swan.

While she was swimming, an elk from the mountains came down to the shore for a drink and then lay down in the water to cool off. The maiden had not seen or heard the elk. When she was ready to rest from swimming, she climbed up into the branches of his spreading antlers, thinking they were the branches of a tree. She did not notice the head below the antlers. At once the elk arose and carried the girl off toward

Mount Adams. But she escaped. In some unknown way, while she was being carried by the elk, she cut off one of his antlers and fell to the ground with it.

Sometime after her return to her home, she gave birth to a strange-looking child. It was an elk-child, half human and half elk. Angry and very much ashamed, the girl killed the baby, hoping that her people would never know about it.

But the elk heard about her deed. He and his tribe were so offended that they hid themselves farther back in the mountains. Never again did they go down to the lake to drink. That is why it was hard for the Indians in the Mount Adams country to find elk when they went hunting.

THE MONSTER

AND

LAKE CHELAN

Lake Chelan—fifty-five miles long and in no place more than a mile and a half wide—lies deep in the Cascade Range of north central Washington. The lake fills a glacier-carved gorge to a depth of more than 1,600 feet, and mountains at the north end rise 7,000 feet above the normal level of the water. The Stehekin River flows into the north end, the head, of the lake; the Chelan River flows out of the south end, into the Columbia River.

The first legend given below was told to the author by Frank Hubbard, long the master of Moore's Inn on Lake Chelan. About 1914 he heard it, through an interpreter, from a grandson of Chief Wapato. The second legend was told to Clarence L. Andrews when he was on a hunting trip in the Chelan country in 1895. Another account of the origin of Lake Chelan is given in "How Coyote Helped the People."

When the world was very, very young, there were no mountain peaks in this part of the country, and there was no Lake Chelan. Instead, there was a great plain covered with tall grass. There my people roamed far and wide, happy with their hunting. Life was easy. Their chief food was deer meat, and plenty of deer roamed on the great plain.

But after many years a monster came into the country. He ate the elk and the bear. He ate the deer. He ate so many that all the other animals fled in terror. My people could not find any deer for themselves, and they became very hungry. At last, weak from starvation, they prayed to the Great Spirit, whose home is in the sky.

The Great Spirit heard their prayer, came down to earth, and killed the monster. Soon the deer came back to feed on the tall grass. The people had food and were happy again.

But after a while the monster came back to life. He returned to the great plain with the tall grass. Again he ate deer, the other animals fled in terror, and the Indians were left with little food. Again they prayed to the Great Spirit for help. A second time he came down from the sky and killed the monster. This time, to make sure that the big monster would stay dead, the Great Spirit cut him into many pieces. The deer came back to the great plain, and the Indians again were happy and well fed.

But after a while the monster came to life again. Once more he devoured the animals which were the Indians' food. Once more they begged the Great Spirit to come and help them.

When he came down from the sky this third time, the Great Spirit was very angry. A third time he killed the monster. Then the Great Spirit struck the earth with his huge stone knife. All the world shook from his blow. A great cloud appeared over the plain.

When the cloud went away, the people saw that the land was changed. Huge mountain peaks rose on all sides of them. Among the mountains were canyons. Extending from the northwest to the southeast for a two days' journey was a very deep canyon between high mountains. The mountains had been formed by the rocks and dirt removed from the canyons.

The Great Spirit threw the monster's body into the bottom of this deep and long gorge. Then he poured much water into it and so formed a lake. Long afterward, Indians called it Chelan. The monster never came to life again, but its tail never died. Sometimes even yet it thrashes around and causes big waves on the surface of the water. The Indians never paddled their canoes on Lake Chelan. They did not fish or swim in its blue waters. No one has ever found the bottom of the lake, it is so very deep.

2

In the days of our grandfathers, a warrior from a Chelan village married the beautiful daughter of the headman of a Methow village. One day they wandered in a canoe to the northern waters of Lake Chelan. At the mouth of the Stehekin River, the young man tried to spear a very large fish. When the spear struck it, it changed into a huge dragon. Lashing the waters into foam, the dragon seized the man and sank with him into the water.

The girl watched the water in horror and great fear. After a time, the dragon rose again. "I am the spirit of the lake," he said. "No one shall again come to my home. I will destroy anyone who dares to come."

Then he sank once more into the water.

Returning to her husband's village near the Chelan River, the girl told his tribesmen what had happened. The old men sat in council. The young men urged war against the monster. Two canoes filled with warriors traveled for two days until they reached the head of the lake.

When they were near the mouth of the Stehekin River, a sudden storm blew up. Again the dragon rose from the water. He seized a canoe and sank with it beneath the waves. He returned to the surface for the other canoe, but the men in it were paddling away furiously. Traveling as fast as possible, they reached the lower end of the lake in safety.

For many, many years, the Chelan Indians dreaded the lake. They believed that a huge dragon hid in its waters, always ready to devour them.

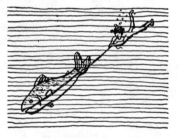

THE LAKES
OF THE
GRAND COULEE

Army officers who used to hunt in the Grand Coulee in the early days reported that bones of strange animals were occasionally found in the mire along certain lakes in the coulee. The Indians gave this explanation of the bones and of the red rocks in the area.

1. THE BLOOD-RED LAKE

Long, long ago, giant sea animals lived in the lakes in the Old Coulee. Our people saw them playing in the water, summer and winter.

One time in the days of our oldest grandfathers, our people had a big battle with the monsters. The battle lasted for three days. Many of the sea animals were killed, and thirteen of our warriors lost their lives. The water of one lake was colored a deep red with the blood of the slain warriors and monsters.

The water remained red for years and years. The shore of the lake also was dyed red, and in some places remains red to this day. The bones you saw are the bones of the monsters.

2. BLUE LAKE

Near Dry Falls, said Bob Covington of the Sanpoil Indians, there is a lake with an island near the middle. It is now called Blue Lake.

One day a man started to swim out to the island. He was a very good swimmer, but when he was about halfway, he suddenly sank. Nothing was seen of him for two or three weeks.

Then his skeleton was found on the shore, across the lake from where he had gone down. There was no flesh on it; only his bones were there. The flesh had not rotted off—it could not have done that in three weeks. The spirits of the lake had drawn him down and had eaten his flesh.

No Indian has gone there since that time.

* * *

At the north end of Nuquispum, which white people call Blue Lake, said Billy Curlew of the Moses-Columbia band, a herd of cattle used to come up every day from below the surface of the water. They would graze on the hills around the lake. At the end of the day they would sink out of sight in the water.

3. DEEP LAKE

Not many years ago, a young man from Snake River married a girl from the Okanogan country. One spring he camped in the Grand Coulee country with her and her parents when they went there to dig roots. While the women dug onions and kouse and other roots, he went hunting with his bow and arrows. Sometimes he brought home a rabbit, sometimes a bird, often nothing. Food was scarce.

When they first came to the Grand Coulee country, his wife said to him, "Never go south of the camp. It is all right to go in other directions, but never go south of here." She did not tell him why he should not go.

When he could find no more rabbits, he began to wonder about her warning. Finally he said to himself, "I will go there today. I will see why she thinks I should not go."

Not telling anyone where he was going, he started off. After a while he came to the edge of a great cliff. Far below, lying on the floor of a wide valley, were some small lakes.

"Where there are lakes, surely there are fish," the young man said to himself. "I will go down and see."

He climbed down the wall of the canyon, and when he reached one of the lakes, sat down beside it on a rock. Looking down through the clear water, he saw many fish.

"Why was I told not to come here?" he asked himself. "We are starving, and here are lots of fish. I will catch some and take them back to camp."

So he cut an elderberry pole, trimmed a hook on it, and went back to the sloping rock at the edge of the lake. He began hooking out the fish, the small ones.

"I do not want these small fish," he thought. "I will catch a big one."

He looked for the biggest salmon and made up his mind to catch it. Soon he had the big fish hooked. But it was too strong for him and soon pulled him into the water. Down, down he went, into the deep lake.

When he did not return home, his people looked for him everywhere. After several days, they went down to the lake. There they found his bow and his case of arrows lying beside the small fish he had caught. The fish had all dried up. The young man's people hunted for days and moons, but they found no more trace of him. Every year when they returned to dig roots in the Grand Coulee, they searched again, but they never found him.

At last they were sure that some monster in the water had taken the man. Never again did they go near Chulananuk, which white people call Deep Lake.

SPOKANE LAKE

OF LONG AGO

More than sixty years ago, Chief Lot, a respected leader of a band of Spokane Indians, told this legend to the army officer who was then the Indian agent on the Colville Reservation. Major R. D. Gwydin reported it in a paper read before the Spokane Historical Society.

A long time ago the country around where Spokane Falls are now, and for many days' journey east of it, was a large and beautiful lake. In the lake were many islands, and on its shores were many villages with many people. The Indians were well fed and happy, for there were plenty of fish in the lake and plenty of deer and elk in the country around it.

But one summer morning the people were startled by a rumbling and a shaking of the earth. The waters of the lake rose. Soon the waves became mountains of water that broke with fury against the shore.

Then the sun was blotted out, and darkness covered the land and the water. Terrified, the people ran to the hills to get away from the pounding water. For two days the earth rumbled and quaked. Then a rain of ashes began to fall. It fell for several weeks.

At last the ashes stopped falling, the waters of the lake became quiet, and the Indians came down from the hills. But soon the lake began to disappear. Dry land rose where the water had been. Many people died, for there was nothing to eat. The game animals had run away when the people fled to the hills, and no one dared go out on the lake to fish.

Some of the water was flowing westward from the lake that remained. The people followed it until they came to a waterfall. Soon they saw salmon coming up the new river from the big river west of them. So they built a village beside the waterfall in the new river and made it their home.

CHIEF JOSEPH'S
STORY OF
WALLOWA LAKE

About 1870, three white men hunting in the Wallowa Mountains of northeastern Oregon were invited to join a group of Nez Perce hunters also in pursuit of elk. Their leader was Eagle Wing, afterward known as Chief Joseph, a famous military leader of his people. While the men were drying their elk meat, Eagle Wing entertained them with this story of the Nez Perce and Blackfeet Indians.

Many years ago, probably as long ago as two men can live, our tribe was strong and had many warriors. Every summer they went over into the buffalo country to hunt buffalo. So did the Blackfeet, who lived east of the Big Shining Mountains.

One summer when Red Wolf, chief of the Nez Perces, and a few of his warriors were hunting buffalo, they were attacked by a large band of Blackfeet. Most of Red Wolf's men were killed.

All the next winter our people made bows and arrows for an attack of revenge. When summer came, Red Wolf and his warriors went to the buffalo country. There the two tribes met and fought again. This time the Nez Perces were strong. Not one was killed, and the band returned home with many horses and many scalps taken from the Blackfeet. Summer after summer the two tribes met in the buffalo country east of the great mountains, and summer after summer they fought. Every boy went to the buffalo country as soon as he was big enough to fight. Old Chief Red Wolf died, and young Chief Red Wolf led the warriors in his place.

One summer, when a large number of our people were in the buffalo country, the Blackfeet attacked them in the night. All our people were asleep. Many Nez Perce warriors were killed. The rest, pursued by the Blackfeet, had to fight again and again as they fled toward home.

The night Red Wolf reached his village, he was worn and weak, and he had only a few warriors left. But the Blackfeet were still powerful. Unable to follow the Nez Perces to their village in the darkness, they camped across the lake. They planned to kill the old men and take the women and children prisoners in the morning.

All night the Blackfeet kept big fires burning, and all night they shouted and danced. But our people built no fires. There was no dancing among them. Instead, there was wailing for the dead. There was sorrow in Red Wolf's tepee.

Chief Red Wolf had only one child, a beautiful daughter named Wahluna. Everyone loved Wahluna, and she loved her people and her father dearly. She knew that he was too weak to fight again, and she knew that not enough warriors were left to fight against the Blackfeet.

Unseen by her family and friends, Wahluna slipped away from the village to her canoe among the willows. Without a sound she paddled across the lake to the camp of the Blackfeet, beached her canoe, and walked toward the biggest fire.

There a huge warrior, with six Nez Perce scalps hanging from his belt, was speaking to the other men. When he had finished, Wahluna came out into the firelight and said, "I am Wahluna, daughter of Red Wolf. I have come to speak to the great chief of the Blackfeet."

"I am Bloody Chief, war chief of the Blackfeet," the big man replied. "What has the daughter of Red Wolf to say to me?"

"I come to plead for my people. They do not know I have come. Our young warriors have been killed. Our women are now wailing for the dead, and we have no fires in our village. My father says that tomorrow you will kill us all. But I know you do not want the scalps of old men and of women and children. I beg you to return to your country without more fighting. We can never fight Bloody Chief again, for our warriors are dead."

Then Wahluna lay down upon the sand and buried her face. Tlesca, the son of Bloody Chief, spread his robe over her shoulders and said to her, "You are brave, and you love your people. My heart grieves with yours. I shall not fight your people again."

These words from the young warrior made his father angry. "Her people are dogs. Pick up your robe, Tlesca. The girl must die."

Tlesca did not move. "Red Wolf is not a dog," he said. "He has fought bravely. For days we have followed him over rough mountain trails. We have seen him stagger from hunger, but when he turned to fight, his heart was brave. I am the only one of our warriors strong enough to fight him singlehanded, and yet my shoulder was broken by his war club. The daughter of Red Wolf is not a dog. I will leave my robe on her shoulders."

Bloody Chief's heart was softened, for he loved the young warrior. "My son's words are good," he said. "I will lay my robe on his."

Wahluna then arose and started toward her canoe. She knew that her people would live. As she reached for her paddle, she found Tlesca standing beside her.

"The daughter of Red Wolf is brave," he said, "and she is beautiful. When twelve moons have passed, listen in the middle of the night. You will hear a great owl hooting down by the lake. Come then, and Tlesca will speak."

Wahluna returned to her village. Her people were not attacked. They could build their fires again.

She counted the moons until twelve had passed. One night when all in the village were asleep, she heard the great owl down by the lake. Leaving her tepee, she slipped through the village and down to the edge of the water. There she found Tlesca waiting.

He said to her, "Some of the Blackfeet daughters look upon Tlesca with favor, because he is a great warrior. But Tlesca's heart is with Wahluna. He wants her to be his wife."

"It cannot be," said Wahluna. "My people would kill Tlesca and give his bones to the wolves, even as the Blackfeet warriors have given our warriors' bones to the wolves."

"When six more moons have passed," Tlesca answered, "Wahluna will hear the howl of a gray wolf. If she will cross the lake, Tlesca will speak again."

Again Wahluna counted the moons. When the sixth one was passing, she heard a gray wolf howl in the middle of the night. She slipped away to her canoe and paddled noiselessly across the lake. Tlesca was waiting.

"I have talked with my father," he said. "His heart has softened. Tomorrow morning, I will bring him and all our chiefs and many of our warriors to the village of Red Wolf. We will smoke the peace pipe with your father and his warriors. We will catch fish in your lake, and you can come to the buffalo country without harm from us."

Next morning Wahluna reported to her father what Tlesca had said. Red Wolf told his men. Together they waited. Bloody Chief and Tlesca and many warriors of the Blackfeet came to the Nez Perce village. They seated themselves around the campfire with Red Wolf and his men. They smoked the peace pipe together and were brothers.

Then the great chief of the Blackfeet said to Red Wolf, "My son's heart is with your daughter. He wants her for his wife. He is a great warrior."

Red Wolf answered, "My daughter has told me. Her heart is with Tlesca. She may go to his lodge."

Then Red Wolf sent runners to the Nez Perce people along the Kookooskia and to his friends among the Yakima and Cayuse. He invited them to a wedding feast.

At sunset on the first day of the feast, Wahluna and Tlesca went out on the lake in a canoe. The people on the shore stood watching them paddle toward the mountains. Suddenly, the waters became troubled. Tlesca and Wahluna began to pull toward the shore. Ripples and then waves came over the lake. The waves became larger. Some demon seemed to be rising from the depths of the lake.

Soon a serpent's head appeared. Then a giant serpent rose out of the water, swam round the canoe, jumped high, and gave the boat a sharp blow with its tail.

Wahluna and Tlesca were never seen again. For days people of both tribes looked for their bodies, but they were never found. With sad hearts the Blackfeet went back to their country. They were sure that the Great Spirit was angry with them and so had taken away the young chief whom they loved.

The Nez Perces also thought that the Great Spirit was angry because they had made peace with their ancient enemy. Fearing that they might be punished a second time, they never again went out on the lake at the foot of the Wallowa Mountains.

*   *   *

When young Joseph of the Nez Perces had finished telling this story at the campfire, George Waggoner, who later recorded it, asked, "Is that a true story or is it just made up?"

"Oh, it is all true," answered Joseph. "I have heard my people tell it many times, and I have heard some of the Blackfeet warriors tell it too."

"But do you believe that a great snake came and swallowed Tlesca and Wahluna?"

"No," he answered. "One big wind. One big wave. That's all."

III.
TALES OF
THE RIVERS
ROCKS AND
WATERFALLS

THE ANIMAL PEOPLE

OF LONG AGO

"Long ago—I don't know how long ago," began Peter Noyes of the Colville Reservation, when recalling some stories heard in his childhood, "the animals were the *people* of this country. They talked to one another the same as we do. And they married, too. That went on for many, many years, and then the world changed."

A Puget Sound Indian once explained to Nels Bruseth this belief in the animal people:

"This time, long time ago, animal just same way like man. He talk, everybody understand. Fur and skin he put on and take off just like coat. Same way everybody—animals, birds, and fish."

These two men expressed a belief once held by the Indians of the Northwest, as well as by other tribes on the North American continent, that before the Indians were created, the world was inhabited by a race of animal people. That was "long, long ago, when the world was very young and people hadn't come out yet."

The animal people in the myths of the Pacific Northwest Indians were giants. Mosquito, Spider, and Ant were larger than our cows. Eagle, Beaver, Fox, Coyote, and others had the characteristics of today's animals, yet they could reason and talk and do many things that neither animals nor people can do now. The animal people in the tribal tales lived exactly as the Indians themselves lived later. They fished and hunted, dug roots and cooked them, lived in lodges, used the sweat lodge, had headmen or "chiefs." In the myth "Origin of the Potlatch," Golden Eagle had a slave, just as the Indians who told the story had slaves. Sometimes these ancient creatures were human in shape, sometimes animal—even in the same story. When telling the tales in English, Indians today refer to these animal persons simply as "the people."

In the mythology of the Indians of the Columbia River Basin, the greatest of these ancients was Coyote. Coyote had supernatural power, which he often used for the good of the lesser animal people. He helped them in many ways, but he did many selfish and foolish things also. He often played mean tricks just for his own amusement. He was often boastful, vain, greedy, and cruel (according to our standards). An endless number of stories are still told about Coyote.

At the end of this mythical period of the animal people, "the world turned over," "the world turned inside out," or "the world changed," often quite suddenly. Human beings were created; the animals shrank to their present size, some tribes believed, and became more numerous. In other traditions, Coyote destroyed the power of the monsters and other evil beings and then changed the good ancients into Indians. He divided them into groups and settled them in different places, giving each group a different name and a different language. These good ancients became the ancestors of all the Indian tribes.

Coyote is the chief character in the myths of the Pacific Northwest, as he is over the whole western half of North America. But in the myths of the Puget Sound and Pacific Coast Indians, other characters play more important roles. The tribes living near the water, in what are now Washington and British Columbia, told many stories about Raven. In some of them, Raven is the culture hero, the Creator and the Changer. In others, Raven is the helper of the Man-Who-Changed-Things. Mink, Fox, Eagle, and Blue Jay are other major characters in the tales of the Pacific Coast and Puget Sound Indians.

Different tribes had different heroes, but seemingly all of them believed that the world was once inhabited by mythological beings and that, in the days long past, some Changer came to transform the ancient world into the world which we know today. Among most of the interior tribes of Washington and Oregon, the Changer was Coyote. Among most of the Puget Sound and Pacific Coast tribes, the Changer was a manlike being with supernatural powers. Not only could he change himself into any form he wished, but he transformed the creatures of the mythological age into animals, birds, fishes, stars, rocks, and trees, in preparation for the race of human beings he was planning to create. The Changer has already appeared in "Mount Rainier and the Olympic Mountains" and in "Kwatee and the Monster in Lake Quinault." He will appear, under different names, in several stories in Sections III and IV.

The next two narratives give additional information about the animal people and about Coyote; many of his exploits are closely connected with the rivers, rocks, and waterfalls of the Columbia Basin. He has already appeared in this volume in "Mount Shasta and the Great Flood," "The Peaks of Central Oregon," and "The Seven Devils Mountains." In some stories, Coyote is an animal, for his tail or his snout is mentioned. In others, he is a man—sometimes old and ugly, sometimes young and handsome. In a Sanpoil myth explaining the origin of the salmon ceremony, Coyote is described as tall and strong—"perhaps a chief of some kind"; his hair was worn in long braids, "his forelocks were carefully combed back, and the few strands of hair in front of his ears were covered with beads."

CREATION OF THE
ANIMAL PEOPLE

"The Earth is our mother" and "the Sun is our father" were common expressions among the Indians of the Pacific Northwest. In southwestern Oregon, Indians prayed to Earth and Sun in gratitude for fruits and berries, roots and grass and salmon. The Klallam along the Strait of Juan de Fuca prayed to Earth as a deity at time of disaster; Klallam women prayed to Earth during childbirth, and after a child was born they offered a prayer of gratitude to Earth. The following myth is from the Okanogan.

The earth was once a human being. Old-One made her out of a woman. "You will be the mother of all people," he said.

Earth is alive yet, but she has been changed. The soil is her flesh; the rocks are her bones; the wind is her breath; trees and grass are her hair. She lives spread out, and we live on her. When she moves, we have an earthquake.

After changing her to earth, Old-One took some of her flesh and rolled it into balls, as people do with mud or clay. These balls Old-One made into the beings of the early world. They were the ancients. They were people, and yet they were at the same time animals.

In form, some of them were like animals; some were more like people. Some could fly like birds; others could swim like fishes. In some ways the land creatures acted like animals. All had the gift of speech. They had greater powers and were more cunning than either animals or people. And yet they were very stupid in some ways. They knew that they had to hunt in order to live, but they did not know which beings were deer and which were people. They thought people were deer and often ate them.

Some people lived on the earth at that time. They were like the Indians of today except that they were ignorant. Deer also were on the earth at that time. They were real animals then too. They were never people or ancient animal people, as were the ancestors of most animals. Some people say that elk, antelope, and buffalo also were always animals, to be hunted as deer are hunted. Others tell stories about them as if they were ancients or half-human beings.

The last balls of mud Old-One made were almost all alike and were different from the first ones he made. He rolled them over and over. He shaped them like Indians. He blew on them and they became alive. Old-One called them men. They were Indians, but they were very ignorant. They did not know how to do things. They were the most helpless of all creatures Old-One made. Some of the animal people preyed on them and ate them.

Old-One made both male and female people and animals, so that they might breed and multiply. Thus all living things came from the earth. When we look around, we see everywhere parts of our mother.

Most of the ancient animal people were selfish, and there was much trouble among them. At last Old-One said, "There will soon be no people if I let things go on like this."

So he sent Coyote to kill all the monsters and other evil beings. Old-One told Coyote to teach the Indians the best way to do things and the best way to make things. Life would be easier and better for them when they were no longer ignorant. Coyote then traveled on the earth and did many wonderful things.

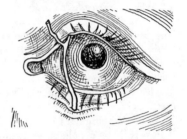

HOW COYOTE

GOT HIS

SPECIAL POWER

This variant of a widely told tale was related by Eneas Seymore, a Lake Indian on the Colville Reservation. In a similar Okanogan story, the chief gave Coyote special power, which was to be in his stomach. In a Karok version, Old-Man-Above made him the most cunning of animals because newly created Man had sympathy for his disappointment; in gratitude, Coyote became the friend of Man and his children.

In the beginning of the world, Spirit Chief called a meeting of all the animal people.

"Some of you do not have names yet," he said when they had gathered together. "And some of you do not like the names you have now. Tomorrow, before the sun rises I will give a name to everyone. And I will give each an arrow also.

"Come to my lodge as soon as the darkness is gone. The one who gets there first may choose any name he wants, and I will give him the longest arrow. The longest arrow will mean that he will have the most power."

As the people left the meeting, Coyote said to his friend Fox, "I'm going to be there first. I don't like my name. I want to be called Grizzly Bear or Eagle."

Fox laughed. "No one wants your name. You may have to keep it."

"I'll be there first," repeated Coyote. "I won't go to sleep tonight."

That night he sat by his fire and stayed awake for a long time. Owl hooted at him. Frog croaked in the marshes. Coyote heard them all. But after the stars had closed their eyes, he became very sleepy. His eyelids grew heavy.

"I will have to prop my eyes open."

So he took two small sticks and propped his eyelids apart. "Now I can stay awake."

But soon he was fast asleep, and when he awoke, the sun was making shadows. His eyes were dry from being propped open, but he ran to the lodge of the Spirit Chief.

"I want to be Grizzly Bear," he said, thinking he was the first one there. The lodge was empty except for Spirit Chief.

"That name is taken, and Grizzly Bear has the longest arrow. He will be chief of the animals on the earth."

"Then I will be Eagle."

"That name is taken, and Eagle has the second arrow. Eagle will be the chief of the birds."

"Then I will be Salmon."

"That name is taken, and Salmon has the third arrow. Salmon will be the chief of all the fish. Only the shortest arrow is left, and only one name—Coyote."

And the Spirit Chief gave Coyote the shortest arrow. Coyote sank down beside the fire of the Spirit Chief. His eyes were still dry. The Spirit Chief felt sorry and put water in his eyes. Then Coyote had an idea.

"I will ask Grizzly Bear to change with me."

"No," said Grizzly, "I cannot. Spirit Chief gave my name to me."

Coyote came back and sank down again beside the fire in the big lodge. Then Spirit Chief spoke to him.

"I have special power for you. I wanted you to be the last one to come. I have work for you to do, and you will need this special power. With it you can change yourself into any form. When you need help, call on your power.

"Fox will be your brother. He will help you when you need help. If you die, he will have the power to bring you to life again.

"Go to the lake and get four tules. Your power is in the tules. Then do well the work I will give you to do."

So that is how Coyote got his special power.

*   *   *

Mr. Seymore gave a unique account of the end of Coyote. Coyote and the Spirit Chief—whom Mr. Seymore always referred to as "God"— had a power contest. Unable to move a mountain except when Spirit

Chief wanted him to do so, Coyote was thus defeated and was taken to an island in the ocean. He and his wife and four children can be seen there now, through a spyglass, but no one can get to them. When the world changes again—in the year 2000—Coyote will come back.

WHY RIVERS
FLOW BUT ONE WAY

The animal people helped in the planning and the arranging of the ancient world. Tribes on the east side of Puget Sound told the first of these two stories; the Quinault on the Washington coast told the second one.

Long ago, before the world changed, all the animal people came together for a big meeting. Eagle was the headman of the gathering. He lived up high, in the top of a tall tree. Whenever the people wanted to decide anything important, they called up to him as he sat in the tree, and he gave them his opinion.

Each of the animal people at the meeting had a chance to say what he thought. Even Raven and Mink, who were slaves, told the others what they believed should be done. Raven's opinion was so good that he became known as a wise man.

For a long time the people argued about the direction in which the rivers should flow. Should they flow up or down, or both up and down? All but Raven thought that one side of all rivers should run up the mountains and the other side should run down. All the rivers should go up as far as the falls, they said, and then should turn round and come back.

"What do you think of our plan?" they called up to Eagle.

"I agree with you," answered Eagle. "If the rivers go both ways, the new people who are to come will have an easy time. It will not be hard to go upstream, and it will not be hard to go downstream. What does Raven think?"

"I don't agree with you," replied Raven. "If the rivers turn round at the falls, salmon will have no chance to stop. They will go up as far as the falls, and then they will come right back again. Where will they spawn? And how will the new people catch them? I think that all rivers should flow but one way."

"Raven is right," agreed Mink. "The people will have a very hard time catching salmon if the rivers run both ways."

"I think the rivers should go but one way," repeated Raven. "And I think that at all the bends in the streams there should be little eddies.

They will make the salmon go slower. The people can fish there, too."

"Raven's reasons seem very good," said Eagle in the tree.

"Raven's reasons seem very good," repeated the people on the ground. So they followed his plan.

That is why all rivers now run but one way. That is why the salmon go all the way up their home river to spawn.

2

Near the beginning of the world, Eagle suggested that Lake Quinault should be a prairie with the Quinault River running through the middle of it.

But Raven replied, "No, that would be too easy for the people. They must work for what they want. If they want camas roots, they should have to go through the woods and find the prairies that are farther away. They should have to carry the camas from the prairies to the river."

And so Lake Quinault has always been a lake. Raven would have it that way. The Quinault River flows into it from the mountains and out of it into the ocean.

Then Eagle said to Raven, "I think one side of a river should flow upstream and one should flow down."

"No," replied Raven, "that would be too easy for the people. When they want to go upstream, they should have to pole up. We can leave some eddies along the banks."

That is why all rivers flow down. Raven would have them that way. The eddies are the only results of Eagle's wishes.

Then Eagle said, "The milt in the male salmon ought to be fat so that the people can use it to cook the fish in."

"No," said Raven, "the fish would be too good for the people if the milt is fat. It should be worthless as food."

Not long afterward, Eagle's child died. In his grief, Eagle went to Raven and said, "It would be better if the people who died should come to life again."

"No," answered Raven, "it is better that they remain dead. They should not come back to the earth."

And that was arranged as Raven wanted it. Eagle's child and the people who died later never came back to the earth world.

HOW COYOTE

MADE THE

COLUMBIA RIVER

An account of the formation of the Columbia River is an important part of the Sleeping Beauty version of the Bridge of the Gods legend. Another is found in "How Coyote Made the Indian Tribes." The following one was related in 1951 by Peter Noyes, a Colville in northeastern Washington. He first heard it nearly eighty years ago.

Mr. Noyes was pleased to read, a few years ago, that geologists see plenty of evidence that in different periods of the geologic past lakes covered parts of eastern Washington now drained by the Columbia River and its tributaries.

Long ago, when Coyote was the big man on the earth, this valley was covered by a big lake. At that time there was no Columbia River. West of us, between the lake and the ocean, was a long ridge of mountains. But the Columbia River did not go through it. Indians today believe that.

Coyote was smart enough to see that salmon would come up from the ocean to be food for his people here if he would make a hole through the mountains. So he went down to a place near where Portland is now, and with his powers he dug a hole through the mountains there. The water went through the hole and on to the ocean.

The water in the big lake up here was drained, and the water flowing out of it made the Columbia River. Coyote got the Columbia to flow through that hole, the way it does today. Then the salmon came up the river to this part of the country. His people after that had plenty to eat.

When he dug that hole through the mountains, Coyote made a kind of bridge. You have heard about it—a broad rock bridge that went across the river. People could walk from one side of the Columbia to the other. A long time afterward, an earthquake broke the bridge down. The rocks that fell into the water formed the Cascades of the Columbia. They made it hard for boats to go up and down the river there.

COYOTE AND
THE MONSTER
OF THE COLUMBIA

In a variant of this story, the monster of the Columbia is said to have lived in the "fishing place above The Dalles," where there used to be several miles of rapids, falls, and eddies. Like Scylla and Charybdis of Greek mythology, this was a female monster; her reddish-brown hair hung down to her waist when she appeared above the water. Nashlah of the following version was a male monster, who also lived near Celilo Falls.

One time on his travels, Coyote learned that a monster was killing the animal people as they traveled up and down Big River in their canoes. So many had been killed that some of the animal people were afraid to go down to the water, even to catch salmon.

"I will help you," promised Coyote. "I will stop this monster from killing people."

But what could he do? He had no idea. So he asked his three sisters who lived in his stomach in the form of huckleberries. They were very wise. They knew everything. They would tell him what to do.

At first his sisters refused to tell Coyote what to do.

"If we tell you," they said, "you will say that that was your plan all the time."

"If you do not tell me," said Coyote sternly, "I will send rain and hail down upon you."

Of course the berries did not like rain and hail.

"Do not send rain," they begged. "Do not send rain or hail. We will tell you what to do. Take with you plenty of dry wood and plenty of pitch, so that you can make a fire. And take also five sharp knives. It is Nashlah at Wishram that is killing all the people. He is swallowing the people as they pass in their canoes. You must let him swallow you."

"Yes, my sisters, that is what I thought," replied Coyote. "That was my plan all the time."

Coyote followed his sisters' advice. He gathered together some dry wood and pitch, sharpened his five knives, and went to the deep pool where Nashlah lived. The monster saw Coyote but did not swallow him, for he knew that Coyote was a great chief.

Coyote knew that he could make Nashlah angry by teasing him. So he

called out all kinds of mean names. At last the monster was so angry
that he took a big breath and sucked Coyote in with his breath. Just
before entering his mouth, Coyote grabbed a big armful of sagebrush
and took it in also.

Inside the monster, Coyote found many animal people. All were cold
and hungry. Some were almost dead from hunger, and some were almost
dead from cold.

"I will build a fire in here for you," said Coyote. "And I will cook
some food for you. While you get warm and while you eat, I will kill
Nashlah. I have come to help you, my people. You will join your friends
soon."

With the sagebrush and the pitch, Coyote made a big fire under the
heart of the monster. The shivering people gathered around it to get
warm. Then with one of his sharp knives Coyote cut pieces from the
monster's heart and roasted them.

While the people ate, Coyote began to cut the cord that fastened the
monster's heart to his body. He broke the first knife, but he kept cutting.
He broke the second knife, but he kept cutting. He broke his third and
his fourth knives. With his fifth knife he cut the last thread, and the
monster's heart fell into the fire.

Just as the monster died, he gave one big cough and coughed all the
animal people out on the land.

"I told you I would save you," said Coyote, as the animal people
gathered around him on the shore of the river. "You will live a long
time, and I will give you names."

Coyote went among them and gave each creature a name.

"*You* will be Eagle, the best and the bravest bird. *You* will be Bear,
the strongest animal. *You* will be Owl, the big medicine man, with
special powers. *You* will be Sturgeon, the largest fish in the rivers. *You*
will be Salmon, the best of all fish for eating."

In the same way Coyote named Beaver, Cougar, Deer, Woodpecker,
Blue Jay, and all the other animals and birds. Then he named himself. "I
am Coyote," he told them. "I am the wisest and smartest of all the
animals."

Then he turned to the monster and gave him a new law. "You can
no longer kill people as you have been doing. A new race of people are
coming, and they will pass up and down the river. You must not kill all
of them. You may kill one now and then. You may shake the canoes if
they pass over you. For this reason most of the canoes will go round your
pool and not pass over where you live. You will kill very few of the new
people. This is to be the law always. You are no longer the big man you
used to be."

The law that Coyote made still stands. The monster does not swallow
people as he did before Coyote took away his big power. Sometimes he

draws a canoe under and swallows the people in it. But not often. Usually the Indians take their canoes out of the water and carry them round the place where the monster lives. They do not pass over his house. He still lives deep under the water, but he is no longer powerful.

*   *   *

The first steamboat the white people brought up the river was stopped by Nashlah. The Indians told the white men to throw food into the river and then they could go. They did so. They threw overboard sugar, flour, rice, and other things. Then Nashlah let the boat loose.

WHY COYOTE

CHANGED THE COURSE

OF THE COLUMBIA RIVER

Clara Moore, who has lived all her life not far from the site of Grand Coulee Dam, often relates this story. It is her Sanpoil great-uncle's version of a tale told by many tribes along the Columbia and its tributaries. With a chuckle, Mrs. Moore states that Coyote's prophecy is being fulfilled through the irrigation project of the Columbia Basin. Her words here were transcribed from a wire recording made on June 30, 1950. Her impersonation of the characters, which added vitality and humor, will have to be imagined.

The last four paragraphs are from the variants related by Mary Summerlin, a Colville, and by Rose Seymore, a Lake Indian, who has lived most of her ninety-four years not far from Kettle Falls. Until the building of Grand Coulee Dam, Kettle Falls was the Indians' favorite fishing place in the upper Columbia.

Coyote had a tepee near the Sanpoil River. Kingfisher had a tepee there too. Four brothers, the Wolves, had a tepee there. So there were three tepees of them.

Kingfisher was having a hard time getting his fish. He could get little fishes, but not enough. They didn't suit Coyote, who expected Kingfisher to do his fishing for him.

The four brothers could get all the meat they wanted because they could kill a deer any time they wanted to. They had plenty of meat, and they gave Coyote plenty of meat. The four brothers, the Wolves, were

Coyote's nephews. But Kingfisher ate no meat. He was having a hard time getting his fish.

Down at Celilo on the Columbia, four sisters had a fish trap. They wouldn't let any big fish come up the river.

Finally Coyote said, "That won't do. I've got to get busy and see into that, so that everybody can have fish. Not just the sisters. I'll have to take a trip down there and see what I can do."

It took him a long time to walk down to Celilo. Before he came to the house where the fish trap was, he tried to think how he would break the dam and bring the fish up without hurting the girls any and without fighting with them. How was he going to fool them? Then he made [called upon] his powers.

He asked his powers, "What can I do to get the fish up the river?"

His powers said to him, "Well, that's too much work. You can't do it."

"I can work all right," said Coyote, "if you will tell me what to do."

One of his powers said to him, "Go down a ways and get in the water and float down. You'll be a little wooden bowl. Go down on the trap. Then the sisters will see you and pick you up and take you back to the house."

So he went down to the water and turned into a little wooden bowl. When he got to the trap, he couldn't float any longer. So he stopped right there. When the sisters came down from the hills where they had been picking service berries, they went to look at the trap and to get some water. They got down there and saw the little wooden bowl on the trap.

One of them said, "O sisters, see this little wooden bowl! Now we can have a nice little dish to put our salmon in."

Two of her sisters ran up and said, "Isn't it pretty? Isn't it lovely!"

But the youngest sister stood off at one side and said, "I don't think that wooden bowl is good for us. Better leave it alone. It might be something that will harm us."

"Oh, you're always suspicious," said one of her sisters. "What is the little bowl going to do? Someone must have tipped over in a canoe up above, and this is part of their stuff. It can't harm anyone. Let's take the wooden bowl to the house."

That's what they did. So they cooked their salmon, ate all they wanted, and after supper put what was left into the little wooden bowl for breakfast. Then they put it behind their little pantry and went to bed.

The next morning when they got up, the wooden bowl was empty. There wasn't a thing in it.

"I wonder what's happened to our salmon?" asked one of the sisters. "There isn't a thing in here."

The youngest sister said, "I told you that wooden bowl isn't good for us. You wouldn't listen. We'd better throw it away."

But the others said, "There must have been a rat or something that came and ate all the salmon. I don't think the dish had anything to do with it."

The youngest couldn't do anything with her sisters. There were three against one. So they cooked some more salmon, ate their fill, put what was left into the wooden bowl, and put it behind the pantry. Then they went up into the hills after more berries.

When they came back about one o'clock, they went to their house and looked at the little wooden bowl. But there wasn't anything in it.

The youngest said, "I told you that bowl is no good for us."

The others began to believe her and walked out of the house. The youngest had the bowl in her hand. She threw it against a big rock. Celilo was pretty rocky. The girl found a big rock and threw the bowl against it, to break it. When the bowl hit the rock, it dropped down on the ground and sat up as a little baby. One of the sisters ran over and picked it up. A little baby was staring at her.

"Oh, it's a little boy baby. Sisters, we'll have a brother now. We'll take care of him, and he'll grow up, and then he can get all the salmon for us. We won't have to get the salmon. All we'll have to do is to dry it and take care of it."

But the youngest sister said, "You'd better leave him alone. We don't want him in the house at all."

But they were three against one. They took the baby up to the house. It was a cute little baby, full of smiles. It was always smiling.

"Isn't he a cute little baby!" said the sisters. "Now we have a little brother."

So they fed it, put it in the bed in the tepee, and went back into the hills to pick berries. As soon as they were out of sight, Coyote changed himself from the little wooden bowl into a man. The man went down and began digging and digging, to break the dam that they had worked so hard to make. When it was about time for the sisters to come back, he would go into the tepee, get into bed, and change himself into a baby.

Well, that went on for quite a few days. Every day he went on digging and digging. One day he said to himself, "Today I think I'll be able to break through this dam." He was working as hard as he could. "It's about time for them to come home, but I'll stay here and finish breaking the dam. They can't harm me."

He had a wooden bowl which he put on top of his head. He kept on digging away and digging away. The sisters got back and went down after water. They saw him there, digging.

"Oh, he's a great big man, and he's breaking our trap!" cried one of the sisters.

The youngest sister said, "You think you know it all. I told you that baby was no good for us."

They picked up a stick and ran over to him. They tried to hit him over the head. But he had on that wooden bowl, so they couldn't hurt him. He gave the dam a few more licks and it was broken through. Then he started running away from the girls.

He laughed at them. "You women never will put it over us men. Men always will put it over you."

When he walked away from them, the salmon followed him. When the dam was broken, the salmon went through the hole he had made. Coyote walked along the shore. Whenever he got hungry or tired, he would stop and call to some of the salmon in the river. A big salmon would jump out. He would catch it, roast it, eat it, and rest awhile. Whenever he stopped, the salmon stopped. So he kept coming up the river that way.

On the way down, he had stopped at the place where Dry Falls are now. At the time, the Columbia River flowed there. He had seen a family camping there and catching little fish to eat. They had two nice-looking girls. They looked good to him. He made up his mind that he would camp there and see what he could do.

He came there that evening and went to their tepee. The girls were out picking berries, so he talked to the old folks awhile. He said to the old man, "You'd better come down to the river with me. I saw a couple of salmon down there that you can have."

So they went down there and caught one and brought it back and cooked it. The girls came home. They all had a big feed on the salmon. He talked with them and then stayed over night. Next morning he went down and caught two more and brought them up to the old man.

After breakfast Coyote asked the old folks if he could have the girls, to marry them.

"Well, I'll have to ask the girls," the old man said. So he asked them.

"No," the girls said, "we don't want to be married yet. We want to be free for a while."

That made Coyote so angry that he broke up the river.

"All right. If you girls won't have me, you can go hungry the rest of your days. I'll just take the river away from you."

So he changed the channel and made the river run down this other way, where it's running now.

He said to the old man, "Some day there'll be some smart man who will run the river through here again. Years from now there will be one man who will make the water run this way again."

Then he came on up the river. He kept coming up, coming up, coming up the river till he reached the mouth of the Sanpoil River. A girl there looked good to him. He put in Hell Gate dam to hold the salmon back for her people. The salmon couldn't get over Hell Gate dam. It was too high; they couldn't get over it, the way he had it fixed.

But that girl wouldn't have him.

So Coyote said, "Four or five kinds of salmon will come up the big river. King salmon will go up the big river, but no big ones will come up the Sanpoil River. Steelheads first, chinooks, then silver salmon, those little salmon smaller than the silver and red on the outside—those four kinds will go up the Sanpoil. But no king salmon—no big ones."

Then he broke up the dam he had made at Hell Gate. Ever since then, there have been rocks and rapids at Hell Gate. He went on up the river and took his salmon with him. He went and went and went and went. He got as far as Kettle Falls. Of course there were no falls there, but people were living on both sides of the river. And he saw a nice-looking girl there. She was one of the Beaver family, and she looked good to him in spite of her big teeth.

"I'm going to see what I can do here," Coyote said to himself.

He caught salmon for the old folks and was good to them. Next morning he asked the old man for his daughter. The old man said, "Yes, you can have her. Then I can have all the salmon I want to eat as long as I'm alive."

So that's where Coyote got his woman—at Kettle Falls. He made the falls there. That's as far as the salmon could go. He would not break those falls. He left them there. So all these years that is as far as the salmon would go up the river.

Coyote was very good to Beaver's daughter. He gave her a beautiful fur coat, the softest and most priceless of furs. He gave her the right to live under the falls. "Whenever you see people or hear them coming," he told her, "you can hide under the falls. There you will be safe."

Coyote piled rocks across the river and cut them, so that there would always be a waterfall. He made three levels of rocks, so that there would be a waterfall whether the river was high or low. When the salmon tried to jump the falls, they could be easily caught by people fishing from the rocks.

Coyote broke down all the dams from the mouth of the river all the way to Kettle Falls. Soon the salmon were so thick that Beaver could not throw a stick into the water without hitting the back of a fish.

Then Coyote made Beaver the salmon chief. "The people of many tribes will come here to fish," Coyote said to Beaver. "You will be chief over all of them. You must share the salmon with everyone who comes. There will always be enough for everyone. You must never be greedy with it, and you must see to it that no one else is greedy."

HOW COYOTE

HELPED

THE PEOPLE

*This is a composite of many tales related by many tribes that once lived
along the Columbia River and its tributaries. For the sake of a unified
story, the author has taken the liberty of weaving together many traditions from several sources. No one tribe told about all these deeds of
Coyote.*

*The part about Lake Chelan and the waterfall was told by Billy Cur-
lew, present titular chief of the Moses-Columbia band of Indians, to the
Forest Supervisor at the agency at Nespelem, with Jack Weipe as interpreter.*

After Old-One had made the earth and the ancient animal people, he
sent Coyote among them, because they were very ignorant and were
having a hard time. Coyote was told to kill the evil beings who preyed
upon them and to teach them the best way of doing things.

First he broke down the dam which five Beaver women had built in
the lower Columbia.

"It is not right," he said to them, "for you to keep the salmon penned
up here. The people farther up the river are hungry."

Then he changed the Beaver women into sandpipers. "You shall
forevermore be sandpipers," he said. "You shall always run by the water's
edge. You shall never again have control over salmon."

By this time so many salmon had come up from the mouth of Big
River that the water was dark with them. Coyote walked along the bank
of the river, and the salmon followed him in the water. At all the villages,
the animal people were glad to see him and the fish he brought. Their
hunger was over.

When he came to the Little White Salmon River, he stopped and
taught the people how to make a fish trap. He twisted young twigs of
hazel brush and hung the trap in the river. Then he showed the people
how to dry fish and how to store it for winter use.

When he came to the bigger White Salmon River, he showed the
people how to spear salmon. He made a spear from the inside bark of a
white fir tree and caught the salmon with the pointed end of the spear.

"This is how you should do it," said Coyote.

Wherever he stopped, he showed the people how to cook fish. They
had always eaten it raw. He showed them how to broil salmon by holding

it over the fire on sticks. And he showed them how to cook it in a pothole. Along Big River, to this day, there is a round-bottomed hole in the rocks, a hole that people call Coyote's Kettle. Coyote put salmon in that hole, poured a little water over it, dropped hot stones into the pothole, and covered everything with green grass to hold the steam. Thus the salmon was steamed until it was tender.

"This is how you should do it," Coyote told the people.

Then he and the people had a big feast—a feast of salmon cooked in the proper way, the way he explained to them. Coyote said to the animal people along Big River and along all the streams which flow into it, "Every spring the salmon will come up the river to lay their eggs. Every spring you must have a big feast like this to celebrate the coming of the salmon. Then you will thank the salmon spirits for guiding the fish up the streams to you, and your Salmon Chief will pray to those spirits to fill your fish traps. During the five days of the feast, you must not cut the salmon with a knife, and you must cook it only by roasting it over a fire. If you do as I tell you, you will always have plenty of salmon to eat and to dry for winter."

Then Coyote traveled farther up the river, and the salmon followed him. Often he came to a smaller stream flowing into Big River. Because the people along the Yakima and Wenatchee rivers treated him kindly, he sent the fish up their rivers and promised them that every spring the salmon would return. Where he was treated very kindly, he made the river narrow in one spot. He would make the two banks of a river almost meet, so that there would be a good place for catching salmon.

When he came to the animal people along the Chelan River, he said to them, "I will send many salmon up your river if you will give me a nice young girl for my wife."

But the Chelan people refused. They thought it was not proper for a young girl to marry anyone as old as Coyote. So Coyote angrily blocked up the canyon of Chelan River with huge rocks and thus made a waterfall. The water dammed up behind the rocks and formed Lake Chelan. The salmon could never get past the waterfall. That is why there are no salmon in Lake Chelan to this day.

Coyote made a waterfall in the Okanogan River because the girls there refused to marry him. He made a waterfall in the Spokane River because the chief along the upper river would not let him marry any girl among his people. Coyote said to the chiefs along the Okanogan and the Spokane rivers, "I will make falls here. I will make falls so that the salmon cannot get past them, to your people farther up the river."

As Coyote traveled up the rivers, he gave names to the streams and the mountains. He killed monsters that were destroying the animal people. He killed the Ice People and defeated Blizzard, so that the winters would not be so cold.

He planted trees, so that when the new people, the Indians, should come, they could burn wood and keep themselves warm. He planted huckleberries in the mountains. "People must climb to get these berries," he said. "It will not be good for them to get all food easily. They will become lazy." He planted strawberries and service berry bushes. He planted camas, kouse, and other roots, so that there would be all kinds of food for the new people.

After the new people, the Indians, came, he showed them how to make fire by twirling sticks between their hands. He made a long knife to cut with, and an ax to chop with. He peeled bark off a cedar tree and made a cedar-bark canoe. "This is how you should do it," he said.

He taught them how to make bows and arrows from young arrowwood, and how to use the weapons. He made dip nets from maple and willow twigs, and showed the Indians how to catch salmon with them. He taught them how to make fishing platforms near the falls of Big River and how to spear salmon from these platforms. He made a basket trap also for catching fish.

Coyote taught the Indians that salmon must always be kept clean. "If you do not keep them clean after you have caught them," Coyote said, "they will be ashamed and not come up the river any more.

"And you must never cook any more than you can eat. If you cook three salmon when you are able to eat only half of one, the salmon will be ashamed and will refuse to enter your river."

Many times he traveled up and down Big River and its branch rivers, teaching the people many useful things. Almost everything the Indians knew, Coyote taught them. He did many good things, but he did many wicked things also.

Some Indians say that when Coyote had done all the good things he could do, he was given a place in the sky. Other Indians say that he was punished for the bad things he had done. He climbed to the sky on a rope. He climbed all one summer and all one winter. Then he fell down for a long, long time. When he struck the ground, he was mashed flat.

Lying there, he heard a voice say, "You shall always be a wanderer and shall forever howl and cry for your sins."

That is why coyotes howl and cry at night. That is why they wander hungry and friendless over the earth.

THE ORIGIN

OF WILLAMETTE FALLS

Willamette Falls, a few miles upstream from the mouth of the Willamette River at Portland, once marked a drop of forty-two feet. It was therefore an ideal place for Indians to fish in with spears and dip nets. During the fishing season, several thousand used to gather there annually to catch and cure salmon for their winter food supply. Now, most of the water is impounded to furnish power for the mills at Oregon City.

The first story given below was told to Professor H. S. Lyman by Louis Labonte, whose father was a member of the Astor expedition of 1811 and whose mother was the daughter of Chief Kobayway, a Clatsop. Mr. Labonte first heard the story in 1834. The second myth was related in April, 1952, by John Hudson, a Santiam, of Grande Ronde, Oregon.

When Coyote came to the Willamette Valley, he found the people cold and hungry and weak. Coyote had been along the coast, teaching the people there.

The Willamette River was full of salmon, but the people could not catch them. Coyote decided to make a *tum-tum,* or waterfall, so that the fish could come to the surface. He began to work at one place but did not like it and so left. A gravel bar shows where he began to work. Then he went to Rock Island and began to make a tum-tum there. But he did not like that place and so left it. The rapids show where he began to work.

The third place he chose he liked. There he made a tum-tum—the falls of the Willamette. There the salmon come to the surface when they try to leap over the falls. There Coyote taught the people how to spear salmon.

"Now I will make a salmon trap," said Coyote.

So he set to work to make a salmon trap, there beside the tum-tum. It was to be a special trap, which would say "Noseepsk" when it was full. Coyote set the new trap near the falls and began to make a fire. He rubbed the fire sticks together, but before he had finished, Trap called, "Noseepsk."

It was already full of salmon. Coyote emptied it, set Trap again by the falls, and began again to rub the fire sticks together. But before he could make fire, Trap called a third time, "Noseepsk! Noseepsk!"

This time Coyote was angry. He was hungry, but Trap would not give him time to make a fire. He said to Trap, "Don't call so soon. Can't you wait until I build a fire and get some salmon cooking?"

Then Trap was angry. He refused to catch any more fish. So the people had to spear the salmon at the falls of the Willamette.

2

"Let us make a waterfall across the river," Meadowlark said to Coyote.

So they made a rope by twisting young hazel shoots. Holding one end of the rope, Meadowlark went on one side of the Willamette River; holding the other end, Coyote went on the other side; and carrying the rope between them, they went down river until they came to a place near where Salem is now. There they stopped.

"Let us make the waterfall here," Meadowlark called across to Coyote.

But she spoke in Clackamas, and Coyote knew only the Kalapuya language. He misunderstood. Instead of making a waterfall, he turned some animals into rocks. They could be seen along the riverbank near Salem until not long ago.

Meadowlark and Coyote walked on down the river until they came to where Oregon City is now.

"Let us make a waterfall here," Meadowlark said. This time she used the sign language too. Coyote understood.

So they stretched the rope tight. Coyote pulled hard. Meadowlark pulled with all her strength and pressed her feet hard against the rock she was standing on. Then Coyote called on his powers and turned the rope into a rock. The river poured over the rock. So that is how Willamette Falls happened to be made at Oregon City instead of at Salem.

Meadowlark pressed her feet on the rock so hard that she made footprints. Her footprints stayed there for hundreds and hundreds of years. They could be seen until the locks flooded the flat rock where she stood.

PILLAR ROCK

Pillar Rock, standing in the middle of the Columbia River a few miles above its mouth, was mentioned in the reports of several early explorers. Charles Wilkes of the United States Exploring Expedition of 1838–1842 was probably the first to record an Indian legend about it. He estimated the rock to be twenty-five feet high and ten feet square at the top.

In the days that are gone, the people used to gather at a certain place along Big River to dig the roots of wapato. Families put up their summer tepees and camped there during the season of wapato digging. Each evening one summer the girls in one tribe sat around the campfires and sang. The people on the other side of the river listened to the singing with much pleasure. One young warrior was so pleased that he said in his heart, "I will go across and ask to marry one of the girls."

As he was getting into his canoe next day, Fox came along. "Why are you crossing the river?" asked Fox.

"I am going to ask to marry one of the girls who sing every evening. If she sings, she will be a cheerful wife."

"Better not go," advised Fox.

So the young man tied up his canoe. But that evening when he heard the singing, he again wanted one of the girls for his wife. He made up his mind that he would cross the river when Fox was not around. After a restless night, he arose early and, not seeing Fox, started to swim across to the other camp. When he was about halfway, he looked back. Fox was on the bank.

"I told you not to go over there," called Fox angrily. "I shall punish you by changing you to a rock. You shall stand out there forever, washed by the waves of Big River. You will be a reminder of what happens to those who disobey my wishes."

There he still stands. If you get close, you can see the outline of a young warrior's face near the top of Pillar Rock.

THE CAVE MONSTER

OF THE

WILLAMETTE VALLEY

This little myth has a feature which is characteristic of many tales told by both the Coast and the Plateau Indians of Washington and Oregon: the making of an arrow rope or arrow trail from the sky to the earth. The rope of arrows has already appeared in "Mount Rainier and the Great Flood." It is found in several stories to follow, and in many variants recorded from other tribes.

A monster was frightening all the people in the valley of the Willamette River. At night he would come out from his cave, seize as many people as he could carry, and return to his cave to eat them.

When Coyote came to the valley, the people left in the villages begged him to save them from the cave monster.

"I will," promised Coyote. "I will get rid of this monster before the new moon comes again."

Coyote did not know what to do, so he talked with his good friend Fox. "The monster always lives in the dark," said his good friend Fox. "He cannot stand the daylight."

Then Fox and Coyote put their thoughts together and made a plan. Next day the sun was very bright. When it was high in the sky, Coyote took his bow and arrows and went to the top of a big mountain. There he shot an arrow into the sun. He shot a second arrow into the end of the first arrow, a third arrow into the end of the second. He kept on shooting until he had a rope of arrows from the sun to the earth.

Then he pulled on the rope of arrows. He pulled very hard. He pulled the sun down and hid it in the Willamette River.

The monster thought that night had come again, so he left his cave to get someone to eat. As soon as he grabbed the first man, Coyote broke the rope of arrows which held the sun down in the river. At once the sun sprang back up into the sky. It made so much light that the monster was blinded. Then Coyote killed him. The people were freed from their terror.

After many, many summers and many, many snows, white people found the bones of the monster and carried them away. The Indians living in the Willamette Valley told them that evil would come from moving the bones of a monster of a long-ago time. But the white people would not listen.

A LEGEND

OF MULTNOMAH FALLS

"All the cliffs and falls of the Columbia Gorge are rich in Indian legendry and enchantment," wrote an Oregon pioneer, "and each has its pretty, tragic story. There are several about Multnomah Falls."

She and two other pioneers wrote the following legend. What changes in the Indian tradition may have resulted from the influences of white man's culture, probably no one now can determine. The motif of human sacrifice, unusual in Northwest Indian stories, is found in one other legend of the same area: "The Maiden Sacrificed to Winter."

Multnomah is the highest of the waterfalls along the Columbia Gorge. It falls from Larch Mountain in a series of cascades.

Many years ago, the head chief of the Multnomah people had a beautiful young daughter. She was especially dear to her father because he had lost all his sons in fighting, and he was now an old man. He chose her husband with great care—a young chief from his neighbors, the Clatsop people. To the wedding feast came many people from tribes along the lower Columbia and from south of it.

The wedding feast was to last for several days. There were swimming races and canoe races on the river. There would be bow-and-arrow contests, horse racing, dancing, and feasting. All the people were merry, for both the maiden and the young warrior were loved by their people.

But suddenly the happiness changed to sorrow. A sickness came over the village. Children and young people were the first to die from the plague. Then strong men became ill and died in one day. The wailing of women was heard throughout the Multnomah village and through the camps of the guests.

"The Great Spirit is angry with us," the people said to each other. "How can we soften his anger?"

The head chief called together his old men and his warriors for counsel. "The Great Spirit is angry with us," he told them gravely. "What can we do to please him?"

Only silence followed his question. At last one old medicine man arose. "We cannot soften such anger. If it is the will of the Great Spirit that we die, then we must meet our death like brave men. The Multnomah have ever been a brave people."

The other members of the council nodded in agreement—all except one, the oldest medicine man. He had not attended the wedding feast and games, but he came in from the mountains when he was called by the chief. He now arose and, leaning on his stick, spoke to the council. His voice was low and feeble.

"I am a very old man, my friends. I have lived a long, long time. Now you will know why. I will tell you a secret my father told me many years ago. My father was a great medicine man of the Multnomah, many summers and many snows in the past.

"When he was an old man, he told me that when I became old, the Great Spirit would send a sickness upon our people. Many would die, he said. All would die unless a sacrifice was made to the Great Spirit. It must be the life of a maiden of the tribe. Some pure and innocent maiden, the daughter of a chief, must willingly give her life for her people. Alone, she must go to a high cliff above Big River and throw herself upon the rocks below. If she does this, the sickness will leave us at once.

"I have finished," the old man said. "My father's secret is told. Now I can die in peace."

Not a word was spoken as the old medicine man sat down. At last the chief lifted his head. "Let us call in all the maidens whose fathers or grandfathers have been headmen."

Soon a dozen girls stood before him, among them his own loved daughter. The chief told them what the old medicine man had said. "I think his words are the words of truth," he added.

Then he turned to his medicine men and his warriors. "Tell our people to meet death bravely. No maiden shall be asked to sacrifice herself. The meeting has ended."

The sickness stayed in the village, and many more people died. The daughter of the head chief sometimes wondered if she should be the one to give her life to the Great Spirit. But she loved the young warrior. She wanted to live.

A few days later she saw the sickness on the face of her lover. Then she knew what she must do. Unless she sacrificed herself, he would die. She cooled his hot face, cared for him tenderly, and left a bowl of water by his bedside. Then she slipped away, alone, without a word to anyone.

All night and all the next day she followed the trail to the great river. At sunset she reached the edge of a cliff overlooking the water. She stood there in silence for a few moments, looking at the jagged rocks far below. Then she turned her face toward the sky and lifted up her arms. She spoke aloud to the Great Spirit.

"You are angry with my people. Will you make the sickness pass away if I give you my life? Only love and peace and purity are in my heart. If you will accept me as a sacrifice for my people, let some token hang in the sky. Let me know that my death will not be in vain and that the sickness will quickly pass."

Just then she saw the moon coming up over the trees across the river. It was the token. She closed her eyes and jumped from the cliff.

Next morning all the people who had expected to die that day arose from their beds, well and strong. They were full of joy. Once more there was laughter in the village and in the camps of the guests.

Suddenly someone had a thought and asked aloud, "What caused the sickness to pass away? Did one of the maidens ———?"

Once more the chief asked that all the daughters and granddaughters of headmen come before him. This time one was missing.

The young Clatsop warrior hurried along the trail which leads to Big River. Other people followed. On the rocks below the high cliff they found the girl they all loved. There they buried her.

Then her father prayed to the Great Spirit, "Show us some token that my daughter's spirit has been welcomed into the land of the spirits."

Almost at once they heard the sound of water coming from above. All the people looked up to the cliff. A stream of water, silvery white, was coming over the edge of the rock. It broke into floating mist and then fell at their feet. The stream continued to float down, in a high and beautiful waterfall.

For many summers the white water has dropped from the cliff into the pool below. Sometimes in winter the spirit of the brave and beautiful maiden comes back to see the waterfall. Dressed in white, she stands among the trees at one side of Multnomah Falls. There she looks upon the place where she made her great sacrifice and thus saved her lover and her people from death.

HORSETAIL FALLS

AND

BEACON ROCK

Horsetail Falls, somewhat in the shape of a horse's tail, springs forth from a wall of basaltic rock 208 feet high. Its spray often drifts across the Columbia River Highway. Beacon Rock, one of the largest monoliths in the world, rises about 900 feet from the river on the Washington side.

Coyote's two sons once fell in love with the same girl, a girl with beautiful hair. One hoped to win her by bravery, the other by trickery. The girl did not know which one she liked better, and so she smiled at both. The brothers soon became jealous of each other, and quarrelsome.

At last Coyote became so tired of their quarrels that he made up his mind to go to the girl himself. So he went to her house and spoke to her fiercely. "Which of my sons do you want to marry? Tell me. I will not have them quarreling any longer."

The girl was angered by the tone of his voice.

"I do not wish to marry either of them," she replied sharply. "The Eagle does not marry with the Wolf."

Then Coyote was angry. He was so angry that he put the girl to death. He buried her spirit in the earth and fastened her body to the side of a mountain. Then he turned her beautiful hair into a waterfall. It is always fleeing but never gets away.

When Coyote returned home, he found his sons still quarreling over the maiden with the beautiful hair. So he turned them into rocks. The one who wanted to win the girl by bravery is Beacon Rock, which rises high above the waters of the Columbia River. The one who wanted to win her by treachery is Rooster Rock, a smaller rock west of Beacon Rock.

The waterfall, which is on the south wall of the Columbia Gorge, is known as Horsetail Falls.

LATOURELL FALLS

AND THE

PILLARS OF HERCULES

Latourell Falls, 6 miles west of Multnomah Falls, drops 224 feet into a pool at the base of an overhanging cliff. A mile away stand the Pillars of Hercules; the tracks of the Union Pacific Railroad go between them.

Long ago, Coyote traveled down the Columbia to break the dam which three Beaver sisters had built. It was keeping the salmon from going up the river, and the people up above were starving. By trickery, Coyote got hold of the key and unlocked the dam.

Then he changed himself into a man, went back to the Beavers' house in the river, seized the youngest sister and ran toward the shore. By this time so many salmon had passed through the unlocked dam that he was able to walk across on their backs. At home, he found the people happy because they could now get all the fish they could eat.

For a long time Coyote's wife seemed to be happy in her new home. But one day she wanted to see her sisters and her old home. Coyote had lost the key to the dam, and the woman who found it made the mistake of giving it to his wife. Coyote's wife kept the key, and whenever she thought about it, she longed to see her sisters.

Coyote would not let her return. In fact, he was so afraid she would leave him that whenever he went away he locked her and their two sons in a cave. There they plotted against him. One day when he was in his sweat house, they broke out of the cave and went down the river.

As they ran along, the Beaver sister stopped now and then to pull a long hair from the crown of her head and stretch it across the trail. Tying the ends of the hair to trees and rocks, she made a snare. If she could trip Coyote with the snares, perhaps she could keep him from catching up with them.

Once mother and sons stopped to see how the plan was working. They saw Coyote trip and fall and bruise his knees. He howled when he heard his family laughing at him.

But he was too sly for them and saw their trick. So he acted more tired than he really was. He crawled along as if too worn-out to move. His wife and sons let him catch up with them, sure now that he was too weak to harm them.

When he was very close, he suddenly jumped to his feet, seized his wife, and shouted, "Give me that key!"

"I will not!" she shouted back.

Coyote was so angered by her stubbornness that he scooped away the side of a mountain and fastened her to it. Then he changed her into a waterfall.

He followed after his sons, who had run toward the river. He begged them to come home with him, but they wanted to visit their mother's sisters first.

"You will stand where you are, forever," said Coyote. And he changed them into two tall rocks.

Today the rocks are sometimes called Coyote's Children, sometimes the Pillars of Hercules. They still stand along the Columbia River. The waterfall is known as Latourell Falls.

WHY THE COLUMBIA

SPARKLES

Five stars once came down from the sky and slept beside the river, near The Dalles. Next morning four of them rose into the air and took four sisters back to the sky with them. When the sisters got to the place where the stars live, they saw that the sky world is just like this one, with grass and flowers.

The oldest of the five stars did not go back with the others, because he was still tired from the long journey. He remained lying there on the ground by the river, but he changed himself into a white flint rock, very large and thick and round and bright. It shone so brilliantly that it could be seen from a long distance.

It became a good-luck rock for the Wishram people who lived near it. The star rock brought many salmon up the river, enough for the Wishram to dry for their own use and also to trade with the people who came to the narrows and to the big falls of the river. The place where the rock lay was a great gathering place for many tribes. Everyone knew the star. The Wishram became known as the Star people.

Across the river on the south side lived the Wasco people. They did not have a star, but they did have a big cup. *Wasco* means "those that have the cup." Near their main village was a rock in the shape of a big cup. Into it bubbled a spring of pure, cold water. The Wasco people prized the cup very highly.

The Wasco, who were always quarreling and fighting with their neighbors, became jealous of the good luck the bright star was bringing the Wishram. One night when the Wishram people were away, some of the

Wasco people crossed the river and stole the star. They wrapped it in an elkskin and threw it into the river.

When the Wishram returned from picking berries, they could not find the star. Months later, when the water of the river was low, some people of the Wishram village saw it shining on the bottom. They got it and put it back on the shore. Always thereafter, someone guarded the star. But three summers later, when the Wishram were again in the Mount Adams country picking berries, Wasco men found the guard asleep one day and stole the star once more. This time they broke it into pieces and threw it into the river.

When the Wishram came back to their winter village, the star rock was gone. Angrily they crossed the river and made war on the Wasco. Some of the young men pounded the big cup until they almost destroyed it. It had been very large and deep. It is now very small.

After the star was stolen and broken, the Wishram lost the name Star people and became very common people. But the broken star rock is still in the river. That is why the water sparkles in the sunshine.

THE EVER-WATCHFUL EYE

The picture writing which this legend explains is on a rock on the north side of the Columbia, opposite The Dalles. It is not far from extensive Indian pictographs and petroglyphs, including those in Petroglyph Canyon, where a high wall is covered with carvings.

On the north bank of Big River, near the village of Wishram, stands a rock shaped like a monument or marker. On it has been painted an eye, large and all-seeing. No matter from what part of the village a person looks at the eye, it appears to watch every movement.

The eye was painted long ago in the days of our grandfathers. One night a medicine man of the Wishram mixed some paint made from roots. Then an unseen power guided his hand and his brush across the stone. The night was dark, without moon and without stars. The man could not see what he was painting.

He worked hard, so that his work would be done before morning came. He was alone, and there was no sound except the splashing of the water on the rocks below. When dawn came, the medicine man had finished. Later he was found, in a trance, at the foot of the rock. A ghostly eye was looking down on him and on the people who came to him. All knew that the Tahmahnawis had painted it.

Ever since then, the eye has watched the village. It protects the people from the evil spirits. It sees everything that everyone does.

For generations, people asked it for help. Bringing it gifts of baskets, mats, weapons, beads, and eagle feathers, men prayed to it for wealth or health or long life. Wives asked that they might have children. Young women asked that the young men of their choice might love them. The all-seeing and ever-watchful eye seemed always to hear their prayers.

THE PAINTED ROCKS

AT NACHES GAP

The origin and the meaning of the numerous picture writings found on rocks along Lake Chelan and along the Columbia, John Day, Santiam, and other rivers of Washington and Oregon puzzle both Indians and archaeologists. The paintings on a basalt cliff near the Naches River—in red, blue, white, and yellow pigments—are the basis for a variety of traditions. The ones that follow were told to Lucullus McWhorter by two old Yakima Indians in 1912.

No one knows how old are the Schoptash, the painted rocks near Naches Gap in the Yakima country. And no one living now knows what they mean. They were painted long ago, after the big flood. Two hands were seen first. They had been painted during the night. Then two heads appeared. Then the rest of the figures appeared, all painted during the night.

The people who made the paintings on the rocks were small—the Wahteetas, my people called them. I am now old. It was before I saw the sun that my ancestors saw the Wahteetas, the little ancient people who lived in the cliff. They were full-grown but were not more than two feet tall. They wore robes woven from rabbits' hair.

My people saw the little people walk from rock to rock, hunting the smooth places and marking the rocks as you now see them. They used four different colored paints: red, white, blue, and yellow. The paintings could not be destroyed.

The Wahteetas are spirits, but they are not evil spirits. They used to watch over the pictures and never let them grow dim. Often the Wahteetas repainted the rocks during the night. If you rubbed the picture paintings with any kind of coloring or any kind of mud, the next morning they would be all bright and fresh as ever. They were the laws of the Yakima, painted there by the ancient little people.

I have never seen the Wahteetas, but some Indians have seen them. Sometimes after the sun has gone down, or just before the sun has risen in the morning, the ancient little people have been seen standing on the cliff. No grown person wanted to see them. Seeing them brought death to a grown person unless one of the Wahteetas was his guardian spirit.

But seeing the picture painters brought power to small children. Often, little children, sometimes not more than five or six years old, were left on the cliff at night. Their fathers and mothers hoped that they would see the picture painters, who usually appeared in the early dawn. If one of the Wahteetas should come to the child, he would be the child's guardian spirit. And he would be a powerful guardian spirit. It was good for a child to see the little picture painters, but it was a warning of death for a grown person to see them.

After white people came, no more painting was done. And now the white man is destroying the painted rocks. That is too bad.

West of the painted rocks, before you reach the bridge, up against the bluff, there is a big flat rock. On it used to be prints of horses' feet. One print was large; four were not so large. The large one was a stallion. Behind him were a mare, three snows old; another one, two snows old; a mare, one snow old; and a newborn colt. In these five tracks was the law given that the Yakima people would raise horses all over this country. That rock with the horses' prints contained the law.

THE ORIGIN

OF THE

PETRIFIED FOREST

The Ginkgo Petrified Forest is in a state park in central Washington. In clay pits near the petrified trees, which are embedded in basalt, fossilized remains of prehistoric animals have been found. White people did not discover the fossil forest until 1931, but Indians used to make arrow points from accessible petrified logs.

This story of the origin of the forest and the fossils was recalled by Mary Summerlin, who learned it from her Colville grandmother.

In the days of Coyote, the Raccoon family lived along the Columbia River, below where the Rock Island Dam is now.

In the family were seven beautiful sisters. When Coyote saw them, he wanted to marry one of them. So he asked Father Raccoon if he could have one of his beautiful daughters for his wife.

"We need all our daughters," answered Father Raccoon. "We need them to bring in sagebrush for our fires. We cannot spare one of them."

"I will see that you have firewood," said Coyote. "Let me marry one of your girls, and I will send you all the wood you need."

"I will talk it over with the girls when they come home with the sagebrush," the father promised.

He told his daughters that Coyote wanted one of them for his wife, and all night the girls tried to make up their minds which it should be. Coyote was so homely that no one wanted to marry him, but the Raccoon sisters did want to stop carrying sagebrush. Half the night Coyote tried to make up his mind which of the seven he wanted to marry. He knew he wanted the prettiest one, but they were all very pretty, with bright eyes, long eyelashes, and soft fur. At last he decided to marry all seven of them. And he used his powers the second half of the night to make all seven of them want to go with him.

Next morning, a great pile of driftwood was washed up on the shore near the camp of the Raccoons. So the father let all of his daughters go along with Coyote. They soon wanted to go back home, but they traveled with Coyote until they were sure there was enough firewood to last for a long time.

As they traveled up the river, Coyote broke off trees and sent them down toward Raccoon. He pushed fallen logs into the river and sent them down as driftwood. He made an eddy in the river so that the logs would be washed in near Raccoon's camp. He planted a new forest on the west bank of the river, so that there would be green wood when the dry wood was all used up. Coyote kept his promise.

By this time the girls were so homesick that they begged Coyote to take them home for a while. So they started back. When they got there, they found great piles of driftwood, and they saw the new forest growing near the camp. They knew that they would not have to carry sagebrush again. So they plotted against Coyote. They told him that they would stay at home, that they would not go with him again.

Coyote became very angry because the girls had tricked him. He scolded and scolded, and then he placed a curse on the Raccoon family. But they did not know about the curse for three years. Although the first two winters were cold, the Raccoons had plenty of firewood. The girls had salmon bakes and clambakes and used the driftwood whenever they wanted a fire.

The third year, Coyote came and told them the curse he had put upon them. "You will all die this winter. All your people who are buried here will some day be dug out. The people digging them will dig out your woodpile."

Then he changed the new forest to rocks. He made his powers and caused a very bad winter. Much snow fell. When spring came and the

melted snow rushed down in the mountain streams, a big flood overflowed the river. The pile of driftwood near Raccoon's camp dammed up
the water and made the river overflow.

The great flood of water knocked down the stone trees. When the
floodwater left, the stone trees were buried underneath sand and soil and
rocks. Many animals were buried with them.

The trees and the bones of the animals still lie where Coyote sent the
flood. Trees are buried in rock. Deer, raccoons, cougars, and many animals
not seen in our country today lie buried there in the clay.

LEGENDS OF

STEAMBOAT ROCK

*Steamboat Rock, 800 feet high and 2½ miles long, stands in the old
channel, the dry coulee, of the Columbia River in central Washington.
Its layers of basalt look like the decks of a huge steamboat. Geologists
think that thousands of years ago, when the river ran through what is
now called the Grand Coulee, Steamboat Rock stood between two tremendous waterfalls, each of them 800 feet high and 2 miles wide.*

*The first of the following stories, obviously of recent origin or a
revised old tale, was related by Peter Noyes, a Colville. The others were
pieced together from fragments remembered by several people thinking
together.*

In the days of the animal people, the Columbia River used to flow
through the Grand Coulee. Coyote had a big steamboat then. One summer he came up from the coast in his boat, bringing many plants his
people here needed for food.

When he got up the river to where the Grand Coulee is now, something—I forget what—made him very angry. He left his big boat out
there in the river and went over to the place where Coulee Dam is now.
There he struck a high rock with his stone hammer, and split it. The
water rushed through the opening, and the river turned north. So Coyote
caused the river to leave its old channel and flow through its present one.

His boat was left in the dry channel. Jack Rabbit sat watching from
the coulee wall, and laughed at Coyote. So Coyote turned him into rock.
You can see him sitting there today, at the left of Steamboat Rock when
you go there from here.

The plants Coyote brought with him still grow on Steamboat Rock—
currants and wild onions, kouse and other roots.

2

The Eagle family once lived on Steamboat Rock. At that time it did not look like an island, as it does today. It was joined to the canyon wall and stretched out into the valley floor.

For a long time the Eagle family had plenty to eat and so were happy. But one summer, food became scarce. Eagles could find no dead fish along the rivers. After a while they could find no snakes or chipmunks. Although they flew up and down the Grand Coulee, they could find nothing to eat. The children became so hungry that they cried all day and all night. Mother Eagle begged Father Eagle to go to Coyote for help.

Father Eagle did not want to ask Coyote, but at last he could not stand his own hunger and the cries of his family any longer. So he went to Coyote and said to him, "Will you help me find some food for my family? My children cry from hunger."

"I will help you if you will do one thing for me," answered Coyote.

"What is that?"

"Give me your oldest daughter for my wife. I will make the coulee rich with food if you will let me marry your beautiful daughter."

Father Eagle, very hungry, answered, "You may have her." Then he flew back to his family on the rock.

Coyote covered the dry bed of the old river with jack rabbits and sage hens and rattlesnakes. The Eagle family had a big feast. When they had eaten all they wanted, Coyote told Eagle to get ready for the wedding. There would be a big wedding feast on top of the rock.

When all was ready, Coyote arrived. He expected to claim the beautiful daughter of Eagle. But when she saw the ugly old Coyote, she began to cry. "I won't marry him. I'd rather starve than marry that ugly old man."

That made Coyote angry. He sang his power song and called for Thunder to help him. With his powers he cut the big rock away from the wall of the coulee, and pushed it out into the center of the valley. Then he seized the women who were standing near him and threw them against the rock walls. The food made ready for the wedding feast he threw against the rocks.

Today when you drive through the Grand Coulee just before dark, you can see women's black braids hanging over the edge of the walls. And you can see the rocks stained with yellow and green and red from the food thrown there long ago.

3

Long, long ago, when Coyote walked the earth, a young woman was left a widow with a small son. For a year after her husband's death, she let her hair hang uncared for, as was the custom of her people. She did not braid it, did not even comb it. She did not paint her face, and she wore her oldest clothes, without any ornaments.

At the end of the year, her period of mourning was over. She washed her hair and rinsed it in water perfumed by sweet-smelling hemlock needles. She braided it and tied pendants to the ends of the braids. She painted her face. She put on her best buckskin dress decorated with elks' teeth, and wore her earrings and necklaces made from shells.

Then her dead husband's parents invited many guests to a big feast on the top of Steamboat Rock. Her appearance and the giving of the feast would show the people that her year of mourning had ended and that her parents-in-law were willing for her to have another husband.

Coyote sat watching her and admiring her beauty. He wanted to marry her, but he knew that he would not be permitted to do so. He had been refused by many girls and their parents. He knew that they considered him very homely, with his long nose and his slanting eyes. He said in his heart, "If I can't get her, I will make it so that no one else will."

Then he changed the young woman to a rock and her son to a smaller rock. While the guests were arriving, he changed them to trees, and he made the walls so steep that people could not easily climb up them. He did not want them to have feasts on Steamboat Rock.

You can see them there today—the stone pillar and the smaller pillar standing up on Steamboat Rock, the scrubby old pines on top of the rocky island and along the steep wall where the trail used to be. Over in one spot is a pile of stones. There Coyote dumped the baskets of food brought up for the feast and changed them all to rocks.

THE HEE-HEE STONE

The Hee-Hee Stone—also called Tee-Hee-Hee Stone, Wishing Stone, and Camas Woman—used to stand about twenty miles from Oroville, Washington, near the Canadian border. Tee-Hee-Hee and Hee-Hee are thought to be corruptions from the Chinook word meaning "to wish." The stone was an upright boulder eight or ten feet high, somewhat in the shape of a human body. For perhaps hundreds of years, Indians when passing always left gifts there, believing that in return their wishes would be granted and they would have good luck. In time, white men also left gifts. Several legends were told about the stone. The one that follows was known by both the Okanogan and the Colville tribes. A variant has been recorded from the Sanpoil and the Nespelem.

Not many years ago, said Peter Noyes, a white man took a hammer and knocked the Hee-Hee Stone to pieces. When Indians warned him that he would have bad luck, he only laughed. A year later, his team of horses ran away with him and he was killed.

Blue Flower was a beautiful maiden who lived in what is now north-eastern Washington. Her father was a chief of the Kalispel Indians.

One day Blue Flower filled her basket with camas bulbs and started west toward the Okanogan country. She knew that in the Okanogan country lived a handsome young warrior named Scrakan. He was the middle one of three brothers, all of whom were great warriors. The girl hoped that Scrakan would like her and would ask her to be his wife.

Blue Flower climbed the mountain range west of her country and saw the Okanogan valley spread out below her. Wanting to look her best when she first appeared, she stopped to make herself beautiful. She took her shell comb from her basket, combed her long hair, and braided it smoothly. She painted her face with paint made from red clay.

Soon she saw the three brothers hurrying to meet her. In a dream they had learned of her coming, and at daybreak had started out. When they saw how beautiful she was, each of them asked her to become his wife. In their jealousy, the two younger brothers fought.

Coyote came along, saw them fighting, and laughed. He thought it funny that two brothers should knock and kick each other because of a girl. His laughter annoyed Blue Flower, and she spoke sharply to him. Then Coyote became angry.

"I'll get even with you!" he said. "I permit no one to speak sharply to me."

Coyote made his powers and turned the lower part of the girl's body into stone. He made his powers again and moved the three brothers back to where they had been when they had their dream. Then he turned them into three mountains.

When he came back to Blue Flower, he found that she had thrown the basket of camas bulbs back into the land of the Kalispel. She wanted no camas to grow in the valley of the Okanogan people. Then she sang her power song and changed the rest of herself into stone.

Coyote turned to her and gave her a special power. "You will help the people who are to come. You will be a wishing stone. People will bring you gifts, and you will make their wishes come true."

Then he faced the three mountains west of him and made three laws. To the middle brother, he said, "You will remain a sharp-pointed peak without shoulders. Women will always like you, just as this Kalispel girl did. They will take pieces of your body, to make ornaments for their bodies. The new people who are to come will call the pieces 'copper.'"

To the oldest brother, Coyote said, "Because you did not fight with the others, you will always stand with your head and shoulders high and proud. You will be known as Big Chopaka Mountain. People will be able to see you for a long distance."

To the youngest brother, Coyote said, "Because you were beaten and laid upon the ground in the fight, you will be a low mountain ridge forever. You will never raise your head high again."

To this day, the three mountains stand where Coyote transformed them. For generations the Kalispel prairies were blue with camas in the spring, and when the blossoming period was over, Indians came from far and near to dig the roots. For many generations the maiden stood near the place where she had stopped to paint her face and braid her hair. The Okanogan people called her *Enamtues*, which means "Sitting on the summit."

THE ORIGIN

OF THE

SPOKANE RIVER

The Spokane Indians once lived in terror because of a huge monster that lived both on land and in the water. He swallowed all the fish and birds and animals that came near him. His claws were so strong that with one pull he could uproot the largest pine trees. His breath was so bad that it killed people. No weapons would stick in his skin, and no hunter had been able to capture him. All people were afraid of him.

One day a girl was picking berries near where the Spokane River now flows into the Columbia River. At that time there was no Spokane River. The girl looked up from the berries and saw the monster. He was lying on a hillside, asleep in the sunshine.

The girl slipped quietly away and ran to her village as fast as she could. "I have seen the monster!" she gasped. "And he is asleep."

The headman of the village called his men together and said to them, "Gather up every cord and rope and every leather thong in all the tepees."

After this was done, the men walked noiselessly to the hillside where the monster still lay sleeping. There they tied him to trees and to rocks. Still he slept, they moved so quietly. Then all the people began to beat him with their weapons of war and their weapons of hunting.

When the monster awoke, he made one big jump. All the cords and all the leather thongs broke, as if they were made of grass. The monster turned and ran eastward like the wind. He ran and ran until he reached Lake Coeur d'Alene. As he went, he tore a deep channel. When he reached the lake, the waters of Lake Coeur d'Alene rushed into the new channel and made a new river.

Ever since then, the Spokane River has flowed from Lake Coeur d'Alene into Big River, and so its waters have reached the sea.

THE ORIGIN

OF PALOUSE FALLS

A few miles above its mouth, the little Palouse River thunders over a cliff 198 feet high, into a circular bowl. From there it plunges southward into a narrow canyon, to join the Snake River not far from where the Snake joins the Columbia. The falls are the scenic feature of a state park.

This myth was told in 1936 to Mr. and Mrs. John McGregor of Hooper, Washington, by Sam Fisher, a Palouse Indian who lived not far from the mouth of the Palouse River. A variant was recorded by Charles Wilkes, of the United States Exploring Expedition of 1838–1842; it explains also the origin of neighboring Indians, with details similar to those in "How Coyote Made the Indian Tribes."

Four giant brothers and their giant sister once lived not far from the Palouse River. They were proud of how they looked, and were especially proud of their hair. They kept it sleek and shining with oil from beavers' tails.

One time they ran out of oil and wondered where they could get some.

"There's a big beaver in the Palouse River," the Wolf people told the giants. "Why don't you get some from him?"

So the four giant brothers looked for Big Beaver. They found him in the river, up above where the falls are now. At that time there were no falls; the water ran smoothly and calmly all the way to the Snake River.

One of the giant brothers wounded Beaver with his spear. Beaver started down the river as fast as he could run, the four giants chasing him. At the first bend in the river, they caught up with him, and the second brother speared him.

But Beaver kept on going. Angrily, he turned to the left, away from the river, and made a new and deep canyon. Again the brothers caught up with him, and the third brother speared him. Beaver shook the spear off and plunged back into the river. As he turned south toward the Snake River, he shook his tail very hard five times. Thus he made the five little falls at that place.

There the fourth brother speared him, but Beaver kept on. He plowed out a deep canyon ahead of the brothers, until they caught up with him and fought with him. In the struggle, Beaver made the rapids you can see there today and turned the canyon sharply to the left.

Again Beaver rushed on down toward the Snake River. At the next bend in the Palouse, he was speared a fifth time. He turned on the four brothers and fought them, in the biggest fight of all. There Beaver tore out a big canyon. The river came over the cliff in a big rush and formed Palouse Falls. The marks of Beaver's claws can be seen all along the canyon walls, even to this day.

But again Beaver escaped from the giants. Soon he reached the Snake River and plunged downstream, sure that he was now free. Perhaps he would have been free if it had not been for Coyote. Coyote was watching from the hills on the south side of the river.

When he saw Beaver escaping, Coyote stood with one foot in the short grass and one foot in the long grass and sang his power song. His power song made Beaver turn round and go back up the Snake to the mouth of the Palouse. There the four giant brothers speared him again and killed him.

You can see Beaver's heart today. It is the big round rock on the west side of the Palouse River, where it joins the Snake.

BEAVER

AND THE

GRANDE RONDE RIVER

The Grande Ronde River flows through the northeast corner of Oregon and the southeast corner of Washington until it reaches the Snake River.

The Nez Perce Indian who permitted this fire myth to be recorded in 1891 gave an example of its practical value. In his boyhood, he and some companions when out fishing wandered too far and had to stay all night; they had salmon and hunger, but no matches. Remembering certain details from this myth, they soon kindled a fire by friction, "in the old way of the Indians."

Before there were any people in the world, the animals and trees moved about and talked together just like human beings. At that time, only the Pine trees knew how to make fire. The Pines were selfish and would not tell anyone what they knew. The other trees did not know the secret of fire. The animal people did not know the secret of fire. No matter how cold the winters were, no people but the Pines could warm themselves.

One winter it was very, very cold—so cold that the animal people feared they would freeze to death. They begged the Pines to warm them or tell them their secret of fire. But the Pines would not tell. Again and again the animal people tried to find out the secret, but they could not.

At last Beaver had an idea. He said to his friends, the other animal people, "I have a new plan. I believe it will work. I believe I can get fire from the Pine trees."

Beaver knew that the Pine trees were planning to have a meeting, a great council, on the banks of the Grande Ronde River. He decided to go to that council. The Pine trees built a big fire on the bank of the river, so that they could warm themselves when they came up from bathing in the cold water. They placed guards around the fire and in other places. The guards were to keep away all the other trees and the animals, because they might learn the fire secret.

Before the guards took their places, Beaver hid himself under the bank. There he waited and watched. After a while a live coal from the fire came rolling down the bank toward Beaver. He grabbed it, hid it under his armpit, and swam down the river as fast as he could swim.

The Pine trees started after him. When they were close behind him, Beaver darted from one side of the river to the other, from one bank to the other. When they stopped for breath, he swam straight ahead. That is why the Grande Ronde River today winds and winds in some places and flows straight along in other places. It follows the directions Beaver took when he was running with the coal of fire.

After a while, the Pine trees were so tired and breathless that they had to give up the chase. Most of them stopped together on the bank of the Grande Ronde River. There they stand today, in a forest so thick that hunters can hardly push their way through. A few trees kept on following Beaver, but they too became tired. So they gave up the chase, a few at a time and one at a time. There they stand today, scattered along the banks of the Grande Ronde River.

One Cedar tree ran with the Pine trees. When he too had to give up the chase, Cedar said to his friends, "I know now that we cannot catch Beaver. I will climb to the top of this hill and see where he goes."

From the top of the hill, Cedar saw Beaver far ahead. Cedar watched him swim into the Snake River, where the Grande Ronde River flows into it. Then the trees knew and Beaver knew that they could not possibly catch him.

Cedar, from the top of the hill, watched Beaver swim down the Snake River. He told the Pine trees down below him what Beaver was doing.

"Beaver is giving some of the fire to the Willow trees on the west bank of the river," Cedar called down to them.

Then he watched Beaver swim across the river.

"Now Beaver is giving some of the fire to the Birches on the east bank of the river," called Cedar. "Now he is giving some to the Cotton-woods."

As long as Cedar could see him, Beaver continued to swim down the Snake River and to share the fire with certain kinds of trees.

Since then, anyone who has wanted fire has been able to get it from those woods. Certain trees have fire in them and they give it to people when pieces of the wood are rubbed together in the right way.

Cedar tree still stands alone on top of a hill near where the Grande Ronde joins the Snake. He is very old and his top is dead. Old Indians point to him and say to their children, "There is old Cedar. He still stands on the spot where he stopped chasing Beaver. Because of Beaver, our grandfathers had fire."

DESTRUCTION ISLAND

AND TATOOSH ISLAND

Tatoosh is a rocky island at the entrance to the Strait of Juan de Fuca. A lighthouse on it warns vessels to stay away from the dangerous rocks near the island. Destruction Island is in the Pacific Ocean, about four miles from the mouth of the Hoh River.

This legend was told by Helen Still Schroeder, who learned it when she was teaching in the school at Neah Bay.

Long, long ago, when the world was new, Destruction Island and Tatoosh Island lived together in the Pacific Ocean, near the mouth of the Hoh River. They had many children—the little rocks and the big rocks along the coast.

The parents often quarreled. At last, after a quarrel more bitter than usual, Tatoosh decided to leave her husband. She put all the children into her boat and paddled up the coast. The farther she went, the angrier she felt toward her husband. She went past the mouth of the Quillayute River and the rocks there, past the points and the capes, to the place now called the Point of Arches.

There she looked at her children and frowned. "You will probably grow up to be just like your father!" she exclaimed bitterly.

So she threw them all overboard and paddled on alone. When she rounded the point now called Cape Flattery, she decided to stop and make her new home there.

She is still there—rocky Tatoosh Island, at the entrance to the Strait of Juan de Fuca. A few miles to the south are her children, the rocks at the Point of Arches.

HOW KWATEE

MADE THE

RIVERS AND ROCKS

Leven Coe and Esau Penn, merry seventy-year-olds, were sitting in the sun, "swapping stories," when I drove into their village on the Washington coast one August morning. Mr. Coe related this story about Kwatee, the Changer; Mr. Penn, the one that follows it.

Kwatee's songs—apparently songs without words, in the usual Indian style—were chanted in the rhythm of the drumbeats which accompany Indian dancing, a rhythm which is punctuated now and then by shouts somewhat like those of Swiss yodelers.

Chief Wolf looked around on the beach early in the morning. He wanted to get anything that was washed in. Chief Wolf sometimes murdered people. When Kwatee learned about the murders, he decided to do something. He put up a cabin near the beach. Under the cabin he dug a well. He planned to murder Chief Wolf.

Later, Chief Wolf had a surf duck for Kwatee. "Here's a surf duck for you," he said.

"I am sick," answered Kwatee. "I can't go out of my house. Will you stay with me tonight?"

Chief Wolf stayed that night. Kwatee made a big fire. When Chief Wolf was snoring, Kwatee took his knife and killed him. He put Chief Wolf's head in the well under the cabin and buried it.

Chief Wolf's family came to look for him. "He passed by late in the evening," Kwatee told them. "Come in. I'll find where he is through my spiritual."

Kwatee sang a song. "Leave the door open wide," he sang. "Leave the door open wide. Stand back, so that there is open space before the door."

Kwatee had his comb and his vessel of hair oil hanging in the doorway.

He sang his song again. In this song he admitted that he had murdered Chief Wolf. Then he ran away. He seized his comb and his hair oil and ran.

The Wolf family followed him. When the Wolf in front reached to grab him, Kwatee stuck his comb in the sand. The teeth became the hills and rocks on the point. Then Kwatee ran down the coast. When the Wolf family came close, he poured hair oil on the beach and made a river. And with the teeth of his comb he made rocks along the shore. That is how he made the Quillayute River and the Hoh, the Queets River and the Quinault—all the rivers along the coast, from Neah Bay down to the Columbia. And he made all the rocky points with his comb.

When he got to his canoe, Kwatee pulled it out into the ocean, out over the breakers. So the Wolf family gave up the chase.

Out in his canoe, Kwatee sang a song about a man-eating shark. He would kill the man-eating shark out in the ocean, he sang. But the man-eating shark swallowed Kwatee and his canoe. From inside its stomach, Kwatee killed the man-eating shark. Its dead body was washed in on the shore.

Early in the morning a man saw that a shark had been washed in. He called to the others, and they planned to cut it up for food, after breakfast. When they started to cut it, Kwatee holloed from inside the shark, "Be careful. Don't cut me."

"What is that?" the men asked. "Someone is inside his stomach."

They cut a hole in the stomach of the shark, and Kwatee ran out. He ran into his house. The people holloed at him, "That's Kwatee! That's Kwatee!"

* * *

"That really happened," ended Leven Coe, trying hard to keep his face straight. "That happened nine hundred and fifty years ago. I followed Kwatee. I was his guide. I am nine hundred and fifty years old."

HOW KWATEE

CHANGED THE WORLD

This story and the preceding one are given here in almost the exact words of the speakers. In telling this one, Esau Penn, like Leven Coe, chanted the songs of the characters in his story. Both narrators talked with twinkling eyes, many chuckles, and expressive gestures. At certain places, Mr. Penn's hands suddenly became big ears; at others, an imaginary club or spear he held became an animal's tail.

Another Kwatee story is among the legends of the lakes: "Kwatee and the Monster in Lake Quinault."

Kwatee went up and down the country changing things. He made deer and elk and beaver and other animals out of the early people. He was getting the world ready for the new people who were to come some day.

As he was walking along, he came to a man making a knife. He had made it out of mussel shells and was sharpening it.

"What are you doing?" Kwatee asked.

"I am making a sharp knife. I am going to use it to kill the man who is changing the world."

"It looks like a fine knife," said Kwatee. "Let me see it."

The man handed it to him, and Kwatee felt the sharp edge.

"That's a good knife. You will kill him quick, that Changer."

Then Kwatee crossed his arms over his head and moved his hands as if they were big ears. He held the knife high over his head and pushed it into the man's ears.

"Now jump into the woods. You will always jump when you run. You will eat brush. You will be Deer. You will be good food for the people who are to come."

And so Kwatee made Deer out of that man.

Soon Kwatee came to a man who was singing as he worked. He was singing a song about the man who was going around changing the world. He had made a club out of stone and was sharpening it. Kwatee sat down beside him while he finished his work.

"What are you doing?" he asked.

"I am making a club. I am going to use it to kill the man who is changing the world."

Kwatee watched for a while. Then he asked, "Will you let me feel your club? It looks good."

The man gave it to Kwatee, and he rubbed his hands over it. "It *is* a good club. You will kill him quick, that Changer. You have made a good club. It is all right up to here."

Kwatee put the club behind his back and moved it up and down.

"Turn around," Kwatee said in a sharp voice. Then he stuck the club into the man's back. "Jump into the water. The club will be your tail. You will be Beaver. Do this way with your tail—flap it in the water. From now on you will always live in the river. If you see people, go into your hole and stay there. You will eat sticks. Nothing but sticks will you eat."

And so Beaver went into the water.

Kwatee walked along until he came to a man who was making a spear. He was singing at his work, too. "What are you doing?" Kwatee asked.

"I am making a spear out of fir wood. I am going to use it to kill the man who is changing the world."

"It looks like a very good spear. That flint point looks sharp. Will you let me feel it?"

The man handed it to Kwatee, and Kwatee felt its sharp point.

"It *is* a good spear. You will kill him quick, that man."

Then Kwatee's voice changed. It was sharp. "Turn around!"

The man turned around, and Kwatee pushed the spear into him. "The spear will be your tail. You will be Land Otter. Your fur will make warm robes for the people who are to come."

And so Kwatee made Land Otter out of that man.

When Kwatee came to the Queets River, he found that no people lived there. So he rubbed his hands over his body until he made little balls of dirt and sweat. Then he changed them into people—the Queets people. "You will eat fish," he told them. "But you will like anything that is good to eat." That's how he made my people—out of his own body.

When he came to the Hoh River, he saw lots of the early people running along on the beach.

"Where are you going?" asked Kwatee. "What are you going to do?"

"We are going to fish for smelt."

"Turn around," said Kwatee. He made a woman with a basket on her head. Then he made a man. They were the first of the new people along the Hoh River.

When Kwatee got to Lapush, he saw a man cutting wood. This man would make a cut in the log, put in wedges, and then knock the wedges with his head. That is the way he split logs.

Kwatee picked up a rock. "Don't use your head. Use this." And Kwatee showed him how to use a rock to pound with.

When he came to Lake Ozette, Kwatee saw no people—only dogs. He made up his mind what he would do. He picked up a male dog and a female dog. He put them together and changed them into people. Then he changed the other dogs into people. So there were no more dogs around Lake Ozette—just people like us. They grew very fast. They grew big in three months. That is why the Makah are big people.

That is the end of the story.

A POTLATCH

ON THE

OREGON COAST

This legend was told many years ago by Old Indian Mary, a Coquille. It explains some curious rock formations along the Oregon coast, near Bandon, at the mouth of the Coquille River.

The word potlatch, *coming from a Nootka word meaning "giving," passed from the Chinook jargon into the speech of all tribes of the Pacific*

Northwest. A few facts about these important ceremonials of the Indians will be found with "Origin of the Potlatch" in Section V.

Seatco, evil spirit of the ocean, caused the storms that blew up and down the coast. He killed fish and threw them on the beach. Sometimes he swallowed canoes and fishermen. The coast people feared him and tried not to anger him.

The mountain tribes did not know Seatco, and so did not fear him. Whenever they came down to the coast to trade or to attend potlatches, they brought with them their families, horses, and dogs; the children brought their pets.

One summer, four chiefs of the coast Indians held a big potlatch in honor of Siskiyou, powerful chief of a mountain tribe. The four tribes planned a big feast, for they wanted to show their guests how prosperous the coast tribes were. The potlatch would he held on the beach, near the mouth of the Coquille River.

For days, the people were busy preparing the feast. The women and girls dug great numbers of clams and mussels and prepared them for steaming beneath sea moss and myrtle leaves. Hunters brought in a dozen elk and several deer. Many salmon were made ready for roasting on spits over driftwood fires. Huckleberries were heaped on cedar-bark trays. When runners announced that Chief Siskiyou and his people were a day's journey away, the roasting and the steaming were begun.

The chief brought with him his beautiful young daughter, and they camped on the potlatch grounds. The daughter, Ewauna, had her pets with her—her dog and a basket of baby raccoons. The girl had never before seen the ocean. All day long, she and her dog, Komax, raced along the beach, excited by the breaking of the waves.

People of the village warned her, "Don't go alone on the bluff. Seatco might see you and take you."

But Ewauna laughed at their warning.

By the morning of the second day all the guests had arrived, and the great feast began. The four chiefs, dressed in their ceremonial robes, welcomed their guests and spoke in praise of the great Chief Siskiyou. All day the hosts and guests feasted. That night they slept where they had eaten.

When all was quiet in the camp, the great chief's daughter, taking her dog and her basket of raccoons with her, slipped away to the beach. She ran and danced along the shore, singing a song to the moon, which hung low over the ocean. She danced nearer and nearer the water, into the silver path. Then she dropped her basket on the beach, told her dog to guard her little pets, and ran into the surf.

She would swim toward the moon, following the silver trail. Her dog barked a warning, but she swam on and on, far from shore. Suddenly a black hand passed across the moon, and she was seized by a creature that came out of the water. Seatco claimed her as his own and started toward his cliff with her.

The dog rushed to rescue her, carrying the basket of raccoons with him. He dropped the basket and sank his teeth into the demon's hand. Roaring with pain and anger, Seatco grabbed the dog and the basket and hurled them down the beach. He held the girl close to him, trying to make her look into his eyes. But she turned her face away and looked at the moon. She remembered that Seatco's power lay in his eyes.

Next morning the chief missed his daughter. He and his hosts rushed to the beach. The tide was out. The girl was lying on the wet sand, her beautiful face looking up at the sky. Near by, her dog stood as if barking. A little west of them were the scattered raccoons and the empty basket. All had been turned to stone.

On a large rock near the shore sits Seatco, still trying to catch the eye of the maiden. He too has been changed to stone.

IV.
MYTHS OF
CREATION
THE SKY
AND STORMS

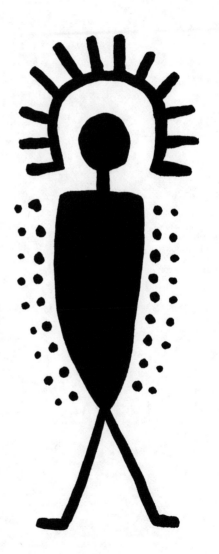

WHY AND WHEN
THE TALES
WERE TOLD

Chief William Shelton, in his little book of Snohomish tales, states this as one of the purposes of storytelling in his family: "My parents, uncles, and great-uncles told me, in days gone by, stories which would create in me the desire to become brave, and good, and strong, to become a good speaker, a good leader; they taught me to honor old people and always do all in my power to help them." The old Indian method, he adds, was to teach through stories.

One of Chief Shelton's stories, "Pushing Up the Sky," illustrates what can be done if people work together. Other lessons which he has pointed out in his family tales are these: "Do not be boastful; otherwise you may come to grief just as Deer did." "Always be on your guard lest a cunning person trick you the way Fox tricked Seal." "Do not look down upon old people just because you are young. . . . If you are always kind to poor people, then you will always have good luck yourself." "Don't go out with anyone if you know he's not good. He'll get you into trouble even if you are innocent, just as Mink got his little brother into trouble." "Don't be greedy," "Don't be wasteful" are obvious lessons in some stories in the present collection.

The recollections of Otis Half-Moon, on the Umatilla Reservation, reveal another kind of instructive purpose in Indian storytelling. In the Nez Perce village of his childhood, special winter lodges were made, one for the boys and one for the girls. Hot rocks kept them warm all day. There respected members of the tribe who were good storytellers—a man for the boys and a woman for the girls—gave the children the information needed for their outdoor living. Mr. Half-Moon recalls animal stories chiefly, with some star myths and other kinds of tribal traditions. An example of the instructive value of a Nez Perce myth is given in the headnote to "Beaver and the Grande Ronde River."

An educated white woman who has lived on the Colville Reservation for twenty-five years says that many of the stories told by her neighbors "were unwritten texts in history, geography, nature study, and ethics." In some families near her, the grandparents used to gather the children round them in the early winter mornings, when it was too cold to play outdoors, and instruct them through the tribal tales. Mrs. Clara Moore's aunt used to relate the old stories to the girls, both to teach them and to amuse them, while they were learning to tan hides and do bead work. Her grandfather and uncles similarly instructed and entertained while the boys were learning to make equipment for fishing and hunting.

A second purpose in Indian storytelling, illustrated again and again in this book, was to explain the phenomena of nature. This has been true, of course, of many early peoples. "Where we propound a scientific theorem," wrote John Fiske years ago in *Myths and Myth-Makers*, "they construct a myth." Fiske defined a myth "as, in its origin, an explanation, by the uncivilized mind, of some natural phenomenon; not an allegory, not an esoteric symbol, . . . but an explanation." "Myths that detail causes are science in infancy," says Hartley B. Alexander in his volume on North American mythology, "and they are perhaps the only stories that may properly be called myths."

Hundreds of explanations of natural phenomena are scattered through the tales of the Pacific Northwest Indians. Some of them are merely incidental: how Blue Jay got his topknot, how Frog lost his tail, why the Grande Ronde River is very crooked in places, why the Columbia changed its channel, why Mount Adams' head is different from Mount Hood's. Some explanations furnish the plots of entire stories. The origin of mankind, of death, of fire, of certain constellations—these have been almost universal themes among the makers of myths. The great rocks and the many trees in the Columbia Gorge, the cut made by the big river through the Cascade Range, the lake in the deep crater on top of a mountain, the eruptions of volcanic peaks, the petrified trees and the bones of prehistoric animals, the ancient picture writings on the rocks—these stimulated the imagination to answer the natural question "Why?"

One of the amazing and fascinating things about several of these explanatory myths of the Pacific Northwest is that in a fanciful way some details parallel modern discoveries and theories of scientists. The parallelism between Indian myths and geologists' theory about lakes east of the Cascade Range in what is now the Columbia River Basin has been pointed out in connection with "How Coyote Made the Columbia River." Several details in "The Origin of Crater Lake," a myth related in 1865 by an old Klamath chief, have striking parallels with the story that geologists have unfolded concerning an ancient peak in southern Oregon. They call it Mount Mazama, and they believe that it once "rose to a height of 12,000 feet, a mile above its present ruins."

Howel Williams, Chairman of the Department of Geological Sciences at the University of California, has graphically described the tremendous explosions that disturbed the area several thousand years ago, the eruptions of ash and pumice that were scattered for many miles, the "glowing avalanches" that destroyed the forests, the "frenzied streaks of lightning" —the "Curse of Fire" in the Indian myth. These were followed by the collapse of the mountaintop into its center, into the void created by the eruptions. Later precipitation and seepage made the lake in the vast crater.

Geologists working in the sagebrush country east of Crater Lake in recent years have unearthed Indian artifacts "beneath deposits of pumice from Mount Mazama."

The myths that explained and the stories that instructed entertained also—entertained the old and the middle-aged as well as the young. And there were many tales, including types not represented in this volume, which were told for enjoyment only. As with the Greek bard, the Anglo-Saxon scop, the medieval minstrel and ballad singer, the Indian storyteller's chief purpose was to give pleasure. This oral art is much older than written literature, in all cultures—much older than history. Until modern civilization changed family life, the telling of stories was one of the most satisfying pastimes for the entire family, among many peoples and on all the continents.

Sometimes a professional storyteller went from Indian village to Indian village, says Peter Noyes, and entertained with tales from his repertoire. Mourning Dove, an Okanogan, recalled vividly a popular storyteller who used to arrive in her village on a white horse; before eager listeners he "would jump up and mimic his characters, speaking or singing in a strong or weak voice, just as the Animal Persons were supposed to have done." Among some tribes, one or two old men or women in each village were recognized as the best taletellers. Such a person was sometimes invited to a host's lodge to entertain for an evening; guests occasionally brought small gifts to the entertainer.

Much more frequently, the legends and myths were told by the best storyteller in the winter lodge, where two or more related families often lived together. Several traditions indicate that this kind of entertainment was for the winter only. "I thought in my childhood that there was a law against telling the stories in the summertime," a Yakima woman recalled with a chuckle. "My grandmother used to tell us," said a Warm Springs woman, "that a rattlesnake would bite us if she told stories in the summer." "My grandfather," added her neighbor, "always said he would get bald and yellow jackets would sting us."

"It is not good to tell myths in the summertime," the Kalapuya of western Oregon used to say. "It is good to tell myths in the wintertime. There are long nights in the wintertime."

During the long winter evenings, while the rain fell or the snow piled high, the log fires which extended the full length of the winter lodges gave light and warmth and cheer. Then the tribal tales, narrated and acted out by the best entertainers in the group, took the place of our books, magazines, movies, radio and television programs. In addition to nature studies, moral fables, and history, the Indians heard fiction— adventure, tragedy, various kinds of comedy. Most Coyote stories among the people east of the Cascade Range and most Fox stories among those west of the range "were good for a laugh," no matter how often they were told.

"For all myths spring from the universal and inalienable desire to know, to enjoy, to teach." These words written by Charles Gayley about the "classic myths" of the Greeks, Romans, and Norsemen apply equally well to the tales once told by American Indians.

These family gatherings around the winter fires, moreover, gave the elders of the group opportunity to pass on to the younger ones some of the sacred traditions of the tribe. When relating the Skagit creation myth, in 1952, Andrew Joe explained that in the old days no one in his tribe could even hope to get spirit power unless he knew that story well; and the securing of spirit power was very important in any Indian man's life. Jack Ward's story about the Thunderbird and the Whale was told with reverence. So was the latter part of Chief Jobe Charley's myth about Mount Adams; he had never before, he said, told the story to a white person. Apparently "The Origin of Crater Lake," "A Legend of Mult-nomah Falls," and "Legend of the White Deer" were precious to the people who created them. If the Indians had had a written literature, some of their stories would have been their "sacred writings." The myths of creation and of the Changer, which follow, and a few other tales scattered throughout this volume would doubtless be a part of their sacred litera-ture.

THE CREATION

OF THE

KLAMATH WORLD

Nearly every people has an explanation of the beginning of the world and of mankind. Among the tales of the Indians of the Pacific Northwest, the explanation is sometimes incidental, as in "Mount Shasta and the Grizzly Bears," "Coyote and the Monster of the Columbia," "How Kwatee Changed the World," and "How Coyote Made the Indian Tribes." Some-times it constitutes the whole story, as in the creation myths that follow. Each "Creator," you will note, begins with something already in existence.

Long, long ago Kemush created the world. Morning Star called him from the ashes of the Northern Lights and told him to make the world.

At first Kemush made the earth flat and bare, without plants or animals. Then he made the hills and mountains, the rivers and lakes. He planted grass and camas bulbs and ferns in the valleys. On the hills and mountain slopes he set out pine trees and junipers.

Then he sent Mushmush, the white-tailed deer, Wan, the red fox, and Ketch-katch, the little gray fox, to run through the forest he had created. Up in the mountains he placed Luk, the grizzly bear. High on the mountains, on the rocks and snow fields, he placed Koil, the mountain sheep. On Mount Shasta he placed Gray Wolf.

Indians were not yet created, but the earth was ready for them. It was all new except the crescent-shaped rock on lower Klamath Lake. On it was the lodge of Sun and Moon. When Kemush had finished his work, he slept in the lodge of the North Wind, on the high mountain east of Klamath Marsh.

While Kemush was sleeping, the Sun Halo called to him and wakened him. "Let us follow the trail of Shel, the sun," said the Sun Halo.

They followed the sun until they reached the edge of the dark. Then Kemush and his daughter, Evening Sky, went to the Place of the Dark, to the lodges of the spirits. There were many spirits; they were as numberless as the leaves on the trees and the stars in the Milky Way. For five nights Kemush and Evening Sky danced with the spirits of the dark, in a circle round a fire in a great pit. But when Shel called to the world and morning came, the spirits became dry bones.

On the fifth morning, after the sun called, Kemush gathered the dry bones and put them in a sack. Then he followed the trail of the sun to the edge of the world. As he followed, he threw away the dry bones, two at a time. He threw them on the mountains, in the valleys, on the seashore.

Some of the dry bones became the people of the Chipmunks. Some became Maidu, the Indians. Some became Maklak, the Klamath Indians. Thus were people created.

Then Kemush followed the trail of Shel, the sun, as it rose in the sky. At the top of the trail he built his lodge. There he still lives. The Klamath call him Old Man of the Ancients. He lives in his lodge at the top of the trail, with Sun Halo and with his daughter, Evening Sky.

IN THE BEGINNING

OF THE

MODOC WORLD

Kumush, Old Man of the Ancients, went down with his daughter to the underground world of the spirits. It was a beautiful world, reached by one long and steep road. In it were many spirits—as many as all the stars in the sky and all the hairs on all the animals in the world.

When night came, the spirits gathered together in a great plain to sing and dance. When daylight came, they returned to their places in the house, lay down, and became dry bones.

After six days and six nights in the land of the spirits, Kumush longed for the sun. He decided to return to the upper world and to take some of the spirits with him. With the spirits he would people his world.

A big basket in hand, he went through the house of the spirits and chose the bones he wished to take with him. Some bones he thought would be good for one tribe of people, others would be best for other tribes.

When he had filled his basket, Kumush strapped it to his back and started up the steep hill road to the upper world. Near the top, he slipped and stumbled, and the basket fell to the ground. At once the bones became spirits again. Shouting and singing, they ran back to their house in the spirit world and became bones again.

A second time Kumush filled his basket with bones and started toward the upper world. A second time he slipped, and the spirits, shouting and singing, returned to the underground world. A third time he filled his basket with bones. This time he spoke to them angrily. "You just think you want to stay here. When you see my land, a land where the sun shines, you will never want to come back to this place. There are no people up there, and I know I will again be lonesome for people."

A third time Kumush started up the steep and slippery road with the basket on his back. When he came near the edge of the upper world, he threw the basket ahead of him, onto level ground. "Indian bones!" he called out.

Then he uncovered the basket and selected the bones for the kinds of Indians he wanted in certain places. As he threw them, he named them.

"You shall be the Shastas," he said to the bones he threw westward. "You shall be brave warriors."

"You also shall be brave warriors," he said to the Pit River Indians and to the Warm Springs Indians.

To the bones he threw a short distance northward, he said, "You shall be the Klamath Indians. You will be as easy to frighten as women are. You will not be good warriors."

Last of all he threw the bones which became the Modoc Indians. To them he said, "You will be bravest of all. You will be my chosen people. Though you will be a small tribe and though your enemies are many, you will kill all who come against you. You will keep my place when I have gone. I, Kumush, have spoken."

To all the people created from the bones of the spirits, Kumush said, "You must send certain men to the mountains. There they must ask to be made brave or to be made wise. There, if they ask for it, they will be given the power to help themselves and to help all of you."

Then Kumush named the different kinds of fish and beasts that the people should eat. As he named them, they appeared in the rivers and lakes, in the forests and on the plains. He named the roots and the berries and the plants that the people should eat. He thought, and they appeared.

He divided the work of the people by making this law: "Men shall fish and hunt and fight. Women shall get wood and water, gather berries and dig roots, and cook for their families. This is my law."

So Kumush finished the upper world and his work in it. Then with his daughter, he went to the place where the sun rises, at the eastern edge of the world. Along the sun's road he traveled until he reached the middle of the sky. There he built a house for himself and his daughter. There they live even today.

THE ORIGIN

OF THE

CHINOOK INDIANS

The Chinook Indians, who lived near the mouth of the Columbia River, and the Chehalis, who lived a little north of them, told this story about their origin. It was probably first recorded by James Swan in 1857.

Long, long ago, when Old Man South Wind was traveling north, he met an old woman who was a giant.

"Will you give me some food?" asked South Wind. "I am very hungry."

"I have no food," answered the giantess, "but here is a net. You can catch some fish for yourself if you wish."

So Old Man South Wind dragged the net down to the ocean and with it caught a little whale. Taking out his knife, he was about to cut the whale and take out the blubber.

But the old giantess cried out, "Do not cut it with a knife, and do not cut it crossways. Take a sharp knife and split it down the back."

But South Wind did not take to heart what the old woman was saying. He cut the fish crossways and began to take off some blubber. He was startled to see the fish change into a huge bird. It was so big that when it flew into the air, it hid the sun, and the noise of its wings shook the earth. It was Thunderbird.

Thunderbird flew to the north and lit on the top of Saddleback Mountain, near the mouth of the Columbia River. There it laid a nest full of eggs. The old giantess followed the bird until she found its nest. She broke one egg, but it was not good. So she threw it down the mountainside. Before the egg reached the valley, it became an Indian.

The old giantess broke some other eggs and then threw them down the mountainside. They too became Indians. Each of Thunderbird's eggs became an Indian.

When Thunderbird came back and found its eggs gone, it went to South Wind. Together they tried to find the old giantess, to get revenge on her. But they never found her, although they traveled north together every year.

That is how the Chinook were created. And that is why Indians never cut the first salmon across the back. They know that if they should cut the fish the wrong way, the salmon would cease to run. Always, even to this day, they slit the first salmon down the back, lengthwise.

IN THE BEGINNING OF THE NISQUALLY WORLD

Long, long ago, some of the Puget Sound Indians used to say, people on the earth became so numerous that they ate all the fish and game. Then they began to eat each other. Soon they became worse than the wild animals had been. They became so very wicked that Dokibatl, the Changer, sent a flood upon the earth. All living things were destroyed except one woman and one dog. They fled to the top of Tacobud and stayed there until the flood left the earth.

From the woman and the dog were born the next race of people. They walked on four legs and lived in holes in the ground. They ate fern roots and camas bulbs, which they dug with their fingers because they had no tools. Having no fire and no clothing, they suffered from both the heat and the cold.

Their troubles were made worse when a giant bear came up from the south. The bear was huge and strong and also had special powers. With his eyes he cast a spell upon whatever creature he wanted to eat. Then that creature was unable to move, and the bear ate him. The people had no weapons. So the bear was about to eat all of them.

At last the Changer sent a Spirit Man over the mountains from the east. His face was like the sun. His voice was like the voice of Thunderbird. He came armed with bow, arrows, and spear. And he had Tahmahnawis powers.

"Why do you weep?" he asked the people.

"We weep because of the bear," they answered. "The beast is about to destroy us. None of us can escape from him."

The Spirit Man did not promise to help them, but he did show them how to walk on two feet. And he told them that there were two powerful spirits. "One of them is good; the other is evil. The Good Spirit sent me to you."

Then he returned to the mountains to talk with the Good Spirit, the Changer. When the Spirit Man came to the people a second time, he brought many strange gifts and stayed for many moons.

First he called all the people together for a big potlatch, the first potlatch of all the Indians. He told them that a potlatch is a big feast and gift-giving celebration. To the young men, the Spirit Man gave bows, arrows, and spears, and he taught all the young men how to use them. To the old men, he gave canoes. He showed them how to make canoes from cedar trees, how to make fishing spears and nets, and how to fish from the canoes.

The Spirit Man taught the girls how to make skirts from the inner bark of the cedar tree, how to paint their faces and oil their hair so that they were more beautiful, and how to sing. He showed the older women how to dig camas roots with the sticks he brought them, and how to make baskets out of cedar bark and seaweed. He showed them how to make fire by rubbing two sticks together, how to cook, how to carry burdens by strapping them across the head. "You will serve man and be useful to him in these ways," the Spirit Man told the women. "He will be your master."

Then the Spirit Man filled himself with strong Tahmahnawis powers, for his next task was to kill the giant bear. First he put seven arrows into his bag. He called together the men of the tribe, and for one whole sun the group chanted over the arrows to make them strong with spirit power.

Then the Spirit Man took one arrow and pushed it into the ground in the center of the plain west of Tacobud. After walking half a day toward the lodge of the great bear, he pushed a second arrow into the ground. He walked for another half day toward the bear's den and pushed a third arrow into the ground. Thus he kept on until he had placed six arrows erect and in a straight line.

With the seventh arrow in his hand, the Spirit Man went up to the bear. The beast tried to cast a spell from his eyes, but the Spirit Man's spirit powers were so strong that the bear could have no effect on him. He shot the seventh arrow into the beast and then ran back to the sixth arrow. The bear followed him. He shot the sixth arrow and then ran back to the fifth. The bear followed him.

They kept running until they reached the first arrow. The Spirit Man shot the first arrow into the heart of the beast and killed him. There the great bear died, in the middle of the Nisqually plain.

All the people were glad when they gathered together near the dead beast that had frightened them for so long. They removed the skin and divided it equally among the different branches of the tribe. The bear was so huge that the skin of one ear covered the whole of Mound Prairie.

The last thing the Spirit Man did for the people on this journey to their land was to make a large building with just one opening. In this big house he placed all the diseases and evil deeds known to the world since then. Then he called a certain family to him and made them guardians of the building. What was in the house he told only to the head of the family.

"You and your children and grandchildren will take care of this house forever," the Spirit Man said. "Remember that the door must never be opened. And remember that only the head man of the family is ever to know what is in the building."

After many years, the only members of the family left were an old man and his wife and daughter. One day, when her father and mother went away from the house, the daughter saw her chance to peek into the Spirit Man's house. She had long wanted to see what was behind that door.

So she undid the fastenings and pushed back the door a little distance. Out rushed all the creatures of the house—all the diseases and evil deeds and sorrows that have been in the world ever since.

The Changer was so angry with the daughter that he created the demon Seatco. Seatco's home is among the rocks in the distant mountains. He sleeps by day. At night he flies over the earth to seize any woman found away from her home.

THE BEGINNING
OF THE
SKAGIT WORLD

On the Swinomish Reservation, in the northern Puget Sound country, a totem pole was carved in the 1930's by men from four families. (The totem pole was not a native art form of the Indians of Washington and Oregon.) The figures at the base of the pole facing the village symbolize the Skagit story of creation. The symbols carved above—bear, whale, seal, salmon, mountain goat—represent the guardian spirits of individuals in the community.

Andrew Joe, whose brother was one of the carvers of the totem pole, tells this story about the figures at the base: A man with a blanket draped over his right arm stands beside a dog sitting at his right. The man represents Doquebuth, the Creator and Transformer in the Skagit religion.

In the beginning, Raven and Mink and Coyote helped the Creator plan the world. They were in on all the arguments. They helped the Creator decide to have all the rivers flow only one way; they first thought that the water should flow up one side of the river and down on the other. They decided that there should be bends in the rivers, so that there would be eddies where the fish could stop and rest. They decided that beasts should be placed in the forests. Human beings would have to keep out of their way.

Human beings will not live on this earth forever, agreed Raven and Mink, Coyote, and Old Creator. They will stay only for a short time. Then the body will go back to the earth and the spirit back to the spirit world. All living things, they said, will be male and female—animals and plants, fish and birds. And everything will get its food from the earth, the soil.

The Creator gave four names for the earth. He said that only a few people should know the names; those few should have special preparation for that knowledge, to receive that special spirit power. If many people should know the names, the world would change too soon and too suddenly. One of the names is for the sun, which rises in the east and brings warmth and light. Another is for the rivers, streams, and salt water. The third is for the soil; our bodies go back to it. The fourth is for the forest; the forest is older than human beings, and is for everyone on the earth.

After the world had been created for a while, everyone learned the four names for the earth. Everyone and everything spoke the Skagit language. When the people began to talk to the trees, then the change came. The change was a flood. Water covered everything but two high mountains—Kobah and Takobah. Those two mountains—Mount Baker and Mount Rainier—did not go under.

When the people saw the flood coming, they made a great big canoe. They loaded it with two of everything living on earth, with the male and female of every animal and plant. When the flood was over, the canoe landed on the prairie in the Skagit country. Five people were in the canoe. After the flood, when the land was dry again, they made their way back here.

A child was born to the man and his wife who had been in the canoe. He became Doquebuth, the new Creator. He created after the flood, after the world changed.

When he was old enough, Doquebuth was told to go to the lake—Lake Campbell it is called now—to swim and fast and get his spirit power. But the boy played around and did not obey orders. Coyote fed him, and the boy did not try to get his spirit power. So his family deserted him. When he came home, no one was there. His family had gone and had taken everything with them except what belonged to the boy. They left his dog behind and the hides of the chipmunks and squirrels the boy had shot when hunting. His grandmother left fire for him in a clamshell. From the skins which he had dried, the boy made a blanket.

When he found that his family had deserted him, he realized that he had done wrong. So he began to swim and to fast. For many, many days he swam and fasted. No one can get spirit power unless he is clean and unless his stomach is empty.

One day the boy dreamed that Old Creator came.

"Take my blanket," said Old Creator. "It is the blanket of the whole earth. Wave it over the waters, and name the four names of the earth. Then there will be food for everyone."

That is how the boy got his spirit power from Old Creator. He waved the blanket over the water and over the forest. Then there was food for everyone. But there were no people yet. The boy swam some more and kept on fasting.

Old Creator came to him again in a dream.

"Gather together all the bones of the people who lived here before the flood. Gather the bones and pile them into a big pile. Then wave my blanket over them, and name the four names of the earth."

The young man did as he was told in his dream, and people were created from the bones. But they could not talk. They moved about but were not quite completed.

The young Creator swam some more. A third time Old Creator came to him in a dream. This time he told the young man that he should make brains for the new people. So he waved the blanket over the earth and named the four names of the earth. That is how brains were made—from the soil of the earth.

Then the people could talk. They spoke many different languages. But where they should live the young Creator did not know. So he swam some more. In his dream, Old Creator told him to step over the big island, from ocean to ocean, and blow the people back where they belonged. So Doquebuth blew the people back to the place where they had lived before the flood. Some he placed in the buffalo country, some by the salt water, some by fresh water, some in the forests. That is why the people in the different places speak different languages.

The people created after the flood prophesied that a new language would be introduced into our country. It will be the only language spoken, when the next change comes. When we can understand animals, we will know that the change is halfway. When we can talk to the forest, we will know that the change has come.

The flood was one change. Another is yet to come. The world will change again. When it will change, we do not know.

THE BEGINNING

AND THE END

OF THE OKANOGAN WORLD

Long, long ago, when the sun was young and no bigger than a star, there was an island far off in the middle of the ocean. It was called Samah-tumi-whoo-lah, meaning White Man's Island. On it lived a race of giants —white giants. Their ruler was a tall white woman called Scomalt. Scomalt was great and strong, and she had Tahmahnawis powers. She could create whatever she wished.

For many years the white giants lived at peace, but at last they quar-reled among themselves. Quarreling grew into war. The noise of battle was heard, and many people were killed. Scomalt was made very, very angry.

"I will drive the wicked ones of these people far from me," she said. "Never again shall my heart be made sick by them. And they shall no longer trouble the peaceful ones of my people."

So she drove the wicked giants to one end of White Man's Island. When they were gathered together in one place, she broke off that piece of land and pushed it out to sea. For many days the floating island drifted on the water, tossed by waves and wind. All the people on it died except one man and one woman.

They floated and drifted for many more days. The sun beat down upon them, and ocean storms swept over them. They became very hungry, until the man caught a whale. Seeing that their island was about to sink, they built a canoe, put the whale blubber into it, and paddled away.

After paddling for many days and many nights, they came to some islands. They steered their way through them and at last reached the mainland. Here they stopped. The mainland was not so large as it is now, because it had not grown much yet. Wandering toward the sunrise, the man and woman came to the country now known as the Okanogan country. They liked that best, and there they stayed.

By this time they were so burned by the sun and whipped by the storm winds that their whiteness was entirely gone. Their skins were tanned a reddish brown. That is why the Indians have that color. All the Indians are the children of this first grandfather and grandmother.

In time to come, the Okanogan Indians say, the lakes will melt the foundations of the world, and the rivers will cut the world loose. Then it will float as the island did many suns and snows ago. That will be the end of the world.

CREATION OF

THE YAKIMA WORLD

Coteeakun, the son of Chief Kamiakin, told this myth to Major J. W. MacMurray, U. S. Army, when the major was among the Yakima in 1884–1885. Coteeakun was a friend and assistant of Smohalla, the originator of what is popularly known as "the Dreamer religion."

In the beginning of the world, all was water. Whee-me-me-ow-ah, the Great Chief Above, lived in the sky, above the water, all alone. When he decided to make the world, he went down to the shallow places and began to throw up great handfuls of mud. Thus he made the land.

He piled some of the mud up so high that it froze hard and made the mountains. The rain, when it came, was turned into ice and snow on top of the high mountains. Some of the mud was made hard, into rocks. Since that time the rocks have not changed, except that they have become harder.

We did not know all this by ourselves; we were told it by our fathers and grandfathers, who learned it from their fathers and grandfathers. We were told that the Great Chief Above made many mountains. He made everything just as our fathers told us. When we are hunting for game or berries in the mountains, we can see that what they said is true.

The Great Chief Above made trees grow on the earth, and also roots and berries. He made a man out of a ball of mud and told him what he should do. He should get fish from the waters, and deer and other game in the forests. When the man became lonely the Great Chief Above made a woman, to be a companion to him, and told her what she should do. He taught her how to dress skins, and how to make baskets out of bark and roots which he showed her how to find. He taught her which berries to gather for food and how to pick them and dry them. He showed her how to cook the salmon and the game which the man brought.

One time when she was asleep, she had a dream. In her dream she wondered what more she could do to please the man. She prayed to the Great Chief Above for help. He answered her prayer by blowing his breath on her and giving her something which she could not see or hear, smell or touch. This invisible something was preserved in a basket. Through it, the first woman taught her daughters and granddaughters the designs and skills which had been taught her.

But in spite of all the things the Great Chief Above did for them, the new people quarreled. They quarreled so much that Mother Earth was angry. In her anger, she shook the mountains so hard that those hanging over the narrow part of Big River fell down. The rocks, falling into the water, dammed the stream and also made the rapids and waterfalls there. Many people and animals were killed and buried under the rocks and the mountains.

Some day the Great Chief Above will overturn those mountains and rocks. Then the spirits that once lived in the bones buried there will go back into them. Now, those spirits live in the tops of the mountains, watching their children on the earth and waiting for the great change which is to come. The voices of these spirits can be heard in the mountains at all times. Mourners who wail for their dead hear spirit voices reply to them, and thus they know that their lost ones are always near.

No one knows when the Great Chief Above will overturn the mountains. But we do know this: the spirits will return only to the bones of people who in life kept the beliefs of their grandfathers. Only their bones will be preserved under the mountains.

THE STORY
OF THE CHANGER

"Star husbands" is a favorite theme in Indian mythology. It occurs in tribal tales all the way from Nova Scotia to the Washington coast. Among the tribes of the Puget Sound and Olympic Peninsula areas it is usually linked with the birth of the Changer, but it is used in another way in "The Earth People Visit the Sky People." A Puyallup variant of the following Puyallup myth was related in August, 1952, by Jerry Meeker.

The bright star in the myth has been identified as Venus in the west in the evening; the red star, as Venus in the east in the morning. In the version written by Henry Sicade, the rope ladder finally fell down from the sky and was turned into Snoqualmie Falls.

Two sisters, working together, dug the fern roots for their family. Often when they were digging roots at some distance from home, they would camp over night. One evening as they lay looking at the sky, the girls wondered what kind of people the Stars were and how they lived up in Star Land.

"Which star would you like to marry?" asked the younger sister. "The big bright one or the little red one?"

"Oh, don't be foolish!" answered the older sister. "Why do you talk that way?"

But her sister was not silenced. "I want to marry the big bright star. You may have the little red one."

She stopped talking, and the two fell asleep.

Next morning, when they awoke, they were surprised to find themselves in Star Land. The older sister was married to the little red star, a handsome young man. The younger sister was married to the big bright star, a white-haired old man.

Just as in the earth world, the sisters spent much of their time digging fern roots. "Do not dig the very long roots," their husbands told them. "They are not so good to eat as the others are."

For a long time the women obeyed their husbands, but one day they decided to dig up the very deepest roots. They knew that on earth the longest ones were best. They dug and dug until at last their digging sticks broke through the ground and made a hole. Looking through it, they saw the earth spread out below them. Then they knew that they wanted to return home.

Quickly they made a plan. While the older sister dug fern roots, the younger sister twisted cedar branches into a rope long enough to reach from the sky to the earth. Both worked hard and fast, the older one digging as many roots as the two girls had been digging.

At last the rope was long enough. They fastened one end to Star Land and then climbed down. Their family was made happy by their return, and people from far and wide came to swing from the rope which hung from the sky. They swung so much that they made gullies on the sides of the near-by mountains, where their feet touched.

Soon after their return to the earth, the older sister gave birth to a son. Whenever she went out to dig roots and camas, she left the baby in care of her blind grandmother, Toad. All day the grandmother worked and sang. All day women came to hear the grandmother sing and to see the baby, the wonderful child of the red star in Star Land.

One day some neighbor women found that the child was gone. The blind grandmother was singing to a swing that had a piece of rotten wood in it. Two women from the north had stolen the baby.

All the family and all the other people of the village looked and looked for the child for months. At last they gave up the search and made a new child from the cradleboard. The new child was thought of as the brother of the stolen baby.

Many years later, Blue Jay, on his travels, reached the edge of the world, far in the northland. There he saw a land beyond the edge of the world. To reach it, Blue Jay saw that he would have to fly below a shelf of land. This shelf rose and fell all the time, and shook the earth with its movement. Blue Jay hesitated, but gathering all his courage, he dashed through, feet first. The shelf of land caught his head and flattened it on both sides. That is why blue jays today have flattened heads.

In the land beyond the edge of the earth, Jay saw but one house. In it he found a man chipping arrowheads from stone. Somehow Blue Jay recognized the man as the child who had been stolen from his grandmother in his babyhood.

"I came to find you," said Jay. "Your mother has been mourning for you for many years."

"I am getting ready to go to your people," replied the man. "I have been making bows and arrows and other things to take with me. Go home to your people and tell that I am coming. I will teach them how to use the things I am making. Then life will be easier for them. And I will change the earth so that it will be less cruel and more beautiful. People will call me the Changer."

Blue Jay returned with the message for his people. In time the Changer came, bringing with him bows, arrows, war clubs, baskets, moccasins, leather garments, and other things which he had made. He showed the people how to use them and how to make them.

He brought seeds of many trees and shrubs. He brought roots and berries and grasses of many kinds. All these he planted on the earth, to make it beautiful and fruitful. He placed animals and birds on the land, and fishes in the water. He made canoes and fish traps and showed the people how to make them.

Up to this time, stones had had life; bees, flies, and other insects had been giants. The Changer removed life from stones and made the insects small and less harmful. Crane had been troublesome to many people by tripping them whenever they tried to cross the river. The Changer transformed Crane into a bird that could do nothing but wade around in the water looking for fish.

As the Changer passed across the land, he came to the house where lived a bad man who sometimes set the earth on fire. "I am the son of Fire," the man kept singing. "I am the son of Flames."

As he sang, his house caught on fire and the flames spread. Soon they reached the Changer. He ran, but Flames followed. Alarmed, he asked Boulders to protect him.

"We cannot," Boulders replied. "If we should try, the heat would break us."

The Changer asked Trees to help him. "We cannot," Trees replied. "If we should try, we would be burned."

As he ran toward the River, he asked River to help him. "I cannot," replied River. "Fire would make my water boil."

At last he came to a hard-worn path. "Lie down on me," called Trail. "Lie down on me, and Fire will pass over you."

So the Changer lay down, and Fire passed over him.

Then he returned to the man and the house where Fire had started. All around him were many snakes. When asked about them, the man mocked him. So the Changer killed the man and split him open. From the man's stomach and from every corner of the house, angry snakes jumped upon the Changer. But he killed them or made them weak. That is why there are few snakes in this country, and why all that are here are harmless.

Thus the Changer traveled over the land, helping the people and getting rid of evil creatures. He taught the people how to make all the things they needed, how to play games, how to cure the sick. He showed them how to get power from the spirits.

One day as he was traveling along a river, he became hungry. He saw a salmon jumping, called it to him, put it on a spit, and placed it beside his fire. While it was cooking, the Changer fell asleep. A wandering creature came and ate all the salmon. Before he slipped away, he rubbed some grease on the lips and fingers of the sleeping Changer, and put some bits of fish between his teeth and lips. When the sleeper awoke, he knew that he had been tricked. He followed the tracks of the creature and soon found him looking at himself in the water. The Changer transformed him into a coyote.

When he went to the home of his blind grandmother, Toad, he saw a mountain of rock. The mountain had been formed from the coils of cedar rope which his mother and aunt had made in Star Land. As he looked up at the sky, the Changer thought that there should be more light. So he went up to the Sky World and traveled across it by day in the form of the sun.

But he made the days so hot that the people could not stand the heat. He called his brother, who had been made from the cradleboard, and made him the sun.

"I will be the night sun," said the Changer. "And I will take with me as my wife the maiden who can lift and carry this great bag of things which I have made."

Only the daughter of Frog could carry such a load, and so she went up to the sky with him. Today the Changer, the Frog, and the bag she carried can be seen in the full moon.

THE CHANGER

COMES TO THE LUMMI

Long, long ago, when the Changer was on the earth, the Lummi Indians of the northern Puget Sound shores heard of his coming. He was traveling among the islands, they were told, in a canoe that moved itself, without paddles. Everywhere he went he was kind to the people, healing the sick and helping the fishermen with their nets. He had the strength of four men, and he could control the winds and the waters.

When the Lummi heard that he was near, they began to get ready for a big feast in his honor. They caught ducks with their nets. They dug clams, gathered crabs, and caught fresh salmon. The women dug fern roots and gathered the summer berries.

At that time people did not know how to make fire. Some of the food was eaten raw. Some of it was cooked by the heat of the sun. Fresh salmon was placed in a cedar bowl filled with water, and the bowl was tipped so that the sun's rays would reach it. As they prepared the feast for the Changer, girls danced round the bowl chanting, "Cook quickly! Cook quickly! Cook quickly!" All day they danced and chanted, from early morning until sunset.

On the morning that the Changer was expected, all the people painted their faces with special care. The men put on their long buckskin shirts, which they wore only for ceremonies. The women put on their fringed cedar-bark skirts. The maidens braided their hair with flowers. Mats were placed on the shore for the Changer to walk on.

Again the cedar bowls of food were tilted toward the sun. Again the maidens began their dance and chant: "Hwonk, quence, quell! Hwonk, quence, quell!" "Cook quickly! Cook quickly! Cook quickly!"

Suddenly the Changer landed on the shore. He saw the mats which had been spread for him. He heard the chanting and saw the dancing. He walked over to the open place where the girls were singing.

"What are they doing, my friends?"

The chief of the village answered him. "A special meal is being cooked for you by our daughters. We wish you to eat with us. We have been waiting for you."

The Changer's heart was touched. "I will gladly eat with you. And in return for your kindness I will give you a great gift. I will show you how to make fire. No longer will you need to dance and pray for the sun to cook your food."

The girls stopped their dancing and chanting. All the people watched while the Changer took a little stick with a hollow in it. This he placed upon the ground. He filled the hollow with some dry, crushed cedar bark. Then he took a sharp stick and twirled the end of it against the cedar bark, rubbing his hands together with the stick between them. Soon there was heat, and a thin curl of smoke began to rise. The cedar bark was on fire.

Then the Changer selected the strongest young man in the village, one skillful with bow and arrow. He put the sharpened stick between the palms of his hands and showed him how to make fire for his people.

The footprints of the Changer can still be seen on the shores of Chuckanut Bay.

PUSHING UP
THE SKY

Chief William Shelton included this Snohomish myth in the little book of family tales which he wrote as explanation of the symbols on the totem pole he had carved for the city of Everett, Washington. The Snohomish name for the Changer was Dohkwibuhch.

In the beginning, the Creator and Changer made the world. He created first in the East. Then he slowly came westward, creating as he came. With him he brought many languages. He gave a different language to each group of people he created.

When he reached Puget Sound, he liked it so well that he decided that he would go no farther. But he had many languages left. These he scattered all around Puget Sound and to the north, along the waters there. That is why there are so many different languages spoken by the Indians in the Puget Sound country.

These people could not talk together, but they soon found that they were not pleased with the way the Creator had made the world. The sky was so low that the tall people bumped their heads against it. Also, sometimes people climbed up high in the trees and went into the Sky World.

One time the wise men of the different tribes had a meeting to see what they could do about lifting the sky. They agreed that the people should try to push it up higher.

"We can do it," a very wise man of the council said, "if we will all push at the same time. We will need all the people and all the animals and all the birds when we push."

"How will we know when to push?" asked another of the wise men. "Some of us live in this part of the world, some in another. We don't all talk the same language. How can we get everyone to push at the same time?"

That puzzled the men of the council, but at last one of them said, "Why don't we have a signal? When the time comes for us to push, when we have everything ready, let someone shout 'Ya-hoh.' That means 'Lift together' in all our languages."

So the wise men of the council sent that message to all the people and animals and birds and told them on what day they were to lift the sky. Everyone made poles to push against the sky, poles from the giant fir trees.

The day for the sky lifting came. All the people raised their poles and touched the sky with them. Then the wise men shouted, "Ya-hoh!" Everybody pushed, and the sky moved up a little. "Ya-hoh," the wise men shouted a second time, and everybody pushed with all his strength. The sky was lifted a little higher. "Ya-hoh," all shouted, and pushed as hard as they could push. They kept on shouting "Ya-hoh" and pushing until the sky was up to the place where it is now. Since then, no one has bumped his head against the sky, and no one has been able to climb into the Sky World.

But a few people did not know about the sky pushing. Three were hunters who had been chasing four elk for several days. Just as the people and animals and birds were ready to push the sky up, the three hunters and the four elk came to the place where the earth nearly meets the sky. The elk jumped into the Sky World, and the hunters ran after them. When the sky was lifted, elk and hunters were lifted too.

In the Sky World they were changed to stars. At night, even now, you can see them. The three hunters form the handle of the Big Dipper. The middle hunter has his dog with him—now a tiny star. The four elk make the bowl of the Big Dipper.

Some other people were caught up in the sky in two canoes, three men in each of them. And a little fish also was on its way up into the Sky World when the people pushed. So all of them have had to stay there ever since. The hunters and the little dog, the elk, the little fish, and the men in the two canoes are now stars, but they once lived on earth.

We still shout "Ya-hoh" when doing hard work together or lifting something heavy like a canoe. When we say "Hoh," all of us use all the strength we have. Our voices have a higher pitch on that part of the word, and we make the *o* very long—"Ya-hoh!"

HOW RAVEN

HELPED THE

ANCIENT PEOPLE

Raven was the benefactor of the mythological people along the shores of Puget Sound and the beaches of the Olympic Peninsula, much as Coyote was of the ancients east of the Cascade Range. Among many other deeds, according to Quillayute mythology, Raven brought the blue-backed salmon to the rivers along the Washington coast. Having eaten some in the underground home of his father-in-law, Mole, young Raven determined to take a blueback salmon home with him. Pursued, he hid the scales of the fish in his mouth and nostrils. He came up to the surface of the earth in the land of the Quillayute and turned south. He threw one scale of the salmon into the Quillayute River, one into the Hoh, and two into the Queets. He washed off all the rest of the scales into the Quinault River. That is why there are a few blueback salmon in the Quillayute and Hoh rivers today, many in the Queets, and very many in the Quinault. "So much for that."

In the following story told by a Puget Sound tribe, Raven is again the benefactor. Two themes universal in mythology are combined in this little tale—the origin of daylight and the origin of fire.

Long ago, near the beginning of the world, Gray Eagle was the guardian of the sun and moon and stars, of fresh water, and of fire. Gray Eagle hated people so much that he kept these things hidden. People lived in darkness, without fire and without fresh water.

Gray Eagle had a beautiful daughter, and Raven fell in love with her. At that time Raven was a handsome young man. He changed himself into a snow-white bird, and as a snow-white bird he pleased Gray Eagle's daughter. She invited him to her father's lodge.

When Raven saw the sun and the moon and the stars and fresh water hanging on the sides of Eagle's lodge, he knew what he should do. He watched for his chance to seize them when no one was looking. He stole all of them, and a brand of fire also, and flew out of the lodge through the smoke hole.

As soon as Raven got outside, he hung the sun up in the sky. It made so much light that he was able to fly far out to an island in the middle of the ocean. When the sun set, he fastened the moon up in the sky and hung the stars around in different places. By this new light he kept on flying, carrying with him the fresh water and the brand of fire he had stolen.

He flew back over the land. When he had reached the right place, he dropped all the water he had stolen. It fell to the ground and there became the source of all the fresh-water streams and lakes in the world.

Then Raven flew on, holding the brand of fire in his bill. The smoke from the fire blew back over his white feathers and made them black. When his bill began to burn, he had to drop the firebrand. It struck rocks and went into the rocks. That is why, if you strike two stones together, fire will drop out.

Raven's feathers never became white again after they were blackened by the smoke from the firebrand. That is why Raven is now a black bird.

HOW THE PEOPLE

GOT THE SUN

Robert E. Lee, a Quillayute, was reading a magazine when I entered his home on the Pacific Coast in August, 1950. His wife was weaving a small basket; she was ornamenting it, as the Indians have done for centuries, with the dyed leaves of a mountain plant which Lewis and Clark said was called quip-quip *(today it is commonly called bear grass). Mr. Lee spoke in fluent English; his phrasing in this story has been followed as exactly as notes in longhand permit.*

A man who was against the Creator put the Sun in his grip [bag]. He opened the grip a little bit toward the way he was going. He took the Sun up into heaven. All the people who were on the side of the Creator began to talk about how they could go up to heaven to get the Sun back to light the world.

Wren decided that they could make a bow and arrows and shoot a ladder to the sky. A stout man split half a hewed log to make the bow with. Then all the stout animals—Whale and Bear and Mountain Lion— and all the deep-sea animals got together to make the bow. They made it, and then they got Man-eating Shark to shoot an arrow up to the sky.

He was the first one to shoot. He couldn't see the arrow when it struck up above. It was too far away. All the people—the land animals, the sea animals, and the birds—tried to see where the arrow was stuck up above. Only Snail could see the arrow Man-eating Shark shot. He was the only one with a good enough eye. Then Snail shot his arrow into Shark's arrow. He shot several times. Mountain Lion, Kingfisher, and Little Hawk—all with good eyes—shot arrows end to end. Then everybody could see the ladder. Everybody shot. The ladder reached from the sky to the ground.

All the people climbed up the ladder to capture the Sun. Everybody went. Eagle, Crane, Robin, Hawk, Raven were the first ones up there. It was so cold that Robin rushed to the Sun to get warm. He went head first and sat by the heat of the Sun.

"Oh, how cold it is up here!" said Robin. "We are the persons coming for war. We are going to kill the man who has the Sun."

So Robin got his breast burned. That is why he has a red breast.

Then all the people came to the man with the Sun—Hawk, Eagle, Raven, Bear, Mountain Lion, and all the rest. They fooled the man. "We are going to roast some *lackamas* [camas]. Won't you come and eat it with us?"

The man who had the Sun was hungry for some lackamas. So he left the Sun and went with part of the people. As soon as he had left, other people grabbed the Sun and ran down the arrow ladder to the earth. The people the man went with were left in the sky. The other people took the arrows down when they reached the earth.

When they got the Sun down, they decided to put it up where it is now, for the whole world.

Then Eagle called a meeting of all the people. They decided to make Snail a slave. They decided to take out the eyes of Snail. Eagle wanted one eye. Hawk wanted the other. That is why Eagle and Hawk have the sharpest eyes. That is why Snail is blind.

The people who were left in the sky are still up there. Skate is the Little Dipper. The stretched-out skin of Bear is the Big Dipper. The stars in the shape of a pancake turner were once Beaver.

The brightest star we can see is from the eye of the man of the ocean who had only one eye. He used to live in the ocean but he is no more.

THE BIG DIPPER

AND THE

MILKY WAY

Lucullus McWhorter, who recorded this Wasco legend in October, 1921, states that the cluster of stars mentioned in the story is the Pleiades, but that he cannot identify the knife, a line of six stars close to them.

Long ago, the five Wolf brothers ran all over the country every day, hunting. They hunted deer and elk and shared their meat with Coyote. Every evening as they ate together, Coyote heard the Wolves talk about seeing something in the sky.

One night Coyote asked the oldest Wolf brother, "What is it you see up in the sky? What is it you are talking about?"

But Wolf would not tell him. The next night Coyote asked the next oldest Wolf brother, "What is it you see up in the sky? What is it you are talking about?"

But the Wolf brother would not tell him. The third night Coyote asked the third Wolf brother the same questions, but the third Wolf brother would not tell him. The next night he asked the fourth brother.

The fourth Wolf replied, "If I should tell you, you would tell my brothers. Then they would be angry at me."

Next morning the fourth Wolf said to his brothers, "Coyote asked me what we were talking about, what we can see up in the sky. What do you think? Shall we tell him what we see up there?"

"It will do no harm to tell him," said the youngest Wolf brother. "Those two things are way up in the sky."

So the five Wolf brothers decided to tell Coyote. The next time he was with them they said to him, "We have seen two animals in the sky. They are 'way up high where we cannot get to them."

"Let's go up and see them," answered Coyote.

"How can we get up there?" asked the youngest Wolf brother.

"That is easy," replied Coyote. "I will show you how we can go up to the sky without any trouble."

Coyote gathered many arrows and cut rings round their shafts. Then he shot one arrow toward the sky. It reached the sky and stuck there. He shot a second arrow. It hit the end of the first arrow and stuck there. He shot a third arrow into the end of the second one. Coyote shot all his arrows, until he had a trail of arrows reaching all the way from the sky to the ground.

When the new sun arrived the next morning, Coyote and the five Wolf brothers climbed up the arrow way. The oldest brother carried their dog. The rings which Coyote had cut in the arrow shafts made it easy for them to have a good hold as they climbed. All day they climbed, and all the next night. Many suns and many nights they climbed. At last they reached the sky safely. There they saw the two animals the Wolves had seen from the earth. The two animals were Grizzly Bears.

"Don't go near them," warned Coyote. "They will tear you to pieces."

But the two youngest Wolves, not afraid, walked toward the Grizzly Bears. The next two youngest Wolves followed them. The oldest brother stayed back with the dog. The two youngest Wolves got closer and closer to the Grizzly Bears. But nothing happened to them. The Grizzlies were not angry. They stood looking at the Wolves, and the Wolves looked at them.

Coyote stood back and looked at all of them. Smiling at the picture they made, he walked about, thinking what he would do.

"They make a nice picture," Coyote thought to himself. "I'm going to make that picture stay there. I want the people who are to come to see it. They will see it and they will say, 'There is a story about that picture up in the sky.'"

So Coyote made them stay up in the sky—the five Wolves and their little dog, with the two Grizzly Bears that had always been up there. Then Coyote started down from the sky, destroying the arrow trail as he came. When he had passed the first arrow, he took it out of the sky. When he had passed the second arrow, he broke it off. When he reached the ground, the arrow trail was gone. So the Wolves could not come down.

Every night Coyote went out and looked at the nice picture he had made in the sky. One night he said to himself, "Who will know about the picture if I die?"

So he called Meadowlark to him. "See the nice picture I have made in the sky. If I die, you tell the people, the new people, what I have done. Soon there will be many stars growing in the sky. It is my work. I want the new people to know that it is my work."

When Meadowlark flies up singing, that is what he is telling you. He is telling you this story, how Coyote made the pictures you can still see in the sky and how the stars came from the two Grizzlies and the five Wolves.

One night after Coyote had been away and had come back to this country, he looked up at the sky and saw many young stars. "Are there too many stars in the sky?" Coyote asked Meadowlark.

"They are very thick, and they are growing fast," Meadowlark answered. "If they grow too thick, they may fall down. If they fall down, this earth will become all frost."

Coyote became alarmed. "I must go up to the sky again. This is my work. I must go up and do something."

Coyote filled five quivers with arrows and shot them toward the sky, making an arrow trail as he had done before. When he had climbed again to the sky, he gathered all the stars together. Then he put them in different places and arranged them in different shapes. Some of them he arranged in squares. Some he pointed toward each other. Many of them he spread across the sky in the Big White Trail.

He said to them, "Do not grow too fast. Keep in the trail together. If you want to go somewhere, fly like the lightning. Speed like the light. But don't grow too fast."

Then Coyote put up a knife of stars. And he put up a bunch of stars. Sometimes this bunch of stars comes up in the evening, just as the sun has set behind the mountains. In the spring, when the bow-and-arrow woods are in bloom, this bunch of stars gives luck.

Coyote left the Wolves and the Grizzlies in the sky as he had first pictured them. Today, people call those stars the Big Dipper. The three older Wolf brothers form the handle; the oldest brother is the star in the middle; he is leading his dog, which is the small star beside him. The two youngest Wolf brothers form the part of the bowl below the handle. The two Grizzly Bears form the opposite side of the bowl. They are the two stars that point toward the North Star.

THE SEVEN SISTERS

OF THE SKY

This Nez Perce myth has striking resemblances to ancient Greek myths about the Pleiades and the "lost Pleiad." The Blackfeet Indians also told a myth about the Pleiades: six poor young brothers went to the sky country and were transformed into a cluster of stars. The Blackfeet also believed that every star was once a human being.

Long, long ago, all things in nature—animals, birds, trees, the sun, moon and stars—were beings much like us. Everything that lives on and under the earth, everything that lives in the waters and in the sky was once a human being.

The sun was the ruler of light and day. The moon was the ruler of night and darkness. They gave life and motion to everything that has life. They were the rulers of all the stars.

In the sky were seven sister stars, each with a different name. Each one believed that love was the greatest thing within herself. Each one loved something in nature and kept her love a secret. She did not tell her sisters. All believed it was wrong to talk about themselves. They thought that if one of them should tell her troubles to the others, she would either die or disappear from the sky.

The next to the youngest sister was called Eyes-in-Different-Colors. She loved a man on the earth, and she kept on loving him even after his death. She told her sisters about her love, and they laughed at her for loving a mortal and for being sad after his death. They made her feel ashamed of herself.

But as time passed, she became more and more sorrowful. She tried to overcome her feelings, but she grew weary with grief. Gradually her eyes became dim. She knew that her sisters were ashamed of her because of her sadness, and so she stayed away from them as much as she could.

Ashamed of the sorrow she was causing them, she thought that it would be best for her to disappear. So she took the veil from off the sky and covered her face with it. The veil hid her face from her sisters and from the world below.

That is why we can now see only six stars in the cluster which white people call the Pleiades.

TWO CANOES

IN THE SKY

Lucullus McWhorter identified the Cold Wind brothers in the following story as the three stars in Orion's belt, the Chinook Wind brothers as the three in Orion's sword. The myth is a fragment of a longer story that is somewhat similar to "The Chinook Wind."

In the sky are two canoes pointing toward a small star, which is a fish. Each canoe is made up of three stars.

The three stars above, closer to the snowland, are the Cold Wind brothers. The three stars below, closer to the warm land, are the Chinook Wind brothers. The little star is a salmon floating in Big River. The canoemen are racing for it. The Chinook Wind brothers are winning the race.

The seven stars tell a story—a story about the earth people. Chinook Wind's grandfather always caught plenty of salmon. Cold Wind wanted salmon, but he always came too late to catch it in Big River. So he took salmon from the old grandfather.

At last the grandson of the old grandfather came from the Hood River country. He hid in his grandfather's tepee. Again the old grandfather caught plenty of salmon. Again Cold Wind demanded some of it. Then the grandson stepped out from the tepee.

"You cannot take my grandfather's salmon," he said.

"Yes, I will, even if I have to wrestle for it."

"That is why I came here," replied the grandson. "To wrestle with you."

So the two wrestled, and Chinook Wind won the match. Because Chinook Wind won, Cold Wind could never again be strong. He could never again take salmon away from the old grandfather.

That is why the three Chinook Wind stars are closest to the salmon star. Cold Wind's canoe is too far away. Cold Wind can never get the salmon.

THE ORIGIN OF

CASSIOPEIA'S CHAIR

In the long ago, five brothers lived here at Lapush. One day four of them went up the river in their canoe, to hunt for elk. When they got near Forks Prairie, they left their canoe and walked off in search of game. On the prairie they saw a big man walking along.

This man of the prairie tricked them and persuaded them to trade their good arrows for his worthless ones. Then the man changed himself into a big elk with long antlers, charged upon the brothers, and killed all four of them.

When they did not return home, their youngest brother, Toscobuk, got into his canoe and went in search of them. At the bend in the river near Forks Prairie, he saw the empty canoe of his brothers. Soon he too met the man of the prairie. The man tried to trick Toscobuk and tried to persuade him to trade his arrows. But Toscobuk's guardian spirit warned him that something was wrong. The youngest brother's spirit power was as strong as the spirit power of the man of the prairie. He could see that the man's arrows were worthless, and so he said, "No, I won't trade."

When the man of the prairie went away, Toscobuk hid behind a tree. Soon a big elk with long antlers came down the trail, the same big elk that had killed the four brothers. Toscobuk shot four arrows into him, then fought with him and cut the animal's throat with his clamshell knife.

When Toscobuk skinned the elk and stretched out the skin, he found that it was bigger than Forks Prairie. So he threw the elkskin up to the sky. You can see it any clear night. Stars mark the holes where Toscobuk drove the stakes when he was stretching the skin. Other stars mark the elk's tail.

This group of stars is called Cassiopeia's Chair.

THE EARTH PEOPLE

VISIT THE

SKY PEOPLE

Harry Shale often tells the old tales of his people, the Queets, or Quinault, to boys and girls who come to his house after school. They lie on their stomachs on the carpet of his modern home, as the children of his boyhood lay on the skins and blankets around the lodge fires when listening to the same stories. He is accustomed to relating them in English because few Indian children today know the language of their grandfathers.

Mr. Shale has lived in two different worlds. At the age of seventy-five, he had tickets for university football games; each season he travels hundreds of miles to see the high school football and basketball games on the Olympia Peninsula.

In early days, women and young girls used to go out on the prairie to dig camas roots. One day two girls went out with their mother and aunt. They dug all day and camped there on the prairie at night. The girls lay and watched the stars. They saw two beautiful ones.

"Oh, how I wish I were up there with that bright star!" wished one girl.

"Oh, how I wish I were up there with that red star!" wished the younger girl.

They said this over and over again until they went to sleep. They were awakened by a voice saying, "I am the star you were talking about."

"I am the bright star," a voice said to the older sister. He was a young man.

"I am the red star," the other voice said to the younger sister. He was an old man.

Then the girls went up to the sky with the stars. In the sky was quite a village, a good-sized river, a fish trap, and all kinds of fish.

The girls' mother and aunt did not know that the girls had gone. So when they awoke the next morning, the mother asked, "What has become of our girls?"

"They must have gone home," answered the aunt.

"We must find out."

But the girls were not at home. Then the mother and aunt remembered their talk about the stars. They told the girls' father, the chief of the village.

"They have gone to the other country," he said.

Then he called all the people together. Birds and animals were people in that day. Fishes also were people, and they were invited to the meeting.

The chief explained what he thought had happened to the girls. "So the question is," he ended, "How are we going to get up there?"

One medicine man said, "My medicine is so strong I can bring the sky down closer. Mountain Lion can make a strong bow, and we can shoot a chain of arrows that will reach from ground to sky."

But Mountain Lion could not make a bow strong enough.

Wren made a bow from a big fir tree. When Wren shot with the big bow, no one could see the first arrow except Wren and Snail. The second arrow Wren shot, the other people could see. He made an arrow chain all the way from the sky to the earth.

Then all the people got ready for war up there. They planned how to make the attack.

Raven was planning to go along. He said to Skate, "How do you expect to do anything? You are so wide they will spear you."

"I challenge you here," answered Skate. "Try to shoot me."

Raven tried, but he missed Skate when he shot. Skate was lying sidewise.

"Now it's my turn to shoot," said Skate. "I'll take a shot at your nose."

Skate shot Raven in the nose. That's why Raven has a big hole in his nose.

That's the way the argument was settled.

Then everyone climbed up the ladder—animals and birds and fishes. All of them were human then.

In the sky land they found a few feet of snow. And they could see the village.

"What shall we do?" people asked the chief. "It is very cold, and we have no way of making a fire."

"Robin, you go up to the village," said the chief. "Get a piece of burning wood and bring it down to us."

Robin flew away to the village and into the house with the fire in it. The girls knew him, but they said nothing. When he got to the fire, he opened his arms wide. Fire gave him his red breast. Robin didn't go back to his people. The fire felt so good he stayed there by it.

When Robin did not come back, the chief said to Beaver, "Jump into the river. Stay away from all traps until you get to the last one. Then let the last trap catch you. You will know what to do next."

Beaver did as he was told. The Sky People carried him into the house.

"We have something strange here," they said. They laid him inside by the fire. The two girls from the earth knew him but said nothing. Robin saw him but said nothing.

While the people were looking the other way, Beaver grabbed some of the fire, rushed back to the river, held the fire up above him, and took it to his people. They made a big fire and planned what they would do.

To Mouse, the chief said, "You and your family will visit every house in the village tonight. Cut all the bow strings."

All the mice were busy all night. They cut all the bow strings. In the morning the Earth People attacked the Sky People. When the Sky People picked up their bows to fight back, they found the strings all cut. They could do nothing. The Earth People took the girls and went down the ladder Wren had made.

Everybody went down except Fisher and Skate. They were left in the sky. Fisher is something like Otter; only he lives in the woods instead of in the water.

Skate is still up in the sky. He is the Big Dipper. Fisher sometimes grabs the sun and the moon and eats a piece of them.

* * *

I remember an eclipse when I was a little boy. The old people made all the noise they could, so as to scare Fisher away from the sun. They got up on top of their houses, pounded on the roofs with sticks, beat their drums, and shot off their guns. They thought they kept Fisher from eating the sun.

THE NORTHERN

LIGHTS

AND CREATURES

OF THE SKY

The Makah Indians, the only members of the Wakashan stock in the United States, live along the Strait of Juan de Fuca, in the extreme north-west tip of the United States. James Swan, who taught among the Makah in the 1860's, reported many of their early beliefs to the Smithsonian Institution in 1869.

The northern lights come from the fires of a tribe of dwarf Indians who live many moons' journey to the north. These dwarfs are no taller than half the length of a canoe paddle. They live on the ice, and they eat seals and whales. Although they are small, they are so strong and hardy that they can dive into cold water and catch whales with their hands. Then they boil out the blubber in fires built on the ice. The lights we sometimes see are from the fires of those little people boiling whale blubber. The dwarfs are evil spirits, or skookums, and so we dare not speak their names.

Stars are the spirits of Indians and of all the animals and birds and fish that have ever lived on the earth. Comets and meteors are the spirits of departed chiefs.

The rainbow is an evil being associated in some way with Thunderbird. It is armed at each end with powerful claws. With these claws it seizes anyone who comes within reach.

Thunderbird is a giant Indian, living on the highest mountain. His food is whales. When hungry, he puts on the head of a huge bird and a pair of giant wings. He covers his body with feathers and ties Lightning Fish round his waist. Lightning Fish has a head as sharp as a knife and a red tongue which makes fire.

When Thunderbird flies toward the ocean, his wings darken the sky, and their movement makes a loud noise. When he sees a whale, he throws Lightning Fish into its body and kills it. Then he carries the whale back to the mountains and eats it.

Sometimes Lightning Fish strikes a tree with his sharp head and tears it to pieces. Sometimes Lightning Fish strikes a man and kills him. Whenever it strikes a tree or anything else on land, the Indians try hard to find some part of it, for Lightning Fish has special spirit powers. Even a piece of its bone, which is bright red, will give the man who finds it skill in whale fishing and in other kinds of work.

THUNDERBIRD

AND WHALE

These two legends come from the Quillayute. The first was related by Jack Ward of Lapush, Washington; he had learned it from his father, who died in 1945 at the age of about 98. The second is a blending of fragments told by two informants, one of whom explained that Thunderbird represented good, and Killer Whale represented evil.

Long ago, as long as two men can live, there was a sad time in the land of the Quillayute. For days and days great storms blew. Rain and hail and then sleet and snow came down upon the land. The hailstones were so large that many of the people were killed. The other Quillayute were driven from their coast villages to the great prairie, which was the highest part of their land.

There the people grew thin and weak from hunger. The hailstones had beaten down the ferns and the camas and the berries. Ice locked the rivers so that the men could not fish. Storms rocked the ocean so that fishermen could not go out in their canoes for deep-sea fishing. Soon the people had eaten all the grass and roots on the prairie. There was no food left. As babies and children died without food, even the strongest and bravest of their fathers could do nothing. They had called upon the Great Spirit for help, but no help had come.

At last the great chief of the Quillayute called a meeting of his people. He was old and wise. In his youth he had been the bravest of the warriors, the swiftest of the runners, the fiercest of a fierce tribe.

"Take comfort, my people," said the great chief to his people. "We will call again upon the Great Spirit for help. If no help comes, then we will know that it is His will that we die. If it is not His will that we live, then we will die bravely, as brave Quillayute have always died. Let us talk with the Great Spirit."

So the weak and hungry people sat in silence while the chief talked with the Great Spirit who had looked kindly upon the Quillayute for hundreds and hundreds of years.

When his prayer had ended, the chief turned again to his people. "Now we will wait for the will of the One who is wise and all-powerful."

The people waited. No one spoke. There was nothing but silence and darkness. Soon there came a great noise, and flashes of lightning cut the darkness. Then the people heard another noise. A deep, whirring sound, as of the beat of giant wings, came from the place of the setting sun. All the people turned their eyes toward the sky above the ocean as a huge, bird-shaped creature flew toward them.

This bird was larger than any they had ever seen. Its wings, from tip to tip, were twice as long as a war canoe. It had a huge, curving beak, and its eyes glowed like fire. The people saw that its great claws held a giant whale—a living, giant whale.

In silence they watched while Thunderbird—for so the bird was named by everyone—carefully lowered the whale to the ground before them. Thunderbird then flew high into the sky, gave one earth-reaching cry, and went back to the thunder and lightning it had come from. Perhaps it flew back to its perch in the hunting grounds of the Great Spirit.

Thunderbird and Whale saved the Quillayute from dying. The people knew that the Great Spirit had heard their prayer. Even today they never forget that visit of Thunderbird, never forget that it ended long days of hunger and death. For on the prairie near their village are big, round stones that the old grandfathers say are the hardened hailstones of that storm of long ago.

2

Thunderbird is a very large bird, with feathers as long as a canoe paddle. When he flaps his wings, he makes the thunder and the great winds. When he opens and shuts his eyes, he makes the lightning. In stormy weather, he flies through the skies, flapping his wings and opening and closing his eyes.

Thunderbird's home is a cave in the Olympic Mountains, and he wants no one to come near it. If hunters get so close that he can smell them, he makes the thunder noise, and he rolls ice out of his cave. The ice rolls down the mountainside, and when it reaches a rocky place it breaks into many, many pieces. The pieces rattle as they roll farther down into the valley.

All the hunters are so afraid of Thunderbird and his noise and his rolling ice that they never stay long near his home. No one ever sleeps near his cave.

Thunderbird keeps his food in a dark hole at the edge of a big field of ice and snow in the Olympic Mountains. His food is the whale. Thunderbird flies out to the ocean, catches a whale, and hurries back to the mountains to eat it. One time Whale fought Thunderbird so hard that in the battle trees were torn up by their roots. Even to this day there are no trees in Beaver Prairie because Whale once fought so hard to keep from being killed and eaten.

At the time of the great flood, Thunderbird fought a long, long battle with Killer Whale. He would catch Killer Whale in his claws and start with him to the cave in the mountains. Killer Whale would escape and return to the water. Thunderbird would catch him again, all the time flashing lightning from his eyes and flapping his wings with a terrible noise. Mountains were shaken by the noise, and trees were uprooted in the struggles.

Again and again Killer Whale escaped. Again and again Thunderbird seized him. Many times they fought, in different places in the mountains. At last Killer Whale escaped to the middle of the ocean, and Thunderbird gave up the fight.

That is why killer whales live in the deep ocean today. That is why there are many prairies in the midst of the forests on the Olympic Peninsula. The prairies are the places where Thunderbird and Killer Whale fought so hard that they uprooted trees.

THUNDER AND LIGHTNING

Enumclaw is the name given by the Indians to a mountain in the Cascade Range, not far from Chinook Pass. Encamped one night at the base of the mountain, says an old legend, some Indians were so terrified by a thunderstorm that they fled. The near-by village of Enumclaw was named for the mountain. Enumclaw *means "thunder."*

Long, long ago, two brothers lived near the peak now called Mount Rainier. The older brother was named Enumclaw. The younger brother was named Kapoonis. Both were great hunters. Often they were gone on hunting trips for many months. They would kill deer and elk, dry the meat, and hide it in the ground to have it ready for use when they returned to the spot.

The men were hunting for something else besides wild game. They were searching for their guardian spirits. Each of them wanted a guardian spirit that would make him a great medicine man. The younger brother often took long trips alone. Early every morning and again at twilight he took a bath in the river, for he must be clean in order to have a vision of his guardian spirit. In that way he at last found a fire spirit, a very powerful spirit. With it he could make lightning.

Enumclaw, the older brother, became very strong. He could throw small stones from peak to peak in the mountains. They made a sharp, cracking sound that could be heard far and near. Sometimes Enumclaw called his younger brother by throwing a small stone against a rock.

Whenever Enumclaw saw people crossing the mountains, he threw stones at the peaks. The noise warned his brother that someone was near, and it also frightened the travelers. The noise was answered by fiery flames. The people said that Enumclaw caused the birds to fly so fast that their wings made a great rumbling sound.

One evening the two brothers had a testing of their powers. On a rocky ridge south of the giant peak they sat facing the sun. Enumclaw pointed to a large white rock across a valley from where they were sitting.

"I will throw stones to the left of that rock," he said to Kapoonis. "I will throw them with such force that the ridge will fall down."

"All right," agreed Kapoonis. "I will throw stones to the right of the great white rock."

They threw stones with all the strength they had. The friendly contest continued until all the ridge was gone except one sharp rock. It still stands high in the air southwest of Longmire Springs. Today it is known as Sawtooth Rock.

The Great Spirit watched the contest from his home in the clouds above the giant peak. "It is not good for human beings to have such power," the Great Spirit said in his heart. So he changed Enumclaw to Thunder and Kapoonis to Lightning.

THUNDER'S SPIRIT POWER

This unusual concept of Thunder and Lightning is given in the words of Andrew Joe, a Skagit on the Swinomish Reservation.

In the beginning of the world, Thunder and his family lived in a lake. His wife was Rain. His children were Lightning and Hail. Then Old Creator placed him up above, to control the weather and to control the air in which everyone would live on earth.

After putting him in the sky, Old Creator gave Thunder a special spirit power and said to him, "Your spirit power will be discovered and will be brought back to earth to be of great use to the human race."

Thunder's spirit power was discovered in our own country. It is electricity, and it *is* of great use to the human race. Nothing can live without the electricity in the air.

THUNDER AND

HIS SON-IN-LAW

Testing a suitor or a son-in-law is a frequent motif in the myths of many peoples. The following story is told by the Quinault.

Thunder's daughter wanted to marry a young man named Sisemo. Thunder thought Sisemo was worthless, and he did not like his family either. So he decided to give the young man some difficult tasks to do.

"Go up to the mountains," he commanded, "and bring me snow from five mountaintops."

Sisemo went to the mountains, came back with a handful of snow, and gave it to Thunder. Thunder was angry because there was so little snow. He scolded and scolded.

"Eat it and see," said Sisemo. "You will find that there is plenty."

Thunder ate and ate the snow, but still there was as much as ever. Then Thunder was angry because Sisemo had got the better of him. In a rage, he threw the remaining snow outdoors. But the handful spread and soon covered the ground and the house and trees.

"Take it back to the mountains," begged Thunder. "Take it back where you found it."

Sisemo picked up the snow—it became only a handful—and carried it back to the five mountains.

When he reached home again, Thunder gave him another task.

"Go to the mountains," he commanded, "and bring me two mountain lions. I want them for pets."

Soon the young man came back from the woods with two mountain lions tied together. He gave them to Thunder, but when Thunder began to play with them, they began to fight him. They tore at him and bit him until he was nearly dead.

"Take them away, Sisemo," begged Thunder. "Take them back to the mountains."

As soon as Sisemo came near them, they were quiet. Quietly they returned with him to the mountains. When the young man got home again, Thunder had recovered from the struggle with the lions and was ready with a third task.

"Go up to the mountains," he commanded, "and bring me two bears. I want them for pets."

Soon Sisemo came back from the mountains with two bears tied together. He gave them to Thunder, but when Thunder tried to play with them, they rose on their hind legs and fought him. Remembering his struggle with the mountain lions, he became frightened and ordered Sisemo to take the bears back.

When the young man returned home, Thunder said to him, "Come to the woods with me and help me split a cedar log."

In the forest, Thunder picked out a long, heavy log. He split one end of it and put in his wedges. Then he said to Sisemo, "Get into the cleft in the log and hold its sides apart."

The young man obeyed. As soon as he was in the split part of the log, Thunder took out his wedges. Sisemo was caught inside the big log.

"Ha! Ha!" laughed Thunder. "Now I have you. Get out of there if you can."

Chuckling to himself, Thunder left the woods and went home. But hardly had he entered the house when he heard footsteps behind him. He listened. Almost at once he heard someone throw something heavy beside the house. Thunder opened the door. There was Sisemo, beside the great log. He had carried it in from the woods. Thunder was so surprised he hardly knew what the next task should be.

At last he commanded, "Go down to the Underworld. There you will find a ball of light which the Underworld people like to play with. They roll it and make lightning with it. I want you to get the ball and bring it to me."

Sisemo went down to the Underworld and there saw the people playing with the ball of lightning. They saw him too and would not let him get near the ball. Sisemo changed himself into smoke, but the Underworld people could still see him. He changed himself into fog, but the people still could see him. They guarded the ball, though they kept on playing with it, rolling it from one group to another.

At last Sisemo changed himself into something they could not see. No one knows what it was. He put himself between the two groups rolling the ball. When it came near him, he picked it up and dashed away to the trail that leads to the upper world.

As Sisemo ran, the Underworld began to grow dark. The people made torches of pitchwood and followed Sisemo by the light of their torches. He ran, but they ran faster. They might have caught him if he had not been helped by Thunder and his friends.

As Sisemo neared the Upper World, Thunder and his friends got water and poured it down upon the people below. The water put out their torches, so they gave up and went back. Sisemo reached home safely with the ball of lightning.

"You have done well, my son," said Thunder at last. "You may marry my daughter. I will not trouble you any more."

Thunder held the ball of light in his hands and looked at it with pride. Then he gave parts of it to his friends. He gave some of it to Hummingbird for its throat, some to Robin for its breast, some to Woodpecker for its crest. He gave some to all the birds and all the animals that now have red on their feathers or on their furs.

But most of it he kept for himself. He put it under his own arms. Whenever Thunder is angry, he raises his wings and shows us his lightning there. His scolding is the thunder which we hear today.

THE BATTLE
WITH SNOW

The conquest of Cold or Snow or the Ice People is the theme of several long and involved myths. The Chehalis myth given here has been selected largely because of its simplicity.

For a long time during the days of the animal people, the Chehalis Indians say, snow was sent by the five Snow brothers. One winter they sent so much that all the houses in the village were buried. The people made tunnels under the snow in order to get from one house to another and to visit their friends.

There was so much snow and the winter was so long that the animal people became worried. "We must do something about it," they said, "or we will starve to death."

"We cannot do anything about it here," replied their headman, their chief. "We'll have to fight the Snow brothers, but we'll have to fight them on their own ground."

"We will fight them," said the people together.

When spring came, the chief told his people, "Before winter comes again, we will go north. That is where Snow lives."

Early that autumn they made preparations. At last everything was ready, and the animal people started north—Rattlesnake, Mouse, and Frog, as well as the big animals. For three days they traveled on land. On the third night, their chief said to them, "Tomorrow we will travel through the air. The rest of our journey will be through the air, up through the sky."

On the fifth morning they all arrived up in the Sky World, where they soon found the house of Snow.

"We will attack early in the morning," announced the chief.

During the night, Mouse slipped away and sneaked into Snow's house. She went to the bow of the oldest Snow brother and cut it to shreds. She went to the bow of the second Snow brother and cut it to shreds. She cut to shreds the bows of the third and the fourth brothers.

But she did not have time to cut the fifth brother's bow. Daybreak came, and she had to leave. She hurried back to her people.

"I am small but I have helped you," she told them. "Now I know that you can beat the Snow brothers."

Early in the morning the animal people attacked Snow's house. The five brothers jumped to get their bows, but four of them found that their bows had been chewed to pieces. The four oldest brothers could not fight. Only the youngest could use his bow against all the bows and arrows of the people from earth. Soon he gave up and fled to the north. Mouse had done her work well.

The animal people hunted through Snow's house and took home with them everything they could find. Snake and Rattlesnake were left in the Sky World to pick up whatever the other animals left. Snake could find nothing but a few red, white, and yellow straws and a piece of smoked buckskin.

Rattlesnake got lost and never found his way home again, but Snake at last returned. Some of his friends thought that he was lost in the Sky World, and so were grieving for him.

His cousin Water Dog was crying because he thought Snake was lost.

So Snake gave him his piece of smoked buckskin. That is why water dogs have tough hides.

Lizard, another cousin, also was crying because Snake was lost. So Snake gave him some basket straws. That is why lizards have stripes.

Frog, another cousin, was crying but at the same time was singing an unkind song:

> Snake is cross-eyed. Snake is cross-eyed.
> That is why he was left behind.

Snake was very angry. "I will not give you any present, Frog," he shouted. "I'll never be a friend of yours again!"

That is why snakes and frogs are enemies to this day. When a snake sees a frog, he bites him and swallows him.

Snake had some of his straws left. So he put them on his own back. That is why snakes have white stripes or yellow stripes on their backs.

Rattlesnake finally found his way down from the Sky World, but he landed in the Yakima country, east of the mountains. He never came back to the Chehalis country. That is why the Chehalis country has no rattlesnakes today.

Thus the Snows were beaten. That is why we have little snow in the Chehalis country today. If Mouse had not cut the four bows, we would still have deep snows. Now only the youngest brother brings the snow.

THE CHINOOK WIND

The Chinook wind is a warm wind of the Pacific Northwest and of British Columbia. In January or February or March, it may overnight melt the ice-locked streams and strip the lower lands and slopes of their snow. The name was first given to a warm wind which blew from over the Chinook camp to the trading post of the Hudson's Bay Company at Astoria, Oregon.

Long, long ago, the warm west wind was caused by five Chinook brothers. They lived far down the Columbia River, near the Pacific Ocean. The cold east wind was caused by the five Walla Walla brothers. They lived east of the mountains, near the meeting of the waters. The grandparents of the five Chinook brothers and the grandparents of the five Walla Walla brothers lived at Umatilla, the place of the wind-drifted sands.

All these wind brothers blew very hard over the country. Sometimes the warm Chinook wind would dash over the camps, blow down trees, tear up the earth, and fill the air with dust. Then the cold Walla Walla wind would come along and freeze everything with its icy breath. So the people led a miserable life.

One day, the five Walla Walla brothers sent a message to the five Chinook brothers. "We challenge you to a wrestling match," they said.

The Chinook brothers accepted the challenge and came up the river to the place decided upon for the wrestling match. Coyote was chosen as judge. He was to chop off the heads of the losers with his big stone knife.

In secret, Coyote whispered to the grandparents of the Chinook brothers, "If your grandsons are about to be thrown, pour oil on the ground. Then they will not be defeated."

In secret, Coyote whispered to the grandparents of the Walla Walla brothers, "If your grandsons are about to be thrown, scatter ice on the ground. Then they will not be defeated."

So the ground was made smooth, and the match began. First, the oldest Chinook brother wrestled with the oldest Walla Walla brother. When the Chinook brother was about to go down, Coyote called out to the grandfather, "Throw on your oil." And the Chinook grandfather threw his oil on the ground. Then the other grandfather threw ice on top of the oil.

The ground became so slippery that the oldest Chinook brother could not keep his feet. He went sprawling, and Coyote cut off his head with a big stone knife.

Then the second Chinook brother and the second Walla Walla brother wrestled, then the third and the fourth and the fifth. Each time, the Chinook grandfather threw oil on the ground. Each time, the Walla Walla grandfather threw ice on top of the oil. Each time, the Chinook brother went down first; and each time, Coyote cut off his head with the big stone knife. So the five Chinook brothers were all killed.

The oldest Chinook brother had a wife and a baby in the Chinook village by the sea. When the child was a tiny boy, his mother said to him, "Your father and your four uncles were killed by the cold Walla Walla brothers. You must make yourself very strong. You must practice wrestling, so that when you are a man you can get even with the Walla Walla brothers for the death of your father."

As the boy grew up, he made himself strong by pulling up trees. He became so strong that he could pull up a large fir tree and throw it away just as if it were a camas bulb. At last he said to his mother, "Now I am strong enough to wrestle with the Walla Walla brothers. Let me go to meet them."

"That is what I have always wanted you to do," answered his mother. So the next night, he started up the Columbia River, tearing up trees as he went. Just before daylight he turned from the big river and went up the Yakima River for a short distance. There he lay down and slept all day. You can still see where he lay, on the south side of a mountain.

In the evening he started out again and went up the great river. Soon he reached the hut of his great-grandparents, at the place of the wind-drifted sands. He found them very miserable, for the Walla Walla brothers had been mean all these years. They had caused the cold wind to blow all the time. And they had often stolen the old man's fish when he returned to shore.

On this day, things were different. Young Chinook went fishing with his great-grandfather, but he lay down in the canoe out of sight. When the boat was full of fish, the old man started back for the shore. The five Walla Walla brothers came down to the shore as usual to steal the fish. But when they reached out to seize the canoe, the young Chinook lying in the stern moved slightly. The canoe shot forward, out of the cold wind's reach. Then the brothers almost seized it again, but the boat shot forward again. This happened five times. Then the old man landed safely.

The Walla Walla brothers watched closely. They saw the grandson get out of the canoe, pick up the fish—big sturgeons—and carry all of them easily on his little finger.

Soon Coyote told all the people that there would be another wrestling match. Again he would be the judge, and again he would cut off the heads of the losers. This time he whispered to the Chinook great-grandfather, "Don't throw your oil on first. Wait until the Walla Walla grandfather throws the ice. Then pour the oil, and your great-grandson will down them all."

The young man wrestled with the oldest Walla Walla brother. "Now throw on your oil!" Coyote said to the great-grandfather. But the old man sat still. Soon the cold-wind brother was almost down. Then his grandfather threw ice on the wrestling ground. The Chinook grandfather threw on his oil. The oldest Walla Walla brother went sprawling, and Coyote cut off his head with the big stone knife.

Then the young Chinook giant wrestled with the second Walla Walla brother until he got him down. He wrestled with the third, and he wrestled with the fourth. Coyote whacked off the four heads with his big stone knife.

Only one Walla Walla brother was left, the youngest. He would not wrestle. "One of us must remain alive," he explained.

Coyote said, "I will let you live. But I make a law that hereafter you shall blow only lightly. You can never again blow so hard and so cold. No longer will you freeze people to death every time you breathe on them."

Then Coyote turned to the young Chinook. "I make a law that you shall blow hard only at night. You shall blow first on the mountain ridges to warn the people that you are coming. Then you shall come down to the valleys and take off the snow quickly."

Ever since then, the cold wind has blown lightly in the winter, and the warm Chinook wind has blown early in the spring. Then it carries off the snow in a rush.

HOW COYOTE

MADE THE

INDIAN TRIBES

At the end of the mythological age of the animal people, when the Changer or Coyote had made the world ready for "the new people" they prophesied would come, human beings appeared. Many tribes of the Columbia River Basin told the creation myth which follows, either with or without the formation of "Big River." In a similar story told in different ways by the Nez Perces, the monster lived near the junction of the Clearwater and the Snake rivers in Idaho. In the variants told by the Palouse, the Spokane, and the Coeur d'Alenes, the monster lived near the junction of the Palouse and Snake rivers.

Long ago, when the animal people walked the earth, a giant beaver monster lived in Lake Cle Elum, high in the Cascade Mountains. His name was Wishpoosh. Under his red eyebrows he had eyes like fire. He had huge, fierce, shining claws, with which he seized everything that came near him.

Lake Cle Elum was full of fish, enough fish for Wishpoosh and all the animal people too. But Wishpoosh would not let the people get any fish. Whenever they came to the lake, he seized them with his giant claws and dragged them to the bottom. There he either ate them or drowned them.

At last the animal people were so hungry and so unhappy that they begged Coyote to help them.

"O Coyote," they begged, "free us from this monster Wishpoosh. If you do not help us, we shall all die."

"I will free you from the monster Wishpoosh," promised Coyote.

But Coyote knew he had a hard task before him. Other animal people had tried to kill Wishpoosh, but he had killed them, instead. What could Coyote do? Though he was very wise, he could not think of a good plan.

He would ask his three sisters who lived in his stomach in the form of huckleberries. They were very wise. They could tell him what to do.

But at first his sisters in the form of huckleberries would not help him. "If we tell you," they said, "you will say that you knew that already."

Coyote knew that they did not like hail. So he looked up into the sky and called out, "Hail! Hail! Fall down from the sky!"

His sisters were afraid and cried, "Stop! Stop! Don't bring the hail. We will tell you whatever you need to know."

Then they told him how he could get rid of Wishpoosh.

When they had finished talking, Coyote said, "Yes, my sisters. That is what I thought. That was my plan all the time."

Coyote made a huge spear with a long, strong handle, just as his sisters had told him to do. He fastened the spear to his wrist with a cord which he had made of twisted flax, just as his sisters had told him to do. Then he went up to Lake Cle Elum to catch some fish with his long spear. Of course Wishpoosh, the beaver monster, saw him and tried to seize him with his huge, fierce, shining claws.

But before the claws grabbed him, Coyote drove the sharp spear into the beaver monster's side. The monster roared with pain and plunged to the bottom of the lake. Coyote was dragged down with Wishpoosh, because the spear was fastened to his wrist with the cord of flax. The two of them tore the water apart.

On the bottom of the lake, Coyote and Wishpoosh fought hard and long. They fought so hard that they shook the mountains around the lake and made a great hole in them. The waters of the lake rushed through this hole, plunged down the mountainside, and soon made a larger lake below, in the Kittitas Valley.

Wishpoosh, still roaring, was carried along with the waters. He tried to drown Coyote, but Coyote hung on. As they tore their way out of the second big lake, they cut a channel for the Yakima River. As the two fighters plunged on down the Yakima River, the waters followed them and made a big lake in the Yakima country. The monster tore through the next ridge and made Union Gap. He plunged eastward across the valley, continuing to dig a channel for the Yakima River as he went. The waters overflowed the new channel and made a big lake in the Walla Walla country.

Then the monster turned sharply toward the west, dragging Coyote after him and cutting the channel of Big River as he went. Coyote tried to stop his journey by clutching at the trees and rocks along the shore. But the trees broke off or came up by the roots. The rocks crumbled away, and the channel which the monster tore out was made wider by Coyote's struggle. Wishpoosh dragged him on and on. The waters of the lakes followed. The monster tore through the high mountains and made the gorge of Big River. Coyote pulled rocks from the shores and made many little waterfalls.

At last they came to the mouth of Big River, where it flows into the ocean. By this time, Coyote was so tired he almost drowned in the waves. Muskrat laughed at him.

Wishpoosh was still very angry and still very strong. He seized many salmon and swallowed them whole. He seized whales and ate them. He threatened to kill everything.

As soon as Coyote had rested a little while, he made up his mind again to get rid of the beaver monster. He said to himself, "I will ask my sisters. They are very wise. They will tell me what to do."

Once more his three sisters who lived in his stomach in the form of huckleberries told him what to do. And once more Coyote said to them, when they had finished talking, "Yes, my sisters, that is what I thought. That was my plan all the time."

Coyote changed himself into the branch of a fir tree, just as his sisters had told him to do. Then he floated out to the beaver monster and the monster swallowed him, exactly as his wise sisters had predicted. Inside the monster's stomach, Coyote changed himself back into his animal shape. He took his sharp knife and began to hack at the heart of Wishpoosh. He hacked and he hacked until the beaver monster was dead.

Then Coyote made himself smaller and climbed out through the monster's throat. Muskrat helped him drag the dead body up on the beach near the mouth of Big River. With his sharp knife Coyote cut up the big body of the monster.

"From your body, mighty Wishpoosh," he said, "I will make a new race of people. They will live near the shores of Big River and along the streams which flow into it."

From the lower part of the animal's body, Coyote made the people who were to live along the coast. "You shall be the Chinook Indians," he said to some of them. "You shall live near the mouth of Big River and shall be traders.

"You shall live along the coast," he said to others. "You shall live in villages facing the ocean and shall get your food by spearing salmon and digging clams. You shall always be short and fat and have weak legs."

From the legs of the beaver monster he made the Klickitat Indians. "You shall live along the rivers that flow down from the big white mountain north of Big River. You shall be swift of foot and keen of wit. You shall be famous runners and great horsemen."

From the arms of the monster he made the Cayuse Indians. "You shall live along Big River," Coyote said to them. "You shall be powerful with bow and arrows and with war clubs."

From the ribs he made the Yakima Indians. "You shall live near the new Yakima River, east of the mountains. You shall be the helpers and the protectors of all the poor people."

From the head he created the Nez Perce Indians. "You shall live in the valleys of the Kookooskia and the Wallowa rivers. You shall be men of brains, great in council and in speechmaking. You shall also be skillful horsemen and brave warriors."

Then Coyote gathered up the hair and blood and waste. He hurled them far eastward, over the big mountains. "You shall be the Snake River Indians," said Coyote. "You shall be people of blood and violence. You shall be buffalo hunters and shall wander far and wide."

From the various parts of the monster Wishpoosh which he had killed, Coyote created all the Indian tribes. Then Coyote went back up Big River.

But two things he forgot. He forgot to make mouths for the new people along the coast. And he forgot to open their eyes.

The first time he returned to the mouth of Big River, Coyote found the people very hungry and wandering about with their eyes shut. He felt sorry for them. Quickly he took his stone knife, opened their eyes, and cut a mouth on each face.

But Coyote was in such a hurry and his knife was so dull that he made some of the mouths crooked and some of them too big. Ever since then, the Indians along the coast have had ugly mouths.

V.
MISCELLANEOUS
MYTHS AND
LEGENDS

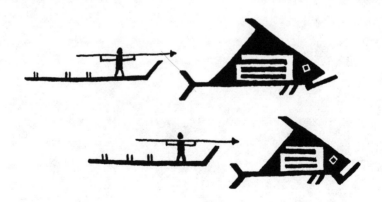

GUARDIAN

SPIRITS

Seven stories in earlier sections—"The Lake on Mount Rainier," "The Elk Spirit of Lost Lake," "The Painted Rocks at Naches Gap," "The Beginning of the Skagit World," "The Origin of Cassiopeia's Chair," "Thunder and Lightning," and "Thunder's Spirit Power"—mention guardian spirits or spirit power. In several other tales appears the expression "made his powers," which means that the character called upon his spirit power to help him.

A guardian spirit was an individual spirit which gave an Indian some special power, protected him from demons, guided and directed him, and came to his aid when he was in need. It lived somewhere in the woods or mountains or water, usually in the form of an animal or a bird. The elk, for example, was the guardian spirit of the hunter near Lost Lake.

The concept of the guardian spirit was inseparably linked with the Indian belief in spirits in all phenomena of nature. The world was full of spirits. It was permeated with a strange, mystical force or power that every spirit possessed. Man might attain this force through fasting and suffering, which would bring him a dream or a vision. Whatever he saw or heard in that dream or vision would be his guardian spirit.

Almost every Indian child, in years gone by, went out in search of his guardian spirit, and that search was a very important experience in his life. It was often called the "power quest," for the guardian spirit was the source of a person's special power, both physical and spiritual.

A child was carefully prepared for his power quest by the instruction and encouragement of some older person, usually a relative. When a boy or girl was between the ages of seven and thirteen, sometimes younger, he was sent into the forest or up on a mountain, or to a point on the beach, alone, for the purpose of seeking his guardian spirit. The child was to stay alone, usually without food, often without sleep. He might be permitted to have a fire, and sometimes kept himself awake by attending a fire. Sometimes he went several nights in succession; sometimes he was gone for three or four or five days and nights.

Although a guardian spirit might come to a child anywhere, most tribes considered certain places better than others. Spirit Mountain, southwest of Portland, was a favorite spot, according to John Hudson of the Santiam; and vigil on Mount Jefferson, he says, brought guardian spirits of special power. White Mountain in northeastern Washington was the usual place among the Colville Indians; numerous piles of rocks on the mountain are reminders of many power quests in days gone by. Peter Noyes, a Colville Indian now past eighty, says that boys between the ages of five and twelve were taken up there by fathers or uncles; they had to stay alone five or six days, without anything to eat, while they waited for the voice of some spirit in the form of an animal or a bird. Each boy made a pile of rocks as proof that he had stayed where he had been left.

In all tribes, cleanliness was an important part of the guardian spirit quest. Unless the young person was scrupulously clean, no guardian spirit would come to him. Rose Purdy, who spent her childhood in a village along Hood Canal, tells about a boy of her tribe who was directed to dive into the water to seek his power. He bathed until he thought he was clean, but when he dived, the rock he held in his fist would not let him go down. Thinking he was not clean, he bathed again, scrubbing himself with a brush of leaves. Four times he came out of the water to make himself cleaner, almost rubbing his nails away with a rock, in his efforts to get fingernails and toenails perfectly clean. When he dived the fifth time, the rock in his hand allowed him to go down.

If the child was in the proper frame of mind, and if he showed courage and perseverance, his guardian spirit would appear to him in a dream or vision. He might see it, or he might hear its song, or it might speak to him. In some tribes it was expected to appear first as a man or a woman, announcing that it was a certain animal. In one of the Puget Sound tribes, a person was considered fortunate if his guardian spirit was an owl, a bear, or a wolf. Among the Okanogan and Colville tribes of north central Washington, the cougar, the grizzly bear, and the eagle were strong powers. Even stronger were Story Chickadee, Story Beaver, Story Mountain Goat, Story Rock—characters which appear in the mythology of the tribes. If a person was so fortunate as to acquire one of these four as his guardian spirit, he would be protected from all harm and might receive some of his guardian spirit's power to perform miracles.

Not every child was successful on the power quest. "My uncle sent me out hundreds of times when I was between eight and fifteen," said a great-grandmother who told me some of her tribal tales. "But I never heard the song of any bird or animal or ground hog. I wasn't lucky enough to hear a song from anyone."

If a woman had acquired a guardian spirit, she was accepted on a par with men, in some tribes; if she had not, she could still live a satisfactory life. But a boy could expect very little from life if he became a man without having been successful in a power quest.

A child fortunate in hearing or seeing his guardian spirit was not to tell anyone of his experience for several years. If he should tell people about it too soon, his guardian spirit would lose some of its power or might even forsake him. In some tribes no person revealed the source of his special power unless death was imminent.

In adult life, he would be helped by his spirit. If an otter were his guardian, he would have special power in swimming. An eel guardian gave him power to escape from his enemies, because it was slippery; rattlesnake power made him immune to rattlesnake poison and gave him the ability to cure rattlesnake bite; both cougar and eagle gave ability to kill deer; thunder gave power for fighting; mouse gave skill in foot racing. Among the Klallam along the Strait of Juan de Fuca, most spirits were supposed to give wealth or some power by which wealth might be obtained.

Legends grew up about these guardian-spirit quests. Rose Purdy relates many about the Tahmahnawis, as she and others always call the spirits. Eneas Seymore, a Lake Indian, tells about a boy whose father commanded him to dive into Twin Lake for his guiding spirit. He tried to dive but came back to a rock overlooking the lake. Directed to dive again, he went down to the bottom of the lake. There he came to a tepee with people in it. The headman said to the boy, "You will have power to catch fish in a trap. These people you see are fish. I give you power to catch fish."

Then the boy went out other nights to get other powers. The more guardian spirits a man had, the more powers he possessed and the higher his place in the tribe.

A seventy-year-old woman I talked with is still helped by her guardian spirit. It comforts her and strengthens her—"lifts me up," she says—when worried about her children and grandchildren. It has protected her from physical danger; its warning kept her from being struck by an automobile. She feels it within her, and she hears its voice. It is truly a guardian spirit, her Tahmahnawis.

THE HAZELNUT,

A GUARDIAN SPIRIT

One time a man was cracking hazelnuts on a large stone, using a smaller stone as a hammer. When he struck one of the nuts an ordinary blow, it sprang away and lighted at a little distance from him. The man picked it up and struck at it a second time, but again the hazelnut sprang away.

"You are brave," said the man as he picked it up. "But I will break you anyway."

He seized the nut firmly and tried to strike it a heavy blow. But a third time it leaped away into the grass. The man hunted and hunted, but he could not find it.

Some nights later, a young boy in search of his guardian spirit came to the hiding place of the hazelnut. He heard a voice speaking to him.

"Look at me, my boy," said the spirit of the hazelnut, "and listen to what I tell you. No enemy can hold me or hurt me, even though I am struck heavy blows. When I hide, none can find me. I am strong, and I can give you strength. If you will always do as I bid you, you will have my power. The enemy may surround you and catch you, but they cannot hold you. You can spring from their grasp and hide before their eyes. They will never find you if you obey me."

The boy told no one about the hazelnut, but ever after he followed its directions and its warnings. When he became a man, he had a strange power of escaping and hiding from anyone who attacked him. Even when he was seized and surrounded by a large band of the enemy, he was always able to break away. He became a great warrior among the Yakima people through the help of the hazelnut, his guardian spirit.

THE ORIGIN

OF GUARDIAN SPIRITS

AND OF SWEAT LODGE

The sweat bath was one of the most important Indian ceremonies. It was not merely a means of cleansing the body and of healing disease; it had religious significance also. The rite included a prayer addressed to the life-giving power of the universe—a prayer for purification and strength and for good fortune in any enterprise of the moment.

Even the construction of a sweat lodge had spiritual value. Sickness or ill luck would strike anyone who built the house irreverently or abused it in any way. A series of arches about four feet high was made by pounding into the ground both ends of birch or willow wands. This framework was covered with skins or blankets if the lodge was for temporary use only— near a summer camp, for instance. It was covered with several layers of bark, earth, and grass if it was for permanent use. The entrance always faced a stream or lake.

The sweating-stones were heated just outside the entrance and were rolled or carried into a pit inside the lodge. Water sprinkled on the hot rocks supplied the steam. As the bather dashed water on them, he chanted prayers to Sweat Lodge. After sweating, he plunged into the stream or lake. Cleanliness was thought to bring good luck.

This myth of the origin of Sweat Lodge and of guardian spirits was told to Verne F. Ray in 1930 by Chief Jim James of the Sanpoil.

Sweat Lodge was a chief long, long ago; but he wasn't called Sweat Lodge then. He was just called chief. He decided to create all the animals and all the birds. So he created them and named them all. He named each animal and each bird. Then he told each one of them: "In times to come, when people have been created, they will send their children out, during the day or during the night, and you will talk with them and tell them what they will be able to do when they grow up. You will tell the boys that they are to get things easily, are to be good hunters, good fishermen, good gamblers, and so on. You will tell the girls that they will be able to get things easily. At that time I will be Sweat Lodge, myself."

Then he spoke to them again: "I'll have no body, no head, nor will I be able to see. Whoever desires to construct me will have the right to do so. The one that builds me may pray to me for good looks, or whatever he may wish—the one that made me. I'll take pity on him, and I'll give him what he requests—the one that made me. People may approach me thus: If anyone is injured, or if he is sick, or if he is poisoned, he may come to me for help and I'll give it to him. Also, when anyone is dying, he may come to me, and I'll help him then also. I'll help him to see the next world. So in this world I am Sweat Lodge, for the help of human beings."

THE ORIGIN

OF THE

ROOT FESTIVAL

A traditional ceremony still observed by Indians in some communities in the Pacific Northwest was held in the spring when the first roots were ready to be dug. In the late spring and summer, the roots of several plants were dried and used in a variety of ways—in soups, for porridge, and for bread. The root festival, held in April, is sometimes combined with the first-salmon ceremony, which has been described briefly in "How Coyote Helped the People."

This account of the origin of the root festival was told by Chief Jobe Charley, a Wasco on the Yakima Reservation.

Long ago, our people went up to the sky every feasting time. There they sang and danced and gave thanks to the Great Spirit for the roots and berries on the earth.

One time Speelyi, the red fox, and Tooptoop, his brother, went up to the sky with the people. All sang and danced and prayed for several days. Speelyi became so tired that he dropped down and fell asleep. Finding him and recognizing him, the people threw him down to the earth, where he belonged.

His brother Tooptoop kept on with the thanksgiving ceremony. After a while he thought of Speelyi down on the earth and went to him with some bitterroot, camas, huckleberries, and salmon. Speelyi had a big feast.

When he had eaten all he could eat, Speelyi raised his hand to the east and made a new law. "My people, no more will you go up to the sky to feast and to give thanks. Many new people are coming to our land, and so we cannot do all that we are used to doing. We must share with our new friends. We must learn to bear our hardships and our sorrows as best we can.

"I am going to put bitterroot and camas and other roots in different parts of the country. You will have feasts here every year. When you begin to dig the roots in the spring, you will sing and dance and give thanks to the Great Spirit. You need not travel up to the sky for that. And as you dig the roots, you will sing songs of thanksgiving. Your children will learn the songs from you.

"I am Speelyi. I have spoken."

And so that is why my people had a root festival every spring, when they began to dig the roots we used for food.

THE ORIGIN OF
THE POTLATCH

The potlatch, an elaborate ceremonial of gift-giving, was an important feature of Indian life from Oregon to Alaska. Differing considerably among different tribes in some details, all the potlatches were marked by the host's giving away quantities of goods. The more lavishly he gave, the more he was respected by his fellow tribesmen and by his guests from neighboring or distant tribes. The giving of gifts was accompanied by several days of feasting, dancing, singing, and athletic contests by day, gambling and storytelling at night.

One concept of the origin of this Indian festival is a detail in the Nisqually creation myth. Below is a condensation of a Quillayute myth about its origin. See also "Potlatch on the Oregon Coast."

A strange bird once appeared in the ocean in front of the village. All the young men of the Quillayute went out and tried to shoot it, but no one could hit it. Every day Blue Jay, a slave of Golden Eagle, watched the hunters try to shoot the strange bird.

One day Golden Eagle said to Blue Jay, "Eh, my children can catch that queer-looking bird."

"Oh, no," replied Blue Jay quickly. "They are girls."

Golden Eagle's daughters overheard the two men, but they said nothing. Next day the two younger sisters went into the woods and stayed all day. Many days they spent in the woods, telling no one what they were doing. Although they were girls, just imagine—they were making arrows!

One morning, before daylight, they went to the forest and brought in the arrows they had made. When they returned to the village, all the hunters had gone out in their canoes to try again to shoot the strange-looking bird. The two sisters disguised themselves by tying their hair in front so as to hide their faces. No one could recognize them. Then they paddled their canoe in a zigzag line until they were near the bird. The older of the sisters killed it with her third arrow.

That evening the girls said to their father, "We caught the bird and then we hid it in the woods. We want to use its feathers as presents, for the feathers are of many colors. Will you tell Blue Jay to invite all the birds to come to our lodge tomorrow?"

Next morning Blue Jay went out with the invitation. Soon all kinds of birds were gathered in the lodge of Golden Eagle. "My daughters caught the strange bird," the host explained, "the bird of many colors. They want to give each of you a present."

The girls gave certain colors to different birds—yellow and brown feathers to Meadowlark, red and brown to Robin, brown only to Wren, yellow and black to the little Finch. They gave to each bird the colors it was to have. They kept giving until they had no more feathers left.

Ever since then, certain birds have had certain colors. And since then, there have been potlatches. This was the first potlatch, the first giving of gifts from the people who invite to the people who are invited.

COYOTE AND CROW

An occasional Indian tale is like a familiar fable from Aesop. The following Yakima story is one example. Another is the counterpart of Aesop's fable about the race between the hare and the tortoise, except that in the Indian version the winner received a prize: his choice of Frog's tail, Bear's tail, or Rabbit's long and bushy tail (as it was when the world was very young).

Coyote traveled through the country, fighting monsters and making the world ready for the new people, the Indians who were to follow. He crossed the Cascade Mountains and came into the Puget Sound country. He was hungry, very hungry.

He saw Crow sitting on the peak of a high cliff, with a ball of deer fat in his mouth. Coyote looked at Crow with this fat and thought how good it would taste. Becoming hungrier and hungrier, he wondered how he could get the fat for himself. He thought hard. Then he laughed.

"I know what to do. I know how I can get the fat from Crow."

Then Coyote came close to the base of the cliff and called. "Oh, Chief! I hear that you can make a good noise, a pleasing noise with your voice. You are a big chief, I know. You are a wise chief, I have heard. Let me hear your voice, Chief. I want to hear you, Chief Crow."

Crow was pleased to be called chief. So he answered, "Caw!"

"Oh, Chief Crow," called Coyote, "that wasn't much. You can sing better than that. Sing a good song for me, Chief. I want to hear you sing loud."

Crow was pleased again. So he opened his mouth wide and called from the cliff in a loud voice, "C-a-a-w!"

Of course the ball of deer fat fell down from Crow's open mouth.

Coyote grabbed it quickly. Then he laughed.

"You are not a wise chief," said Coyote. "You are not a chief at all. I called you 'Chief' just to fool you. I wanted your deer fat. I am hungry. Now you can go hungry because of your foolishness."

HOW COYOTE

BROUGHT FIRE

TO THE PEOPLE

Like other myth-making peoples, Indians of the Pacific Northwest told many stories about the origin of fire. One of these has already been presented in this volume under the title "The Bridge of the Gods." "Beaver and the Grande Ronde River," "The Origin of Mount Si and the Forests," "The Changer Comes to the Lummi," and "How Raven Helped the Ancient People" are other examples. The two which follow are representative of the patterns most frequently found in the fire myths of the region. The first was known all the way from the Karok along the Klamath River in northern California to the Plateau tribes of northern Washington.

At the beginning of the world, people had no fire. The only fire anywhere was on the top of a high mountain, guarded by evil spirits, or skookums. The skookums would not give any of their fire to the animal people. They were afraid that if people should become comfortable, they might become powerful—as powerful as the spirits.

So the people had no heat in their lodges, and they had to eat their salmon raw. When Coyote came among them, he found them cold and miserable.

"Coyote," they begged, "bring us fire from the mountains, or we will die from the cold."

"I will see what I can do for you," Coyote promised.

When the new sun came up, Coyote began the long climb to the snow-covered top of the mountain. There he found that three old, wrinkled skookums watched the fire all day and all night, one at a time. While one guarded, the others stayed in a lodge near by. When it became another's turn to watch, the one at the fire would come to the door and say, "Sister, sister, get up and guard the fire."

At dawn, when the air was chilly, the new guard was slow in coming from the lodge. "This is my time to steal a brand of the fire," Coyote said to himself. But he knew that he would be chased by the three skookums. They were old, but they were very swift runners. How could he get away from them?

Though Coyote was very wise, he could not think of a good plan. So he decided to ask his three sisters who lived in his stomach in the form of huckleberries. They were very wise. They could tell him what to do.

But at first his sisters in the form of huckleberries would not help him. "If we tell you," they said to Coyote, "you will say that you knew that yourself."

Coyote remembered that his sisters did not like hail. So he looked up into the sky and called out, "Hail! Hail! Fall down from the sky."

His sisters were afraid and cried, "Stop! Stop! Don't bring the hail. Don't bring the hail. We will tell you whatever you need to know."

Then his three sisters told him how he could get a brand of fire from the three skookums and how he could bring it down the mountain to the people.

When they had finished talking, Coyote said, "Yes, my sisters. That is what I thought. That was my plan all the time."

When Coyote had come down from the skookums' fire, he called all the animals together, just as his sisters had directed. He told each animal —Cougar and Fox and Squirrel and others—to take a certain place along the mountainside. Each place was in a line between the people's lodges and the fire guarded by the skookums.

Then he climbed the mountain again and waited for the sun to come up. The skookum guarding the fire saw him, but she thought him just an ordinary animal skulking around the lodge.

At dawn, Coyote saw the skookum leave the fire and heard her call, "Sister, sister, get up and guard the fire."

As she went inside the lodge, Coyote sprang forth and seized a burning brand from the fire. Down across the snow fields he ran. In an instant the three skookums were following him, showering ice and snow upon him as they ran. He leaped across the huge cracks in the ice, but soon he could hear the skookums behind him. Their hot breath scorched the fur on his flanks. One of them seized the tip of his tail in her claw, and it turned black. Ever since then, coyotes' tails have been tipped with black.

Panting and hot, Coyote reached the tree line and sank to the ground, tired and out of breath. There Cougar jumped from his hiding place behind some little fir trees. He seized the burning brand and ran down through the scrubby trees and the rocks. When he came to the taller trees, Cougar passed the fire to Fox. Fox ran with it until he came to the thick underbrush.

Then Squirrel seized the hot brand and leaped from tree to tree. The fire was still so hot that it burned a black spot on the back of Squirrel's neck and made his tail curl up. You can see the black spot and the curled tail on squirrels, even today. The skookums, still chasing the fire, hoped to catch Squirrel at the edge of the forest.

But under the last tree, Antelope was waiting to run with the brand across the meadow. Antelope was the fastest of all the animals. One after another, the animals carried the fire. All hoped the skookums would soon be tired out.

At last, when only a coal was left, it was given to squatty little Frog. Squatty little Frog swallowed the hot coal and hopped away as fast as he could hop. The youngest skookum, though she was very tired, was sure she could catch Frog. She seized his tail, and held tight. But Frog did not stop. He made the biggest jump he had ever made. And he left his tail behind him in the skookum's claws. Ever since, frogs have had no tails.

Still Frog did not stop. He made a long, deep dive into a river and came up on the other side. But the skookum leaped across. A second time she caught up with Frog. He was too tired to jump again. To save the fire, he spat it out of his mouth on Wood, and Wood swallowed it. The other two skookums joined their sister. All three stood by, helpless, not knowing how to take the fire away from Wood. Slowly they went back to their lodge on top of the mountain.

Then Coyote came to the place where the fire was, and the people came close, too. Coyote was very wise. He knew how to bring fire out of Wood. He showed the people how to rub two dry sticks together until sparks came. He showed them how to use the sparks to make chips and pine needles burn. And then he showed them how to make a bigger fire from the burning chips and pine needles.

Ever after that, the people knew how to use fire. With fire they cooked their food, and with fire they heated their houses.

HOW BEAVER

STOLE THE FIRE

This fire myth is given in the words of Clara Moore, transcribed from a wire recording made in June, 1950. Now a great-grandmother, she first heard it from her Sanpoil great-uncle. In other variants, some other "little fellow" shoots the arrows—Woodpecker or Boy Sapsucker or Wren.

In the early days of the animal people, there was no fire on the earth. The people ate their food raw or cooked it by the heat of the sun. They had no fire in their tepees.

"There is fire up in the sky," Eagle said one day. "Let us go up to the sky and get it."

So the animal people had a big gathering. They came from all over the country.

"We must have a war dance before we go," someone said. "Someone sing a song that we can dance to."

So different ones would sing.

"Oh, that isn't good enough," someone would say. "We can't dance to that."

Magpie sang his song. It wasn't good enough. Mr. Crow sang his song. That wasn't good enough. They couldn't dance to that. Wolf sang his song, but it wasn't good enough. Then the people called on Grizzly Bear to sing his song.

"Oh, that is too ugly! We can't dance to that."

The people kept on singing until it was Coyote's turn to sing his song. It was a good enough song, but the people didn't like it.

"It's good enough," they said, "but we can never depend on Coyote. He doesn't know what he is doing. He is liable to do anything and lose out anyway.

"There are two little fellows who haven't sung yet—Mr. Bat and Mr. Chickadee—two little fellows."

So they called on them. They called on Mr. Chickadee, but his song wasn't good enough. Then they called on Mr. Bat.

"Oh, I can't sing any song."

"But you've got to sing." They kept after him.

"All right. I'll try."

So he started out with his song. When he had finished, all the people holloed, "That's the song we want! Sing it again."

So they jumped up and war danced to Mr. Bat's song.

"Now we'll have to fix a road to get up into heaven."

Of course they all had bows and arrows. "We'll have to try to make a road of arrows to climb up on."

They tried and tried and tried to make a road. The big animals used all their arrows, but they couldn't reach the sky. So they came to Mr. Bat and Mr. Chickadee again.

The big animals laughed when Mr. Chickadee stepped up with his bow and arrow. He took aim and shot carefully. All the people watched. His arrow reached the sky and stuck there. He shot another arrow. It stuck in the first arrow and stayed there. He shot a third arrow, and it stayed in the second arrow. He kept on shooting. When he had emptied his two bags of arrows, the chain reached almost to the ground. He used other people's arrows to finish the road.

Then they climbed up to heaven to steal fire and bring it down to earth. Grizzly Bear was the last one to start up the arrow road.

"I must take a bag of food with me," he said. "There may not be any food up there."

So Grizzly Bear started up the arrow road with a big bag of food. But he was so heavy that he broke the ladder and fell flat on the ground. Grizzly Bear had to stay at home.

When all the other people got up in the sky, Mr. Eagle was boss. He was the one who had the idea of getting the fire and bringing it down here. Like all bosses, he stayed behind, and he sent his peepers out, to look around. It was night when the people got up there.

"Who's going to see about the fire?" asked Eagle.

Then he sent people out in pairs. Dog and Frog were partners. They were too lazy to look. They lay and lay, and lay and lay, and of course didn't find anything. Then they went back.

"We didn't see anything," they said.

Eagle got tired and disgusted. "We've got to do better than that. I'll go myself. Beaver, you come along with me."

"All right."

Beaver traveled on water, and Eagle flew overhead. He got on a big tree close to the Sky People's houses. Beaver swam down the river to a trap. He went into the trap and played dead.

Early next morning, a man went down to see what was in his trap. "Oh, there's a fine beaver dead here!" So he took it up to the chief's house.

"See this beaver," he said. "Isn't this a nice, soft fur? I'm going to skin him right away."

Eagle was up in a cottonwood tree looking down. He moved, and some men saw him. "Oh, what a pretty bird! We've got to get that bird. We must kill it so that we can have its feathers for a headdress."

The men went to their lodges to get their bows and arrows.

The man with Beaver took him into the chief's house. That's the house the fire was in—where they took Beaver. Soon they had him almost skinned. Beaver was afraid they were going to take his hide entirely off. If they took it off, then he couldn't put it back on again.

Outside the house, Eagle was scared that the men were going to hit him. Their arrows were coming close. Just as Beaver's skin was all off except around his jaws, the men outside called out, "Come on and shoot. See who can hit him. Eagle's going to fly away soon."

The man skinning Beaver heard them hollo. He ran out with his knife in his hand. Mr. Beaver jumped up, rolled over and over in his hide, and got it back on him, just as good as it ever was. He took the fire, stuck it under his fingernails, and rushed to the river. Everybody was looking at Eagle, 'way up there in the air. No one saw Beaver until he was almost in the water.

Eagle saw his partner come out of the house. He kept on dodging the arrows shot by many people until he saw Beaver going into the river. Then he flew away. "Oh, we have missed Eagle," the Sky People holloed. "We have missed Eagle."

The man who had been skinning Beaver ran back into the house. Beaver was gone. Fire was gone too. "Oh, we've lost our fire," he holloed. "Our fire is gone."

Eagle and Beaver rushed back to their people. They were gathered near the top of the arrow road.

"We have the fire," said Eagle. "Let us get down before the Sky People get here."

"The ladder is broken," the people told him. "Grizzly Bear and his bag of food were too heavy for it."

"The birds can fly down," said Eagle, who was the boss. "The little animals can ride down on the big birds' backs. The rest of you get down the best way you can."

So the little animals rode down on the big birds' backs. Coyote made his powers and turned himself into a pine needle and floated down. But soon the pine needle was going very fast, too fast to suit Coyote. So Coyote made his powers again and changed himself into a leaf. Then he floated down slowly. He made a nice landing.

But Sucker did not. He jumped from the last arrow, where Grizzly Bear had broken them. Sucker landed on a rock, face first, and flattened his mouth. Suckers have flat mouths to this day, and so have to suck their food.

When all the people had reached the earth, they had a big gathering at the place where they had war danced to Mr. Bat's song.

"Who has the fire?" they asked. All looked at Mr. Eagle.

"*I* don't have the fire," sang Mr. Eagle.

"*We* don't have the fire," sang Magpie and Crow.

"*We* don't have the fire," sang Chickadee and Bat.

They all sang with their hands spread out, open. Then Beaver stepped out in front. He spread his hands out, wide open, and began this song.

"I am holding what we went after. I am holding what we went after."

But no one could see anything in his hands. His daughters went up to him and looked at his fingers. His oldest daughter looked at his first finger, but there was no fire there. Beaver kept on singing, "I am holding what we went after. I am holding what we went after."

His second daughter looked at his second finger, but there was no fire there.

"I am holding what we went after," sang Beaver.

His older daughter looked at his third finger, and there found some fire hidden in his double fingernails. His second daughter looked at his fourth finger and found some fire hidden in his double fingernails.

Beaver stored the fire in the wood of many trees. What Beaver brought down from the sky is still with us. Fire is in every tree. Whenever we want fire, we can get it from wood.

COYOTE AND EAGLE
VISIT THE LAND
OF THE DEAD

Like other early peoples, most of the tribes of the Pacific Northwest whose tales have been recorded have done some philosophizing on the subject of death. Several tribes have handed down myths about the origin of death. Several have presented arguments, usually dramatized, over whether death should be temporary or permanent. In a Wishram myth, Eagle and Coyote go to the World of the Spirits to bring back their wives, very much as Orpheus of Greek mythology went to Hades to bring back his Eurydice. As Orpheus was warned, when leaving, not to turn round to look at her, so Eagle and Coyote were warned, "You shall not look in any direction."

The two myths about death which follow were recorded on the Yakima reservation in the 1870's by Dr. G. B. Kuykendall.

In the days of the animal people, Coyote was sad because people died and went away to the land of the spirits. All around him was the sound of mourning. He wondered and wondered how he could bring the dead back to the land of the living.

Coyote's sister had died. Some of his friends had died. Eagle's wife had died and Eagle was mourning for her. To comfort him Coyote said, "The dead shall not remain forever in the land of the dead. They are like the leaves that fall, brown and dead, in the autumn. They shall come back again. When the grass grows and the birds sing, when the leaf buds open and the flowers bloom, the dead shall come back again."

But Eagle did not want to wait until spring. He thought that the dead should be brought back without any delay. So Coyote and Eagle started out together to the land of the dead, Eagle flying along over Coyote's head. After several days they came to a big body of water, on the other side of which were a great many houses.

"Bring a boat and take us across the water!" shouted Coyote.

But there was no answer—no sound and no movement.

"There is no one there," said Eagle. "We have come all the way for nothing."

"They are asleep," explained Coyote. "The dead sleep during the day and come out at night. We will wait here until dark."

After sunset, Coyote began to sing. In a short time, four spirit men came out of the houses, got into a boat, and started toward Coyote and

Eagle. Coyote kept on singing, and soon the spirits joined him, keeping time with their paddles. But the boat moved without them. It skimmed over the water by itself.

When the spirits reached the shore, Eagle and Coyote stepped into the boat and started back with them. As they drew near the island of the dead, the sound of drums and of dancing met them across the water.

"Do not go into the house," warned the spirits as they were landing. "Do not look at the things around you. Keep your eyes closed, for this is a sacred place."

"But we are hungry and cold. Do let us go in," begged Eagle and Coyote.

So they were allowed to go into a large lodge made of tule mats, where the spirits were dancing and singing to the beating of the drums. An old woman brought to them some seal oil in a basket bottle. Dipping a feather into it, she fed them from the oil until their hunger was gone.

Then Eagle and Coyote looked around. Inside the lodge everything was beautiful, and there were many spirits. They were dressed in ceremonial robes, beautifully decorated with shells and with elks' teeth. Their faces were painted, and they wore feathers in their hair. The moon, hanging from above, filled the big lodge with light. Near the moon stood Frog, who has watched over it ever since he jumped into it long ago. He saw to it that the moon shone brightly on the crowd of dancers and singers.

Eagle and Coyote knew some of the spirits as their former friends, but no one paid any attention to the two strangers. No one saw the basket which Coyote had brought with him. In this basket he planned to carry the spirits back to the land of the living.

Early in the morning, the spirits left the lodge for their day of sleep. Then Coyote killed Frog, took his clothes, and put them on himself. At twilight the spirits returned and began again a night of singing and dancing. They did not know that Coyote, in Frog's clothing, stood beside the moon.

When the dancing and singing were at their gayest, Coyote swallowed the moon. In the darkness, Eagle caught the spirit people, put them into Coyote's basket, and closed the lid tight. Then the two started back to the land of the living, Coyote carrying the basket.

After traveling a great distance, they heard noises in the basket and stopped to listen.

"The people are coming to life," said Coyote.

After they had gone a little farther, they heard voices talking in the basket. The spirits were complaining.

"We are being bumped and banged around," groaned some.

"My leg is being hurt," groaned one spirit.

"My legs and arms are cramped," groaned another.

"Open the lid and let us out!" called several spirits together.

Coyote was tired, for the basket was getting heavier and heavier. The spirits were turning back into people.

"Let's let them out," said Coyote.

"No, no," answered Eagle quickly.

A little later, Coyote set the basket down. It was too heavy for him.

"Let's let them out," repeated Coyote. "We are so far from the spirit land now that they won't return."

So he opened the basket. The people took their spirit forms and, moving like the wind, went back to the island of the dead.

Eagle scolded at first, but soon he remembered Coyote's earlier thought. "It is now autumn. The leaves are falling, just as people die. Let us wait until spring. When the buds open and the flowers bloom, let us return to the land of the dead and try again."

"No," replied Coyote. "I am tired. Let the dead stay in the land of the dead forever and forever."

So Coyote made the law that after people have died they shall never come to life again. If he had not opened the basket and let the spirits out, the dead would have come to life every spring as the grass and flowers and trees do.

MEMALOOSE ISLAND,

THE ISLAND

OF THE DEAD

Memaloose Island, in the lower Columbia, was for many generations, perhaps for centuries, an Indian burial place. When it was learned that the backwater from the Bonneville Dam would submerge the island, the bones were removed and placed in other burial places along the river.

When passing Memaloose Island and other cemeteries, the Indians used to steer their canoes as far away as possible and to remain silent or speak only in whispers. The spirits of the dead were thought to dwell in those places.

Long ago, a young warrior and a beautiful maiden were deeply in love and very happy. But sickness came to the warrior. He died, and his spirit went to the land of spirits. There he mourned for the girl, and she mourned for him in the earth world. A few nights after his death, a spirit from the land of the dead came to her in a dream and spoke to her.

"Your lover is longing for you," said the voice of the spirit. "Even though he is in the beautiful land of the spirits, he is unhappy without you. He cannot be happy again unless you come to him."

The girl was so troubled by the dream that she told her parents. They too were troubled and did not know what she should do. The next night, and again a third night, the spirit spoke to the girl in a dream. After the third vision, her parents decided that they would send their daughter to her lover, lest some harm come to them from the land of the spirits.

So in their canoe they took the girl down the river to the island where all the dead are gathered in the happy spirit land. Darkness was falling as they drew near. From the island came the sound of drums and of spirits singing as they danced to the music. Through the twilight haze, lights gleamed on the island.

Four spirits met the family at the shore, helped the girl out of the canoe, and told her parents to return to their home among the living. The spirits guided the girl to a great dance house, a large lodge made of tule mats. There she saw her lover, more handsome and noble looking than he had been on earth and dressed with the richness found only in the land of the spirits.

All night the singing and dancing continued, and the young couple were among the happiest of the dancers. When dawn began to break and the first bird songs were heard, the spirits went to their rest. Spirits sleep during the day and are active during the night. The maiden also closed her eyes on the joyful spirit world and went to sleep.

But, unlike the spirits, she did not sleep soundly. When the sun was high above her, she awoke and looked around. Beside her lay a skeleton— the skeleton of her lover. His skull, with hollow eyes and grinning teeth, was turned toward her. All around her were skeletons and skulls. The air was filled with the smell of death, for the beautiful spirits of the night hours had become bones.

With a scream, the girl sprang from her bed and ran to the shore. After a little search she found a canoe and rapidly paddled back to her home village. But her family and friends were alarmed. They feared that the spirits would be offended by her leaving their land and that they would punish the village.

"You have done wrong to the spirit people," they told her. "You should have slept all day, as they do. You must go back to your lover, for he has claimed you."

So the maiden returned to the island that evening and again joined her lover at the dancing lodge. He was again a handsome and happy spirit. Next day, and every day after that, she slept until evening. When darkness came, she went forth to be happy with all the spirits during the night.

In course of time a child was born to her, a child of unusual beauty, half human and half spirit. The young father was so eager for his mother on the earth to see the baby that he decided to send for her. He found a spirit messenger and gave him this message:

"Tell my mother that we are very happy in the spirit land and that we have a beautiful baby. We want her to see him. Ask her to come back with you. Then the baby and his mother will return home with her to the land of the living. I will soon follow, taking with me all the dead people so that they may live on earth again."

The message made the grandmother happy, and she gladly went to the island of the dead. Her son welcomed her but warned her that she could not see the baby yet.

"Not for ten days can you see him."

The grandmother waited patiently at first. But the longer she waited, the more eager she was to see her grandchild. After a few days she decided that she would peep at him. It would do no harm to anyone, she thought, if she should lift up the cloth covering the baby board and take one glance.

She lifted the cloth and saw the sleeping child. The punishment came swiftly, for the baby sickened and died. The spirit people were so displeased that they have never since permitted the dead to return to the living.

The grandmother was sent back to her village and never heard of the young couple again.

THE MORTAL
WHO MARRIED
A MERMAN

This folk tale of the Oregon coast has some interesting parallels with an old Danish tale that Matthew Arnold retold in his poem "A Forsaken Merman."

Many years ago, in a village on the Oregon coast, a girl lived with her five brothers. Several young men asked to marry her, but she was not willing to marry any of them. Her brothers chose a young man for her, but she told them she did not want any husband.

She liked to be alone, and every day she went swimming by herself in a little creek near the village. One evening as she was returning home from swimming, a man suddenly appeared and walked beside her.

"I live in a village in the bottom of the sea," the strange man told her.

"I have been watching you for many days. Will you return with me and be my wife?"

"Oh, no," answered the girl. "I cannot go so far away that I would never see my brothers again."

"I will let you see your brothers," the man promised. "You may come back to visit them. You will not be far away."

"I will go with you if I may come back."

"Hang onto my belt," he said. "And close your eyes tight."

She did so, and down, down, down they went into the sea. At the bottom of the ocean she found that her husband was one of five sons of the chief of the village. In the village lived many Indians. There the girl lived, contented and happy for several years.

She and the man of the sea had a child. As soon as the boy became big enough, the mother taught him to shoot with bow and arrows, which she made for him. Often she said to him, "Up on the land above us, you have five uncles. They have many arrows, much better than the ones I can make down here."

One day the little boy said to her, "Let us go up to the land people and get some arrows from my uncles."

"We will ask your father," she replied.

The father would not let both of them go, but he finally let the mother make the journey alone. Early the next morning she put on the skins of five sea otters and started out. When she came out of the water, her brothers saw her and thought she was a real otter. They shot at her and hit her again and again, with their bows and arrows. Again and again she came to the surface, without any arrows sticking in her fur.

The brothers were puzzled. Up and down, up and down, near the beach, the otter swam, followed by many people in canoes. Many shot at her, but no one harmed her. They could not understand what became of the arrows. None of them stuck in the otter's fur.

At last all the people gave up except the oldest brother. He followed when the otter turned in toward the beach. Soon he saw someone moving around close to the shore. When he came nearer, he saw it was a woman. A little closer, he saw that the woman was his lost sister.

"I am the sea otter," she told him. "I came up here to get some arrows for my little boy."

And she showed her brother all the arrows that had been shot at her. Then she told him about her husband and their home in the bottom of the sea. She told him all about their little son.

"We live not far from here," she said. "Whenever the tide is low, you can see our house right in the middle of the ocean. I brought you these five otter skins to trade for some other things."

Her brothers gave her as many arrows as she could carry, and she got ready to return to her husband and her little boy. Just as she was leaving, she said, "Tomorrow morning on the beach in front of your landing place, you will find a whale."

On the next day the whale was on the beach. The brothers divided it among all the people of their village.

A few moons later, the woman came again to the beach village, bringing her husband and child with her. This time the brothers noticed that her shoulders were turning into the shoulders of a dark-colored sea serpent. Long after she and her family had returned to the ocean village, a large number of sea serpents came near the beach. But the woman did not come ashore a third time. She was never seen again.

The sea serpents had come after arrows. The five brothers shot at them the arrows they wished. They never came back. But every summer and winter for a long, long time, they put two whales ashore as a gift to their kinsmen above the sea.

THE MAIDEN OF
DECEPTION PASS

Deception Pass is a narrow, high-walled gorge between Whidbey and Fidalgo islands in Puget Sound. It was named by Captain George Vancouver in 1792 when he learned that it did not lead to a closed harbor. The tidewater rushing through the channel makes navigation difficult even for motor boats today.

The story of the maiden of Deception Pass is represented on the Samish side of the base of the totem pole on the Swinomish Reservation. Alexis Edge, one of the carvers of the pole, said (in 1952) that the Indians who once lived on the islands had no trouble bucking the swift current if they would think about the maiden; if they did not keep their minds on her, their canoes would get caught in the whirlpool and they would sink. Sometimes they saw the girl come up from the water; with her hands on her hips she would wade around in the current behind the canoes.

In the days that are gone, the Samish Indians lived near the narrow channel now called Deception Pass. Most of their food came from the sea, where they usually found plenty of clams, crabs, mussels, and salmon.

One day, a group of maidens was on the beach gathering some of the shellfish. In the group was a very pretty girl. Once, a clam she had in her hand slipped from her grasp, and she followed it into the water. Again and again it slipped from her, and she went out farther and farther until she was in water up to her waist.

Then she realized that a hand was grasping her hand. When she screamed with fright, a voice coming from the water said softly, "Do not be afraid. I will not harm you. I only want to look at your beauty."

Soon the speaker let go her hand, and she went back to her home. Again and again she had the same experience. She would be drawn into the water, a hand she could not see would hold her hand, and a voice would say loving things to her. The voice told her about the beautiful world at the bottom of the sea, about the beautiful plants and the colored fishes which she could never see from the earth. Each time, the hand held hers a little longer, and the voice spoke to her a little longer.

One day a young man rose from the water. He went with her and asked her father if he might marry her.

"Oh, no," said the father. "My daughter cannot live in the sea."

The young man told the girl's father about the beautiful world at the bottom of the ocean, but the father would not say yes.

"You will be sorry," warned the young man. "If your daughter cannot be my wife, I will see to it that you and your people cannot get sea food. Then you will be very hungry."

Still the father would not let his daughter marry the young man.

In a short time, shellfish became scarce. Then salmon became scarce. Then the streams flowing into the salt sea dried up, and the people could get no fresh-water fish. Soon the springs dried up, and the people had no water to drink.

Then the maiden went to the beach and out into the water. There she called to the young man. "Let my people have some food," she begged. "And let them have water to drink."

"Not until your father will let you marry me," replied the young man of the sea. "Not until you are my wife will there be plenty of food in the waters again."

So to keep his people from dying of hunger and thirst, her father at last gave in. He asked one thing of the young man from the sea: "Let my daughter return to us once each year. Let us see that she is happy with you."

The young man was willing to do as the father asked, and so the maiden walked out into the bay. The people on the beach watched until she disappeared from sight. The last they saw of her was her long hair floating on the surface of the water.

Soon water returned to the streams. The shellfish and the salmon returned to the sea. The Samish people were well fed. True to his promise, the man of the sea let his wife go back each year to visit her people. Four years she came. And before each visit, the fish were more plentiful than ever before.

Each time, the people saw a change in her. First they noticed that barnacles were growing on her hands, then on her arms. On her fourth visit, they saw that barnacles had begun to grow on one side of her beautiful face, and that she seemed unhappy when she was out of the water. A chill wind came from her whenever she walked among them.

The people talked among themselves and then gently said to her, "We release your husband from his promise. If it makes you unhappy to leave the sea, you need not visit us each year. Do not come unless you wish to come."

And so the woman did not come again from the water. But always she was the guardian of her people. Because of her they always had plenty of sea food and plenty of pure water in the springs and streams. Her people could see that she was watching over them. As the tide passed back and forth through Deception Pass, they could see her long hair drifting on the surface of the water. They knew that the maiden of the sea was watching over her people.

THE MAIDEN

SACRIFICED TO WINTER

A winter colder and harder than any before came to the land of the Chinook people. Snow lay on the level as deep as half a man's height. The time for spring came, but the snow did not melt. Ice floated down the river in huge masses, grinding and crashing. Every night more snow fell, filling up places the wind had swept clean. Snowbirds were everywhere.

One day a bird flew over with something red in its bill. The people so frightened it that it dropped the red thing—a ripe strawberry. Then they knew that somewhere not far away spring had come. Around them it was still winter. The earth was frozen.

Something was wrong. So the chief of the village called a meeting at his lodge. All the people came. The old men asked each other, "Why does the winter not end? What can we do to end it?"

After much talk, the oldest man in the village arose and spoke. "Our grandfathers used to say that if a bird should be struck by a stone, the snow would never stop falling. Perhaps some child has stoned a bird."

The headman asked that all the children be brought in before the council. When they came, they were questioned one by one. Each child spoke for himself. Every mother was in fear, lest her child be the guilty person. One by one, the children said they had not struck any bird. Some of them pointed to a little girl. "She did it."

"You ask your daughter if the children speak the truth," the old men of the council said to her father and mother.

In terror the little girl answered that she had struck a bird with a stone.

The chief men of the village sat in council for a long time. The child and her parents waited, trembling.

Slowly the chief arose. "Give us your child. We will not kill her as we first thought we would do. Instead, we will give her to Winter. Then he will cease to be angry, and Summer will come."

The hearts of the little girl's father and mother were sad and heavy. This was their only child. But they realized that the wise men of the village knew best, and that the good of all was more important than the life of their little one. Many people brought them gifts in payment for the child, but their hearts were not lightened. As the headmen led her away, her father and mother cried aloud. They mourned for her as if for the dead.

Some young men were sent to the river to get a large block of ice. The headmen would place the maiden on it and thus give her to Winter. Finding a large piece in an eddy in the river, they pulled it to shore.

While the young men did that, all the other people dressed in their finest clothes, as if for the winter dances. The little girl was dressed best of all. Then the headmen led her to the river, and all the people followed.

At the water's edge they spread a thick layer of straw on the block of ice, and over that a covering of many tule mats. They placed the girl on the ice and pushed it out into the swift current. Swirling with the rise and fall of the water, the ice block drifted down the river. The crying of the child and the wailing of the parents could be heard above the noise of the water and the crashing of the ice. When child and ice block were out of sight, the people returned to their lodges, chanting.

Very soon they felt a warm wind. In a few days the snow had gone. Then the people knew that the old men of years gone by had spoken the truth.

When spring came, the people moved to their fishing place, to catch and dry the salmon. In the fall they went back to their winter village. Snow and ice came again. One day some old men stood by the riverbank watching the ice drift by. Far down the stream, as far as their eyes could see, a block of ice swirled round and round in an eddy. On the ice was a black spot.

The headmen of the village sent a young man out to look at it. "It looks like a body!" he called back as he drew near the ice block. The people who were watching brought long poles and drew the ice to the shore. On it was a young girl—the one who had been sacrificed as an offering to Winter.

The people lifted her up and carried her to the lodge of her father and mother. Wrapped in warm furs, she fell asleep by the fire.

Ever after that, she was able to walk barefoot on ice and snow. People thought she had special power. They called her *Wah-kah-nee*, meaning "She drifts."

LEGEND OF

THE WHITE DEER

In the early days of southwestern Oregon, the Colvig family, who had come west in a covered wagon, settled on land along the South Umpqua River. Near them was a small village of Umpqua Indians. One day, one of the white men killed and brought home a most unusual animal—a snow-white deer. When an old Indian neighbor saw it, he was distressed. "The man who killed that has a bad heart," he told the white family.

"Why?" they asked. (Both groups spoke in Chinook.)

"Because that deer is the angel of the Great White Spirit," said the old man, pointing toward the sky. Then he explained by telling this legend.

A long time ago, a dreadful sickness spread throughout the Umpqua tribe. Many of the people died. Few who had the illness lived. For many days and nights the sad death chant was heard in the tepees. Both young and old, hundreds of them, slept their last sleep.

At last the medicine men of the tribe decided what should be done. "We will leave our village," they told their people. "We will go up to the top of the Big Mountains. There we will be nearer the Great Spirit, and he will hear our prayers and our cries."

So the people took up their tepees and climbed to the top of the Big Mountains. The Big Water is just beyond the mountains. There in a mountain meadow they put up their tepees. But the death sickness followed them. It looked as if the whole tribe would be wiped out.

Then Teola, the chief's daughter, became ill with the death illness. Teola was loved by all her people. She was tall and straight as the arrowwood and as graceful as the willow tree. She was called the Little Mother of the Umpqua. All of her people grieved when the dreadful sickness touched her.

One dark night they thought that Teola would die. Around the fire in front of her tepee, the men of the tribe sat with their heads bowed and their hands clasped before them. Inside the tepee, the women chanted the death song as they marched round the bed of the dying girl.

Then a strange thing happened. A deer, white as snow, came out of the dark forest beyond the fire. Unafraid, it walked across the meadow to the people near Teola's tepee. Silent, wondering, the men watched the deer walk round the tepee three times. Each time it looked in at the dying girl.

The third time, the white deer entered the tepee, and the girl stretched out her hand toward it. The deer came close to her, kissed her lips, and then walked off into the darkness.

As soon as the white deer had gone, Teola rose from her bed and walked among her people. "I am well! I am well!" she called to them. "The angel of the Great White Spirit has kissed away my sickness!"

Since that time, my people, the Umpqua, have never killed a white deer. The white deer is sacred, to be protected and loved.

THE COMING

OF THE

WHITE PEOPLE

This prophecy of the coming of the white people was a tradition of the Wasco, who lived along the Columbia River near The Dalles. On the Warm Springs Reservation, Walter Miller's father used to tell about Coyote's prophecy of the coming of a different race of people. They would be pale and would have iron birds that could fly. The following narrative was recorded by Jeremiah Curtin many years ago.

A long time ago my people at the Cascades learned that white men would come. One old man, I believe, learned of it at night. He dreamed. He saw strange people, and they spoke to him and showed him strange things. And he heard something that sounded like Indian songs.

In the morning he spoke to all the people. And then everybody gathered to hear him—old men, men, women, and children—everybody. He told them what he had seen in his sleep at night. The people were glad. They danced every day and every night, they were so glad because of his story.

"Soon all sorts of strange things will come," the old man said. "No longer will things be as before. No longer will we use these things of ours. Strange people will bring to us everything strange. They will bring to us something—if you just point it at anything moving, that thing will fall down and die."

As it turned out, it was a gun he spoke of.

"They will bring us a bucket to boil things in. No longer will we use stone buckets."

As it turned out, they really brought to us what he spoke of.

"No longer will you make fire by drilling with sticks as before."

Still more were the people glad. They danced with vigor.

"Certain small pieces of wood will be brought to us. We will make a fire with them."

As it turned out, it was matches he spoke of. The people danced with more vigor. For days and nights they danced. They were not at all hungry. Truly they did their best in dancing. They saw everything he spoke of—ax, hatchet, knife, stove.

"Strange people will bring us these things. White people with hair on their faces will come from the rising sun. You people must be careful."

Then my people would jump up and down. They danced their best.

And truly things are just so today, even as the old man dreamed. White people soon brought these things to the people living along the river.

THE FIRST SHIP

Indians told explorers and early settlers in Oregon about several shipwrecks and landings which seem to have occurred a generation or two before Captain Robert Gray discovered the Columbia River in 1792. The Indian traditions are supported by these facts, among others: in 1806, Lewis and Clark found near the mouth of the river an Indian with freckles and reddish hair, and they saw beeswax in the hands of natives; in 1811, Gabriel Franchère talked with an old man near the Cascades who said that his father, a Spaniard, had been wrecked at the mouth of the river; several tons of beeswax, including a few tapers, have been found buried along the Oregon coast. The following Chinook tradition was recorded in 1894.

An old woman in a Clatsop village near the mouth of Big River mourned because of the death of her son. For a year she grieved. One day she ceased her wailing and took a walk along the beach where she had often gone in happier days.

As she returned to the village, she saw a strange something out in the water not far from shore. At first she thought it was a whale. When she came nearer, she saw two spruce trees standing upright on it.

"It is not a whale," she said to herself. "It is a monster."

When she came near the strange thing that lay at the edge of the water, she saw that its outside was covered with copper and that ropes were tied to the spruce trees. Then a bear came out of the strange thing and stood on it. He looked like a bear, but his face was the face of a human being.

"Oh, my son is dead," she wailed, "and now the thing we have heard about is on our shore."

The old woman returned to her village, weeping and wailing. People hearing her called to each other, "An old woman is crying. Someone must have struck her."

The men picked up their bows and arrows and rushed out to see what was the matter.

"Listen!" an old man said.

They heard the old woman wailing, "Oh, my son is dead, and the thing we have heard about is on our shore."

All the people ran to meet her. "What is it? Where is it?" they asked.

"Ah, the thing we have heard about in tales is lying over there." She pointed toward the south shore of the village. "There are two bears on it, or maybe they are people."

Then the Indians ran toward the thing that lay near the edge of the water. The two creatures on it held copper kettles in their hands. When the Clatsop arrived at the beach, the creatures put their hands to their mouths and asked for water.

Two of the Indians ran inland, hid behind a log awhile, and then ran back to the beach. One of them climbed up on the strange thing and entered it. He looked around inside it. He saw that it was full of boxes, and he found long strings of brass buttons.

When he went outside to call his relatives to see the inside of the thing, he found that they had already set fire to it. He jumped down and joined the two creatures and the Indians on shore.

The strange thing burned just like fat. Everything burned except the iron, the copper, and the brass. The Clatsop picked up all the pieces of metal. Then they took the two strange-looking men to their chief.

"I want to keep one of the men with me," said the chief.

Soon the people north of the river heard about the strange men and the strange thing, and they came to the Clatsop village. The Willapa came from across the river, the Chehalis and the Cowlitz from farther north, and even the Quinault from up the coast. And people from up the river came also—the Klickitat and others farther up.

The Clatsop sold the iron, brass, and copper. They traded one nail for a good deerskin. For a long necklace of shells they gave several nails. One man traded a piece of brass two fingers wide for a slave.

None of the Indians had ever seen iron and brass before. The Clatsop became rich selling the metals to the other tribes.

The two Clatsop chiefs kept the two men who came on the ship. One stayed at the village called Clatsop, and the other stayed at the village on the cape.

SOURCE NOTES

Oral sources have been indicated in the headnotes. The following references are to the printed and manuscript sources listed in the Bibliography.

I: MYTHS OF THE MOUNTAINS

The Spirits in Nature: Sampson and Whitney, p. 8; Boas (*b*); Wickersham; Silas Smith, p. 259; Parker, p. 476; Sapir (*a*); Stevens; Bruseth, p. 12; Alexander, pp. 132–138, 268–273; Cline, p. 133; Swan (*b*), p. 61; Eells (*b*), p. 672; (*d*), pp. 69–71. *Mount Shasta and the Grizzly Bears:* Miller, pp. 264–265, 272–276; Bancroft, pp. 91–93. *Mount Shasta and the Great Flood:* Dixon, p. 36. *The Chief's Face on Mount Hood:* Bushnell. *White Eagle:* McWhorter MSS, folder 1; for headnote: Crandall MS (*b*). *The Bridge of the Gods:* Crandall. *The River Spirit and the Mountain Demons:* Ranck. *Indian Names for Mount Rainier:* Seattle MS; Curtis, VII, 6; Evans (*b*), pp. 63–64; Flett, in Denman, p. 6; W. D. Lyman (*c*), pp. 377–378; Stanup; McWhorter, p. 28; Sicade (*a*), p. 252. *Mount Rainier and the Olympic Mountains:* (1) Waterman MS; (2) Meany (*b*); (3 and 4) Sicade (*a*). *Mount Rainier and the Great Flood:* W. D. Lyman (*a*), p. 53. *The Lake on Mount Rainier:* Ballard, pp. 143–144. *The Miser on Mount Rainier:* Winthrop, pp. 131–154. *The Origin of Mount Si and the Forests:* Hunt and Kaylor, pp. 515–516; for variant: Bertelson. *Kulshan and His Two Wives:* Buchanan (*b*); Stern, p. 112. *Mount Baker and the Great Flood:* Johnson, pp. 53–58. *Other Traditions of the Great Flood:* (3) Reagan and Walters, p. 322; (4) McWhorter MSS, folder 5; for headnote: Eells (*a*). *The Valley of Peace in the Olympics:* Semple. *The Seven Devils Mountains:* Maynard.

II: LEGENDS OF THE LAKES

Spirits and Animals in the Lakes: Wickersham, p. 350; Ballou, p. 455; Kuykendall, pp. 71, 75–76; Meany (*a*), pp. 127–128; oral traditions. *The Origin of Crater Lake:* Colvig MS (*a*). *The War between Lao and Skell:* O. C. Applegate; Moray Applegate letter. *Crater Lake and the Two Hunters:* Moray Applegate MS. *Another Crater Lake Legend:* Steel (*a*), pp. 15–17; (*b*), pp. 35–37. *The Elk Spirit of Lost Lake:* Roberts; Curtin (*a*), pp. 257–259. *The Demons in Spirit Lake:* Finke; Kane, pp. 199–200; *Wash. Guide,* p. 496; McKee, p. 207. *Kwatee and the Monster in Lake Quinault:* Reagan and Walters, p. 312. *The Origin of Lake Crescent:* Reagan and Walters, pp. 324–325. *Nahkeeta:* Morse, pp. 31–35: *Mason Lake and the Crying Loon:* Wickersham, p. 351. *The Lake*

on Vashon Island: Van Olinda, pp. 82–83. *The Lake and the Elk-Child:* Kuykendall, pp. 71–72. *The Monster and Lake Chelan:* (2) Andrews. *The Lakes of the
Grand Coulee:* (1) Steele and Rose, p. 1017; (2) Ray (*b*), p. 185; Scheffer letter;
(3) McWhorter MSS, folder 6. *Spokane Lake of Long Ago:* Durham, p. 645. *Chief
Joseph's Story of Wallowa Lake:* Waggoner, pp. 191–199.

III. TALES OF THE RIVERS, ROCKS, AND WATERFALLS

The Animal People of Long Ago: Bruseth, p. 12; Teit (*a*), pp. 65–82; (*b*),
pp. 176–177; Sapir (*b*), pp. 2–117; Goddard, pp. 135–141; Ray (*a*), p. 72; *Crea-
tion of the Animal People:* Teit (*a*), pp. 80–82; for part of headnote: Gunther, p.
289. *How Coyote Got His Special Power:* For variants mentioned in headnote:
Spier (*b*), pp. 199–200; Bancroft, p. 90. *Why Rivers Flow But One Way:* (1)
Haeberlin, p. 396; (2) Farrand, p. 111. *Coyote and the Monster of the Columbia:*
McWhorter MSS, folder 3; for variant: Kuykendall, pp. 75–76. *How Coyote
Helped the People:* Curtis, VIII, 107–116; Gill, p. 317; Jacobs (*a*), pp. 238–243;
Kuykendall, pp. 68, 79; Ray (*a*), pp. 71–75, and (*b*), pp. 157–171; Sapir (*b*), pp.
3–48; Teit (*a*), pp. 65–67. *The Origin of Willamette Falls:* (1) H. S. Lyman (*a*),
pp. 183–184. *Pillar Rock:* McClay; for headnote: Hines, p. 195; Wilkes, V, 120.
The Cave Monster of the Willamette Valley: Judson, pp. 116–117. *A Legend of
Multnomah Falls:* Susan Smith; Wells; Higginson. *Horsetail Falls and Beacon
Rock:* H. S. Lyman (*b*); Lapham, p. 41. *Latourell Falls and the Pillar of Hercules:*
Saylor; *Oregon,* p. 274. *Why the Columbia Sparkles:* Crandall MS (*b*); Curtin
(*a*), pp. 240, 302; Curtis, VIII, 145–146. *The Ever-watchful Eye:* Ranck; Curtis,
VII, 146; for headnote: Glassley, pp. 147–149. *The Painted Rocks at Naches Gap:*
McWhorter MSS, folders 5 and 6. *The Hee-Hee Stone:* Mourning Dove, pp. 193–
196; for variant: Ray (*b*), pp. 171–172. *The Origin of the Spokane River:* Durham, p. 645; Steele and Rose, p. 1001. *The Origin of Palouse Falls:* McGregor letter; for variant: Wilkes, IV, 466. *Beaver and the Grande Ronde River:* Packard,
pp. 327–329. *How Kwatee Made the River and Rocks:* For variants: Reagan and
Walters, pp. 307–308; Farrand and Mayer, pp. 253–254. *How Kwatee Changed
the World:* For variants: Andrade, pp. 82–85; Eells (*b*), pp. 680–681; Farrand
and Mayer, p. 251. *A Potlatch on the Oregon Coast:* Kronenberg; for part of
headnote: Hodge, Part 2, p. 298.

IV: MYTHS OF CREATION, THE SKY, AND THE STARS

Why and When the Tales Were Told: Shelton (*a*), pp. 3–4; (*b*), pp. 416 ff.;
Mrs. William Shelton (interview, Aug., 1950, Tulalip Reserv.); Buchanan (*a*);
Fiske, p. 21; Alexander, p. xviii; Williams (*a*), p. 115; (*b*), pp. 45–49; Kuyken-
dall, p. 72; Mourning Dove, pp. 10–11; Commons, p. 185; Jacobs (*b*), p. 51;
W. D. Lyman (*e*), p. 222; Gayley, p. xxxiii. *The Creation of the Klamath World:*
Gatschet, pp. lxxix–lxxxiv. *In the Beginning of the Modoc World:* Curtin (*b*), pp.
42–45. *The Origin of the Chinook Indians:* Eells (*c*), pp. 329–330; Swan (*a*),
p. 203. *In the Beginning of the Nisqually World:* Eells (*d*), pp. 74–77. *The Beginning and the End of the Okanogan World:* Ross, pp. 287–288. *Creation of the
Yakima World:* Mooney, pp. 722–723. *The Story of the Changer:* Curtis, IX,
117–121. Variants: Farrand and Mayer, pp. 264–266; Farrand, pp. 107–109;
Haeberlin, pp. 373–377. *The Changer Comes to the Lummi:* Lambert; Stern,

pp. 108–109. *Pushing up the Sky:* Shelton (*a*), pp. 11–12; (*b*), p. 417. *How Raven Helped the Ancient People:* W. D. Lyman (*e*), p. 232; for headnote: Andrade, pp. 27–31. *The Big Dipper and the Milky Way:* McWhorter MS, folder 3. *The Seven Sisters of the Sky:* Armstrong MS; for headnote: Clark (*a*). Variant: Wissler, p. 3. *Two Canoes in the Sky:* McWhorter MSS, folder 3. *The Origin of Cassiopeia's Chair:* Reagan and Walters, pp. 325–326. *The Northern Lights and Creatures of the Sky:* Swan (*b*), pp. 7–9, 87–91. *Thunderbird and Whale:* (2) Reagan and Walters, pp. 320–321. *Thunder and Lightning:* Sicade (*b*); for headnote: *Wash. Guide,* p. 383. *Thunder and His Son-in-Law:* Farrand, pp. 113–114. *The Battle with Snow:* Adamson, pp. 76–77. *The Chinook Wind:* Kuykendall, pp. 78–79; W. D. Lyman (*d*), pp. 24–28. *How Coyote Made the Indian Tribes:* Kuykendall, pp. 62–63; W. D. Lyman (*e*), pp. 227–229; for headnote: H. S. Lyman (*c*), pp. 104–107, and Wilkes, IV, 466.

V: MISCELLANEOUS MYTHS AND LEGENDS

Guardian Spirits: Interviews with John Hudson (Santiam), Clara Moore (Sanpoil), Peter Noyes (Colville), Rose Purdy (Skokomish), and Eneas Seymore (Lake); Boas (*b*); Cline, pp. 131–162; Gunther, pp. 289–291; Ray (*a*), p. 182; Swan (*b*), pp. 63–66. *The Hazelnut:* McWhorter MSS, folder 6. *The Origin of Guardian Spirits and of Sweat Lodge:* Ray (*b*), p. 132: for headnote: Alexander, p. xvi; Spier (*b*), pp. 41–42, 167, 193–194. *The Origin of the Potlatch:* Andrade, pp. 173–175; for headnote: Hodge, Part 2, p. 293, and Gunther, pp. 306–310. *Coyote and Crow:* McWhorter MSS, folder 1; for headnote: Mourning Dove, pp. 81–83. *How Coyote Brought Fire to the People:* Bancroft, pp. 115–117; H. S. Lyman (*c*), pp. 137–138; Kuykendall, pp. 73–74. *Coyote and Eagle Visit the Land of the Dead:* Kuykendall, pp. 80–81; for headnote: Sapir (*b*), pp. 107–117, and Gayley, pp. 165–168. *Memaloose Island:* Kuykendall, pp. 81–82. *The Mortal Who Married a Merman:* Frachtenberg and St. Clair; for headnote: Clark (*a*). *The Maiden of Deception Pass:* Sampson and Whitney, pp. 10–13. *The Maiden Sacrificed to Winter:* Curtis, VIII, 147–149; Curtin (*a*), pp. 244–245. *Legend of the White Deer:* Colvig MS (*b*). *The Coming of the White People:* Curtin (*a*), pp. 229–231. *The First Ship:* Boas (*a*), pp. 275–278; for headnote: Clarke, pp. 154–179. *Glossary:* Berreman; Hodge; *Idaho Guide;* W. D. Lyman (*c*); McArthur; Meany (*a*); *Oregon;* Phillips; Ray (*c*); Spier (*a*); *Wash. Guide.*

BIBLIOGRAPHY

PRINTED WORKS

(Abbreviations used: BAE—Bureau of American Ethnology; CUCA—Columbia University Contributions to Anthropology; JAFL—*Journal of American Folklore;* MAFS—Memoirs of the American Folklore Society; OHQ—*Oregon Historical Quarterly;* OTM—*Oregon Teachers Monthly;* UWPA—University of Washington Publications in Anthropology.

Adamson, Thelma. *Folk Tales of the Coast Salish,* MAFS, XXVII, 1934.

Alexander, Hartley B. *North American* (L. H. Gray, ed., *The Mythology of All Races,* Vol. X). Boston, 1916.

Andrade, M. J. *Quileute Texts,* CUCA, XII (1931).

Andrews, Clarence L. "A Chelan Legend," Seattle *Times,* December 21, 1895, p. 12.

Applegate, O. C. "The Klamath Legend of La-o," *Steel Points,* I (January, 1907), 75–76.

Ballard, Arthur. *Mythology of Southern Puget Sound,* UWPA, Vol. III, No. 2 (December, 1929).

Ballou, Robert. *Early Klickitat Valley Days.* Goldendale, Wash., 1938.

Bancroft, Hubert Howe. *The Native Races.* 5 vols. San Francisco, 1883. Vol. III.

Berreman, Joel V. *Tribal Distribution in Oregon.* Memoirs of the American Anthropological Association, No. 47, 1937.

Bertleson, Ernest B. "The Mountain That Was a Rope," Seattle *Sunday Times Magazine,* March 18, 1951, p. 3.

Boas, Franz. (*a*) *Chinook Texts,* BAE Bulletin 20 (1894).

(*b*) "Religion," in Hodge, Part 2, pp. 365–371.

(*c*) ed. *Folk-Tales of the Salishan and Sahaptin Tribes,* MAFS, XI (1917).

(*d*) "Mythology and Folktales of the North American Indians," in Boas, Dixon, Goddard, Radin, and others, *Anthropology in North America.* New York, 1915.

Bonney, W. P. *History of Pierce County.* 3 vols. Chicago, 1927. Vol. I.

Bruseth, Nels. *Indian Stories and Legends of the Stillaguamish and Allied Tribes.* Arlington, Wash., 1926.

Buchanan, Charles M. (*a*) "The Indian: His Origin and His Legendary Lore," *Overland Monthly,* 2d ser., XXXVI (1900), 114–122.

(*b*) "The Origin of Mounts Baker and Rainier," *The Mountaineer,* IX (December, 1919), 32–35.

Bushnell, Grant. "The Chief's Shadow," *OTM*, Vol. VII, No. 5 (January, 1903), pp. 22–23.

Clark, Ella E. (*a*) "The Mortal Who Married a Merman," *JAFL*, LXIX (1949), 64–65.

   (*b*) "The Pleiades: Indian and Greek Versions," State College of Washington, *Research Studies*, XIX (1951), 203–204.

   (*c*) "The Bridge of the Gods in Fact and Fancy," *OHQ*, LIII (March, 1952), 29–38.

Clarke, Samuel A. *Pioneer Days in Oregon History*. 2 vols. Cleveland, 1905. Vol. I.

Cline, Walter. "Religion and World View," in Spier (*b*), pp. 131–182.

Commons, Rachel S. "Diversions," in Spier (*b*), pp. 183–194.

Crandall, Lulu. *Pageant of Wascopam*. The Dalles, Ore., 1923.

Curtin, Jeremiah. (*a*) "Wasco Tales and Myths," in Sapir (*b*), pp. 237–314.

   (*b*) *Myths of the Modocs*. Boston, 1912.

Curtis, Edward S. *The North American Indian*. 20 vols. Cambridge, Mass., 1907–1930. Vols. VII, VIII, IX.

Denman, A. H. *The Name of Mount Tacoma*. Tacoma, Wash., 1924.

Dixon, Roland. "Shasta Myths," *JAFL*, XXIII (1910), 8–37, 364–370.

Durham, N. W. *History of the City of Spokane and Spokane County, Washington*. 3 vols. Chicago, S. J. Clarke Publishing Co., 1912. Vol. I.

Eells, Myron. (*a*) "Traditions of the 'Deluge' among the Tribes of the North-west," *American Antiquarian*, I (1878), 70–72.

   (*b*) "The Twana, Chemakum, and Klallam Indians of Washington Territory," Smithsonian Institution, *Annual Report*, 1887, pp. 605–681.

   (*c*) "The Thunderbird," *American Anthropologist*, o.s., II (October, 1889), 329–336.

   (*d*) "The Religion of the Indians of Puget Sound," *American Antiquarian*, XII (March, 1890), 69–84.

Evans, Elwood. (*a*) *History of the Pacific Northwest: Oregon and Washington*. 2 vols. Portland, 1889. Vol. II, chap. lx.

   (*b*) "Thoughts on the Name 'Tacoma,' " in Steel (*a*), pp. 59–65.

Farrand, Livingston. "Traditions of the Quinault Indians," *Memoirs of the American Museum of Natural History*, IV (Anthropology, III, Pt. III), 77–132. (Also published as *Publications of the Jesup North Pacific Expedition*, Vol. II, Pt. III.)

Farrand, Livingston, and Theresa Mayer. "Quileute Tales," *JAFL*, XXXII (1919), 251–279.

Finke, Mary Jane. "St. Helens, the Haunted Mountain," in Powers, pp. 30–31.

Fiske, John. *Myths and Myth-Makers: Old Tales and Superstitions Interpreted by Comparative Mythology*. 21st ed. Boston, 1896.

Frachtenberg, Leo, and Hull St. Clair. "Traditions of the Coos Indians of the Oregon Coast," *JAFL*, XXII (1909), 25–41.

Gatschet, Albert S. *The Klamath Indians of Southwestern Oregon*. Contributions to North American Ethnology, Vol. II, Part I. Washington, D.C., 1890.

Gayley, Charles M. *The Classic Myths in English Literature and in Art*. Rev. ed. Boston, 1911.

Gill, John. "Superstitions and Ceremonies of the Indians of Old Oregon," *OHQ*, XXIX (December, 1928), 311–322.

Glassley, Ray H. *Visit the Pacific Northwest*. Portland, Binfords & Mort, 1948.

Goddard, Pliny E. *Indians of the Northwest Coast*. American Museum of Natural History, Handbook Series, No. 10. New York, 1924.

Gunther, Erna. *Klallam Ethnography*, UWPA, I (1927), 177–310.

Haeberlin, Herman. "Mythology of Puget Sound," *JAFL*, XXXVII (1924), 371–438.

Higginson, Ella. "Along the Columbia," *Pacific Northwest* (Portland), Vol. I, No. 3 (1896), p. 3.

Hines, Gustavus. *Oregon, Its History, Condition and Prospects*. New York, 1859.

Hodge, Frederick W., ed. *Handbook of American Indians North of Mexico*. Washington, 1907–1910. Part 1, A–M; Part 2, N–Z.

Hunt, Herbert, and Floyd Kaylor. *Washington West of the Cascades*. 3 vols. Chicago, S. J. Clarke Publishing Co., 1917. Vol. I.

Idaho: A Guide in Word and Picture. (American Guide Series.) Caldwell, Idaho, Caxton Printers, Ltd., 1937.

Jacobs, Melville. (*a*) *Northwest Sahaptin Texts*, UWPA, Vol. II, No. 6 (1929).
(*b*) *Kalapuya Texts*, UWPA, XI (June, 1945).

Johnson, E. Pauline. *Legends of Vancouver*. New ed. Toronto, McClelland & Stewart, 1922.

Judson, Katherine B. *Myths and Legends of the Pacific Northwest*. Chicago, 1910.

Kane, Paul. *Wanderings of an Artist among the Indians of North America*. London, 1859.

Kronenberg, O. K. "The Legend of Face Rock near Bandon, Oregon," *Oregon Motorist*, Vol. X, No. 12 (September, 1930), pp. 9, 23–24.

Kuykendall, G. B. "The Indians of the Pacific Northwest—Their Legends, Myths, Religion, Customs," in Evans (*a*), II, 60–95.

Lambert, Eva C. "Legend of the Lummi Indians: Khaelts, the Wonder-working Man," *Puget Sounder* (Bellingham, Wash.), Vol. I, No. 23 (December, 1935), pp. 1 and 5.

Lapham, Stanton. *The Enchanted Lake*. Portland, J. K. Gill Co., 1931.

Lyman, Horace S. (*a*) "Reminiscences of Louis Labonte," *OHQ*, I (1900), 167–188.
(*b*) "The Indian 'Arabian Nights,'" *Pacific Monthly*, III (1900), 220–221.
(*c*) *History of Oregon: The Growth of an American State*. 4 vols. New York, 1903. Vol. I.

Lyman, William D. (*a*) "Indian Legends of Rainier," *Mazama*, II (December, 1905), 203–207.
(*b*) "Indian Myths of Mount Adams," *Mazama*, IV (December, 1913), 14–17.
(*c*) "Indian Myths of the Northwest," *Proceedings of the American Antiquarian Society*, n.s., XXV (1915), 375–395.
(*d*) *The Columbia River*. New York, 1917.
(*e*) "Myths and Superstitions of the Oregon Indians," *Proceedings of the American Antiquarian Society*, n.s., XVI (1903–1904), 221–251.

McArthur, Lewis A. *Oregon Geographic Names*. 2d ed. Portland, Binfords & Mort, 1944.

McClay, Max. "Pillar Rock," *OTM*, VII, No. 5 (January, 1903), 21–22.

McKee, Ruth Karr. *Mary Richardson Walker: Her Book*. Caldwell, Idaho, Caxton Printers, Ltd., 1945.

MacMurray, J. W. MS quoted in Mooney, pp. 722–723.

McWhorter, Lucullus. *Tragedy of the Wahk-shum*. Yakima, 1937.

Maynard, Madge. "The Seven Devils," *OTM*, Vol. IX, No. 9 (May, 1905), p. 9.

Meany, Edmond S. (*a*) *Origin of Washington Geographic Names*. Seattle, University of Washington Press, 1923.

    (*b*) "Mount Rainier in Indian Legends," *The Mountaineer*, XXIII (December, 1930), 23–25.

Miller, Joaquin. *Unwritten History: Life amongst the Modocs*. Hartford, 1874.

Mooney, James. "The Ghost-Dance Religion," BAE, *Fourteenth Annual Report* (for 1892–1893), Part II, pp. 653–828.

Morse, Mary Gay. *Lore of the Olympic Land*. Port Angeles, Wash. (?), 1924.

Mourning Dove. *Coyote Stories*. Caldwell, Idaho, Caxton Printers, Ltd., 1933.

Oregon: End of the Trail. (American Guide Series.) Portland, Binfords & Mort, 1940.

Packard, R. L. "Notes on the Mythology and Religion of the Nez Percés," *JAFL*, IV (1891), 327–330.

Parker, Samuel. *Exploring Tour beyond the Rocky Mountains, 1835–1837*. 3d ed. Ithaca, New York, 1842.

Phillips, W. S. *The Chinook Book*. Seattle, 1913.

Powers, Alfred. *Legends of the Four High Mountains*. Portland, Junior Historical Journal, 1944.

Ranck, Glenn. "Tribal Lore of Wisham Indians Rich in Traditions of the Columbia," Portland *Oregonian*, February 7, 1926, sec. 3, p. 9.

Ray, Verne F. (*a*) *The Sanpoil and Nespelem: Salishan Peoples of Northeastern Washington*, UWPA, V (December, 1932).

    (*b*) "Sanpoil Folk Tales," *JAFL*, XLVI (1933), 129–187.

    (*c*) "Native Villages and Groupings of the Columbia Basin," *Pacific Northwest Quarterly*, XXVII (1936), 99–152.

Reagan, Albert, and L. V. W. Walters. "Tales from the Hoh and Quileute," *JAFL*, XLVI (1933), 297–346.

Roberts, Ella. "Lost Lake," *Mazama*, VI (December, 1920), 79–80.

Ross, Alexander. *Adventures of the First Settlers on the Oregon or Columbia River*. London, 1849.

Sampson, Martin, and Rosalie Whitney. *The Swinomish Totem Pole Tribal Legends*. Bellingham, Wash., 1938.

Sapir, Edward. (*a*) "Religious Ideas of the Takelma Indians of Southwest Oregon," *JAFL*, XX (1907), 33–49.

    (*b*) *Wishram Texts, together with Wasco Tales and Myths*, collected by Jeremiah Curtin. Publications of the American Ethnological Society, Vol. II. Leyden, 1909.

Saylor, Fred. "Latourelle Falls and the Pillars of Hercules," *The Pacific Monthly*, VII (March, 1902), 135–136.

Semple, Eugene. "The Olympic Mountains," *The West Shore*, XVIII (August, 1888), 428–429.

Shelton, William. (*a*) *The Story of the Totem Pole*. 2d ed. Everett, Wash., 1935.

    (*b*) "Origin of the Exclamation 'Yahu!'" in Haeberlin, p. 417; also morals of other stories, pp. 416–417, 420, 421.

Sicade, Henry. (*a*) "Aboriginal Nomenclature," *Mazama*, V (December, 1918), 251–254.

(*b*) "Two Brothers Are Transformed into Thunder and Lightning," in Haeberlin, pp. 417–418.

Smith, Silas B. "Primitive Customs and Religious Beliefs of the Indians of the Pacific Northwest Coast," *OHQ*, II (1901), 255–265.

Smith, Susan. *The Legend of Multnomah Falls*. Portland, 1905. (Verse.)

Spier, Leslie. (*a*) *Tribal Distribution in Washington*. General Series in Anthropology, No. 3. Menasha, Wisconsin, 1936.

(*b*) ed. *The Sinkaietk or Southern Okanagon of Washington*. General Series in Anthropology, No. 6, Menasha, 1938.

Stanup, Peter. "Statement of Rev. Peter Stanup," in Steel (*a*), pp. 57–58.

Steel, William G. (*a*) *The Mountains of Oregon*. Portland, 1890.

(*b*) "Legends of the Llaos," *Steel Points*, I (January, 1907), 35–37.

Steele, Richard, and Arthur Rose. *An Illustrated History of the Big Bend Country, Washington*. Spokane, Western Historical Publishing Company, 1904.

Stern, Bernhard. *The Lummi Indians of Northwest Washington*, CUCA, XVII (1934).

Stevens, Hazard. "The Ascent of Mount Takhoma," *Atlantic Monthly*, XXXVIII (November, 1876), 513–530.

Swan, James G. (*a*) *The Northwest Coast, or Three Years' Residence in Washington Territory*. New York, 1857.

(*b*) *The Indians of Cape Flattery*. (Smithsonian Contributions to Knowledge, Vol. XVI, art. 8.) Smithsonian Institution Publication 220. Washington, D.C., 1869–1870.

Teit, James. (*a*) "Okanagon Tales," in Boas (*c*), pp. 65–97.

(*b*) "The Salishan Tribes of the Western Plateaus," BAE, *Forty-fifth Annual Report* (for 1927–1928), pp. 23–396.

(*c*) *The Middle Columbia Salish*, UWPA, Vol. II, No. 4 (June, 1928).

Van Olinda, O. S. *History of Vashon-Maury Islands*. Vashon, Wash., 1935.

Waggoner, George A. *Stories of Old Oregon*. Salem, 1905.

Walters, L. V. W. "Social Structure," in Spier (*b*), pp. 71–99.

Washington: A Guide to the Evergreen State. (American Guide Series.) Portland, Binfords & Mort, 1941.

Wells, Harry D. (*a*) "The Legend of Multnomah," *Pacific Northwest* (Portland), Vol. I, No. 8 (January, 1897), pp. 1–3.

(*b*) *Multnomah, a Legend of the Columbia*. Portland, 1923. (Verse.)

Wickersham, James. "Nusqually Mythology," *Overland Monthly*, 2d ser., XXXII (1898), 345–351.

Wilkes, Charles. *Narrative of the United States Exploring Expedition during the Years 1838 . . . 1842*. 5 vols. Philadelphia, 1845. Vols. IV and V.

Williams, Howel. (*a*) *The Geology of Crater Lake National Park, with a Reconnaissance of the Cascade Range Southward*. Carnegie Institution of Washington Publication 540. Washington, D.C., 1942.

(*b*) *The Ancient Volcanoes of Oregon*. Eugene, Oregon State System of Higher Education, 1948.

Winthrop, Theodore. *The Canoe and the Saddle; Adventures among the Northwestern Rivers and Forests*. Boston, 1863.

Wissler, Clark. *Star Legends among the American Indians*. American Museum of Natural History, Guide Leaflet Series, No. 91. New York, 1936.

MANUSCRIPT MATERIALS

Applegate, Moray L. (*a*) "A Legend of Crater Lake." MS dated February 13, 1898, in University of Oregon Library.

(*b*) Letter to his cousin, Rachel Applegate Swan, 1941.

Armstrong, Chief Ralph. "The Pleiades." From a manuscript owned by Mrs. Joe Evans, Spalding, Idaho.

Colvig, William M. (*a*) "The Legend of Crater Lake." MS dated 1892.

(*b*) "The Legend of the White Deer." Both are among the private papers of Judge Colvig and are used by permission of his daughter, Mrs. William Warner.

Crandall, Lulu. (*a*) Scrapbooks of Lulu Crandall, in the Wasco County Library, The Dalles, Oregon. (Newspaper clippings and MS notes.)

(*b*) The Lulu Crandall Collection, Holland Library, the State College of Washington.

McGregor, John. Letter to Department of Anthropology, State College of Washington, dated March 12, 1936. Lent by Professor Herman Deutsch, Department of History and Political Science.

McWhorter, Lucullus. The L. V. McWhorter Archives, Holland Library, State College of Washington. Manuscript Collection, Exhibit 8:

Folder 1: "Coyote and the Crow" and "Pah-to, the White Eagle."

Folder 2: "Legend of the Great Dipper and the Big White Road across the Sky."

Folder 3: "Orion."

Folder 5: "The Painted Rocks of the Naches"; "Coyote and the Monster of the Columbia"; and "Yakima Tradition of the Flood."

Folder 6: "Pictured Rocks of the Naches Puh-tuh Num," "Deep Lake," and "The Boy and the Brave Hazelnut."

Scheffer, Theodore H. (*a*) Letter to the author, December 19, 1950, with detail from Billy Curlew about Lake Chelan and about Blue Lake.

(*b*) Letter of January 14, 1951, about Indian food plants found on Steamboat Rock.

Seattle, Matthew. "Mt. Tacoma." MS written in summer of 1900, in Washington State Historical Library, Tacoma, Wash.

Waterman, T. T. "The Mountain Who Had Three Wives." MS in private library of Arthur Ballard, Auburn, Wash.

ORAL SOURCES

White: John S. Coie, Frank Hubbard, Helen Still Schroeder.

Indian: See the last page of the Introduction.

Research for this study was financed in part by a grant from the State College of Washington Research Fund.

GLOSSARY

There is no standardized spelling of Indian tribal names. In the present volume this principle has been followed: whenever the name of the Indian tribe is the same as that of the river on which it had its winter villages, the standardized spelling of the name of the river has also been used for the name of the tribe.

The diacritical marks indicating pronunciation are the same as in Webster's dictionaries.

arrowwood (or bow-and-arrow wood)—Any of several shrubs having tough, pliant shoots formerly used by the Indians in making arrow shafts. In the Pacific Northwest, the three favorite shrubs for the purpose are known as service berry, ocean spray, and syringa. The lower slopes are white with their blossoms in the spring.

camas (căm′ăs)—A plant of the lily family, with blue flowers, growing in low, wet meadows; the bulbs are a staple food of the Pacific Northwest Indians. The name came from a Nootka word meaning "sweet" or "fruit," into the Chinook jargon used throughout the region, and thence into English. Botanical name—*Camassia*.

Cayuse (kī ūs′)—A Shahaptian tribe in northeastern Oregon. Because these people were breeders of horses, Indian horses became known as cayuses.

Celilo (sê lĭ′lō)—A waterfall in the lower Columbia River, a few miles up the river from The Dalles. Site of ancient fishing stations of several Indian tribes.

Chehalis (chê hā′lĭs)—The collective name for several Salishan tribes along the Chehalis River in southwestern Washington.

Chelan (shê lán′)—A long lake and a small river in north central Washington. Three meanings have been given for the word: "deep water," "beautiful waters," "land of bubbling waters."

Chemakum (chĕm′á kŭm)—A small tribe in the northeast corner of the Olympic Peninsula; related to the Quillayute.

Chinook (chĭ nŏŏk′)—(1) A tribe on the Washington side of the mouth of the Columbia River. (2) A jargon made up of Indian, English, and French words, used chiefly for trade. (3) chinook (shĭ nŏŏk′)—A warm southwest wind of the Pacific Northwest.

Chinookan (chĭ nŏŏk′an)—A linguistic family made up of tribes along the lower Columbia and lower Willamette rivers.

Chopaka (shō pä′ka)—A mountain peak in the Okanogan highlands of north-eastern Washington.

Clackamas (clăck′å màs)—A Chinookan tribe along the Clackamas River in northwestern Oregon.

Clatsop (clăt′sòp)—A Chinookan tribe on the Oregon side of the mouth of the Columbia River.

Cle Elum (klē ĕl′ŭm)—A lake in the Cascade Range in central Washington. The name means "swift waters."

Coeur d'Alene (kûr dà lān′)—A Salishan tribe once living chiefly along Lake Coeur d'Alene and the Coeur d'Alene River in the Idaho Panhandle, and in Washington along the Spokane River above the falls. These Indians called themselves Skitswish. *Coeur d'Alêne,* probably "awl-heart" or "sharp-hearted," from the French, seems to have been a derisive term used by French-Canadian traders and by the Skitswish; which group used it first for the other is uncertain.

Colville (kŏl′vĭl)—(1) An Indian reservation in northeastern Washington, be-tween the Okanogan River and the upper Columbia. The name came from Fort Colville, an important trading post along the upper Columbia, established by the Hudson's Bay Company in 1826 and named for Andrew Colvil, a governor of the company. (2) All the Indians now living on the Reservation, except the Nez Perces, "even though they belong to many divergent groups."

Coos (kōōs)—A tribe of the Kusan linguistic family once living along Coos Bay, in southwestern Oregon.

Coquille (kō kēl′)—A small tribe of the Kusan family once living near the mouth of the Coquille River in southwestern Oregon. Probably an Indian word with French spelling.

Dahkobeed (däh kō′bēd)—Duwamish name for Mount Rainier.

Dalles, The (dălz)—An Oregon city on the bank of the Columbia River. The name is from the French *dalle,* meaning "flagstone." It was applied to the nar-rows of the Columbia by French-Canadian employees of the North West Fur Company and the Hudson's Bay Company. The word meant to them "river rapids swiftly flowing through a narrow channel over flat rocks."

Doquebuth (dō′quê bŭth)—Puyallup name for the Changer.

Dosewallips (dō sê wŏl′ŭps)—A river flowing from the Olympic Mountains into Hood Canal, western arm of Puget Sound.

Duwamish (dü wä′mĭsh)—A small body of Salishan people once living along the Duwamish River, on the present site of Seattle. The word means "the people along the river."

Enumclaw (ē′nŭm claw)—Thunder.

hiaqua (hē ä′quà)—Shell money and ornaments highly prized by the Indians of the Pacific Northwest coast. Chinook jargon.

Hoh (hōh)—A small tribe, or subtribe of the Quillayute, living near the mouth of the Hoh River on the Washington coast.

Kalapuya (kăl à pōō′yà)—A group of related tribes living formerly in the

Willamette Valley of western Oregon. Also the language spoken by those tribes. (Spelled also Calapuya, Kalapooia, Calapooia.)

Kalispel (kăl'ĭ spĕl)—A Salishan tribe in northern Idaho and northeastern Washington.

Kamiakin (kà mī'à kĭn)—Chief of the Yakima and of federated tribes in the 1850's.

Keechelus (kĕch'ĕ lŭs)—A lake in the Cascade Range in Washington, near the summit on U.S. Highway 10.

Kittitas (kĭt'tĭ tăs)—A flat valley surrounding the present city of Ellensburg, Washington, once the territory of the Kittitas tribe.

Klah Klahnee (klăh klăh'nē)—The Three Sisters peaks in central Oregon; "three points" in the language of the Warm Springs Indians.

Klallam (klăl'làm)—A Salishan tribe on the Washington coast, along the Strait of Juan de Fuca. (Also spelled Clallam.)

Klamath (klăm'àth)—A tribe of southern Oregon, near Crater Lake; their principal villages were on Upper Klamath Lake.

Klickitat (klĭck'ĭ tăt)—A Shahaptian tribe of southwestern Washington, once living mainly along the headwaters of the Cowlitz, Lewis, White Salmon, and Klickitat rivers.

klootchman (klōōtch'măn)—Chinook jargon for "woman."

Komo Kulshan (kŏ'mō kŭl'shăn)—Lummi and Nooksack name for Mount Baker. It means "white, shining mountain" or "great white watcher."

Kookooskia (kōō kōōs'kĭ à)—The Clearwater River in northern Idaho; the Nez Perces lived along it. The name means "clear water."

kouse (kowse, rhyming with "house")—Chinook jargon for a plant of the parsnip family; the root was second to the camas in importance to the Indians of the Pacific Northwest. Often called biscuit-root today. Botanical name—*Lomatium*.

Kwatee (kwă tē')—The Changer in the Quinault myths. Esau Penn and Leven Coe pronounced it with a very guttural K and prolonged *ee*.

Lapush (là pōōsh')—Indian village at the mouth of the Quillayute River. The name is probably a corruption of the French *la bouche*, "the mouth."

Latourell (lă tôr ĕl')—Waterfall along the Columbia Gorge, Oregon side. Named for a pioneer in the locality.

Llao (lă'ō)—High cliff overlooking Crater Lake. Named for a spirit that once lived in the lake (Klamath mythology).

Loo-wit (lōō wĭt')—Mount St. Helens, a volcanic peak in the Cascade Range in Washington. Last eruption in 1842.

Lummi (lŭm'mĭ)—A Salishan tribe living formerly on some islands in northern Puget Sound and on the adjacent mainland.

Makah (mà käh')—A tribe in the extreme northwest corner of Washington, the only tribe of Wakashan stock in the United States. The word means "cape people."

Mazama (mà zä' mà)—A prehistoric mountain in southern Oregon, in the caldera of which Crater Lake is now. The Spanish name, meaning "mountain goat," was applied to it by the Mazamas, an organization of mountain climbers in the Pacific Northwest.

Memaloose (mĕm'á lōōs) —The largest of several burial islands in the Columbia River, situated near The Dalles. Lewis and Clark called it "Sepulcher Island," because of the thirteen burial huts they counted on it.

Methow (mĕt'how) —A Salishan tribe of eastern Washington, once living between Lake Chelan and the Methow River.

Metolius (mĕ tōl'ĭ ŭs) —A river in west central Oregon. Its source is large springs at the base of Black Butte.

Modoc (mō'dŏc) —A tribe related to the Klamath, once living in southern Oregon and adjacent California.

Multnomah (mŭlt nō'mäh) —(1) A Chinookan tribe that formerly lived on and about Sauvies Island in the lower Columbia River; it probably has been extinct since sailors brought an epidemic of measles in 1832. (2) All the tribes once living along or near the lower Willamette River, Oregon. (3) A waterfall of the Columbia Gorge.

Nespelem (nĕs pē'lĕm) —A Salishan tribe that once lived along Nespelem Creek, a tributary of the upper Columbia River, in northeastern Washington. The name means "desert country."

Nez Perce (nĕz pûrs') —A large Shahaptian tribe once living in what is now southeastern Washington, northeastern Oregon, and central Idaho. The French words mean "pierced nose," but since these Indians never pierced their noses, it seems likely that *nez pressé* ("flattened nose") was intended by the French-Canadian traders.

Nisqually (nĭ skwôl'lĭ) —A Salishan tribe and a river near the southern end of Puget Sound.

Nooksack (nōōk'săk) —(1) A river in northwestern Washington flowing from Mount Baker into Puget Sound. (2) A Salishan tribe formerly living along the Nooksack River. The name means "mountain men."

Nootka (nōōt'kà) —The language of several tribes once living on and near Vancouver Island, British Columbia.

Okanogan (ōk á nŏg'án) —(1) A river in north central Washington and adjacent British Columbia, a large tributary of the upper Columbia. (2) An important division of the Salishan family formerly living along the Okanogan River and along Okanagan Lake in British Columbia.

Ozette (ō zĕt') —A lake in the northwest corner of the Olympic Peninsula; on its shores was a village of the Makah or of a separate tribe.

Pahto (päh tō') —Mount Adams, a major peak of the Cascade Range, in southwestern Washington. The word means "standing high." The mountain is called Klickitat in some myths.

Palouse (pá lōōs') —(1) A small river in southeastern Washington, tributary to the Snake River. (2) A Shahaptian band once living along the Palouse River. (3) A large area of land in southeastern Washington thought to have been called *pelouse*, "the grass lands," by French-Canadian voyageurs. The Palouse River flows through it. The tribal name is usually spelled Palus.

Puyallup (pū yăl'lŭp)—An important Salishan tribe once living along the Puyallup River and adjacent Puget Sound. (According to Henry Sicade, *Puyallup* means "generous people"; according to Elwood Evans, it means "shadows from the dense shade of the forest.")

Queets (kwēts)—A small tribe or subdivision of the Quinault, along the Queets River on the Washington coast.

Quillayute (kwĭl'lā yūte)—(1) A river only six miles long, in Washington; the fishing village of Lapush is at its mouth. (2) Often spelled *Quileute*—a Chimakoan tribe living along the Quillayute River.

Quinault (kwĭn ält')—A Salishan tribe living along Lake Quinault and on the Washington coast between the Quinault River and the Chehalis River.

Salishan (sā'lĭsh ăn)—Pertaining to an American Indian linguistic family which includes more tribes of Washington than any other linguistic family does.

Samish (să'mĭsh)—A Salishan division once living along the Samish River and Samish Bay of the northern Puget Sound region.

Sanpoil (săn poil')—A Salishan tribe along the Sanpoil River and the Columbia immediately below the Big Bend. *Sanpoil* is a corruption of the name of the principal village of the tribe.

Santiam (săn'tĭ ăm)—A tribe of the Kalapuyan family once living along the Santiam River in western Oregon.

Seatco (sê ăt'cō)—An evil spirit (or evil spirits) greatly feared by the Indians of the Washington and Oregon coasts.

Shahaptian (shā hăp'tĭ ăn)—Pertaining to an American linguistic family which included, among other tribal groups, the Klickitat, Nez Perce, Walla Walla, Palouse, Umatilla, and Yakima. (Also spelled Sahaptin and Sahaptian.)

Shasta (shăs'tà)—(1) A tribe of the Hokan linguistic stock formerly living in southwest Oregon and adjacent California. (2) A volcanic peak in northern California.

Shuksan (shŭk'săn)—A high peak in the northern part of the Cascade Range, near Mount Baker. The name means "the place of the storm wind."

Si (sī)—A peak in the northern part of the Cascade Range.

Siskiyou (sĭs'kĭ yū)—(1) A mountain range in southern Oregon and northern California. (2) The chief invited to the "Potlatch on the Oregon Coast."

Skokomish (skō kō'mĭsh)—A Salishan tribe formerly living at the mouth of the Skokomish River, which flows into the northern end of Hood Canal. The name means "river people."

Snohomish (snō hō'mĭsh)—A Salishan tribe once living on the south end of Whidbey Island and along the adjacent east coast of Puget Sound. The city of Everett, Washington, is at the mouth of the Snohomish River.

Snoqualmie (snō kwôl'mē)—(1) A Salishan tribe along the upper branches of the Snoqualmie River, western Washington. The name means "people who came from the moon." (Spelled also Snuqualmi.) (2) Snoqualmie Falls, a 270-foot cataract in the northern Cascade Range, near U.S. Highway 10.

Spokane (spō kăn')—A Salishan tribe or group of tribes formerly living along the Spokane River in the area of the present city of Spokane.

Squamish (skwä′mĭsh)—A Salishan tribe living along Howe Sound, British Columbia.

Stehekin (stĕ hē′kĭn)—A small mountain river which flows into the head of Lake Chelan. The name means "the way" or "pass."

Steilacoom (stĭll′á kŭm)—A small lake near Tacoma, Washington. The name is a corruption of the name of an Indian chief.

Stillaguamish (stĭll á guä′mĭsh)—A Salishan tribe once living along the Stillaguamish River in northwestern Washington. The name means "river people."

Suquamish (sû kwä′mĭsh)—A Salishan tribe formerly living on islands west of Seattle and possibly along the adjacent shores of Puget Sound.

Swinomish (swĭn′ó mĭsh)—(1) A Salishan tribe once living on Whidbey Island, Puget Sound, and the adjacent mainland. (2) An Indian reservation in northwestern Washington.

Tacobud (tä kō′bŭd)—Nisqually name for Mount Rainier.

Tahmahnawis (täh mäh′nä wĭs)—A word from the Chinook jargon, both noun and adjective, meaning "supernatural," "supernatural power," "beings endowed with supernatural power," "anything beyond human understanding."

Taholah (tä hō′läh)—Indian village on the Washington coast, at the mouth of the Quinault River..

Takkobad (täk kō′bǎd)—Puyallup name for Mount Rainier.

Tatoosh (tä tōōsh′)—A small island one-half mile off the Washington coast, at the entrance to the Strait of Juan de Fuca. Named for the Indian chief who welcomed Captain John Meares in 1788.

Toppenish (tŏp′pĕn ĭsh)—A band of Yakima or of Klickitat formerly living on Toppenish Creek, a branch of the Yakima River. The name means "people of the trail coming from the foot of the hill."

Tyee Sahale (tī ē säh′hä lē)—Chinook jargon for "chief up above," used by missionaries for the Christian concept of God. Often interpreted as the "Great Spirit."

Umatilla (ū má tĭl′lá)—A Shahaptian tribe once living along the Umatilla River in northern Oregon and along the adjacent banks of the Columbia River. The name means "lots of rocks," or "water rippling over sand."

Umpqua (ŭmp′kwä)—An Athapascan tribe, long extinct, formerly living along the Umpqua River in southwestern Oregon.

Vashon (vǎsh ŏn′)—An island in Puget Sound, named in 1792 by Captain Vancouver in honor of a friend in the British Navy.

Wallowa (wôl lou′wá)—A mountain range, a lake, and a river in northeastern Oregon. The name is a Nez Perce word for a particular kind of fish trap the Indians used in the Wallowa River.

Wapato (wä′pá tō)—An Indian family of the Chelan group, living near the south end of Lake Chelan.

wapato (wä′pá tō)—A tuberous root, eaten boiled or roasted by almost all North American Indian tribes. In the Chinook jargon, a plant still called *wapato;*

also called broad-leaved arrowhead and Indian potato. Botanical name—*Sagittaria*. (Also spelled *wapatoo, wappato, wapata*.)

Wasco (wäs′cō)—A Chinookan tribe along the Columbia River, near the present city of The Dalles, Oregon.

Wenatchee (wĕ năch′ė)—A tributary of the Columbia River, in central Washington, and the Salishan people once living beside it. The name means "issuing from a canyon."

Whulge (whŭlj)—Puget Sound. The name means "salt water."

Willamette (wĭl lăm′ĕt)—A river of western Oregon, flowing northward into the Columbia. Portland is at its mouth. From *Wäl lämt′*, Indian name for a place on the west shore of the Willamette, near Oregon City.

Wishram (wĭsh′răm)—A Chinookan tribe on the Washington side of the Columbia River, immediately opposite the Wasco.

Wyeast (wī ēst′)—Mount Hood, the highest peak in Oregon.

Yakima (yăk′ĭ mȧ)—An important Shahaptian tribe of central Washington, once living along both sides of the middle Columbia River and along the northerly branches of the Yakima and Wenatchee rivers.